THE
WAR
BENEATH

THE RISE OF OCEANIA

Distributed in Canada by
Fitzhenry & Whiteside Limited
195 Allstate Parkway
Markham, Ontario L3R 4T8
Phone: (905) 477-9700
e-mail: bookinfo@fitzhenry.ca

Distributed in the U.S. by
Consortium Book Sales & Distribution
34 Thirteenth Avenue, NE, Suite 101
Minneapolis, MN 55413
Phone: (612) 746-2600
e-mail: sales.orders@cbsd.com

Library and Archives Canada Cataloguing in Publication

Johnston, Timothy S., 1970-, author
        The war beneath / Timothy S. Johnston. -- First edition.

(The rise of Oceania ; 1)
Issued in print and electronic formats.
ISBN 978-1-77148-471-8 (softcover).--ISBN 978-1-77148-472-5 (PDF)

        I. Title.

PS8619.O488W37 2018   C813'.6   C2018-904662-7
                                               C2018-904663-5

CHIZINE PUBLICATIONS
Peterborough, Canada
www.chizinepub.com
info@chizinepub.com

Edited by Leigh Teetzel
Copyedited and proofread by Kate Campbell Moore

Canada Council   Conseil des arts
for the Arts   du Canada

We acknowledge the support of the Canada Council for the Arts which last year invested $20.1 million in writing and publishing throughout Canada.

ONTARIO ARTS COUNCIL
CONSEIL DES ARTS DE L'ONTARIO
an Ontario government agency
un organisme du gouvernement de l'Ontario

Published with the generous assistance of the Ontario Arts Council.

Printed in Canada

TIMOTHY S. JOHNSTON

THE
WAR
BENEATH

THE RISE OF OCEANIA

Books by Timothy S. Johnston

ChiZine Publications

THE WAR BENEATH
THE SAVAGE DEEPS (forthcoming)
FATAL DEPTH (forthcoming)

Carina Press

THE FURNACE
THE FREEZER
THE VOID

TIMELINE OF EVENTS

2020 Despite the fact that global warming is the primary concern for the majority of the planet's population, still little is being done.

2042 Ocean levels rise higher and faster than expected.

2055 Shipping begins to experience interruptions due to flooded docks and crane facilities. World markets fluctuate wildly.

2061 Rising ocean levels swamp Manhattan shore defenses and disrupt Gulf Coast oil shipping; financial markets in North America become increasingly unstable due to flooding.

2062 Encroaching water pounds major cities such as Mumbai, London, Miami, Jakarta, Tokyo, and Shanghai.

2063 The Marshall Islands, Tuvalu, and the Maldives disappear.

2065 Refugee problem escalates in Bangladesh; millions die.

2069 Shore defenses everywhere are abandoned; massive numbers of people move inland. Inundated coastal cities become major disaster areas.

2071 Market crash affects entire world; economic depression looms.

2072 "Breadbasket" regions of North America, South America, Europe, and Asia experience less precipitation than previous years; desertification intensifies.

2073 Led by China, governments begin establishing settlements on continental shelves. The shallow water environment proves ideal for displaced populations, aquaculture, and as jump-off sites for mining ventures on the deep ocean abyssal plains.

2080 The number of people living on the ocean floor reaches 100,000.

2088 Flooding continues on land; the pressure to establish undersea colonies increases.

2090 Continental shelves are now home to twenty-three major cities and hundreds of deep-sea mining and research facilities. Resources harvested by the ocean inhabitants are now integral to national economies.

2091 Over five million now live in undersea colonies.

2093 Led by the American undersea cities of Trieste, Seascape, and Ballard, an independence movement begins.

2099 The CIA crushes the independence movement.

2128 Over ten million now populate the ocean floor in twenty-nine cities.

MARCH 2129 Present day.

TRIESTE CITY UNITED STATES CONTINENTAL SHELF

30 KILOMETERS WEST OF FLORIDA

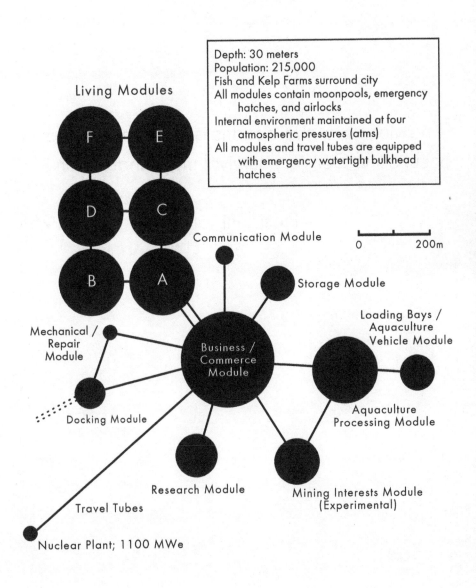

Depth: 30 meters
Population: 215,000
Fish and Kelp Farms surround city
All modules contain moonpools, emergency hatches, and airlocks
Internal environment maintained at four atmospheric pressures (atms)
All modules and travel tubes are equipped with emergency watertight bulkhead hatches

Living Modules

F E

D C

B A

Communication Module

Storage Module

Mechanical / Repair Module

Loading Bays / Aquaculture Vehicle Module

Business / Commerce Module

Docking Module

Aquaculture Processing Module

Research Module

Mining Interests Module (Experimental)

Travel Tubes

Nuclear Plant; 1100 MWe

0   200m

"Knowledge of the oceans is more than a matter of curiosity. Our very survival may hinge upon it."

—President John F. Kennedy, 1961

part one: the gulf of mexico

CHAPTER ONE

IT ONLY TOOK TWO SECONDS TO realize someone was following me.

He'd been on my tail from the moment I left work. It had been another grueling shift, hauling in kelp from the massive farms on the perimeter of Trieste City and loading it into the farming module in the southeast quadrant. The stuff grew fifty centimeters a day in the nutrient-rich environment of the continental shelf just off Florida's west coast—the warm water, abundant sunlight, and organic material that washed off the landmass and settled on the shallow seabed generated perfect growing conditions— and was one of the reasons why economies and populations of the world's undersea cities were booming. Harvesting the plants was a daily routine. We then prepared it for export topside for food, or shipped it out for further processing into methane. It was our main source of income.

I didn't mind the manual labor, even though I had trained for a far different type of work. Nevertheless, Trieste City's continued survival and expansion required such efforts. The flooding on land had pushed us to the shelves. It was a harsh environment for people, but I saw it as the future of humanity, and I would do almost anything to see the city thrive. Just as my father had, though his strategy had been far more aggressive. He had *fought* for the city, and died as a result.

Now, at this point in my life, I just wanted to work hard for it.

The man following me watched from a side passage as I left the aquaculture sector and stepped onto the travel tube's conveyor leading to the Commerce

Module. The tube was three meters high with curved bulkheads. A belt also ran in the opposite direction; it carried people toward the processing facilities or the farms for the next shift. They wore either laborer's clothing or wetsuits. All had the same desire as me; you could see it in their features. They wanted Trieste City to continue to grow and prove its necessity to the world's economy. After our short and troubled history, I knew they too would do anything for the colony, even if it meant endangering their own lives. It was hazardous as hell outside, where a work accident, an equipment malfunction, or even some seemingly innocuous creature could take your life in an instant.

Above me, expansive windows looked into the sea. The sun's beams cut through the thirty meters of water to Trieste easily enough. Hundreds of species of fish darted by, and divers and seacars surrounded the city. In the distance, kelp rose toward the surface and languidly swayed in the currents. And, only a kilometer away, a menacing *Reaper* class US warsub—USS *Impaler*. Just close enough for people to see they were always nearby, watching, waiting for trouble.

I snorted and looked away.

A few seconds later I pretended to recognize a woman coming toward me on the opposing conveyer, and I turned as she passed to say a few words to her. She was a school teacher leading a class of seven- and eight-year-olds on a field trip to the farms. They were excited and chattering amongst themselves. As my gaze shifted away from them, I glanced behind me.

He was still there, about twenty meters away.

In the brief second I saw him, I realized there was something oddly familiar there. The shape of his jaw perhaps . . . or the pierce of his eyes. It was a feeling I just couldn't shake, and I had learned long before to trust my hunches. The thought that he was a foreign agent—of a land nation or an undersea city—flashed through my mind, but I disregarded it almost immediately. That part of my life was well behind me now. A member of the United States Submarine Fleet, then? Perhaps, but unlikely. Soldiers were everywhere in the city—we were still a part of the United States, after all—patrolling or on leave, and they could have watched me if necessary. Still, there weren't many other options.

Someone abruptly nudged me in the side and I turned to see what they wanted.

"Hey, Mac, just off work?" the man asked.

My name is Truman McClusky, though most people just called me Mac. It was easier that way, especially as a laborer when a hundred people a day have to yell to get your attention. The man was an old acquaintance, someone

I had worked with while building one of the Living Modules a few years back. I grunted and kept my tone casual. "Yeah. Going to the entertainment district. You?" I knew he wasn't the type to visit that area, so we would be going our separate ways in less than ten seconds.

"Back to my bunk," he replied. "I'm exhausted, you know. This business is draining." He laughed at himself and an instant later left the belt and began to march in a different direction.

His joke made me groan inwardly. However, such a thing was typical of the people here—despite the back-breaking life, they were quite happy to be a part of what had begun as a grand experiment to alleviate the disasters in coastal areas of the planet and the loss of primary breadbasket regions. In fact, seafloor colonization had grown into a venture boasting almost thirty major undersea cities with a combined population of ten million. There was still much to be done, but it seemed as though we were indeed winning the battle. The only real remaining problems were malcontents upset with the increasing military presence of our colonizing nations. Things were coming to a head once again, as they had back in 2099, and that was something that I desperately wanted to avoid.

The Commerce Module was the largest one in Trieste. Four stories up—the highest we could go, otherwise we risked surface vessels scraping the top of the structure—and five stories down, it contained all the business and recreational facilities for the city. The central area was open from floor to ceiling, and with the ceiling mostly window, sunlight penetrated right to the lowest level. Offices and shops that bordered this nine-level atrium had glass fronts that allowed the natural light to filter toward the outer bulkheads. The main walkways that ringed each deck had plants, trees, and vines growing in recessed pots, which helped maintain the atmosphere. It was the most beautiful area of the city; in fact, it was the most famous module of any American colony. We were all proud of it.

The entertainment district was in the lower levels. I marched along the steel grating of the outer walkway to the escalators that led downward. In the reflection of a storefront window I could see the man still behind me, walking casually and doing a fair job of being unobtrusive. He was a professional, there was no doubt of that. He had picked up a newspaper chip at a stand and was reading the latest top stories—most likely about the increasing tension between the United States and China—and only glanced up to track me every fifteen seconds or so.

Down on a lower level, I made my way into a tavern and found a corner where I could conceal myself. I kept watch out the window. Sure enough, a minute later, the man approached. He sent a fleeting glance in, but it was impossible for him to see anything. With the natural sunlight in the atrium and the bar's darkened interior, all that he got was his own reflection.

He would have to come in if he wanted me now.

He entered.

I crouched farther into the corner as he moved to the bar and ordered a drink in low, mumbled tones. The feeling that I knew this person came back in a surge, for the way he held his body and perched on the stool seemed so damn familiar. I strained to place his face, but still it was impossible. It was as if the man had made an appearance in a dream I'd had a decade earlier, and I had never really known him.

He looked over his shoulder and searched the establishment. There were only a few other patrons there—all US military—but at first he didn't catch sight of me. Then his glare lingered on my corner.

I stepped out of the shadows and stalked toward him. We made eye contact and he rose from the stool in tentative jerks.

Without thinking, my hand darted to his neck and I poured on the pressure. It was something I shouldn't have done—I was just a civilian now, after all, and security could arrest me for assault—but it just happened. The bartender's jaw dropped at the suddenness of the assault.

"Who are you?" I hissed.

The man's eyes bulged and he struggled to speak. "Mac—don't—" he finally managed.

Startled, I immediately backed off; that voice didn't match the face. "Blake?"

He nodded as he massaged his throat. "Damn it, man. You didn't have to do that."

"You don't look quite the same as you used to," I mumbled.

"That was Shanks's idea. We found out that the other intelligence services have detailed dossiers on me, including photos." He gestured to his face. "So we changed it."

I looked closer. The nose was different. The eyes a dull brown where they used to be a dazzling blue. The hairline had receded, and the ears protruded a bit more. The cheekbones were also more pronounced. But there was no doubt about it now—it was indeed Daniel Blake, an operative of Trieste City Intelligence.

One of my former colleagues.

"Why are you following me?" I whispered as I ushered him to a table and away from the bartender.

"Shanks wants you for something important. A job."

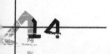

I growled. George Shanks was the Director of TCI. He had recruited me into the intelligence business after my graduation from university eighteen years earlier. I had left the organization, however, following a colossal disagreement with him over TCI policy. He and I were not on good terms, to say the least. I didn't want anything to do with him—or the job—anymore.

"Why follow me? Why not just track me down at my cubicle? Call me?"

"Too scared of tipping off other agents. They've probably bugged your place already, as well as the comm lines. We decided to grab you after work, bring you in that way."

"What other agents?"

He looked cagey. "Another city, of course."

"Chinese? French?"

He shook his head. "Sorry. We have to go see Shanks. He'll fill you in."

I looked my old friend up and down. It all seemed very bizarre, but he had piqued my interest. Still, the prospect of dealing with Shanks again was not something I wanted.

Eventually I gave a reluctant nod. "All right then. Let's go."

"STILL WORKING THE FARMS, MCCLUSKY?" SHANKS rumbled at me ten minutes later. "Slugging kelp around? It's a little beneath you, isn't it?"

I clenched my teeth as I stared at the man. He hadn't changed much since last I saw him, seven years earlier. He was still a tall, broad-shouldered, and imposing figure. His hair was now salt and pepper, which gave him a distinguished look. But the sneer on his face said volumes. And my own expression, I knew, screamed that the distaste was mutual. Despite my feelings toward him, however, I knew that he was no idiot. He had managed to run Trieste City Intelligence for over twenty years without our own military discovering it, which was no small feat. At least when it came to his job, I knew Shanks was professional enough. I just had serious questions about his morals.

TCI's function was to protect the interests of the city and prevent other intelligence services from compromising our security. We couldn't rely on American forces for that. Not since 2099, anyway. TCI's headquarters were located in the Communication Module, but only a handful of people knew that. There were approximately forty operatives, most of whom were usually out on assignment at any given time.

Blake had escorted me through security and into the tiny office concealed inside a normal relay station. Equipment cluttered it and there was barely room for a desk and two chairs. We stood in silence, guardedly watching each other. Behind the desk a small window looked out into the ocean; the sun above was setting and twilight had reached the undersea city.

"I'm doing a job and helping Trieste," I finally ground out. "Any way possible."

"Anything except staying with TCI?" Shanks said.

"You know why I left. It was your fault."

"That the Chinese caught you? Hardly. We all know who really turned you over."

I winced at the memory. "He had his reasons. I don't pretend to agree with them, but it was your fault he did it, and your fault I quit."

He snorted. "Nonsense. You could have stayed."

"After what I found out about you? I could never have—"

"Your father would have condoned what I did! I've saved this city countless times, and I'm not about to apologize for it!"

A sudden jolt shot through me; the mention of my father had taken me aback. Partly because I didn't think Shanks had a right to even think about him, let alone mention him in open conversation, and partly because deep inside, in a place that I didn't even want to admit to myself existed, I knew that Shanks was right. My father would have disagreed with my decision. Still, the accusation stung. I knotted my fists. "How dare you bring him into this!"

By now Shanks's face was red with anger. "He wanted the best for Trieste! I should know—I served with him when you were just a kid!"

I took a step toward him, not really sure what I was going to do. Then a cough from the side caught my attention, and I stopped suddenly, aware that I had let my composure crack because of a longstanding feud I had thought was gone forever. For seven years I had thought this part of my life was behind me. Now, in less than thirty minutes, it was back in full force. And it shook me to the core.

Blake had been wise to interrupt us. "Why don't you brief him, sir?" he said with a hint of apprehension.

Shanks glared at the man for a hard moment. The only sound was from the ventilation fans in the ceiling. Then, finally, he deflated. "You're right. I don't want to push him away." He turned back to me. With a pained expression, he continued, "To put it bluntly, we need your help."

"For what?" I gestured at Blake. "You've got other operatives."

"You have special knowledge that could mean the difference between success and failure, McClusky."

I rolled my eyes. "It's always about life or death, isn't it? Don't you think you tend to overstate things a bit, Shanks?"

He slammed his palm on a nearby shelf and a handful of electronic components clattered to the deck. "Dammit, the danger here is real! If you don't help, it could mean the end of the city!"

I paused as I sized him up. He had started to sweat and tendons had popped out on his neck. Apart from his hatred of me, I had never seen him quite like this.

"What is it?" I asked.

He took a breath and gathered his thoughts. "Someone stole some sensitive information from us yesterday. Specifically, the plans for a crucial piece of technology that we can't let any other country or undersea city get their hands on. If they do, they will have dominance over every other nation involved in the colonization of the seafloor. *We* developed it, and *we* need to be the ones to put it to use. If they beat us to the punch, say goodbye to mining the seafloor, to control over our own conshelf, even to the currently accepted sealanes that we use for travel. It'll all be over." He hesitated, then added, "It could even lead to war, both in the ocean and on land."

I glanced at Blake for an instant, but his face was blank. He didn't know either. I turned back to the director. "What could be so important?"

He shook his head. "No way. Not until you agree to help, and even then your access to information will be limited. I'll reinstate your position as Operative First Class, and you'll go get the information back from the people who stole it."

I thought for a long minute. I didn't want back in this business, but I knew that Shanks wouldn't have asked for help unless he really needed it. Perhaps it was that important, after all.

"So why me? At least explain that much."

He turned to his desk and touched a button on his computer. An instant later an image filled a display screen. "Here's the man who stole the information."

It was a security video. I peered closely at the figure on the monitor. The room he was in wasn't well lit and the image was slightly blurry. Regardless, for the second time in less than an hour, I had the impression that I knew who it was, that something deep within me *already* knew, and that my conscious mind was just a step behind. It was the way he moved. The way he jerked his head to the side when he thought there was danger nearby.

TIMOTHY S.
JOHNSTON

The broad shoulders. The dark hair. He was in a lab of some sort, clearly anxious that someone might catch him where he shouldn't be. He turned slightly and Shanks abruptly froze the picture.

I gasped. The face on the screen was clear.

I knew who it was.

That man was the reason the Chinese military had interrogated and tortured me ruthlessly for four months in Sheng City. He was Johnny Chang, former operative of TCI. Seven years earlier he had betrayed and given me up while on a covert mission. He was a traitor to Trieste—and a former colleague—and until today I had thought he was still at Sheng. I thought I'd never see him here again.

My arms tightened at my sides and my heart pounded. Despite my hatred for Director Shanks and my claim that he was the real reason I had left the service, the complete truth was far more complicated. Suffice to say that Johnny Chang had also played a huge role, not the least of which was the torture I had suffered while in captivity.

In the years since, I had known that if I ever saw Johnny Chang again, I would kill him.

And now I had my chance.

CHAPTER TWO

WE STOOD IN THAT OFFICE AND stared at the frozen image on the display without speaking for what felt like an eternity. The revelation had stunned even Blake.

I turned to him. "You didn't know?"

"I knew the Chinese were involved. But this . . ." He shook his head. "This is huge. I wish I were the one going, Mac. I owe him for what he did."

We all owed him, but I most of all, and Blake knew it. He glanced away from the screen and fixed me with a penetrating glare. "Are you going to do it?" There was an unspoken message in that question. If I declined the mission, he would go in my place.

"I'll do it," I said in a soft voice.

I was back. After a seven year absence from TCI, I was in the game again. When I had awoken that morning, I'd assumed it would be the same as any other day. Now here I was, mentally preparing myself to pursue and kill a traitorous operative of TCI. A former friend. It was surreal.

There was an unmistakable look of relief on Shanks's face. "I had hoped you would agree. You are, after all, the best person for the job."

"Why's that?" I mumbled, but I already knew the answer.

"You know the Chinese. You've been on more missions to Sheng, Lau Tsi, Hanzhou, and New Kowloon Cities than any other person I've got. If they're going back to one of those places, you're well-equipped to follow them."

"What if this is a mainland China operation and the cities know nothing about it?"

He winced. "We'll have to hope that's not the case. Johnny Chang crossed us and defected to Sheng City. According to our information, he still works for them."

"But of course you want me to stop him before he gets anywhere near the city."

"Yes. Which brings up the real reason we contacted you. You *know* Johnny Chang. You worked closely with him on numerous occasions. You know where he'll be going, what he'll be doing, and why he'll be doing it."

But it was more than that, I realized. He had been my closest friend. I knew him better than any other operative.

At least, I *thought* I had. Until his betrayal.

Shanks continued, "On this mission, you're our secret weapon, McClusky. He doesn't know you're involved. It'll shock him, throw him off guard. I'm hoping you'll nail him before he makes it too far."

"And when I get him?"

"Bring him back here."

I tried not to let my face show disappointment. I would have to make it look like an accident, then.

"We have a seacar prepped and ready in the Docking Module. One other person will accompany you."

"It'll be good to work with Blake again."

Shanks shook his head. "Not him. A scientist. The person who developed the stolen technology."

My jaw dropped. "What? A civilian? Come on, Shanks. On this mission I could use help from someone trained in these things—an operative. This is ridiculous."

"Like it or not, that's the way it is. Blake will escort you to your cubicle and then to the docks. You'll meet your companion there."

I glared at him for a heartbeat, but could tell there was no use. Blake looked equally angry at missing out on the opportunity, but held his objections in check.

Finally, I muttered to Shanks, "How much does the civilian know?"

"About TCI? A little. You don't have to conceal anything, if that's what you're asking. I've granted full security clearance." He paused for a moment, as if he were struggling with a decision about something. And then, "Contact us in the usual manner. We'll be waiting for your word. Bring him back to us."

BLAKE'S FACE WAS DRAWN AS WE marched from the office. "How much did you know?" I asked him.

He shrugged. "A little. But as I said, I didn't know anything about Johnny." He swore. "I couldn't have kept that from you, and Shanks probably realized it and kept it from me too. We all want revenge for what happened." He paused. "Don't you?"

"Perhaps."

"Are you going to bring him in?"

It was a loaded question, and I stopped just meters from the travel tube leading to the habitat modules. Blake pulled up next to me, and together we moved through the lines of people stepping onto the conveyer. The deck was steel grating that hid conduits and pipes and wiring. Our footsteps clanged as we stalked to a large window set into the bulkhead. The lights had come on outside, flooding the sea with brilliant beams that sparkled and danced as plankton and fish passed through them. Darkness at Trieste was often even more beautiful than day; the lights attracted creatures of all kinds, and also outlined the modules and tubes of the city. Seacars with their lamps added to the scene as they soared through the water either on approach to the docking port, on departure, or as their operators performed routine maintenance on the city.

"I don't know," I finally whispered.

"I wouldn't."

"But orders are orders."

"No one will ever know."

I hesitated. "I will."

Another silence fell over us as we watched the cityscape through the window. It was so beautiful that it reminded me why I sacrificed so much. Still, hidden forces were always at work to prevent us from prospering.

"What's happened lately?"

He sighed. "Things are worse than when you worked for TCI, Mac."

"Between China and the States. The papers call it the Second Cold War."

"Well, you know that's been true since 2067, but things are getting out of hand now. Almost every mission Shanks sends me on is in some way related to a Chinese underwater city."

The two largest superpowers on the planet couldn't keep growing stronger and developing greater militaries without eventually coming into conflict with each other, and since the Second Korean War in 2067, tensions had grown substantially. When China led the charge to ocean colonization, the States had been forced to follow. We only had three cities to their six, a fact that rankled most of our politicians.

He continued, "It flares up all the time. Sometimes into outright fighting underwater that's kept silent in the press. Warsubs have even been sunk! It's a miracle those events haven't led to a land war."

"Fighting over The Iron Plains, I assume?"

He nodded. "Right."

I grimaced. And things were only going to grow worse. The Pacific seafloor just east of the Philippines was incredibly rich in iron. It was a discovery made only five years earlier, and both China and the United States had been quick to claim ownership. Each had declared solitary mining rights to the entire region. The flat and desolate abyssal plains there had a greater concentration of iron nodules than anywhere in the world, and with the human race now pushing out into the solar system as well as the oceans, the mineral was more valuable than ever.

"Last year the Chinese lost a few subs in the region. Three *Jin* class vessels, a *Yuan*, and even a *Kilo*. They blamed the States."

I blinked. "Were they right?"

He shrugged. "You know our military. Itchy trigger fingers. Anyway, suddenly we started losing subs as well. A couple of *Houston* classes and a *Matrix*."

"It sounds like a goddamned war."

If the Second Cold War was common knowledge, the fact that the Chinese and the Americans were actually coming to blows in the oceans was definitely not. Lives were being lost, the undersea cities were on the front lines, and most people had no idea. American troops had flooded our shelves, their subs were everywhere, and their troops were in our corridors on a daily basis. They weren't aware of our own struggles against the Chinese cities, however, or about TCI and the other intelligence services. That was why we couldn't contact the USSF and have them track down Johnny Chang for us. We had to do it on our own.

No one in Trieste liked the American military's presence. We saw it as a move that inflamed the current political situation and made us even more of a target to the Chinese. But after Trieste's drive for independence from the United States had failed in 2099, we knew the military was here for reasons other than Chinese tensions. They were trying to keep a lid on the situation, to maintain the status quo. We provided large amounts of kelp and fish for the topsiders, and they would do anything to keep us a part of the nation.

Trieste citizens, on the other hand, often felt otherwise, though they kept it to themselves nowadays. Loose lips sink ships, as they used to say—and at this time in history it had proved to be a more appropriate saying than ever.

I nudged Blake. "Come on. Let's get my things from my cubicle. Time's running out."

We stepped onto the conveyer and let it take us into the Living Modules of the undersea city.

MY BUNK WAS IN THE UPPERMOST level of Living Module B, one of the first constructed, and now home to single men and women. Module A was also home to single people. Families with children occupied C through F. As Trieste grew, we simply added more modules to accommodate the burgeoning population. Most people assumed they were domes, but they were actually squat cylinders, and when we added levels it was similar to putting another layer on a cake. We didn't require domes in this shallow environment.

Living space was so tight in the undersea cities that personal space for a single man was limited to a recessed bunk in a bulkhead with a tiny area next to it that contained a desk, a comm, and a computer. Bathrooms, recreation lounges, and eating areas were all in communal sectors. My own cubicle was only four square meters. At first it seemed tight, but I had gotten used to it. I rarely spent time there, anyway—it was just for sleeping or working in private. The rest of the day was spent putting in hours working.

I ducked into my cubicle and pulled open the drawers above the bed to grab a change of clothes and my personal hygiene travel kit. I shoved the items into a duffel. Blake stood waiting in the corridor outside, and I slid the plastic partition shut.

"Just want to make a call," I muttered to him. I recalled his warnings of possible listening devices nearby; I would have to be careful.

At the desk, I punched the code for Blue Downs, Australia's only underwater colony, into the comm. A few seconds later the connection came through, and a pretty, freckled face filled the screen.

My sister.

We were twins, forty-four years old. She had left Trieste in 2103. After our father had died, the stress of living in a place that regarded him a hero had grown too much for her. She hated what Dad had done, hated the path that he had chosen, and resented every occasion when someone tried to console her by telling her he had been a great man and had done the right thing. It drove her mad. And so, as soon as we turned eighteen, she left for

Blue Downs, located on the shelf between Australia and the island of Tasmania.

I understood why she ran, but missed her terribly. I hadn't seen her in a few years now.

Her eyes widened and a grin cracked her face as soon as she saw me. "Tru!" she cried. "How are you?"

I couldn't help but smile. "Fine, Meagan. You?"

"Couldn't be better. Things are great here. The city is booming and our aquaculture projects can't keep up with demand. Business for me is fantastic."

"Sounds a lot like here."

"The failing cropland topside has basically ensured us a position on the world market. What are you doing now?"

"Still working the farms. Doing what I can."

She tilted her head. "Ever gonna fill me in on what you've been into since university?"

This was an ongoing area of friction between us. I couldn't discuss my involvement with TCI—couldn't even mention that it existed—and she knew that I was secretive about my past for a reason. And after what had happened to our father and his quest to achieve independence for the city, she naturally assumed that I was part of that movement as well. I wasn't, but couldn't come out and say it.

"There's nothing to tell, sis."

She chuckled. "At least you've gone straight now. Working for a living, staying away from trouble."

I clenched a hidden fist. "Right."

Meagan worked as a sub engineer. She repaired engines, sealed fractured hulls, restored power systems, fixed electronics. She was a wunderkind when it came to subs, and owned a repair shop in Blue Downs. People everywhere in that city knew her as the best person for a tricky job, and paid her well for her skills. I was proud of her.

"What can I do for you? Or are you just calling to chat?"

I hesitated. "I'm going on a trip, wanted to let you know. I should be back soon."

She grinned again. "About time you took a vacation. Where to?"

I had already prepared the answer. "Just sticking around the Gulf. Might travel to Ballard or Seascape City."

"Staying near the States, eh? Why not be adventurous? Go to a European or South American city." She leaned forward. "Or even more daring, why not go topside and lie on a beach for a while?"

I frowned. "The decompression from this depth is over a hundred hours, Meg. You know that. Half the trip spent in a chamber?"

She laughed. "I know. Just kidding. But thanks for keeping me updated."

"Talk to you later, kid."

"Don't say that. We're the same age."

"I'm older."

"By thirty seconds, maybe."

"Still your older brother." I smiled at her. "I love you, Meg."

"Love you too. Enjoy your trip." She tilted her head as she said it, and in that instant, I knew that she hadn't believed a word that I'd said.

I ended the call and sat silently in front of the darkened screen. She could see right through me. Whatever happened, I had just wanted to talk with her in case this was the last trip I ever took.

I slid the partition aside; Blake was still outside in the windowless hall, keeping watch. "Ready?" he asked.

"Sure." I threw the duffel over my shoulder.

Footsteps came to us suddenly and I turned to see who was approaching. It was a group of men—five of them—marching quickly toward us in the narrow corridor. They had just come up the ladder; five seconds later and they would have missed us. They were wearing wetsuits, their hair slick from outside.

I swore.

They were Chinese.

THEY BROKE INTO A RUN AND I dropped the duffel. I savagely thrust aside the thought that they were simply citizens of Trieste and that this was just coincidence.

Beside me, Blake pulled his gun.

"Freeze right there!" he cried.

They ignored him.

"Fire," I hissed.

He lowered his aim and got off four quick rounds; each sounded as harmless as a puff of air, but they were deadly. One of the men cried out and sprawled to the deck, his kneecaps a shattered ruin. Blood and bone sprayed outward and the men on either side leaped away from him.

And then they were on us.

A few more shots went off—I couldn't tell who had fired—and I backed away as two of them came at me. I ducked a fist, then another, and with the next one, I grabbed my attacker's wrist, turned my body, and wrenched the arm down across my shoulder. There was only a slight resistance before the arm snapped backward and his elbow splintered. He screamed in agony. I spun back toward him and struck at his neck with a quick jab. His cries turned to gurgles and he fell to the deck writhing in pain.

The other one pressed the attack and I backed off to avoid his kicks. Damn, he was fast as hell. Three crescents, a front kick, then a stomp aimed at my left knee. I jerked to the side and threw an elbow deep into his kidney. He yelped in surprise and fell away, arching his body to absorb some of the impact. I wrapped an arm around his neck, pinning one of his arms in the process, and began to squeeze.

He brought a knee into my midsection. It hurt, but didn't break my grip. I squeezed tighter and waited for the struggle to stop.

I hadn't fought in a while and thought I would be rusty at this. However, to my surprise, it all came back fairly quickly. My training as a recruit in TCI was still intact, and the work on the farms had toughened me, increased my musculature. I could probably take more damage now than I ever could have as an operative in my early years.

My attacker tried one last move to break free. His right hand grabbed at a nerve cluster at the base of my neck, and he applied intense pressure. I gritted my teeth and twisted away from him.

A second later it was over.

He fell with a dull thud.

The last two men stepped back and took in the situation. We had hopelessly injured two of them—one had lost his knees, the other his arm—and another was dead.

They spun on their heels and sprinted away.

I lunged to Blake to check him; he was uncharacteristically quiet.

And then I saw why.

There was a blade buried in his chest.

In his heart.

I couldn't believe the man was still standing. But as soon as our attackers disappeared from sight, their ringing footsteps descending the ladder, he fell into my arms and then collapsed to the deck.

His last breath was the death rattle, that final bit of air sighing out from a lifeless corpse.

I paused for just a second. Two of the Chinese on the deck were still alive and I needed to take them in for questioning, before someone else called for help or a USSF sailor happened to come along. But the two men who had run were only a short distance away; I still had time to catch them.

It took only another instant to make up my mind.

I bolted to my feet and pursued.

CHAPTER THREE

I MADE SURE TO GRAB BLAKE'S PCD—his Personal Communication Device—and thumbed the call button as I rocketed down the ladder. Each level in the habitation modules had an airlock in case of emergency, but the two remaining attackers had ignored it in order to get to the lower levels. There was no doubt about it: they were headed for the moonpool.

An instant later a voice came to me from the small device. "Report, Blake. Did everything go—"

"Blake's dead!" I yelled as I rounded a corner and started on the next ladder. The moonpool was on seafloor level. "Two men remaining; I'm on them!"

Shanks wasted no time asking for explanations. "I'll send a team immediately. Is there anything to clean up there?"

His question was cryptic but its meaning was unmistakable. "Outside my quarters, yeah," I said, breathless. I hit another landing and turned the sharp corner.

Since all modules were kept at a standard four atmospheres, and the water pressure outside was also at four atmospheres, it allowed us to have a hatch in the deck through which we could access the ocean quickly. No water came in, and no air went out. If there was a depressurization emergency, however, the water would immediately surge in, but that was why we had bulkhead doors and airlocks throughout the city. Still, living under pressure the way we did meant that we could never shoot straight for the surface if there was a disaster. We would die within minutes as the dissolved gases in our tissues expanded and bubbled out of our blood like soda on a hot day. Just as in all other major undersea cities around the world, we lived thirty meters down, essentially performing one long saturation dive. This meant that our cells had absorbed the maximum amount of gases possible at this depth. Unless we depressurized slowly, we could go no shallower. You could say that we were willing prisoners of the deep.

What made living underwater significantly easier was the fact that every seacar, sub, and facility also had its life support at four atmospheres. Nations had mandated this decades ago to allow for easy travel through the oceans.

The Chinese had most likely entered through the pool in this module. That was, after all, how I had infiltrated the Chinese cities on most of my missions. Their gear was either on the deck beside the pool, or they had left it on the seafloor just outside. It would take them a moment or two to put it on, and in that time, I hoped that I would be able to catch them off guard.

At seafloor level I sprinted through the corridor and passed through the watertight hatch. There was no one around. My feet clanged with each impact on the deck; I realized suddenly that this was not going to be much of a surprise. As I came to the lip of the pool, I pulled to an abrupt halt and looked down into the water. I could see the ocean floor. The sun above had set, but the lights of the city were at full illumination and the area below was quite visible. I arrived just in time to see two shadows disappear to the west; they were swimming like hell. I shot a glance at the lockers in the room; my scuba gear was there, but it would take a few minutes to suit up.

The decision was easy to make.

Grabbing a nearby weighted belt to keep me from floating to the surface, I sucked in a deep breath and dove in.

The water was cold—even at this latitude, the temperature at the bottom was only about fourteen degrees Celsius—and it stung for a second as I entered. At that moment, the fact that I wasn't wearing a wetsuit and was without a tank didn't bother me in the least. I'm not sure why. I could only hold my breath for three minutes, at most, and after the fight and pursuit down the ladder, my heart was already pounding and I was short on oxygen.

The adrenaline had taken over, I guess.

I plunged downward and came to rest on the sandy bottom, just a few meters under the lip of the pool. I never tired of feeling weightless when outside the city. The immense mass of water above was not a problem as the air in my lungs and sinuses was already at four atmospheres. My hair swirled about in the current, my limbs splayed out effortlessly. The seagrasses partially obscured me, but the maintenance personnel kept it trimmed so it didn't grow too high and interfere with the pool. However, my entrance made enough noise that the two men turned to look behind them as they swam away and saw me almost instantly.

Shit.

They jerked to a halt and gestured toward me. Their transparent facemasks covered their mouths, and I could see them debating what to do. Since it was obvious I had no equipment, I knew it would be a simple choice for them.

They started toward me.

I searched the area nearby and saw, hidden in the swaying grasses, the gear belonging to the men we had injured or killed. I could swim to it and pull it on, but by then the two would be on me.

I had to face them before I could breathe again.

Their faces were tight as they moved toward me. Earlier I had marveled at the beauty of the city at night, but now I resented the floodlights—there was no place to hide.

The lead attacker reached to his thigh and drew a gun.

My heart nearly exploded.

The large, square barrel was as clear as day.

A needle gun.

Highly effective for underwater combat.

And I had nothing.

AND THEN THE LIGHTS WENT DARK.

Shanks, you son of a bitch, I thought. The bastard had brains, after all, and knew where I had gone. He had given me a fighting chance.

I pushed off the bottom and arced up two meters before I brought myself to a stop. Two huge kicks later, I figured that I was directly over the first one. It was impossible to see anything. The afterimage of the bright lights had blinded me. If the moon had been in the sky up top there might have been some faint light to see by, but for the moment, everything was pitch black.

I kicked savagely and plunged downward. My outstretched hand touched something metallic, and I grasped and hauled myself toward it.

A scuba tank.

I wrapped my legs around the man's torso and clutched his facemask in my right hand. I tore it away with a quick jerk and a rush of bubbles shot past me on their way to the surface. There was a brief yelp, then he fell silent as he held his breath.

He twisted to the side; it was obvious that he was trying to bring his weapon to bear.

Snap!

Snap!

Snap!

He fired three times and the needles lanced past my left ear.

Fuck! I almost screamed out loud; I had come close to buying it just there.

I pulled myself closer to him and snaked an arm around his neck. I flexed my biceps and squeezed with everything I had. He began to writhe like crazy. He was panicking.

He knew that he was seconds from death.

The problem was he most likely had more air in his lungs than I.

I remained calm and maintained my grip. With eyes closed, I began to count in my head. If I had ripped the mask off after he had taken his last breath, I was done for. If I had removed it just after he *exhaled*, however, I would be fine. But already my lungs were screaming for air and I realized that I only had about twenty seconds left.

I opened my eyes. Above and to the right was a dim glow. It was the moonpool. There was safety there . . . and air, if I could reach it.

Only a few moments left. . . .

The thrashing body stopped suddenly, convulsed twice more, then fell still.

I released my grip and struggled to find his facemask. It had fallen free during the struggle, but within seconds I located the tube leading to the regulator. I yanked it up and hurriedly placed it over my face. I activated the airstream and the mask cleared.

I took a massive gulp of air.

Then another.

A voice came to me through an earphone attached to the mask. It was Chinese. "Where are you, Tsui? I can't see anything." It was a throaty whisper—the man was terrified.

I could understand and speak the language—something I had needed for my missions in my earlier life—and I considered responding. The water on the faceplate muffled and distorted the sound of a person's voice slightly, and it might just trick him. But my accent was the problem. I had no idea what part of China the dead man had come from, or what undersea city. My own was fairly innocuous and passable, actually, but it would be a huge gamble.

But I had nothing to lose.

It was still dark, and I had drifted down to the seafloor with the body. I began to search blindly for the man's needle gun. As I did, I said in Chinese, "I'm here."

Pause. "Where?"

"Near the moonpool. I got him."

"How?" He sounded guarded.

"Shot him. There must be blood everywhere. We should leave." They had to have some method of transport nearby. Some personal scooters, probably. They would ride them thirty kilometers or so until they were picked up by a small seacar or warsub. Our own traffic controllers would detect them, but they'd seem no larger than small sharks. They might hear them, but often the sounds of other seacars in the area masked the low thrum of a scooter.

If I could use the one remaining man to lead me to his transport, I knew he might also take me right to Johnny Chang. I could end this tonight, possibly.

If this worked.

"You don't sound well," the other said.

"He pulled my mask off. I almost died."

Another pause. Longer this time. "What's my name?"

Oh, shit.

I shrugged inwardly. "The morgue will list you as *John Doe*, I'm guessing."

There was a sudden gasp, then the earphone went dead. I looked around but still couldn't see much.

My hand touched hard plastic, and I clutched it eagerly.

The gun.

I tore the holster from the corpse's thigh and tightened it around my own. Then I holstered the weapon and removed the PCD from my waist. It had multiple communication capabilities. With it I could surf the net, take photos, make audio calls, communicate visually, read books and newspapers, and create documents. I had taken Blake's because I knew it would be easy to contact Shanks with its preprogrammed codes.

It could also send text.

I pushed it down to the sandy floor and scrolled through the menu. Hopefully the seagrasses would obscure the screen, but just in case, I nudged the backlight level to its lowest setting. I called up Shanks's number and sent a single, simple message.

LIGHTS BACK ON, TEN SECONDS.

I pocketed the device and waited calmly.

THE FLOODLIGHTS WERE ALMOST BLINDING. I had to fight to keep from shutting my eyes against the powerful illumination.

But there he was.

Fifteen meters from me, swimming frantically.

I ripped the tank off the corpse and pulled it on. I couldn't let this one get away, not after getting so close to Chang's trail.

Not after they killed Blake.

I decided to take the flippers too. They were just too great an advantage underwater. Had I tried to pursue without them, my prey would have ended up out of sight within moments.

My ragged breath and heaving lungs threatened to terminate the chase within five short minutes despite the flippers, but I pressed on. He was twenty-five meters from me now, but his lead wasn't increasing. In fact, I was beginning to close the gap. The problem was, as we left the modules of the city behind, it was getting darker and darker. I would lose him soon in the murky water.

I had to chance it.

I removed the gun and brought myself to a stop in the cold water.

I took aim.

I breathed in and held it.

I fired.

Snap!

The man jerked to the side and arched his back in pain. Bubbles exploded from his mask. Shit, that wouldn't have been nice. The needles—five of them in each shot—were twenty centimeters long and each the thickness of a spaghetti noodle. I had just nailed him in the legs, feet, and possibly groin.

I approached him silently. He was searching himself now as he tried to find the sharp projectiles to pull out. Most often, however, the needles buried themselves completely in flesh.

It was a deadly—and *painful*—weapon.

But I had no reservations about using it. Hell, one of these assholes had shot at me only minutes earlier.

He seemed to have forgotten that I was nearby. When I was within ten meters, he suddenly looked up. He touched his ear and I heard a click in my own mask.

"Mission failed! Abort!" He had spoken in Cantonese this time, as opposed to Mandarin, hoping that I would not understand. But of course, I did.

He realized that it was all over. He reached for his gun.

"Don't do it!" I shouted, bringing my own to bear.

He ignored me.

I gritted my teeth, and squeezed the trigger.

The needles stabbed out and plunged into his abdomen. It was such an agonizing injury I knew it would be hard for him to press his attack. I approached, removed his gun, and let it drop to the bottom to retrieve later.

"What do you want?" I growled. "Why are you after me?"

He could only groan in pain.

And then he seized my mask and pulled with everything he had left.

I fired again.

And again.

At this range the needles probably penetrated his chest and shot out the other side into empty water.

He shuddered and then fell still.

I gasped. That one had been close. I was lucky.

The body slowly drifted downward and I stared at it, silently debating what to do. He had warned his friends, and they were probably already on their way out of the Gulf. Finding his scooter didn't make sense anymore. I would have to return to Trieste and try to pursue Johnny with the seacar Shanks had prepared for me.

Still, the situation was puzzling. What had they been after? Why me? How had they known that I would be the one selected for the mission? Whatever the case, it was clear that a Chinese city was making the attempt at securing the technology Trieste had developed. If Shanks's stunted explanation before hadn't spelled out the seriousness of this mission, the attack certainly did. They were willing to kill for it, whatever *it* was, and openly at that. It might even start an international incident! I had never heard of five foreign operatives infiltrating one of our cities at the same time, in the same group, and assaulting a US citizen in the corridor of a habitat module with the intent to kill.

Cold war, my ass.

Blake had been right: the subterfuge and espionage between the US and China would likely start an all-out war, and when it happened, it would not only involve the undersea cities, but the nations on land as well. It would be a world war, most likely fought with hydrogen and neutron bombs, and there would be *billions* dead.

I searched the second body quickly but found nothing other than standard scuba gear. I retrieved the needle gun from where it rested, turned, kicked out hard, and began the swim back to Trieste. When lit, the modules and travel tubes were visible for hundreds of meters in the shallow water. They would lead me home.

If Shanks couldn't contain word of these attacks, or if someone other than TCI retrieved the bodies, then I had a potential war to stop.

And a man still to kill.

CHAPTER FOUR 四

I DRIED OFF QUICKLY IN MY cubicle and threw on a change of clothes. My duffel was nowhere in sight, and neither were the bodies. All evidence of the struggle, in fact, was gone. A TCI crew had scrubbed away the blood on the deck and bulkheads.

Shanks worked fast.

I stalked quickly through Living Modules B and A, through the tubes into the Commerce Module, along the outer bulkhead past expansive windows with lounges and restaurants arrayed before them, and down the long tube into the docks.

I sprinted on the conveyer.

Trieste's docking facilities were typical of most underwater cities. Seacars approached along a very visible path of lights on the seafloor, much like a runway. They entered the module through a large hatch and came to a halt in a wide shaft that led upward. They blew their ballast, changing their buoyancy to positive, and ascended the few meters into a moonpool far larger than the ones divers used. It was nearly the size of a football field. There were over fifty berths within. Platforms completely surrounded each berth for people to walk on, perform routine maintenance, and load their vessels. There was little disturbance in the water at this location on the shelf, so the main hatch that led outside was open almost all of the time.

Due to their size, submarines, on the other hand, such as the warsubs of the United States Submarine Fleet, could not enter and dock here. Umbilicals stretched out to those ships' airlocks and people could cross into the city that way.

I entered the module and scanned the interior, looking for a hint as to where to go. Shanks stood on the other side of the large bay beside a seacar. He motioned to me. His face was grim. Standing with him was a short, heavyset woman with dark hair and severe features. I sighed. Mayor Janice Flint. Technically Shanks was her Administrative Assistant—a cover for his real job as head of our intelligence service. The mayor was fully aware of its existence, and in fact often initiated its operatives' missions to foreign cities. She was stubborn, arrogant, demanding, forceful, and extremely self-assured. All wonderful qualities to have in a leader, I supposed. But damn difficult to work for.

Shanks and Flint, standing together waiting for me, I thought. Just great.

I walked across the docks, past numerous seacars. The sound of waves sloshing against the platforms echoed in the large chamber and created a pervasive low drone. As I moved toward Shanks and Flint, the seacar they stood near stole my attention. Its tanks had been partially flooded to lower its profile in the water, but even so, I could see that there was something odd about its design. In the post-nuclear era, most seacars and submarines were cigar-shaped. Beforehand, subs had mostly sailed on the surface and only submerged during battles, such as the subs of World War II. But when militaries started using nuclear power plants, their submarines often stayed submerged for months at a time. Engineers soon realized that the vessels needed to be more streamlined and suited to underwater travel, and so, starting around 1950, they'd redesigned hulls with the now familiar shape. It meant that they weren't very seaworthy on the surface, but they performed far better underwater.

This seacar, however, did not resemble a cigar. It had a flat, blunt nose, and the cockpit was covered by a large span of ultra-dense acrylic glass. The stabilizers looked more like wings than stern planes. They were thicker than most—perhaps for ballast?—and each had a flap at its rear for tilting the stern of the seacar up or down. There were two thrusters at the end of each stabilizer. Most seacars had these closer to the main body of the vessel. This ship's long stabilizers meant the thrusters were quite far from the hull—at least three meters. A cylindrical shield housed the screws to prevent damage should a collision occur. The stern of the hull narrowed to a dull point. There were also two bow planes used to tilt the nose up or down, as well as the vertical stabilizer and rudder that looked more like it belonged on an airplane than an ocean-going vessel.

The lettering on its hull identified it as *SC-1*.

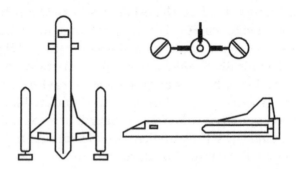

It didn't look like the most conventional seacar around, but it did look highly maneuverable. Still, the odd shape of the bow would make this slower than most, I figured. Unique seacars were not uncommon, but I was shocked Shanks would have us use something that stood out. Usually we traveled in something a little less conspicuous.

He ignored my scrutiny of the vessel. "We took care of the mess outside your cubicle. They're all dead now. Too bad about Blake."

My earlier confrontation with the director still perturbed me. I had hated this man so bitterly for so long, and it was difficult to get past that. But finally I managed to ask, "What did you do with the bodies?"

"Took 'em out the airlock. I have a team picking them up right now, along with the other ones you left for us."

Mayor Flint's expression was more cordial than usual. "Tough way to start the mission, Mr. McClusky."

"I wish we had been more prepared for it."

"Blake will receive our highest commendation."

Too bad no one but us will ever know that, I thought. The drawbacks of a life in espionage. . . .

"They were all Chinese?" Shanks asked.

"Yes. After me specifically. Know how they found out?"

He shook his head. "We've been concerned about other agencies bugging our offices and operatives. We'll have to do a complete check."

Flint turned to him. "Are you sure you want to send just him out after this man?"

Shanks looked slightly annoyed. "The more we send out, the more notice they draw. You know that. Other cities are always watching us, the same way our operatives watch them."

Flint seemed like she was about to disagree, then thought better of it. A brief silence fell over us. Shanks seemed uncomfortable; it was almost as if he felt unsure of how to act around me.

"This seacar," I remarked, pointing at it, "might make us a little more noticeable than I had hoped."

He shrugged and didn't say anything.

A shadow in the water passed under the vessel. I peered at it for a moment—a shark or dolphin inside the module.

Mayor Flint barked abruptly, "Don't fuck this up, McClusky. Shanks may think this mission is up your alley, but as far as I'm concerned, you're too close to this. We need that information back, intact. Johnny Chang as well. Bring that asshole to us in one piece so we can deal with him."

I almost took a step back. Her brutal demeanor had returned in full force. Thankfully, I hadn't had much contact with her since resigning from TCI, back when she was merely one of the elected officials on city council. She had risen to the top quickly; rumor had it she had used blackmail to destroy the lives of her political competitors. And Flint had done very well with the strategy. She was currently in her second three-year term.

Shanks suddenly looked toward the entrance of the docking facility. "Oh, shit. Here comes trouble."

Two men in neatly pressed blue uniforms had entered and were marching directly toward us. US military. The USSF, to be precise.

"Keep watching them," Shanks muttered. "Don't look suspicious." He pulled out his PCD and acted as if he was receiving a call. "Take her down two meters," he muttered into the device. "Run some ballast trim tests—but don't surface."

It was obvious he was speaking to the pilot of the seacar—my scientist companion for the trip. I could barely see him in the command seat through the large cockpit port. It stretched clear across the hull of the seacar, exposing a large array of multicolored lights on the control console inside.

A second later the hatch on top of the hull slid shut and the vessel disappeared beneath the waves. It was still visible, but it was now only a blurry shape.

The two soldiers halted before us. "Mayor Flint," one of them said in a deep voice. "I'm Commander Schrader of USS *Impaler*." He was tall and broad with dark hair and a five o'clock shadow. He had heavily muscled arms and thick legs. He looked like a wrestler of some sort, and not the type to spend his career in a military submarine.

Impaler was the *Reaper* class warsub I had seen earlier outside the city.

"Can I help you?" Flint responded. There was no warmth in her voice.

"We had a report of some odd transmissions a short time ago."

A shock ran through me. I wondered if my hair was still wet from the incident outside. I noticed Schrader's eyes flick toward me, but it seemed to be merely idle curiosity.

Flint frowned. "Such as?"

"It seemed as though a confrontation of some sort occurred."

"Between who?"

"We're not sure."

"What did your people hear, exactly?"

"I'm not at liberty to discuss it."

The mayor looked displeased. "Then why ask?"

Schrader's face grew hard. He did not look like the type who would take shit from anyone, let alone a civilian. "Orders," he ground out.

Beside me, bubbles broke the surface. The ballast test. The two USSF officers glanced at them only briefly; their attention was on Flint at that moment.

"When did this happen?" she asked.

"Within the last hour. Someone also ordered the outside floodlights cut. Why?"

She shrugged. "I've been here at the docks with my administrative assistant, and have heard nothing from Trieste City Control."

A long pause. "Does that mean you don't know anything?"

"That's what it means. Perhaps I'll read a report about it in the morning, if one of my security people noticed something peculiar. But since I can't give you answers, and you're not willing to fill me in, is there something else I can help you with?"

The soldiers' eyes were like ice. "No ma'am," the commander growled after a heartbeat.

Flint turned from him. "Good evening." She began to talk with Shanks about some trivial city matter—construction on the Storage Module—and completely ignored the two USSF officers.

Their faces clearly showed their anger, and they spun on their heels and stalked away. I didn't feel any sympathy for them.

Shanks muttered, "You could have been a bit more diplomatic, Jan."

Flint snorted. "I don't care for them, you know that. And you know why. Have you seen *Impaler*? She arrived last week and her crew have been traipsing through the city causing trouble ever since. They're only here for one reason, anyway. Concern for their feelings is at the bottom of my list of priorities."

Although I didn't care for her manner, I appreciated her attitude. We couldn't involve the military in this matter. First, they were also our competitors in the oceans, and we couldn't allow important new technology to fall into their hands. Second, they didn't know about TCI's existence, and we had to keep it that way.

I suspected Mayor Flint had come to the docks to *motivate* me to do the best job possible. She knew all about my past troubles with Shanks, and by her comments earlier I could tell that she also questioned my loyalty. I didn't need her brand of encouragement, but I understood. So, I kept my mouth shut.

Shanks ordered the seacar to surface. He handed me a computer chip for the PCD. "Here are the details on Johnny's last known position, the make of seacar he was in, and his course. Your bag is inside, as is your companion."

And with that, they turned and left.

They didn't look back.

I CLIMBED ONTO THE HULL OF the seacar and the hatch opened for me. There was a short ladder down, and I descended the five rungs quickly.

My feet hit the deck with a clang.

The hatch closed.

Inside it smelled slightly metallic, of oil and grease and canned air. I was in a narrow passageway that ran the length of the vessel. As I moved forward I passed two bunks recessed into the bulkheads on opposite sides of the passage. Aftward was a small lounge, kitchen, eating area, and a sliding door that hid a washroom, and behind me, at the other end of the hall, was the engine room. I decided to have a look around there in the morning, to familiarize myself fully with the vessel.

The thrum of the thrusters reverberated through the hull, into the deck, and up my legs. It sounded smooth, powerful. It felt *good*. I enjoyed being out in the open ocean. The danger of the mission was foremost in my mind, especially after the attack, but being in this vessel was pleasant and enjoyable.

I walked toward the control cabin and pushed the hatch aside. A woman turned to look at me.

"You better be as good as they say you are," she snapped. Then she turned back to the console.

Water splashed over the canopy as the sub descended.

I SAT NEXT TO HER. SHE was African American and had long, straight hair and stunning features. I had to force myself to study the console before me.

"Get used to the controls," she said. Her voice was melodious and rich, even though her tone was clipped and sharp at that moment. Had it not been for her appearance, I probably would have already snarled back at her. She continued, "It could be a long journey."

"My name's Truman McClusky, TCI Operative First Class," I said eventually.

"I know."

She said no more, and I turned from her. If she wanted to act like Shanks and Flint, I thought, then let her. I would just ignore her and focus on the mission.

She peered out the port before us as she navigated from the Docking Module. She had set the ballast to neutral buoyancy, and used the airplane-like yoke to tilt the nose of the seacar up. We ascended fifteen meters and powered over the habitat modules, on an eastward course. She banked the seacar and we passed the Storage Module that Flint had mentioned only minutes earlier. It had been undergoing construction now for over two years, and came up often in city council debates due to frequent delays and cost overruns. It was a common complaint people had of the council, along with other trivial items such as the expense of materials needed for batteries, such as lithium. We seemed to import a great deal of lithium—more than any other colony—and no one really knew why.

The lights of the city fell away behind us, and we moved into deeper water. I felt the thrill of adventure surge within me again; the canopy almost completely surrounded the control cabin, and it was as if *SC-1* did not exist. It was exhilarating. It had taken centuries of exploration, disasters, innovations, and lost lives to bring us to this point. The oceans stretched out before us, ours for the taking.

If only we could colonize without it leading to war, I thought. That would ruin the oceans, contaminate them beyond hope. We could do it peacefully. I knew we could. If only someone could convince those short-sighted people of the necessity of living together on the planet, of using her resources wisely.

I sighed. Wishful thinking. Father had been one of them—someone who'd thought that armed conflict was the solution to our troubles. Even the best of us can make mistakes, I reminded myself. But if that were true, how could we possibly avoid war? Perhaps it was inevitable.

"Can you pilot her?"

I pulled myself back to the present and studied the controls before me, but found the question slightly insulting. I was no stranger to piloting a seacar. "Sure. There's the thruster power levers on the left side of the pilot's chair—one for starboard, one for port. The yoke controls the bow and stern planes. The pedals operate the rudder." I pointed to a panel between the two chairs. "There are the ballast controls." I shrugged. "Easy enough."

She flipped a toggle on the panel before her, next to the navigation and shipboard status readouts. It was the autopilot function. "You know where that bastard went?"

I held up the chip that Shanks had given me.

"Then get us there fast." And with that she stood and pushed her way past me into the passageway that led to the living area. She disappeared into a bunk and yanked the curtain shut.

I turned back to the controls. Shit. She was right. It was going to be one hell of a long journey.

As *SC-1* powered through the ocean and headed east through the Florida strait, few people in Trieste noticed USS *Impaler* quietly detach from her umbilical in the early morning hours and depart the city.

Her four massive screws churned the waters violently.

Her course: east.

". . . when I first arrived in that incredible undersea environment, I realized immediately how tenuous the undersea colonists' hold is to life. A violent confrontation between well-armed ships could possibly end within seconds. The key is to make sure you strike first . . . for if you give them a chance to shoot back, it could end before you know it."

–Frank McClusky, Citizen of Trieste, Mayor, and Freedom Fighter

PART TWO: THE ABYSSAL PLAINS

CHAPTER FIVE 五.

WE PASSED THROUGH THE FLORIDA STRAIT without incident, and five hours after our departure we hit the shallows of the Great Bahama Bank, 350 kilometers from Trieste. I turned the seacar northward to the Blake Plateau, an area of flat relief one hundred kilometers east of Florida. When we reached the Plateau, I would shift to the northeast and begin the long haul to the massive mountain range in the middle of the ocean known as the Mid-Atlantic Ridge. That was the course Johnny's vessel had taken; that was where we had to follow.

When I first pushed the throttle forward and watched the readout, my eyes widened in shock. The top speed of *SC-1* was seventy kilometers per hour. The maximum velocity any undersea vessel could travel was eighty, a limitation caused by the massive drag and friction of water against steel. In the era of submarines that had followed World War II, the fastest a nuclear attack submarine could travel was roughly thirty-five knots, or sixty-five kilometers per hour. This was still considered quite fast. Modern warsubs of the USSF could exceed that velocity, but not by much. The fastest warsub in the fleet was the *Houston* class—also known as the *Hunter-Killer*—at seventy-eight kph, and rumor had it that the Chinese had hit the maximum limit with their counterpart warsub, the *Jin* class, also known as the *Fast Attack*.

The speed of *SC-1* surprised me because of the hull's odd shape. Whoever had built her had done a fine job, after all, as a speed of seventy kph was nothing to laugh at. I wondered if perhaps the placement of the thruster pods had something to do with it. They were farther from the hull than was standard, and were also quite a bit longer, perhaps to contain extra batteries for her electric motors.

A quick glance at the depth gauge made me admire her further; the crush depth was listed at 4000 meters. This fact interested me because most seacars could only descend to depths of about 2000 meters. Since our cities were all at thirty meters, there was no real need to go much deeper. The bottom of the Atlantic was around four to five kilometers in most places, though there were some areas even deeper, such as the ocean trenches and rift zones. I almost wanted to take us down simply to have a look around.

We generally lived near the surface and rarely went much deeper except for exploration or deep-sea mining ventures. But this seacar's abilities were phenomenal. To compare with the twentieth century: most subs in World War I could descend no deeper than a hundred meters. World War II subs doubled this—still a minuscule range. And by the end of the century, warsubs had reached maximum depths of about 1500 meters; still nothing compared to the deepest parts of the ocean, at around 11,000 meters.

The water outside the canopy was pitch black; I sailed by instrument alone, turned off the running lights, and kept my eyes on the sonar. There was something on the console called the Virtual Imaging Display, which sounded interesting, but I decided to wait until I could ask about it later. The sonar picked up numerous boats and seacars on the same route—we were currently in a common sealane—but nothing that matched the description of Johnny's sub. It would take us days to catch him; he was traveling at sixty kilometers per hour and had a head start of several hours.

When I looked back at the control console, I noticed one area covered by a sealed panel, beside which was a thumbprint scanner. I left it alone for now. I added it to the list of things I would ask my companion about later.

I snorted to myself. *My Companion.* I needed a name for her, and soon. I also hoped she would be a little more courteous after a night's rest. Granted, it was her discovery Johnny had stolen, and she had a right to be upset, but still, I was there to retrieve it for her. A little gratitude or respect instead of scorn and derision would have been nice. My life was at risk, after all.

There was no indication of the sun rising overhead. Since the Gulf Stream flowed northerly in this region, as part of the North Atlantic Gyre, northbound vessels stayed shallow to take advantage of the current. We were at a depth of only two hundred meters, but even there it was always dark. It was the lower limit of the euphotic depth, which meant that light levels were less than one percent of those at the surface. No plants could grow; it was essentially as black as the darkest night sky, even when the sun was at its zenith.

Eventually I decided that it would be a good idea to get a look at the engine room in the aft compartment. I toggled on the autopilot and stalked through the central passageway, past the bunks and the living area, and punched the button to open the watertight hatch. Inside was a mechanical area quite ordinary in appearance. There were banks of powerful batteries for the electric thrusters, which were quick to charge when docked and capable of generating high underwater velocities. Ballast control and environmental air and water recycling systems were also in the engine room. The ceiling and bulkheads were bare steel that curved inwards. The space seemed smaller than it should; I had thought that the aft portion of the hull was several meters beyond this chamber.

There was one curious feature: large pipes in the ceiling, at head level, that stretched from forward to aft. They were for the ballast system, to transfer water from one tank to another to help stabilize, or trim, the seacar. But their presence in the engine room was odd.

I frowned at that and headed forward again.

She was there, back in the pilot's seat. She turned to look at me with a somewhat sheepish grin on her face. "McClusky, I'm sorry about my behavior last night," she said in that wonderful voice. "I'm in a bit of a stressful situation right now."

"I'd say we both are." I attempted a small smile to let her know I understood.

"I just want to catch this guy and get my material back."

"Me too," I muttered, still staring at her.

She paused for a moment, and then reached her hand out suddenly, as if she had forgotten earlier. "My name's Katherine Wells. I'm a specialist in undersea colonization and I have a doctorate in aquanautic engineering."

"You're not from Trieste." I shook her hand and sat beside her.

She frowned. "How can you—"

I gestured at her hair. "Most people here keep it short. It's easier to dry. Yours is long."

A nod. "You're right. I've only been in Trieste for a month. I had been doing all my work topside until just recently."

An awkward silence ensued, perhaps because her behavior the previous evening still perturbed me, or maybe because I was once again in awe of her beauty. Her dark skin was perfect, her hair shiny and straight. Her eyes seemed so black they absorbed all light that hit them. I could lose myself in those, I thought.

"Problem?" There was another smile on her face.

"No," I said abruptly. "I was just back looking at the engine room. I noticed some interesting things." I paused. "This seacar, in fact, is quite unique. Its shape, its maximum speed and depth, the position of the thrusters."

"It's not made by one of the common manufacturers. A company in Clearwater built it for me." She stopped and said nothing more.

"How can it get a top speed of seventy with such a design?"

"Ah. The batteries."

"I saw them. But there don't seem to be enough."

She gestured out the canopy. "The thruster pods are longer than usual—did you notice?"

"There are more batteries there?" Just as I had thought.

"Yes. The ones you saw in the engine room are partly for the living compartments, the controls, and so on, but most are for the engines. The ones in the pods, however, are dedicated solely to the thrusters."

"I see. Just pure, brute force gets this vessel though the ocean so quickly. If the shape were more streamlined for water—"

"We'd hit eighty fairly easy."

I considered that. "I noticed something else odd in the engine room."

Her eyebrows rose. "What?"

"The ballast pipes. Since they carry water, they shouldn't be anywhere near electronic components."

Her face remained blank. She didn't say a word.

I hesitated. "In case there's an emergency . . ."

Still she didn't respond. In fact, she was beginning to look angry again.

"Hey," I said, "don't get defensive. I know this is your seacar. But there should never be water pipes in those areas. We learned our lesson almost two centuries ago with USS *Thresher*."

In fact, everyone who piloted the depths knew the famous story. In 1963, one of the newest nuclear subs in the United States arsenal underwent sea trials in the Atlantic following an overhaul at the naval yard in New Hampshire. After the sub began her test dive, her radioman broadcast the following: "Experiencing minor problem. Have positive angle." And later: "Attempting to blow." Those listening heard air under high pressure, followed by fourteen minutes of silence, until: "—test depth." The sound of wrenching metal and collapsing bulkheads followed. The sub had imploded.

What had happened seemed clear: at some point in her dive, she began to take on too much water. The crew had used the bow planes to tilt the sub up and tried to power her to the surface. The ballast system failed, however, and the sub descended, eventually hitting her collapse depth, more popularly called crush depth.

Although authorities knew the sequence of events, the exact cause took years to ascertain, though doubts still remain. They theorized the ballast pipes in the engine room broke at poorly joined seals, the spraying water shorted out sensitive electronics, and as a result, the nuclear reactor automatically shut down. Without it for power, the engines simply couldn't force the vessel to the surface, especially as water flooded the engine room. At that depth, the ballast-blow system couldn't clear the water from her tanks to make the sub lighter. It sank.

Carrying with her 129 souls.

It was one of the worst disasters in US Naval history, caused by a design flaw.

Just as with *SC-1*.

Katherine Wells now looked positively furious. She knew the story, and my mention of it had bothered her for some reason.

This is one prickly customer, I thought. *What the hell is her problem?*

"I'm not suggesting this seacar will sink," I offered. "Just that the design is—"

"What?" she snapped. "Poor?"

"No, just *flawed*."

She closed her mouth and stared at me for several long seconds. It made me uncomfortable, and I wondered what I could do to ease the tension.

Finally she said, "Look. The engines on this vessel are battery driven. Each thruster has batteries in its pods, well away from the engine room. Even if there is water spray there, it won't affect those batteries or the thrusters."

"I'm just saying—"

"You're not saying *anything*, you're just making dumb statements."

I frowned. "Miss Wells, *Thresher* was a great lesson for us all. You lived on land until just a month ago, right? Well—"

It was the wrong thing to say. She bolted to her feet. "I may have been on land, but I have devoted my life to the oceans. I had my first doctorate at twenty-one. I earned a second at twenty-four. I've instructed at UCLA, Harvard, and Honolulu. I also spoke to Congress about continuing the ocean colonization program. So don't tell me what I don't know about living in the oceans. I know a hell of a lot more than you!" Her nostrils had flared and her face was drawn.

I raised my hands. "I didn't mean that you weren't smart, just that down here, in the undersea cities, in a saturation environment, we learn about these things as a matter of course, you know? Everyday talk is about this stuff."

She paused and looked away. She took several breaths and looked as if she were forcing herself to be calm. Then, "Sorry I got so angry. I understand what you're talking about, and I know all about *Thresher*. I wish I had been able to come here sooner, but events in my life prevented it."

"That's unfortunate. I'm sorry."

"Well. I'm here now. I'm officially a citizen of Trieste."

I nodded. "Fine. Let's just catch Johnny and we'll be done with this."

There was another uncomfortable break; we sat in the command chairs next to one another and simply stared out the canopy. Eventually she said, "If Trieste is ever going to be a free city, we need that information. And don't worry about *SC-1*. There is no design flaw."

I started at that. "*Free city?* What are you talking about?"

She looked at me, puzzled. "I thought everyone down here wanted to be a free nation. Trieste fought for independence against the United States once."

I grimaced. "I know all about it. My father led the fight. He died during it."

She blinked. "How?"

"The CIA assassinated him in 2099. I don't want anything to do with the independence movement now."

She cocked her head to the side. "That's interesting, because the information that Johnny Chang stole is going to help Trieste gain independence from the States, once and for all. And your job, McClusky, is to retrieve it."

And with that she stormed past me, back to the aft compartment.

CHAPTER SIX 六

I SPENT AN HOUR GOING OVER the conversation in my mind, trying to figure out exactly what had happened, why she had grown so angry. She seemed to take my criticism of the seacar personally. Then the mention of independence and my desire to stay away from that fight, and she had left, more upset than ever.

Her behavior the night before seemed clear. She was mad at Johnny Chang. She desperately wanted to catch him, but her desire for revenge had come across as resentment toward me. But something else had motivated her more recent outburst. Something that I failed to grasp.

Independence.

It was nonsense, as far as I was concerned. People always strive to be free. However, Trieste was part of a free nation, the United States. It was the presence of the military and ships like *Impaler* that drove people to talk about independence. It was merely a pipe dream though, one that would only cause heartache, as it had for me and my sister. Meagan had run from Trieste after Dad's death. She hated what he had done, thought he had died for nothing. I agreed with her. Why try for independence when we already had a good life? Why end up like those nations in Africa and Central America, burdened by dictatorships and poor governments because they achieved independence too quickly? If Trieste wanted to be free, I felt we should earn it, and slowly. Let the States grant it to us when we're ready. We just weren't there yet.

Still, I understood the desire.

The USSF had harassed us ever since 2099. They were always in the area, clearly keeping their eyes on us. Admiral Benning of the *Terminator* class USSF warsub *Devastator* was the CO of the forces in the Gulf and Caribbean region. He was well known around the undersea colonies as being a non-compromising, hard-edged soldier who did not negotiate with the enemy. If there was an engagement that he was involved in, he would fight until the other side either surrendered or until he utterly destroyed them. He did not care about the death of innocent civilians. He had gone on record several times as saying emotions were the reason nations lost wars. "You can't be afraid to kill," he would growl to the press. "If you're at war, then death is the result. There's no room for feelings." He had been involved in skirmishes with the Chinese a decade earlier, and had won handily. The Chinese were still upset about it. Needless to say, to have this man as the US representative in Trieste's immediate vicinity was not a measure geared toward alleviating tension.

What furthered the strain between the US and Trieste was that their troops angered and abused our citizens and caused trouble in the city when they were on leave. Our produce and minerals went to the US economy instead of our own. Meanwhile the federal government gave us very little support. Katherine had gone to Congress to fight for us; that much pleased me, at least. But the very fact we *had* to do things like that for our own fair share irritated our people.

There was an uncomfortable feeling in the pit of my stomach. The mission was going to be more difficult than I had thought. Not just because of Johnny—but now because of Katherine Wells, who seemed to be a part of a new independence movement.

I SET THE AUTOPILOT AND FOLLOWED her to the living area. She was preparing breakfast—for herself. She had removed a precooked meal from the tiny pantry and was reheating it. "What the hell are you talking about?" I asked. I could have been more delicate, I guess, but at that moment I just needed an explanation.

She didn't even look up. "Exactly as I said, McClusky. Are you hard of hearing?"

I knotted a fist. "What does your invention have to do with Trieste?"

"I'm not permitted to tell you about it."

"Shanks told you that?"

"He did." She sat, began to eat, and completely avoided eye contact with me.

I felt my temperature rise. Not just at her behavior, but at the way Shanks had manipulated me. He had used Johnny Chang's involvement as a way to convince me to help, trapped me on this seacar, and now expected me to follow through with my mission even though it might result in something that I didn't believe in.

Then again, I wanted Johnny Chang for my own reasons. I would have taken the assignment regardless.

A sudden shock surged through me, and I sunk slowly to a chair. "Oh my God," I whispered.

She finally looked at me. "What?"

I hesitated before, "I just realized that maybe Johnny Chang isn't involved in this at all. Perhaps it was a setup. A fake video to get me to commit."

Neither of us spoke. The seacar's thrusters vibrated the deck and bulkheads; the ventilation system hummed quietly in the background. Water sighed against our hull as the vessel cut through it. I closed my eyes and thought hard for a minute. Shanks could have made the video as a backup, in case I refused the first time he asked. When we met in his office, he had started by appealing to my patriotism for Trieste . . . he had mentioned that if we failed to get the technology back, it could mean the end of the city and our place in the oceans. He then stated it could even lead to war. And he followed that up with . . .

Johnny Chang.

He had saved that bit of information until the very end.

Was it possible? Had he duped me?

There was one major problem with that, however: Why? Shanks could have just sent Blake or some other TCI operative. Instead he specifically called for me, and his reasoning made sense. I did know Johnny better than anyone else in the agency.

Katherine was watching me silently. Then, "Are you serious?"

"It's possible," I muttered.

"But the video. I saw it too. Shanks told me that man was Johnny Chang, an operative of Sheng City Intelligence."

"It was him. I recognized him."

"But why would he fake that?"

"To convince me to do this." I shrugged. "But that doesn't make sense."

"No. It doesn't."

The whole setup seemed strange. Chinese operatives had known that I was involved almost immediately. They had tried to stop me from going on the mission. Something else was going on that Shanks had not filled me in on. And now Katherine's claims that this all had to do with independence.

I glared at her. "Look. I need to know the truth. What are we really chasing here? And did Johnny Chang really take it?"

She shook her head. "I can't tell you what it is. But was it Johnny? I believe so. There's no reason for Shanks to lie about that."

"Is it a weapon of some sort?"

"What?"

"Perhaps a new torpedo?"

She turned back to her food. "I told you I can't say anything about it."

I frowned and watched as she resumed eating. There had to be a way to get the information from her, but I didn't yet know much about her, and to figure out this mystery, I needed to learn as much as possible.

Even if I didn't want anything to do with her.

I sighed inwardly. It had to be done. I made some tea slowly—dried kelp, of course, though a variety that did not taste fishy—and debated how to begin. I had to be casual about it. I returned to the chair beside her. "Where did you get your doctorate?" I asked.

"MIT," she said instantly. "The second one too. After that I branched out into other fields."

"You said earlier that something in your life prevented you from coming here sooner."

She swallowed her mouthful and leaned back. "That's true." She paused. "I fell in love with the ocean as a child. There was just something about it that attracted me. The risk, the danger, the nobility. The fact that humanity's immediate future lies here. One day we'll go to the stars, but for now, this is our best hope, especially at the rate that global warming has affected us. I devoted myself to the oceans and our future here."

"And you really spoke to Congress about our efforts?"

"Sure. Remember after 2099 they wanted to cut payments to the colonies? Well, I was part of the movement on the mainland that convinced them not to give up on you. We used China as the principal reason."

"We couldn't let them take the oceans. I remember."

"Well, it worked. They didn't cut the funding, and you're still here."

I blinked at that. Even if the States completely disassociated themselves from us, we'd still be here. That was the whole point of the independence movement. "Don't get a swelled head," I said. "We'd do fairly well without the federal government and the military presence at Trieste, I think."

"But you don't want independence. You're scared of it."

I stumbled slightly. It was obvious what she was attempting: she was manipulating me into saying that I *wanted* independence. I realized suddenly that Katherine Wells didn't have two doctorates for nothing. She wasn't just smart; she was cunning. I had to be careful around her. "I'm not scared of it. I just don't want it too soon. I want Trieste to be ready for it when it comes."

She snorted. "Ah, I see. When it's given to you, right?"

"That's right. It's happened to other nations, and they've been successful. Look at the nations that got it before they were ready, or those that fought for it."

"You mean like the United States."

"No," I snapped. "The nations of Africa, for instance. Or in the Caribbean, like Haiti."

"What about Israel? Back when it was Palestine on world maps, it was really a British colony. But some Jewish people who lived there were bombing British government offices and forced a solution on England. They got their homeland back. It worked for them."

"There were other circumstances there. The UN was involved. The Balfour Declaration. The Holocaust." I leaned back for a minute and considered what she had said. She was right about the United States and Israel. But still, so many nations around the world that achieved independence too early had suffered hugely as a result. Military dictatorships, warlords, death squads. Too many murdered civilians to count.

"You haven't answered my question," I said finally.

She sighed. "My dad was very ill. He held on for a long, long time, and during his illness, I kept up with my education and learned everything I could about how to live underwater. And finally . . ." She trailed off.

She didn't have to finish. She had felt compelled to stay for her family. To help a dying father. And when he was gone, she had come to work for Trieste. I looked at her now in a new light. There was a sensitive, caring side there after all. "Did Shanks recruit you?"

A nod. "He knew me by reputation. Said he'd followed my career closely. He had contacted me before my dad's passing, but I had politely declined. A few years ago, he tried again and I accepted."

I put a few facts together in my mind. She had said that she had only come to Trieste a month earlier. "So you were topside for some time before you finally came down here. Still lecturing?"

"No, I was in Florida."

"What were you doing?"

Her face grew tight and she shot me a wicked glare. "Are you attempting to be nice, or are you trying to figure out what we're chasing?"

I shrugged. "Both."

She scowled. "Well . . . I guess I can't blame you for trying. But I still can't tell you what I was doing." She rose to her feet and began to clear her mess. "But I appreciate your attempts to get to know me. And I'm sorry about earlier."

"Once again."

She seemed contrite. "I'm a touchy person, I know. I get upset at little things." She suddenly turned and offered me her hand. "Truce?"

I frowned. How good would such a thing be? Surely she would be angry again in just a few short minutes. Or snap at me in some way. Shanks had stuck us on this seacar together though, and I wanted to at least be civil with her. I forced a smile. "Sure."

We shook hands and she offered me a dazzling grin. Christ, she could really turn it on when she wanted.

Just don't let her affect your judgement, Mac, I told myself.

I HAD A QUICK SHOWER IN the cramped washroom—the water was pleasantly warm—and grabbed a bite to eat. All we had were ration packs, which made for an extremely bland and unappetizing meal. An hour later I was back in the control cabin next to Katherine, checking our course against Johnny's.

"This man works for Sheng City, right?" she asked as I stared at the charts on the navigation screen.

"Yes."

"And yet we're going east."

I nodded. I had noticed the same thing. Had he wanted to run straight for his city, he would have gone west to the Panama pass-through and into the Pacific. Instead he was headed to the middle of the Atlantic Ocean.

According to the maps, we were now over the Blake Plateau, just east of Florida. It was a stretch of relatively flat seafloor that reached depths of about 2000 meters. As Katherine watched, I turned *SC-1* to the northeast, and within three hours we were off the bank. The ocean bottom was now four kilometers or more below us. If something happened to the vessel and we sunk, we would land on the bottom, exceeding our crush depth.

Our hull would creak and groan at first. Then, somewhere along a seal or join, it would give just a few nanometers.

And that would be it.

The ocean would surge in and crush us to pulp in an instant. We probably wouldn't even see it coming.

Many people were scared of ocean travel because the maximum depths that our vessels could withstand were not equal to the depth of the ocean's floor. When *Titanic* sank, for example, it took six minutes for it to finally hit bottom.

A six minute fall for an object that weighed over 20,000 tonnes.

The immensity of the ocean was difficult to comprehend.

And we still weren't at the deepest points of our journey. Johnny was headed for the Mid-Atlantic Ridge for some reason . . . and depths in the rift zone were far greater than four kilometers.

"WHAT'S THE VIRTUAL IMAGING DISPLAY?" I asked Kat later. She had been quiet, and until then I had been happy to let the truce exist as complete silence between us. I needed to know as much about this vessel as possible, however, and felt compelled to finally ask.

She glanced at the console. "The military invented it a few years back. Not many private seacars have one, though that's changing now. The intelligence services all have them. In essence, it converts sonar information into a Heads-up Display for the pilot. It projects it onto the canopy." She gestured at the acrylic before our eyes.

I gasped. "You mean it presents a three dimensional view of everything that the sonar detects?"

She nodded. "To a point. The active sonar on this seacar has a range of a hundred kilometers. The VID, however, can only project objects that are within five kilometers. But its range will grow as new designs come out."

"Five kilometers. That's right to the bottom."

"If the seacar angled downward, an image of it would appear on the canopy, yes." I watched her silently, and she extended a small smile. "Want to try it out?"

"Of course."

She flicked it on.

The water outside was dark, and we couldn't see the sun overhead. There was a display on the console for sonar contacts showing twenty-three objects in a thirty kilometer radius. It was currently set to passive mode, which meant it simply listened for screws in the water around us. If we switched to active mode, the range would be significantly larger. The sonar system would send out a strong audio pulse, which would reflect off of other objects and return to *SC-1*.

An image immediately appeared on the canopy. Since the acrylic was so expansive—I could see out the seacar to the port, starboard, and bow—the display almost completely surrounded us. Seacars appeared. Some of them appeared quite close, projected as large images. It was a stylized visual, so bright white lines showed their shape and size, and their hulls, stabilizers, and screws were clearly visible. In the distance were other vessels so small I could only make out blurry white shapes on the blue background. There was even a group of dolphins nearby, swimming leisurely away from us.

It was remarkable.

It would change the way people perceived submarines and seacars as being essentially blind. Even strong floodlights could only penetrate a few meters in really deep water.

Until now.

The VID made it look as clear as day. It was like flying an airplane.

"You can zoom in," Katherine said.

Her voice startled me. I had forgotten that she was there.

She used a control on the console and a small box appeared on the image. She moved it to one of the smaller seacars on the display, which according to the sonar was just under five kilometers away. She pressed a button and the square expanded to show the seacar within, one of standard design, headed west toward land. I could see her single thruster, the bow planes, the rear stabilizers.

I must have gasped, for Katherine laughed. "You'll get used to it."

"It's revolutionary." I hesitated for a heartbeat. "Do you think there's anything else you should tell me about this vessel? I should know for when we get close to Johnny."

There was a slight pause. "I can't think of anything."

I glanced at her. "Okay."

"Want to see the bottom?"

I answered by pushing the yoke away from me. The rear ailerons lowered hydraulically and the nose dipped. We passed twenty degrees, thirty . . .

Forty . . .

Fifty . . .

Sixty . . .

Something appeared on the lower portion of the canopy. A white grid of polygons. It was unmistakable what they represented: the terrain of the ocean floor. Granted, it was fairly flat, but there were some variations in bathymetry there. A few peaks, a hundred meters high. Some depressions. A small canyon came into view, and at the extreme range of the VID, a crater, probably an extinct volcano. The display only showed three-quarters of it; the rest was out of range.

"Easy now," she warned. We were at a seventy degree down-angle and had secured our safety straps to keep from falling onto the control console "Watch your depth."

I glanced at it. "A kilometer. Not even close to maximum." Still, I backed off and pulled the yoke toward me. *SC-1*'s dive angle returned to zero, and I held it there. I blew some ballast to make the seacar positively buoyant, to bring us to a shallower depth.

"I think I remember people talking about this a long time ago."

She shrugged. "Oh, we could have developed it a while back. In the twentieth century even. But it's only recently that the military started putting it on their smaller vessels, like the *Hunter-Killers*, which are so fast and maneuverable that their pilots need to see their surroundings. The larger subs don't need this system. Instruments are more than enough."

Something flashed on the sonar. "Oh, oh," I whispered.

"What?"

"Our little move got someone's attention."

Just on the limits of the passive sonar, a contact had appeared. It was a seacar headed toward us; at current velocity, both vessels would intersect in forty minutes.

"What is it?"

I glanced at the display. "According to the sound of the screws, it's a Chinese vessel."

THE BLIP ON THE SCREEN WAS as clear as day. Next to it, an identifying flag had popped up that labeled it as a Chinese Submarine Fleet *Jin* class military warsub, also known as the *Fast Attack*. Its current velocity was an astounding eighty kph.

I called up everything we had on her from the computer's library. Twenty-two meters long and cigar-shaped, she had five torpedo tubes, mines, and complete countermeasures. A crew of ten. Three thrusters: two at the ends of the horizontal stabilizers, like *SC-1*'s, and one was at the top of the hull, attached to the vertical stabilizer. Analysts had estimated her top speed at eighty. I snorted—looked like the military theorists had been right on that one. But it also implied that our fleet hadn't known for sure, that the Chinese had never run it up to top speed while in a US warsub's sensor range. Strangely enough, here was one running at eighty just off the US coast.

They must want us pretty badly, I thought.

I realized with a shock that it was probably the vessel that the five now-dead operatives who had attacked me had come from.

Their comrades would want blood.

We had one torpedo tube to their five, with a complement of only eight torpedoes.

"Are you going to turn and run?" Katherine asked.

It wouldn't make sense to. Their speed was ten kph higher than our own. The confrontation was going to happen sooner or later, and if we diverted course, it would allow Johnny more time to get away. We had to stay with him. "No," I said finally. "But look at this." I pointed at the *Fast Attack's* specifications. "Their max depth is only 2150 meters, only half of ours. We can go deep to avoid her."

She frowned. "How accurate is that information?"

"Can't say for sure. There's a good chance it's off by a bit. Our spies are the ones who got these stats, remember, and the Chinese might have fed them false data. However, our spy boats listen and watch very closely while they're running drills. If it's off, it might be by only a slight margin. We'd still have them beat."

"So we go deep, and stay on course."

"That's our best bet." I shoved the ballast controls to negative and watched as bubbles spewed from valves on the hull of the seacar. There was the distinct feeling of falling.

"How deep are you going?"

I pursed my lips. "Three thousand should be good."

"They have mines, don't forget."

Don't worry, I wanted to say. *I haven't.*

My heart was pounding.

THIRTY MINUTES LATER THE WARSUB WAS within five kilometers and closing every second. I had left the VID on, and there was now an image of the Chinese vessel on the canopy above me, to our starboard and at a forty-five degree angle upwards.

When the warsub attacked, we would have to change course to avoid her mines as she dropped them in our path and her torpedoes as they fired at us on a downward angle. It would probably throw us off course, so I decided to get a more accurate reading on Johnny's current position.

I prepared the active sonar.

I could send a pulse out, and if his ship was within a hundred kilometer range, we would know within a few seconds.

The sonar system was a standard design, and I simply switched the toggle to ACTIVE. It could be set to send a pulse—or a ping—every second. I only wanted to send out two: the first to get a position, the second to get a new position about ten seconds later to calculate his course. As soon as he detected the first pulse, he would realize what was happening and try to change direction so we couldn't get a fix on his trajectory. Hopefully this would catch him off guard, however, and he would not be able to adjust his bearing quick enough.

I activated the pulse.

A few moments later the display expanded and a multitude of new contacts appeared. There were now seventy-three on the screen. I had already programmed into the system the ship I was specifically looking for.

He was there. Just at the outermost range of our sonar, ninety-eight kilometers away.

We were on the right track.

The second pulse soon went out and the computer calculated the new position. His course had changed slightly since he left the Gulf area, though it was still toward the Mid-Atlantic Ridge. I recorded it and shut down the active mode. The problem was every ship on the screen now knew someone had tried to identify them; it was not a subtle way to chase someone.

Johnny probably now knew that we were on his tail.

THE *FAST ATTACK* WAS ALMOST ON us. We were now at a depth of 3000 meters, and sure enough, our pursuers were at just over 2000. It looked like the military analysts had been right about her maximum depth, and the Chinese didn't want to push her any further.

Then she started to dive.

I looked up at her in horror. She was a kilometer over our heads, and the VID clearly showed her on the same course, though she was now diving at least ten meters per second, her thrusters still on maximum.

She was coming straight for us.

"Oh shit," I muttered. I pushed the yoke forward and began our own steep descent. We had to stay below her, but even so, her torpedoes could probably reach any depth in this area. She would probably just stay up there and try to damage us enough to sink us.

"Three thousand two hundred," Katherine reported. "Four hundred. Five hundred." She glanced at me. "Careful, we can't go any deeper than—"

"I know! But we have to stay away from her!"

A second later a surge of turbulence shot from the computer-generated image on the VID above my head, and at the same instant a shriek came from the sonar console between us.

She had fired torpedoes.

Two of them.

On an intercept.

I heeled the ship to port and increased the angle of descent. I rammed my hand on the ballast and switched it to full negative. The sound of the valves opening to allow water into the tanks vibrated the ship. Bubbles surged outward as we began to plummet.

Like a rock.

"Three thousand eight hundred!" Katherine yelled. "Slow descent!"

"Not yet," I growled.

"Four thousand! That's our max!"

There had to be a safety margin built in, I thought. Every seacar and sub could go deeper than the specified maximum, though usually it was only by about ten percent. If I was right about that, then we could theoretically hit 4400 meters—but no deeper.

The hull creaked.

"Stop it!" she bit out. "Four thousand two hundred!"

I switched ballast to neutral and pulled the yoke back to level her out. I had kept my eyes on the torpedoes the whole time; they were still headed straight for us.

"What countermeasures does this seacar have?"

"Standard!" she yelled. "Sound and turbulent."

"Launch some."

She stabbed at a button on the console and ejected two devices from the hull of *SC-1*. They would stay in place and spin violently, emitting bubbles to simulate the cavitating screws of a seacar.

Hopefully, the ploy would trick the weapons into thinking they had locked to a vessel.

I turned the yoke to starboard and pushed the right pedal to move *SC-1* as hard as possible to the side. We were already at maximum speed, so there was nothing else I could do.

I held my breath.

Ten seconds later a shock wave hit us and the vessel shook violently. The yoke jumped in my hands and I struggled to hold on. I stared at the control console, silently praying for no red lights to appear.

None did.

We were safe.

The countermeasures had worked.

Three hundred meters above me, the *Jin* had once again matched our course. Clearly their maximum depth was 3900 meters, 1750 deeper than she should have been able to go! Either the Chinese had completely fooled our analysts, or this was no ordinary *Jin* class vessel. It could be some type of experimental warsub.

The thought made my skin crawl.

They had us outclassed by a massive margin.

"ARE THEY HERE TO PROTECT JOHNNY?"

"Partly. I think the crew of that sub had orders to kill me. They failed earlier, and now they're trying to finish the job."

"We could fire our own—"

"That would be a waste of our weapons. Not unless we had them dead to rights and they had exhausted their own countermeasures. That's a warsub up there." I gestured at it directly overhead. "*SC-1* is barely more than a civilian seacar. Our only chance is to avoid them, but they have a higher top speed."

Katherine glared at me. "You sound like we have no hope here."

"I didn't say that. I'm just trying to think of options."

Her gaze flicked to the console, and I followed with my own. "What?"

She shook her head and watched the sonar. "Nothing." A pause, and then, "What about one of those nearby ships? There are at least twenty close enough. Maybe one could help."

"Against a CSF *Fast Attack*? Unlikely. The only help out there is from a USSF warsub, and we don't want anything to do with them, remember? We have to keep them out of this."

She snorted and turned away. "So let's just give up then, shall we?"

I growled in response.

The hull groaned again, and we both jumped in our seats, startled.

The fathometer listed the bottom under us at roughly 1200 meters. That meant the total depth here was 5400 meters. We would not survive hitting it.

Another shriek from the sonar. More torpedoes, on the way.

I jerked the yoke toward me and jammed my fingers on the ballast controls. I blew all ballast—thankfully the system could clear the tanks at this depth, even though it was greater than the vessel's stated maximum—and started an emergency climb. We were now at a sixty degree up-angle, our thrusters churning at seventy kph, and our ballast tanks completely devoid of water.

The ascent seemed incredibly fast.

The torpedoes could not adjust in time. The *Fast Attack* had fired on a downward trajectory, and we climbed steadily past the weapons. Their noses tilted toward us as we soared past, and Katherine launched more countermeasures.

The shudder of a nearby, gigantic explosion rattled everything in the control cabin. Behind me, in the living area, supplies and food fell from cupboards and smashed to the deck.

The lights flickered and the sound of the thrusters stuttered for a second. *Oh, shit.*

Please don't lose the thrusters! I thought. I almost yelled it out.

Beside me, Katherine screamed.

"We're not dead yet," I snarled. I pushed the yoke forward and our climb leveled out at around 3000 meters. We were now *above* the warsub. Our buoyancy was still lifting us, however, and I slammed it back to negative, water flooding the tanks as we began to descend again.

"What are you doing?" she shrieked.

"Keeping us alive! Do you want to pilot?"

Her eyes were frantic. "No, but I don't understand why you're—"

"I'm following an erratic course so they can't get a good lock on us! Our countermeasures are working, and we can go deeper than them, though not by much."

We were headed down again. I steered us away from the *Jin*, still on a northeasterly course.

"A few more concussions like that and we've had it," she said. "Did you hear the thrusters there?"

I had indeed. But I didn't really know what to do. In the short term I was just trying to stay away from the Chinese warsub, but in the end, I knew she would beat us.

We raced down into the dark depths.

Our attacker was behind us, matching our course and rate of descent.

The bathymetry of the ocean bottom appeared on the VID. The terrain was relatively flat, still at a depth of 5400 meters.

Then I saw something.

A seamount, rising just over a kilometer from the floor. Its top was right at our limit—with the safety margin included—but we could probably make it.

And perhaps trick them into thinking we had drowned.

I steered toward it, and maintained the downward angle.

The sonar screamed for attention; two more torpedoes.

"Oh, fuck," I whispered. Not now. Not now.

Not now.

"Countermeasures!" I cried.

Katherine pressed the button and ejected the devices. The torpedoes collided with them a mere five seconds later.

"Hold on!" I bellowed.

The shock wave hit us almost instantly and the entire seacar seemed to convulse like a tortured animal. Even my teeth rattled. Alarms blared from the console and numerous lights turned from green to red and began to flash.

I smelled smoke.

"Fire!" Katherine said as she leaped into action. She grabbed an extinguisher from an emergency compartment and wrenched a panel beside her open. Electrical flames surged out. She pressed the breakers to cut power to those controls, multiple indicators and readouts on the console winking off. She sprayed the fire retardant, smothering the flames. The smell was acrid; it burned my nostrils.

"Cutting thrusters," I said into the mayhem. First I shut down the port; five seconds later, the starboard.

"What?"

I maintained our negative buoyancy and kept us angled toward bottom. Our velocity quickly diminished without the propulsion, but there was no doubt that we were going down. The seamount was directly before us now, still illuminated in the Heads-up VID. It was a mountain that rose from the abyssal plains—an extinct volcano, from the time when this section of the ocean floor had been at the tectonically active rift in the Mid-Atlantic Ridge. Its sides were steep—about forty degrees—and I desperately hoped we could find a ledge on which to land.

Otherwise we would hit the side and slide to the bottom of the seamount, 1000 meters beyond our capability to survive.

Our depth was now 4100 meters. We were almost there. I tried to blow some ballast to lessen our rate of fall, but the system failed to work. We were now permanently heavier than the water we displaced. This was not a good development, but I would have to worry about it later.

We continued to fall.

The hull creaked every five seconds now. It was an ominous sound, something that submariners since the beginning of ocean exploration dreaded. It was thunder in a lightning storm.

It foretold terrible death.

"Does this thing have landing gear of some sort?"

Katherine's eyes were fixed to the VID as she watched the mountain approach. "Landing skids, yes."

"Deploy them."

They were similar to the gear on a plane that could land on snow or ice, and designed to slide across the ocean bottom and keep a seacar from sinking in the muck and getting trapped by the suction. Thankfully the electrical short hadn't affected the system, and the sound as they lowered vibrated the deck at my feet.

"Here we go," I muttered.

The side of the mountain now completely filled the screen. Outside, the sea was pitch black, but the VID did a nice job of projecting its features, although not in great detail. A small protrusion drew my attention, and I steered toward it. The rudder on the vertical stabilizer didn't seem to respond as quickly as it had earlier, but I managed to get the seacar over the ledge. I pulled up on the yoke and we leveled off directly over it. We continued to descend under the negative buoyancy of the ballast, and the seacar shuddered as it finally made contact.

We slid forward; the sound of the skids scraping the bottom rumbled through the vessel.

I held my breath.

We continued toward the edge.

Another five meters, and still we moved forward.

Still more, and then—

Finally, we ground to a halt.

We had landed. Our depth, 4380 meters. The numbers on the display were an angry red.

According to the sensors, the pressure on our hull was just over 450 kilograms per square centimeter.

Almost half a metric tonne per square centimeter!

I looked up at the acrylic over our heads. It was extraordinary that it could withstand this kind of stress.

The *Jin* was up there, circling. It was half a kilometer away, waiting. Watching. I hoped they thought we were dead. I held my finger to my lips; Katherine understood immediately. We didn't want them to hear us.

A minute later the warsub began searching with her active sonar, pinging away once every couple of seconds. No doubt they had detected us heading for the seamount and had heard our thrusters cut out. Since we were now a part of the bottom terrain, however, I hoped that they could not see us.

And then the unthinkable happened.

She started to drop her mines.

THERE WERE FOUR OF THEM FALLING toward us. The VID system displayed them as white stars on a dark blue background; they left a faint streak of luminescence as they plunged downward.

We were completely, utterly, silent. Thankfully, Katherine had studied the ocean and its inhabitants for most of her life, and knew sound traveled far better in water than it did in air. Right now there were people on the CSF warsub listening to every noise in the immediate vicinity. We couldn't throw our lives away by making some pointless remark.

The first mine detonated a hundred meters above the seamount on the other side of the peak. It was a clear miss. Still, the floor under our seacar trembled from the concussion. I shot a glance to the port, at the ledge that we were dangerously near. If we slid toward it and fell from the precipice . . .

Another mine actually hit the mountain and exploded instantly. The projection showed it as a brilliant white flash. Rock crumbled underneath the wave and a large slide began to flow downslope toward the plains a kilometer below.

The third disappeared behind us and rolled down the mountain another five hundred meters. We barely felt it when it went.

The fourth, however, nearly incinerated our seacar.

It fell directly behind us, about thirty meters away, on the very outcropping on which we were perched so precariously. The ship heaved and slid meters to the port.

Toward the ledge.

Katherine's eyes went wide.

I gripped the yoke tightly, as if it would do anything.

The seacar rattled to a halt a mere two meters from the edge.

Shit, that was close.

The lights in the cabin had dimmed dramatically; in fact, emergency illumination was the only thing running at that moment. A haze had filled the interior—smoke from the fire—and until the environmental system was up and running, I knew we would just have to live with it.

The *Fast Attack* was still up there, but she dropped no more mines.

We watched her in silence for another hour, just sitting there in our control seats, hardly moving a muscle. My eyes were burning and I yawned again and again. I had been up since the night before this whole adventure began; since before Blake had contacted me and brought me to see Shanks. I was exhausted.

I considered my options. Until that warsub left, there was little we could do. I hoped that her crew would assume we were dead after hours of silence. It seemed reasonable; after all, we were now at a depth that few manned seacars had ever attained.

The question was, how long would they wait?

I rose to my feet shakily and crept from the cabin. A few meters back, I stopped at the bunk, looked at Katherine, and gestured inside. She understood my meaning and nodded. I climbed in, slowly slid the curtain shut, and put my head on the small pillow.

Sleep came instantly.

NOISE FROM THE CONTROL CABIN WOKE me. I poked my head out from the bunk and saw Katherine working in the panel where the fire had occurred. She had a tool box in front of her and was rewiring the system. I admired her for a few moments; she was handy with the tools and clearly knew what she was doing. With a doctorate in aquanautic engineering, she was more than equipped to repair wiring damage.

The ventilation system was operating again, and the smoke was gone.

It was a relief, but I was more concerned with the mechanics of the ship *outside* the hull.

My feet hit the deck and I padded toward her. She looked at me.

"They left," she said. "An hour ago."

It was late afternoon; I had slept for six hours. It had rejuvenated me, but the amount of work before us was sickening. The entire living area was a shambles, covered with smashed cartons of food, rations strewn about. It looked as though someone had ransacked the place. I dreaded thinking about the engine room.

Those pipes on the ceiling . . .

I shuddered.

"I've got the control console up," she said, "but there are still circuits out. It'll take hours longer to repair the connections."

I peered through the opening at the wires concerning her. I traced them back to the main panel, under her watchful gaze, and noticed that they were not a part of the seacar's control system. Their breakers were unlabeled. Except for one, which read: CONTAINMENT.

I pointed that out to her.

She looked surprised. "You're right." She lowered her tools. "We can ignore that for now, I suppose. I'll get to it later."

I settled into my chair and studied the readings before me. Everything seemed to be working. The sonar had several contacts on it, but none appeared to be the CSF warsub.

"We could call for help," I muttered, "but it wouldn't do us any good. We need to get off this seamount and back on Johnny's tail." I looked at the ballast system readout to my left. It was still set to negative. I moved the toggle to neutral and listened for the sound of water expulsion from the tanks.

Nothing.

According to the readout, they were completely full of water, at the same pressure now as outside.

Flooded.

We were too heavy to rise.

Still, our thrusters were powerful enough to propel us forward, and we could use the bow and stern planes to angle the nose upward. We could take her up under sheer power.

I activated the thrusters and pushed the throttle toward full. The engines vibrated the hull and deck, but there was now something distinctly different—a rattle where there used to be a smooth hum.

The mines had damaged something in that last explosion, probably the screws themselves. If they had twisted under the shock wave—the most reasonable explanation—they would never generate enough force. Hell, they wouldn't get us *close* to seventy kph, let alone off that ledge.

I looked into Katherine's dark eyes. They were somber.

"Useless," she murmured. "We're stuck, unless we can figure out a way to fix them."

I LEANED BACK IN THE CHAIR. "There must be some other way to get to shallow water." I knew surfacing was not the thing I truly wanted, however, for at sea level we would be in just as much trouble as here. We couldn't just rush up there and open the hatch and jump out. Our tissues were saturated with dissolved gases at four atms. We had to decompress slowly, let the gases move to our lungs safely and exhale them naturally. The process at our level of saturation would take over a hundred hours.

We were confined underwater.

I just wanted to get us off this ledge and back on the hunt for Johnny.

"What about the emergency ballast?" I said suddenly. Every seacar and submarine carried some sort of dead weight for this exact situation. Lead pellets, usually. "We could jettison enough of it here and float upward. We could resume the search. . . ." As I said it I realized how silly it sounded. They had damaged our screws. Johnny's top speed now seriously outclassed ours. There would be no catching him.

I started to feel uneasy.

Katherine opened the seacar's operation manual and showed me the section with the vehicle's specifications. There was a chart displaying various details such as sensor range, air supply, airlock capacity, carbon dioxide scrub rates, and so on. I located the ones that were currently important.

SC-1	Value
Length:	17 m
Height:	4 m
Beam:	9 m
Draft:	2 m
Displacement:	10,030 kg
Gross Weight:	9,669 kg
Gross Weight (with flooded tanks):	11,212 kg
Emergency Ballast:	500 kg

It took only a second for the figures to sink in.

"Oh, shit," I muttered.

"You picked that up fairly quickly," she said.

"You don't have to be a sub engineer to realize what it means." We displaced 10,030 kilograms of water. However, the seacar's weight when her tanks were full was 11,212 kilos. That meant that the vessel was 1182 kilos heavier than the water it displaced. This made it negatively buoyant, meaning it would sink without compressed air in its ballast system. We could drop the emergency ballast, which weighed 500 kg, to try to make the ship positively buoyant, but even if we did, the seacar would still be 682 kg heavier than the water it displaced.

It would sink, even with the ballast jettisoned.

I wanted to scream. What kind of *emergency* ballast was that? There should have been more lead *without* increasing the overall weight of the seacar while the tanks were full of water!

"Who the hell designed this thing?" I growled. "That's ridiculous!"

"Hey, you were marveling at it a few hours ago," Katherine said.

"Yeah, before I realized it was a deathtrap."

Her nostrils flared. "It's a good seacar—you've seen what it can do!"

"Well now that we're trapped in over four kilometers of water and the emergency ballast won't take us up, perhaps my opinion has changed!" I paused to take a breath as I stared at the page before me. *Don't panic*, I thought. *There's always a solution.* "Maybe there wasn't enough space in the compartment," I theorized a moment later. "But still, they could have used something heavier than lead. Uranium, mercury, or osmium would have been useful substitutes."

"Maybe it is one of those. And perhaps the engineers thought that in an emergency, our tanks wouldn't be *completely* full."

I sighed and threw the book to the side. Whatever. It didn't matter. The fact was that the emergency system was damned useless to us.

WE SAT IN THE CONTROL CABIN for almost ninety minutes in complete silence. I went over every scenario in my head multiple times to no avail: the ballast-blow system wasn't working—the explosions had damaged the exterior valves on the hull in some way; the emergency ballast couldn't get us off the seamount; the screws had twisted and couldn't produce enough thrust, and even if they did manage to get us off the ledge, they might not be able to power us up to safer waters. We would sink to crush depth.

It seemed hopeless.

The air would run foul, and we would choke to death on carbon dioxide.

Or the hull would give, and we would implode.

Except I knew we had one option remaining to us.

We could go outside to fix the screws and the ballast valves.

I looked at Katherine, and realized that she was thinking the same thing.

It was the only way.

"THE PROBLEM IS," SHE SAID TO me, considerably calmer now, "we don't have the right air mix to go outside. And we're far too deep."

Once again, her temper had flared and almost pushed me over the edge as well. It was not a good way to function. I needed to be at my best, and she kept snapping at me. The next time it happened, I knew I would probably blow up at her.

I focused on what she was saying. Under thirty meters depth it was okay to breathe normal canned atmosphere from the surface. However, deeper than that, it grew extremely dangerous. First, our atmosphere was seventy-eight percent nitrogen, and higher pressures would force more of it into our blood, where it would act like a narcotic—laughing gas. Euphoria would overcome anyone who attempted to use normal air at depths greater than thirty meters; Jacques Cousteau had once called it "Rapture of the Deep." Divers had died performing illogical acts—shoving limbs in turning screws, for instance—never realizing that such things would result in death.

Second, oxygen in normal air makes up twenty percent of the mix. But oxygen was actually a corrosive gas, dangerous if too much was absorbed. Death resulted from breathing too much oxygen at depths greater than those of our conshelf cities.

So, both nitrogen and oxygen were harmful. The solution to this was actually fairly simple: reduce the proportion of these gases in the mix so the body absorbs just the right amounts, and replace the rest with another inert gas like helium.

"Has anyone ever dived at 4400 meters before?" I asked Katherine.

Her eyes were wide. "No way."

I snorted. "Well, there's a first time for everything."

OUR BODIES WERE MOSTLY WATER, AND water did not compress. That was the good news. I could go outside without too much damage—provided the breathing mixture was right. The bad news was the pressure in the exterior environment would crush any spaces in my body if the air in there wasn't at the same pressure. Specifically, my lungs, middle ears, and sinus cavities. The only solution was to go into the airlock and pressurize it with the proper air mixture to match the outside. At this depth that was an astounding 440 atmospheric pressures.

"You couldn't survive that," Katherine whispered.

"We have no choice."

"But the chances—"

"*We have no choice*," I repeated. I had to try.

Die trying, if necessary.

"If I can't do it," I continued, "you'll have to give up the mission. Call for help. Hope someone can get down this far. You can use the canned air from the scuba gear for a while, I guess, if it takes a long time."

Her forehead crinkled. "Why risk yourself like this?"

I shrugged. "It's my mission. I need to get Johnny."

"Just for the technology? Even though it will help Trieste try for independence, which is something that you don't believe in?"

I wondered how much I should say. She didn't know the full story. "I have other motivations."

"Such as?"

I frowned. "A long time ago, seven years now, he did something to me that I can never forgive."

"What?"

I did not want to tell her the story right then, 4400 meters down, as the pressure wormed its dangerous tendrils into every microscopic flaw in the seacar's hull. "Later. For now, we need to figure out how we're going to do this." I got to my feet in the cramped cabin and marched back through the passageway to the aft compartment. "Show me the exterior hatches."

She followed and came to a stop in the living area. She pointed at the deck. "There's the moonpool." There was a sealed hatch that opened downward. There was no way we could open it now; the pressure in the interior of the seacar had to match the exterior for it to open.

"Okay. And the airlock?"

She led me back to the engine room. Just before it and off to the side was a tiny compartment with a watertight hatch. "Here it is." She swung it open. "It's narrow in there."

It also meant that when I returned from the repair mission—*if I returned*—I would have to stay in there as I depressurized back to four

atmospheres. I removed the dive tables from a cardboard envelope on the bulkhead next to the airlock and tried to calculate how long decompression would last for an hour outside.

It was off the chart.

"Shit," I muttered. "The table doesn't go this deep."

Katherine looked at the ceiling and did the calculation in her head. "For thirty minutes, you can depressurize in about twenty-five hours, I think."

I shot a look back inside the chamber. "*In there?*" Then I sighed. "But I guess people have endured worse before." I paused as the enormity of what I was about to do set in. Then, "Where are the gases for the mix?"

"That's something I've been thinking about for a while now." She seemed hesitant. Nervous.

"Why? Are they in the stores?" I pointed at the locker where the scuba gear and tanks were kept.

She pursed her lips. "Yes, but we have nothing for this depth. We need to create our own custom mix, and we don't have any helium."

"What do you mean? You just said—"

"It's mixed already for different depths. We can't just remove the helium from a bottle. We have no equipment for that."

I stared at her for a long minute. "Are you saying we have no hope here?"

She looked directly into my eyes. "That's exactly what I'm saying."

OF COURSE IT WAS EASY ENOUGH to vent gases from the scuba tanks, separate them into their component parts, then create a new mix with more helium and less oxygen and nitrogen, but we did not have the necessary equipment to do it on the seacar.

We went over everything that we *did* have on the seacar, but there simply wasn't much there that could help.

It didn't look good.

We were in the engine room, staring at the banks of batteries, the equipment on the bulkheads, and the backup controls on the central console. No ideas.

"We might have to call someone for help after all," Katherine said. She was still skeptical about my idea, and seemed downcast. Johnny had stolen her discovery, and we had no idea who he was going to hand it over to. Still, a nagging part of me believed that there was some way to do this. Some way to get outside and repair the damage with the tools at hand.

"Let's go over what we have again," I suggested.

She sighed. "Tanks of mix for a much shallower environment. Some pure oxygen for emergencies. Damaged thrusters. Batteries have a strong charge. Water and food for days. Ventilation and environmental seems okay, for now." Pause. "I can't think of much else."

"It doesn't sound like a lot, you're right." Something she had said, however, was useful. I had heard a story from long ago . . . a tale that people sometimes told one another in the conshelf cities. "You know," I said finally, "it's weird that we use helium for deep dives."

She frowned. "Why's that? It's common practice. It's inert and can replace nitrogen in our air supply. It doesn't have any harmful side effects, as long as there is enough oxygen present."

"It does change our voices."

"That's not a problem. People have lived with it for years now. Decades."

"But why helium? Why not some other inert gas?"

"What else—" She stopped suddenly and looked at me. "I suppose we could use a substitute. But we just don't have anything in storage."

I thought back to the story as I remembered it. In the 1940s, a Swedish inventor named Arne Zetterström invented a hydrogen-oxygen mix which he used to dive 162 meters in the Baltic. The mix worked, but during his decompression ascent, his assistants made an error and the Swede died as a result. Following this, people mostly abandoned the use of hydrogen in deep dives, though it was the best of the inert gasses to use. His death was now associated with hydrogen.

Katherine was looking at me. "You're thinking of using hydrogen, aren't you?"

I blinked. "Yes."

She paused for a long moment. "Instead of helium?" I could tell she had just said it as a delay while she considered the idea.

"Sure. We can manufacture it easily. We have battery power. All we'd have to do is pass an electric current through water, which will separate it into its component parts."

"Hydrogen and oxygen."

"That's right. We take the hydrogen and bottle it. Compress it to the point where I'll be able to breathe it outside. Combine with a tiny percentage of nitrogen and oxygen, probably even lower than one percent."

"I'll have to calculate that," she murmured.

"And voila," I continued. "We've got a mix that will help me survive long enough to fix the screws and repair the ballast valves."

She turned to the batteries and remained silent for quite a while. "McClusky," she finally whispered, "it's a death sentence. Nobody has been out this deep before. Not even *close* to it."

I spread my arms out. "It's either try or the chase ends here and now. Hell, we might both die if we don't do something, and fast. The pressure could kill us at any minute, and even if it doesn't, we might be too deep for any nearby rescue vessels to get us. We're currently beyond the listed crush depth of this seacar."

"Still . . ."

"It's our only hope."

She sighed. "It is indeed."

"Then let's get started. Help me hook up a lead to the batteries. We'll need a catchment system for the gases."

We began to work on the problem, but I couldn't help but notice the drawn expression on her face.

It seemed to be more than fear.

It looked like guilt.

WITHIN AN HOUR WE WERE BUILDING up a nice supply of hydrogen, and we began to use the ship's air compressors in the airlock to bottle the gas. Katherine had calculated the percentage of oxygen needed; it was less than point-four percent. It astounded me that such a small amount would be able to keep me alive. The pressure outside was almost incomprehensible.

Another hour and I was ready to go. Katherine prepared the airlock to match the outside environment; at that point, while breathing our exotic blend of gases, I would go outside and conduct the quick repairs.

If this hare-brained scheme worked.

"You should only stay out twenty minutes, no longer. At this depth, and for that short amount of time, the decompression will still be over twenty hours."

Twenty hours, stuck in that tiny airlock. Ugh.

But a part of me didn't even think I'd make it back. I was past the point of caring about conditions in the lock after the repair. I could only think about being outside, with almost a half-tonne of pressure on every square centimeter of my body.

"Your lungs, ears, and sinuses will hurt like hell as you're pressurizing. Try to equalize as frequently as possible. We'll get through that period in thirty minutes. Then I'll flood the chamber. Go out and proceed to the starboard thruster first. Use this torch." She pointed at the deck where a handheld flashlight lay; it seemed fairly standard, though its lens was six centimeters thick. "I'll also turn on the hull lamps and the running lights. Each pod has a panel that you can open with this tool." She showed me a large wrench, custom fitted with a hexagonal head, though it was far wider than the standard ones. "Inside the pod are the spare parts. There are new screws in each. Remove the damaged propeller and use the same tool to replace it with the new one. Seal the panel and then move to the port thruster."

"You make it sound like it'll go quickly."

"An experienced technician can get the screw off in under two minutes. Luckily this is a new seacar, so there won't be any corrosion to prolong the process."

Too bad Meagan's not here, I thought. She would have been a huge help. My sister was a wiz at things like this.

"Once you've replaced both, you can get back in here immediately. I'll be watching from the closed circuit. I'll seal the door, drain the chamber, and start depressurizing you immediately."

"What about the ballast valves?"

She shrugged. "As long as the screws are working, we can propel ourselves up, even with the flooded tanks."

But we would need forward momentum to keep from sinking—and to repair those valves while moving would be tricky. "And if I feel well enough?"

She hesitated. "A replacement valve is in the airlock. Simply unscrew the eight bolts, pull it out, and put that one in. The ballast tanks are at the same pressure as outside. It should slide out smoothly."

I exhaled. "Fine. Let's—"

The hull suddenly groaned and creaked; it was the loudest one yet.

I glanced up, and swallowed. "Let's get this over with, as soon as possible."

She grabbed my shoulder and turned me to face her. I looked into her dark eyes, and felt slightly uncomfortable doing so. Our time together so far hadn't exactly been pleasant. She said, "I'm sorry I've been a jerk to you. I'll try to be less temperamental after."

If there is an after.

I nodded. "Don't worry about it, Katherine."

"It's Kat. Call me Kat."

I gave her a weak smile. "See you soon."

THE TEMPERATURE OUTSIDE WAS FOUR DEGREES Celsius, or thirty-nine Fahrenheit. I would freeze to death in minutes without a chemically-warmed wetsuit. Even then it would feel extremely cold. I pulled it on, barely able to control my trembling limbs. Kat had retreated to the control cabin and was yelling instructions at me.

"Outside floodlights are on. The mix is ready for compression in the airlock."

I stepped into the lock and swung the hatch shut.

It clanged loudly behind me; the lock mechanism ground into place.

I heard the hiss of air and immediately felt pain in my ears. "Hey, slow down a bit."

"You're only at ten atms." Her voice came from a concealed speaker; it sounded distant and tinny. "Still four hundred and thirty to go."

I swore. What the hell was I doing here?

I realized, at that moment, that this was suicide.

But it was too late to back out.

"Twenty," she said. "Thirty."

I squeezed my nose and forced air into my middle ears until they popped. It was called the Valsalva Maneuver. I would have to do that again and again to prevent a deadly rupture. "I feel light headed," I murmured after another minute.

The air being forced in sounded very loud.

"You're now breathing nitrogen, oxygen, and hydrogen. At your current pressurization you still need a larger proportion of oxygen than in the final mix. I'm adjusting as you pressurize."

"You know what you're doing?"

"Trust me."

I grunted. "Guess I have to."

"Don't worry. I'm not about to kill the guy who's going to get my invention back. Forty atmospheres."

"What is it, anyway?"

"Hah. Nice try."

"I might die here. Why not tell me?"

Silence. And then, "Fifty."

Minutes passed as the pressure continued to rise. "Can the interior airlock hatch take this?"

"Should be able to. It's rated the same as the outer one. You're doing great. Over one hundred now."

"Damn."

"What?" She sounded instantly concerned.

"I said, 'Damn.'"

"I can't understand you, McClusky. You're slurring."

I tried again.

"That's better," she said. "I adjusted the mix a bit there."

"Call me Mac," I muttered.

More time passed. My head had begun to throb. It was agonizing. My chest heaved; I suddenly found it difficult to breathe. Each inhalation was a struggle.

I couldn't believe what I was doing.

Still the pressure built. The sound of air was driving me mad. It was like torture.

"One fifty," she said. "Keep equalizing."

She didn't have to tell me. If I failed to do it, my sinuses would implode.

It was absolutely necessary to go through this process. If I just left the seacar without preparing, the pressure would squash my chest flat. The air in my lungs had to be at an equal pressure as the outside to prevent that from happening, and the air in the tank also had to be at the same pressure, otherwise I would never be able to draw a breath.

It took time to get there; I had to work my way to it in stages.

Some animals dove this deep, but evolution had worked out ways for them to withstand the crushing forces on their lungs. Sperm whales, for instance, had collapsible chests; thick coats of mucous in their lungs allowed them to compress and re-inflate again as they surfaced.

The pain was incredible. I had closed my eyes and was focusing on the task at hand, on the reason why I was doing this.

He had betrayed me seven years ago. . . .

All that torture, because of what he had done. . . .

I needed to deal with those unhealed wounds.

"Two fifty!" I heard eventually. "A new record, Mac!"

I didn't respond.

I felt my hand on something cold. I opened my eyes to see what it was. It was the deck. I was on my knees in the cramped space.

"What's wrong?" she cried.

"Nothing," I grumbled. "But I don't remember kneeling."

"You might have passed out for a second there. I'm stopping the pressurization for a minute."

"No! Keep going." *Don't give me an opportunity to back out now. We have to press on.*

Pause. "Very well." And then, "Three fifty!"

My ears were in great pain. It felt like someone was driving knives into them. I groaned.

"Equalize!" she yelled. "Your eardrums will burst!"

"I'm trying." Finally I managed it, and the stabbing sensation diminished, but not by much. I did it again.

And again.

And again.

Finally: "Four twenty!"

"Open the outer hatch," I mumbled.

"We're not there—"

"Do it," I said. I could barely hear the words. Had I whispered?

"Put your mask on."

"It is."

"No, it's not! Mac, are you sure you want to—"

"Don't stop me now. Putting my mask on." I fumbled with it and clumsily pulled it over my head. "Air mixture is on."

"I'm flooding the chamber."

Water began to rise up my ankles, to my knees, my thighs. With the interior pressurized to match outside, it flowed in quite slowly. Had the pressure within been at the standard four atmospheres, the water would have pounded in like a canon, crushed me to pulp, and burst the inner airlock hatch right off its mounting.

The exterior hatch opened.

It was pitch black outside.

AT THE EDGE OF MY MASK, the water felt like a cold blade peeling at my skin where there was no protection. I took a step out and stood on the platform that had automatically lowered when the hatch opened. I looked down at the seafloor, but couldn't see it.

"Turn on the lights," I said. It was difficult to speak; I had to focus on each breath. It was a struggle to take in air.

"Give it a minute for your eyes to adjust," she responded.

"I can barely hear you."

"The amount of air in your mask is making it difficult for the sound to reach your ears. Turn the volume up on your headset."

I did as she suggested. "It's black out here. Blacker than night."

"The floodlights are on, full intensity."

I estimated the distance to the bottom. The hatch was about a meter from the underside of the hull, but I reminded myself that we were currently resting on the landing skids. Perhaps I was two meters up. I wore weights to help me sink and walk around out there, but it was difficult to tell exactly how far I would fall.

I shrugged inwardly and stepped off into blackness.

There was no time to waste.

I hit bottom with a slight jar, and immediately lurched forward, toward the thruster. The bottom was mushy, like mud. It took an effort even to lift my foot from the stuff.

"Don't forget your flashlight."

I touched the switch and a dull glow appeared from the lens. Incredible. There were thousands of watts of light there, and I could barely see the beam. It traveled *maybe* a meter before it diminished into nothing. It wasn't going to be much help. I dropped it.

But Kat was right—it did seem a little lighter now around the seacar. I could make out the dull shape of the hull. And there, just over my head, was the starboard thruster. The water was hazy with suspended sediment, probably from deep currents, though perhaps my presence had already disturbed the bottom.

The fogginess in my head had cleared somewhat, and I thought that I was beginning to move a little faster. I located the panel and reached up to open it with the wrench.

I couldn't touch it.

Shit.

The landing gear had raised the seacar too far above the bottom. It was a meter too high.

"Uh, Kat."

"Yes? Can you hurry?"

"I can't reach the ship."

"But why? It should—" She stopped. "Oh, that's dumb of me. Of course you can't. Let me lower the landing gear a bit, but I won't fully retract it. Stay out of the way, just in case it collapses."

A faint whine reached my ears, and I watched as the seacar lowered on its hydraulic skids. A moment later it was within reach. I opened the panel. Inside was a neatly organized system of shelves that looked like boxes, and within each was a piece of equipment, a tool, or piping of some sort. The spares were easy to see; they were well-marked and strapped into place.

"Cut the binding," she said. "Use the other side of the wrench; it has a sharp edge. Pull the first screw out."

It was difficult to maneuver the metal piece from the opening. It was about a meter long, from tip to tip, but thankfully easy to carry underwater. I walked to the rear of the pod and studied the damage.

"The screw is completely fucked," I grumbled as I set to work removing it. "Warped. No wonder it didn't push any water when we tried."

"The other is the same, I'm sure."

It took a lot longer than two minutes for me to remove it. Closer to six.

"You have to work faster," she said.

"I'm trying." But I had begun to feel sick. Nauseated by something. Perhaps the mix was making me ill. Perhaps my lungs and sinuses were tired of the punishment. She was right—I needed to finish, and fast.

Finally it was done. I dropped the damaged screw to the seafloor, unconcerned about whether we might need it again at some point in the future. I sealed the panel and began the difficult journey to the other pod. It was less than nine meters away, but it seemed to take forever. My legs were heavy, sluggish. My vision was starting to fade in and out, and my breath came in ragged gulps. I could tell that Kat was concerned. I could hear it in her voice.

"Same as the other side," she murmured in a soft tone. "The panel first."

I did exactly as I had earlier, though it took a hell of a lot longer. But finally the new screw was out, the old screw was off, and I was tightening the nut as best I could. I just wanted to get this over with and start depressurizing. The cold had set in; it felt like a dull ache through my entire body. My head pounded with each beat of my heart. It sounded similar to a baby's heartbeat on an ultrasound. It was just the blood in my ears and head, I knew, but it was lulling me to sleep. I could just close my eyes and take a brief rest. . . .

"Mac!" Kat screamed. "Hurry up! What are you doing?"

"Nothing," I muttered.

"Get back in, quickly!"

"The ballast valve first."

"Are you sure?"

I ignored her and lurched to the hull and searched for it in the murky environment. There weren't any creatures or plant particles suspended out there; it was just thick, dirty, dangerous, black water.

There were four valves in total on the hull, and apparently the shock wave of an explosion had damaged them all. My plan was to replace just one, then take care of the others later. It would reduce the rate we could blow the tanks, but at least we could change our buoyancy.

I finally found one and began to unscrew the bolts with the same wrench.

"You've been out now for twenty minutes," Kat warned. "Your tank is running dry; we didn't make enough hydrogen for any longer."

"I'm almost done."

"You have to hurry. It might take some time to get back to the airlock."

I focused on the job. Within a minute all the bolts were off. I wedged the sharp end of the tool under the valve and used it as a lever to lift it out. It came up with little resistance. Surprisingly easy. I could see the interior of the valve now, from the other side, and it was obvious that the fins within had bent. Some had been forced right down on themselves, constricting the flow of air and water. No wonder it hadn't worked.

I slid the other one in its place, plugging the opening in the hull. "Replacing the bolts."

A few minutes later I was done. I staggered to the side and crouched to walk under the hull. I stumbled and fell to the bottom, seemingly in slow motion; mud and sand churned up and further obscured my view.

"Get up!" she yelled.

My hands disappeared into the muck as I attempted to push myself up. My arms felt weak. My lungs were on fire.

"MOVE IT!"

One last push and I rose shakily to my feet. I had lost the wrench and the damaged valve. I didn't care. Three steps later I was on the other side of the hull and before the platform into the airlock. It was at waist height.

I fell forward, grabbed the grill in the deck of the lock.

I hauled myself in.

"Your legs are in the way!"

I pulled them toward me.

"More! Dammit, your legs! I can't shut the hatch while you're in the way!"

I heaved again, but my vision was going fast. I could still hear her screaming. I felt weaker than ever before.

Everything went black.

I'M NOT SURE HOW LONG I lay on that deck in the small chamber. The sound of air under pressure as it exited or entered the airlock was always there. My legs were crunched up underneath me; somehow I had managed to get them into that enclosure, though I wasn't sure how. Pushing up with my left arm, I managed to lift my torso somewhat and fall to the side to take the pressure off my lower extremities. A voice came to me, distorted and faint. I couldn't tell what it said. A part of me realized it must have been Kat, but I ignored it.

Hours passed. My head pounded. It was more than a simple headache; my skull felt bruised, battered. Breathing was still difficult. There was a ringing in my ears. Every time I woke I regretted it instantly. I drifted in and out of consciousness.

The deck shifted beneath me. *SC-1* was moving again. The thrusters reverberated the ship. It was a good feeling.

Eventually I heard a clang and the hatch swung open. Cool air from the seacar's interior washed over me. I struggled to say something, but all that came out was a low mumble. There was a jab of pain in my arm, and Kat said something about morphine. Her voice still sounded so far away.

Somehow she got me into my bunk. I must have helped, though I have no recollection of it. She gave me a few more injections and muttered something about my eardrums. My head now rested on the soft pillow, and

I finally got to stretch out my cramped legs. After hours on the cold steel of the airlock deck, it was heaven.

I tried to speak. "Everything okay with the screws?" Except what came out was more like, "Eggrydin ohmay widah shrews?" I never heard her response.

I was asleep again.

ANOTHER NOISE WOKE ME FROM THE deep slumber. A clatter of metal on metal. I fought to open my eyes—they were sticky with sleep and mucous and grime—and stared at the ceiling of the bunk barely thirty centimeters above my face. Another bang. Kat was working in the control cabin of the seacar, probably finishing repairs.

My body hurt like hell, but things were not as bad as they had been earlier. My ears felt better. Sounds didn't seem so distant anymore. My eardrums had not burst, thankfully. It was easier to breathe now, although I did feel a lancing pierce in my chest with each inhalation. The headache was still there, even with the morphine, but it was more tolerable now. I used an elbow to push myself up and stuck my head out the curtain. I craned my neck and looked up the passageway toward the control cabin; it took almost every ounce of energy I had, but somehow I managed. Sharp pains shot through my skull and into my sinus cavity. I groaned.

Kat pulled her head out of the wiring panel where the fire had damaged the control circuits. I thought she had repaired everything before I went outside, but I guess there was more to do than I had thought. Her forearms were black with grease and there was a sheen of sweat on her forehead. At that moment, she was the most beautiful sight I could have imagined. A surge of elation filled me; strangely enough, I was happy to see her.

I had survived.

"How do you feel?" she asked. There was genuine concern in her voice.

"Been better," I finally managed. My words sounded far more intelligible than they had earlier.

"You've damaged your eardrums. Bruised lungs too—I think—and you'll probably find it difficult to breathe for a few days." She got to her feet and walked toward me. "But other than that, you seem to be all right." She smiled; it seemed warm and sincere.

"I can't believe we did that."

"*You* did that. It's a new record, Mac."

"I don't want to go through it ever again."

"Thank God you managed to get your legs past the threshold of the lock."

I shook my head. "I don't remember."

"It was damn close."

I just wanted to stop talking about it now, and get back to the job. "Are we on course?"

"Yes, at two hundred meters."

I glanced at the canopy over the pilot seats; the VID system had altered the background color to a lighter blue to represent the shallower depth.

"I went outside and checked your repairs."

I blinked. "Really? I've been asleep for that long?"

She laughed. "You were in the airlock for twenty-six hours! I did it then. Brought us up to thirty meters and went out the moonpool. Set the controls for station-keeping. Tightened the screws a bit. Checked the ballast valve that you repaired. Replaced the three other damaged ones."

"Did the new one work?"

"Yes, though it took longer to blow the tanks with just that one." She shrugged. "We're almost back to a hundred percent operational capability now. Just a few more repairs needed on the control console, and we're all done."

She had been busy.

"Then I brought you inside, got you in your bunk. That was—" She checked her watch. "Eighteen hours ago."

My eyes widened. Wow. The excursion had really affected me. "What's our speed?"

"Back to seventy. I set our course to intercept Johnny; I used his new course to calculate it, based on the information our active sonar gathered before the attack."

A sense of gratification flowed through me. We were back on his tail.

I lay my head on the pillow. I felt as weak as a kitten.

"Keep resting," she said. She laid a hand on my arm. She seemed so different, as if, before, she had resented my presence and doubted my dedication. As if she was the only one who cared about the mission. I guess I had now proven to her that I wanted Johnny just as badly as she, perhaps even more so.

"He's heading for the Mid-Atlantic Ridge for some reason," Kat muttered.

I nodded. He hadn't altered his course. We had to get there before he could hand off the technology. If his meeting lasted several hours, it would be our chance to ambush him and stop the transaction.

It would also give me an opportunity to kill him.

I closed my eyes and slept.

OVER THE NEXT DAY I SHOWED remarkable improvement. The first steps I took were wobbly and I nearly fell several times in the confines of the living area, but I soon got my feet under me. I still ached, though that began to get better within hours as well. I stopped taking the morphine, got a good night's sleep—which was weird because I had been unconscious for all those hours—and the next day I felt almost human once again. It had been almost seventy hours since I had gone outside.

When Kat looked at me now there was respect in her eyes. She said once, after my first outing from the bunk, "That record could stand for centuries. People have died in far shallower environments."

"I can't take total credit. People have theorized that hydrogen is the better gas to use. Safer. Maybe we just proved the concept. Deep divers everywhere might switch to it now."

When I felt well enough, I began spending more time in the control cabin watching the sensors and keeping an eye on our position. The depth finder showed a vastly different seafloor than the one just east of the State's coastline: this was quite rugged with peaks kilometers above the bottom, huge canyons, and myriad valleys. It was the outskirts of the Mid-Atlantic Ridge, part of the chain of mountains that encircles much of the Earth. It is the largest mountain range on the planet, some 64,000 kilometers in length—if you connected the Andes, the Rockies, and the Himalayas in one long mountain system, the Mid-Oceanic Ridge would be longer. Either Johnny was running toward it to hide, his meeting was to take place somewhere on a seamount or guyot in there, or he was simply passing through on his way to the Mediterranean or Europe. That was doubtful, however; he was out of the regular sealanes.

It was time to risk another position check with the active sonar. Kat agreed with me, and together we triggered the system and watched the display with bated breath.

"There he is," I said. The contact marked in yellow was in the ridge system, now headed due north.

"Speed still sixty," Kat reported.

I took a minute to study the list of contacts in the hundred kilometer radius. It didn't take long to find the Chinese *Fast Attack* that had almost sunk us. She was sixty kilometers to the southeast. Headed to the coast of Africa or the Cape of Good Hope.

A part of me felt a moment of fear.

She now no doubt knew that we were still alive.

And she would be coming.

"It's okay," I muttered. "By the time she catches up to us, we'll be in the Ridge and able to evade her."

I hope, I added to myself.

THE DISTANCE FROM THE LOCATION WHERE we had confronted the Chinese *Fast Attack* and the seamount where we had hidden, to the central rift in the Mid-Atlantic Ridge, was 3000 kilometers. It was the dividing point of the Atlantic Ocean. There, the oceanic crust was fissured straight down to the Upper Mantle in the Earth's interior. Superheated liquid rock rose to the surface and spewed out into the ocean through a multitude of undersea volcanoes and thermal vents. New ocean floor was constantly forming in the rift. The ocean crust there, acting under immense planetary forces, split apart at a rate of three centimeters per year. The deep water in that region was warm and turbulent; explorers had discovered life there decades ago, existing where the sun could not penetrate. Most of the life forms were beyond imagination. Indeed, we only knew about ten percent of the creatures that lived in the world's oceans.

We descended to 2000 meters and began the long trek northward though the rift. Undersea currents created by flash-cooled magma at the bottom of the canyon buffeted our tiny seacar and tossed us about with mighty force. The ocean conveyer system that flowed south, driven by salinity and temperature differentials, fought with the other currents and created an environment quite difficult to navigate. To make matters worse, the Chinese had damaged our vertical stabilizer in the attack, and there was little we could do about it. I compensated for the slow response time with my own piloting, but it was difficult.

We strapped ourselves in and kept our gazes fixed to the instruments.

We were out of the sealanes, traveling where few dared.

Where the hell was Johnny going?

The VID system had a playback function, and I decided to take a look at the record of the attack by the Chinese vessel. Kat set the image on the canopy to replay the entire incident. It was like watching a movie unfold before our eyes. The *Jin* class vessel circling above . . . torpedoes surging down into the depths . . . mines plunging toward us . . . It was surreal.

Kat froze the image and I zoomed in on the warsub. It was just an outline, but it was enough. Our computer records had all known information on the *Jin* class, and I brought it up on a split screen view to compare the two. They were similar, there was no doubt about it. It *looked* like a *Jin*—or a *Fast Attack*—but there were subtle differences.

"The thrusters are closer to the hull," I said. "And it's a little sleeker."

"Our sonar identified it as a *Fast Attack*."

"Right. It's using the same engines, so it sounds the same. But it's a new variant."

"Experimental?"

I shrugged. "No way to tell. It could be . . . or it could be an entirely new model." One thing was for sure, however: our information on its maximum depth had been dead wrong. "I'll have to tell Shanks about it. TCI needs to know."

"And the American military?"

I hesitated. "I'll leave that up to him." I pondered the situation for long minutes. We were chasing Johnny north, through the rift. At the same time, the *Fast Attack* would be back on course for us, coming from the south. But when would they reach us?

I decided to risk another active sonar pulse. Kat didn't object, and a few seconds later, we had the results.

They were on us again, now also in the rift. We were slowly overtaking Johnny, but the other vessel was slowly overtaking us. I hoped that wherever he was going, we would be able to deal with him before the *Fast Attack*—or whatever it was—reached us.

Then I noticed something else on the screen that took my breath away. Perhaps I had seen it because there were fewer contacts. Or maybe it was just fortunate that I happened to glance at that quadrant of the display.

It was an American warsub.

USS *Impaler*.

Reaper class, the largest attack sub in the US arsenal.

She was just under a hundred kilometers away.

And on an intercept for us.

"I realized the undersea world was as unknown and as perplexing as that of any alien planet. One could simply disappear in those depths, and no soul on Earth would ever know what had become of you."

—Jessica Ng, Naturalist, Oceanographer, and
Freedom Fighter

PART THREE: THE CHARLIE GIBBS FRACTURE ZONE

CHAPTER ELEVEN +−

THE CENTRAL RIFT IN THE MID-ATLANTIC Ridge was twenty kilometers across and over five kilometers deep—an enormous tear in the crust of the planet. In some places the volcanoes were so immense that they emerged above the water. Places such as Iceland, Ascension Island, and the Azores. Imagine living in such a place, where the land beneath your feet is actually tearing in different directions and an eruption could kill thousands at any moment.

We were within that giant canyon, forging north, toward Johnny and his imminent meeting. He knew that we were on his tail, that his time was running out.

And that meant he would be dangerous prey.

The currents continued to buffet the seacar; sometimes we would heel to the port or starboard, at others we would suddenly ascend or descend tens of meters without warning. Just as airplanes experience turbulence over intensely heated land, we now faced the same conditions. Pilots generally try to avoid this type of environment, but it was impossible for us. We had to stay on the trail, even if it meant a day or two of difficult travel.

It was necessary to contact Trieste City Intelligence and inform Shanks of the situation. Along the most common sealanes were vast networks of fiber optic cables, and every twenty kilometers there was a junction to receive and transmit communications. As we crossed the sealane between England

and the Northeastern United States, I knew that one of them would be within range. I brought the seacar up above the lip of the rift so a message could get out of the canyon, and keyed the code into the comm system. We had encrypted both sides of the transmission. Minutes passed before Shanks appeared on the screen. He looked tired, but anxious for news of any sort. His face was grim, as usual, and there were no pleasantries between us.

"Report," he said in a brusque voice.

I filled him in on the events of the past four days. A look of concern flashed across his features as I related the news of the attack, and he clenched a fist on the table before him.

"Those bastards," he muttered. "They're either trying to stop you from catching Johnny Chang, or they know that Doctor Wells is with you."

"They want her dead?" I shot a look over my shoulder; Kat was in her bunk, getting some sleep before we caught up with Johnny.

"Maybe."

"What has she invented that's so damn important?"

"That's not relevant. Just bring Johnny back."

"What are you talking about?" I snapped. "Not relevant? They're trying to kill us, Shanks! I want to catch Johnny, but I need to know the whole truth to do my job properly!"

"No you don't. You just have to get him."

My jaw clamped shut; I was fuming. I had to force myself not to speak because I knew that it would just escalate the argument.

"You did well to escape from that ship," he said, trying to mollify me. "And you're still on track, which is a good thing." He paused, and then, "And you say it was a *Jin* class vessel?"

I nodded. "That's how the sonar identified it, but it appears slightly different. It has enhanced capabilities, as well."

"Such as?"

"It dove to a depth of almost four kilometers."

He blinked. "A *Fast Attack*? Incredible. A new model maybe."

"I'm sending you the information that we've gathered on it now." I pressed the SEND DATA key on the comm, and the burst transmission instantly relayed the file to him.

"How far are you from Johnny?"

I glanced at the display. "He's within our passive range now; thirty kilometers. We should overtake him in three hours."

A hint of a smile spread across the director's features. "Good. Make sure you get that son of a bitch and bring him back to us, McClusky."

I nodded, but said nothing.

"Anything else?"

"There's a *Reaper* class USSF warsub also on our tail."

The *Reaper* was the largest SSN warsub class in the fleet. Four massive thrusters gave her a maximum speed identical to our own. I wasn't concerned with her overtaking us, but when we stopped to deal with Johnny, it would give them time to catch up. She was at the limits of our active sonar range, and she could make that distance in ninety minutes. What I was really concerned with was her firepower. She had more than fifteen torpedo tubes, mines, and grapples. She was a carrier for smaller fighter-subs that could exit and attack multiple targets simultaneously. The warsub was 250 meters long and could reach a stated depth of 3850 meters. There were ten of them in the fleet, each with a crew of 400. She was an intimidating vessel.

Shanks's face grew hard. "She's headed for you?"

"Without a doubt. When we reach Johnny, both the *Reaper* and the Chinese *Fast Attack* will be on us. It's going to get dicey." Understatement of the year.

"Is it *Impaler*?"

I nodded. "According to sonar."

He winced. "She pulled out of Trieste hours after you did." He tapped his fingers on the desk before him as he considered the situation. "We can't let the information that Johnny has fall into USSF hands. This is too big for them."

I leaned forward. "Why?"

A scowl. "As I said earlier, it could mean the end of Trieste's position in the oceans. It will give other nations and cities the edge. We can't allow that." I studied his expression as he spoke; he noticed my scrutiny and his face flushed. "Everything depends on you. Don't let us down."

I snorted. "Kat's discovery is that—"

"It is. Now go do your job." He reached out to cut the transmission.

"Wait! What does *Impaler* know—why is she following us?" This was crucial. Was the USSF after Kat's discovery too?

"Frankly, we're not sure. But they don't know about TCI, so they might just be curious about what you're doing."

It sounded flimsy. Why follow me if they didn't know about the mission? Or Kat's invention?

"They might also be after the new Chinese *Fast Attack*," he continued. "To gather more information. Maybe that's what scared her away from you."

That was a more likely scenario.

Still, the fact that they were on an intercept with us was bothersome.

"And if they attack?" I whispered.

His face tightened. "I'll leave that up to you. But if things do get rough out there, we can't claim knowledge of you or your mission."

"You'll disavow me." It wasn't a question.

Pause. "We'll have to, to preserve TCI's secrecy. You know that." He glared at me for a long minute. Then, "Keep me informed."

The transmission ended.

I SAT IN SILENCE AND CONSIDERED the dilemma. I still didn't know what I would do when I confronted Johnny. I felt loyal to Trieste—I wanted nothing more than for the city to continue to grow and prosper—but if I did what Shanks had ordered it would mean losing my opportunity to pay Johnny back for what had happened all those years ago. At the same time, he had stolen TCI property, and if I did retrieve it, it could mean that Shanks and Mayor Flint would take the city down a road that I did not want to follow.

Kat stirred in her bunk behind me, and a few moments later I heard her feet hit the deck lightly. She entered the control cabin and sat beside me. She laid her hand on my arm as she did so, and I glanced at it, surprised.

She ignored my expression.

"How is everything?" she asked.

"Fine." I had descended back into the rift, and the currents were again rocking the seacar from side to side. "Did you get some sleep?"

"Surprisingly, yes." She looked out the acrylic canopy and a silence fell over us for several minutes. I glanced at her to see what she was doing, and saw an expression of peace and happiness on her features. She had pulled her hair back into a ponytail and was now in a black jumpsuit. Without taking her eyes from the view, she said, "I love the ocean. Everything it represents, everything that lives in it. I always have."

"Why?"

"I just felt myself drawn to it, even as a young child. We would go to the coast, on family trips, and I would just sit and watch the waves for hours on end. Dream of what it might be like to live under the water, to use the resources there, and not have to depend on anybody else."

I understood the notion well, and found it just as compelling a force.

She continued, "I applied to MIT in a field that I knew would get me into an underwater city. My dad got sick soon after, however, and . . ." She trailed off.

"You said he held on for a long time."

"Yes." She sighed. "I loved him so much. It got to a point, however, where I began to resent him for being sick. It was terminal, we all knew it. But it stretched on for years. Then I felt guilty for feeling the way I did, and I had to go into therapy to understand if it was normal or not."

"Your dreams were on hold."

A tentative nod. "But don't get me wrong. I didn't want him to die. I didn't want him to be sick." She paused again; her eyes had welled up. "I miss him so much."

I didn't know how to respond, so I said nothing. Instead I dimmed the cabin lights and let her experience the ocean as we powered through it. We were in the middle of one of the most remarkable features on the planet, and she knew it. Hell, it was her lifelong dream, and she had only been in water for a month now. Despite the danger of the mission and her stolen property, she must have been loving the experience.

She turned to me suddenly. "What about you?"

"What do you mean?"

"How did you get involved in this?"

I shrugged. "It's a long story."

She laughed. "We have a bit of time."

I couldn't help but return the smile. "We lived in Texas until I was eight. Myself, my parents, and Meagan, my sister. Like you, Trieste recruited my dad and we went to live there in 2093."

"What did they want him for?"

"He told us that it was for his engineering expertise. It was a lie." I hesitated. "My father did a lot of things I don't agree with. He had another agenda that we didn't find out about for some time. He had been in the military for decades before Meg and I were born. He fought the Chinese and North Koreans in the Second Korean War. He was a great strategist and a member of Special Forces, though I'm not sure what section. Someone in Trieste heard about him and recruited him to work for the city."

"As an engineer."

"That was the official reason, but in reality they were planning independence. This was back in the '90s when everyone in the three American colonies was clamoring for it. My father joined TCI and led the fight, although it was pretty brief. The people even elected him mayor in 2095." My chest tightened at the thought. In 2099 the CIA had infiltrated Trieste and simply assassinated the leaders of the city and the entire city council. It put an end to the independence movement. Meg and I were fourteen at the time. It devastated our mother, and she never fully recovered. She passed away in 2111, the year I joined TCI.

"Did the CIA know about TCI back then?" Kat asked.

"No. At least, we don't think so. They still don't, as far as we know."

"If you don't agree with independence, why join TCI?"

I shrugged. "I still wanted to help the city. I felt the lure of the intelligence business, same as my dad. Shanks actually worked there at the same time as him. He helped bring me into the agency. A lot of people remember my father and what he did; they respect him for it. During my time in TCI I went out on a lot of missions, did a lot of great things for the city." I had been trying to live up to his reputation, I thought. Tough shoes to fill.

"Such as?"

"Espionage, mostly. Observing what the other cities were up to. Sometimes stealing important information or discoveries."

"Like Johnny Chang?"

"Yes. I used to do precisely what he did to you. That was our thing; that's the game. We sometimes even worked together. We were friends."

She seemed shocked at that. "Why'd he turn?"

I paused. It was a tough question. "I still don't fully understand why. He was a Chinese American and a lot of our missions were to Chinese cities. Things between the two nations were tense; they still are."

"Worse now."

"Yeah. Maybe someone turned him, or maybe he just did it on his own."

"How did it happen?" Her voice was soft. She could tell that the topic bothered me.

"We were on a mission to Sheng City. It was a simple assignment. We were to observe their military and report any changes or sudden buildup of arms or vessels. It was standard. Right now there are TCI people in other undersea cities around the world doing the same thing."

"Are there foreign operatives in Trieste watching us?" Her eyes were wide.

"Undoubtedly."

"But why?"

"Everyone wants the biggest piece of the ocean possible. Everyone wants that one bit of technology or information that will give them the edge." I studied her. "Like yours, I'm sure."

"And that's created all the tension?"

"No. The troubles between the States and China go back decades. But the undersea cities are a frontier for them to compete with one another. Hostilities flare up on occasion. It's also a place for them to test new technology, unseen and unheard on land."

Her brow crinkled. "But why—"

I had anticipated the question. "The resources down here are the key to the future, Kat. You know that. The mineral deposits, the aquaculture potential. The future of the superpowers is down here." The Iron Plains was the contested area today, but tomorrow it would be something different. It would never end.

"Which is why we need to keep it to ourselves," she said.

"How? By declaring independence? The US will squash us like bugs, and you know it."

"We aren't as weak as we were when your dad . . . I mean, as we were in 2099."

"It doesn't matter. They're too powerful."

"But a war on land would involve us. Do you want to be a part of that?"

"Of course not. It would be a disaster for us."

"Independence would prevent that."

"Independence would *cause* that. Don't you see?"

"No. I don't."

I sighed and turned away from her. "I guess it doesn't matter if we disagree. Shanks and Flint will do what they want, even if it destroys the city."

"I'm hoping it will make Trieste better, in the long run."

I didn't respond to that. I just couldn't see it happening. The USSF was massive, and there were only three American undersea cities, so they weren't about to let one go. Independence didn't seem possible; it would only bring the military down on our heads worse than ever, and they would never leave us alone afterward. They would probably insert a puppet government. Take full control of us.

"So what happened when Johnny turned?" she asked.

I winced. "It happened seven years ago now. We were conducting surveillance when suddenly the Chinese military swooped down on us. Johnny was in on it; he gave me up. They took me prisoner and tortured me for months."

She gasped. "Why?"

"They wanted to know about TCI. Names of our operatives, how the agency worked, and so on."

"Did you talk?"

"I wanted to some days. It was tough. The pain was excruciating. I've never felt anything like it since."

"And Johnny?"

I hesitated, then, "Sometimes he conducted the sessions."

Her jaw dropped. "What?"

"I'm not sure why. Maybe his new bosses made him, but he didn't seem to mind."

"How'd you get out?"

"Prisoner exchange." This was the source of my anger toward Shanks. It turned out that he had had Chinese operatives imprisoned at Trieste. He had been torturing them. I suspected that this was why Johnny betrayed us and defected to Sheng City. It was Shanks's fault. He had escalated things, and the Chinese cities had simply followed suit.

And caught me in the middle.

I hadn't believed Johnny when he told me about the Chinese prisoners at Trieste. I refused to during the entire four month period. And then the prisoner exchange occurred, and I realized he had been right all along. I saw them with my own eyes. Withered, skinny, beaten. Their eyes seemed dead when I looked at them.

I couldn't forgive Shanks for what he had done to those people. They were just doing a job. They didn't deserve torture. He had said earlier that my father would have approved, and maybe he was right. But I just could not accept it.

Two major events in my life had made me the man I am. First was my father's death. After the assassination I had withdrawn and become a loner, rarely interacting with people on a social level. I didn't even spend much time with women, although there had been a few. I had dedicated myself to Trieste, perhaps to keep my father's dream alive, even though I was still bitter about what he had done. The second event had been the incident with Johnny. Afterward I had grown even more distant. I resigned my commission as an operative and began to work as a laborer. The only people I dealt with were my coworkers, and only then if it was during a shift. It seemed easier that way. The work I was doing made me feel that I was helping the city. The anger at Shanks and Johnny had simmered for seven years, and when the opportunity came to get revenge, I had jumped at the chance.

My readiness had surprised me, in fact.

I wanted blood for what had happened, and the more I thought about it, the more I knew I had to kill him.

CHAPTER TWELVE

FORTY-FIVE MINUTES LATER THE CONTACT WE were chasing abruptly disappeared. We had been closing in on a major feature in the Ridge—a canyon thirty kilometers wide and a thousand long—called the Charlie Gibbs Fracture Zone. Some parts were three times deeper than the Grand Canyon, and it ran perpendicular to the central rift in the Mid-Atlantic Ridge, at the midpoint between Iceland and the Azores. The canyon was 4500 meters deep, though some seamounts within it hit only seven or eight hundred meters below the surface.

And Johnny had gone in there.

He had been on our passive sonar, just a few kilometers ahead of us. Although we were in his baffles, or "wake," which made it difficult for him to hear us, we had already used our active sonar to identify him a few times. It must have alerted him to our presence.

As he turned west into the Fracture, the contact cut off immediately.

"What happened?" Kat asked.

"The rock walls are shielding his noise. As soon as we turn the corner, we'll pick him up."

But when we turned into the canyon, his signal was gone.

THE BOTTOM OF THE FRACTURE WAS at the limits of our crush depth. I considered taking on water and descending to look for him, when I noticed a seamount in the VID three kilometers away. It rose from the bottom, equidistant between the canyon walls, to a depth of about one kilometer. He might have gone to the other side of it to hide from us.

I steered the seacar toward it and made our depth 1000 meters. I decreased speed to only ten percent; no point alerting him to our exact location. Make him search for us, I thought. Our thrusters were fairly quiet at such low speeds.

I studied the VID as we approached the seamount. It was actually a guyot—a mountain with a flat top. At some point in the past, the ocean level had been low enough so that wave action had eroded it. It was possible that—

"Holy shit," Kat whispered.

There was a structure on the guyot's top. It was a dome, set on stilts. If it hadn't been for the VID system, we would never have noticed, even with our lamps on. Its dark color blended in perfectly with the rock that it rested on.

Johnny had connected his seacar to the structure with an umbilical. He had already entered the dome.

The meeting was underway.

I CUT ALL POWER TO THE thrusters and changed our buoyancy to negative. We descended to the plateau, and I took a minute to study the base. I had to be careful about how to get in there, but I knew my time was limited. There was another seacar there, and if the meeting ended and both parties went their separate ways, there might be no way to get the information back.

We had to act fast.

The facility was probably pressurized at four atmospheres, so it would be a simple matter to hook up an umbilical and march straight into the base. To go outside would take far longer. We were a kilometer down. We had mix for that depth, but I couldn't just go outside then straight into the base. I would have to decompress. No, I needed to use an umbilical. The question was: Did the base have another entrance point? And if we used it, would it alert the people within?

Kat was studying the facility on the projected display. She pointed at the two seacars and their links into the dome. "There are two entrances here. Both already have umbilicals secured." She shook her head. "There's no quick way in."

But I was looking somewhere else. "There is a way." I pointed at the second seacar, the one belonging to the people who Johnny had come to meet. It

was significantly larger and there were two airlocks on its hull, one on each side. Only the starboard airlock was currently mated to the base. I could enter the vessel from its other side—through its port airlock—then enter the facility through the umbilical already attached.

A smile appeared on Kat's face. "And since nations have standardized airlocks, we can connect ours to theirs."

"Exactly." I just hoped that there was nobody in the vessel right now.

I nudged power up on the thrusters and slowly brought us toward the parked seacars. There was a strong current running across the top of the guyot, however, and I had to compensate for it with more thruster power. After mating with the other vessel's airlock, I strapped a holster and gun to my thigh. I had found it in my bag earlier; Shanks had put it there for me.

Nowadays there were thousands of facilities in the ocean. Some were major cities, some just small settlements, usually based around the exploitation of a mineral deposit or a rich fishing region. Some were experimental installations to test new technology for living in the deep. Some were research bases. It was impossible to determine which this was, or which nation it belonged to. There was no lettering of any kind on the dome. There was, however, a name on the vessel that was there to meet Johnny: *Patriote*.

French.

That's why Johnny had sailed northeast instead of just bolting for Sheng City to the west. He was dealing the technology to the French. Were they working together, perhaps? If so, to what end? Or was he just there to sell it?

I gritted my teeth and stalked to the airlock.

Time to find out.

"HEY, WAIT A MINUTE," KAT HISSED. Her hand was on my arm, and she was pulling me back from the hatch. "What do I do here?"

"Seal the lock. I'll contact you with the PCD." I had already retrieved her code if I needed to message her. "But don't call me under any circumstances. You might give me away."

Her eyes were wide. "And if someone comes?"

"Disconnect from the airlock. Don't let them in."

"What about you?"

I paused. "If they come for you, it might mean I'm already dead. If I don't contact you, destroy this base."

Her mouth hung open. "Say again?"

"This seacar has eight torpedoes. Use one."

"But why?"

"It'll eliminate the information that Johnny has. It'll prevent the transaction from taking place. Your discovery will be safe." The only reason I hadn't already done so was because I needed to confront Johnny. If I was going to kill him, I wanted to talk to him first. I needed to know what had happened to him. "Do you understand?"

She nodded after a heartbeat. "Be careful."

I turned and slapped open the hatch.

THE FRENCH SEACAR WAS LARGER AND more luxurious than ours. Comfortable couches in the living area, cabins instead of bunks set into the bulkhead, and a control cabin that could seat four. I spent a minute looking around, but did not find anything of interest. I marched to the second airlock and the umbilical that led to the facility. The hatches slid open and shut at my touch; they hadn't thought to arm the security system. Odd, but it was possible that Johnny had not warned these people I was on his tail. Unlikely, but possible.

The umbilical was characteristic of most—one person could pass through at a time—and my head almost hit the top of the curved tube as I walked. Once inside the base, I sealed the hatch behind me. The interior of the facility was also typical. Metal bulkheads and decks, everything polished steel. Harsh, fluorescent lighting. Emergency lights in the ceiling, covered by red translucent panels. Watertight doors every fifteen meters. My feet clanged with each step; I had to crouch somewhat and move slowly.

All was silent inside.

The dome was three levels high; I had entered from the bottom. I circled the entire level, poking my head into each room. Most of the operational equipment was there, such as the atmospheric system, waste and water recycling, and the batteries for electrical power. There might also have been a small nuclear plant, but it was not in the base. It would be underground, perhaps, or located elsewhere on the guyot and connected to the facility with buried cables.

Up to the second level.

This was the living and working area. Recreational lounges. Cabins with bunks. A kitchen and mess. A few research labs. There was nothing of

interest; the labs looked not only unused, but as if they had been empty for a decade.

This was a deserted research base of some sort.

I gripped the gun tightly in my hand.

The top level.

Everything was still completely silent, with the exception of the hum of the ventilation system, and the occasional creak and *thunk* caused by the weight of water overhead. This was a much smaller level, being at the top of the dome, and there were only a few spaces to search. Most were control rooms, such as the communications station.

I stood before the last hatch. A sign marked it as: *Module de Commande*.

I listened intently. Still nothing.

A surge of fear suddenly coursed through my body. What if they were all down in Johnny's seacar? I hadn't checked it yet—I had only looked at the French one as I moved through it—and if they were there, they would be able to run easily.

Damn. I should have checked that first.

I opened the hatch.

My breath caught in my throat.

There were six people inside. They were sitting around a table in the center of the chamber. Along the room's exterior were panels and switches and displays necessary to run and control the facility. In the ceiling over the table was a large stretch of acrylic—a "skylight." Above, the ocean was dark.

One of the men at the table was sitting so that he faced me directly.

Johnny Chang.

"Hello, Mac," he said. "I've been waiting for you."

CHAPTER THIRTEEN 十三

He had a smirk on his face, and I glared at him for a long, hard moment. He looked the same as he had last I saw him. Lines around his eyes, square jaw, broad shoulders, short hair, almost a brush cut. His appearance screamed military.

There were five others in the room with him. The only other Asian was most likely his partner. The rest were all Caucasians. Three of them were women of varying ages, and last was an older man. They looked more like dignitaries or government delegates than spies or people who would conduct a secretive exchange.

I studied Johnny closely in the silence. It had indeed been a long time since we had last worked together for Trieste. The man I had known then was loyal and trustworthy, though a tad secretive when away from work. He hadn't had many friends, although there was a family that he visited frequently in the city. They were Chinese as well, and I always attributed their friendship as a need for Johnny to remain connected to his culture. He would see them for meals or holidays, or sometimes just for tea and a chance to talk. He had never invited me along when he visited them, a fact that sometimes annoyed me. I hadn't had much in the way of friends either—it was difficult in our line of work. We were often away for weeks or months at a time. And since my sister had left Trieste and our parents had died, I'd felt almost completely alone. Johnny had been one of the people closest to me. And for that reason, his betrayal had hurt more than anything. He hadn't just turned against the city—he had stabbed me in the back.

I mostly ignored the other people in that room, except to growl at them to stay still and keep their palms on the table. The gun was steady in my hand, aimed directly at Johnny's head. He could see the tension in my body. Unfortunately, he didn't seem surprised or nervous at my presence.

"Don't pretend like you're happy to see me," I finally snapped. "Our last meeting is still burned in my memory. Remember?"

"Old times, Mac. No reason to bring those up now."

I almost pulled the trigger right then and there. He was utterly calm, serene. He didn't have a care in the world. The others, however, were visibly terrified. They hadn't moved a muscle. I'm not sure if they knew mine and Johnny's history, but they could tell that my anger was very real.

"You betrayed me," I ground out. "Betrayed Trieste. Put us back ten years in the intelligence business."

"I told you why I did it. You didn't believe me at the time. Do you now?"

I hesitated. I remembered the faces of the tortured Chinese as they shuffled past me during the prisoner exchange. They had been through hell, as I had. "I didn't know anything about it. It was all Shanks. I quit when I found out."

He nodded. "Noble of you."

"I couldn't stand working for that man."

"And yet here you are."

I took a step toward him. A part of me screamed, *Be careful! Don't let him get under your skin!*

I didn't pay any attention to it.

"I'm here for other reasons." I gestured with the gun. "Get the picture?"

"Revenge." He winced. "Such a dangerous emotion. You need to distance yourself from your primal brain, Mac. It'll just get you into trouble."

"I'm also here for the stolen technology."

His face remained blank as he paused for a moment. "You mean you don't know what it is? Shanks didn't tell you about it?"

I ignored the question. "Where is it? Have you handed it over to them yet?" I studied the others in the room. I had assumed they were French. But just to make sure . . . "What are you doing here?" I said to the oldest. He withered under my glare. His hair was white and he wore round-framed glasses. He was so scared that he didn't answer. I shifted my aim. "*Speak,* or I start shooting."

He finally attempted to say something, but all that came out was a croak. Then he gave another try, and managed a feeble, "To meet him." He pointed at Johnny.

And he had spoken with a very recognizable accent.

"You're in this with the French," I said to Johnny. "Why? What's your plan?"

"Which one? There are so many."

"Don't play games. I'd rather kill you all now and search your bodies for the information. It would be far easier that way."

One of the French started to speak, but Johnny shushed her with a sharp motion. "He doesn't mean it," he said. "He's angry, but he doesn't have it in him."

I held my aim on the older man. "You don't believe I'll do it, Johnny? After everything you put me through? Four months of torture, of agony at your hands, and you don't think I'll kill you and the pieces of shit that you're dealing with?" My voice trembled with rage, and I could feel a sheen of perspiration on my forehead. I realized, deep down inside, that I was close to losing it.

And I didn't care.

A pregnant pause ensued. The old man appeared as though he would faint at any moment. Finally Johnny said in a quiet voice, "I guess you do."

"Damn right. Now answer my questions, or people start dying."

"There's a lot you don't know, Mac. I'm willing to talk."

"Tell me what it was like to torture your friend."

For the first time, his face betrayed his emotion. A flash of regret. "I didn't want to do that. They made me."

"You turned. Did they make you do that too?"

"No. That was my choice, because I knew what Shanks was up to. I tried to tell you during those four months, but you couldn't accept it."

"Of course not! Would you? Your supposed *friend* turns you over to your enemies and starts zapping your nuts with a thousand volts? I couldn't believe anything you said."

He winced. "It was a test. They wouldn't have taken me had I not done it. Then where would I have gone? Back to Trieste? Ha." He spat the last word.

"I would rather the whole incident had not occurred, actually."

"In a perfect world. However, this ain't it. And George Shanks would be the first to admit it."

I ground my teeth and considered what to say. Finally, "Look. I disagreed with what he did. You were right about it. But you didn't have to betray us."

He spread his arms out. "What should I have done? Challenged Shanks to a duel? I did the only thing possible. I joined up with Sheng City."

"You could have just left TCI, like me."

"It wouldn't have saved those prisoners. What I did achieved that."

A part of me realized he was right, but it still hurt that he had cast my friendship aside so easily.

"You see?" he said. "You understand now, don't you? I used *you* to save *them*."

I didn't respond to that. Instead I said, "Where's the technology you stole? Do you still have it?"

"Before I answer, let's talk about *why* I stole it."

I glanced at the French contingent in the room. If he wanted to talk about what they were doing here, I wouldn't stop him. "Go ahead."

"Shanks and Mayor Flint are planning something for Trieste, Mac. Did you know that?"

A jolt shot through my body. After what Kat had told me, I had considered the possibility that they were up to something. And now Johnny was confirming it.

He continued, "They're not working in the best interests of their people. They have their own agenda. And you're a part of it. So is Doctor Wells."

"What did you take from her?"

"Something she invented. The reason Shanks recruited her." He paused and glanced at his comrade, the other Asian in the room. "We went to Trieste to steal it. But I also went for another reason."

I started to feel uneasy about all of this. "And that is?"

He paused for a heartbeat; there was a slight smile on his face. Then, "I engineered the entire theft for your benefit, Mac. I *wanted* Shanks to use you for this. You see, I *wanted* him to send you . . . to bring you here, to me."

THE OTHERS IN THE ROOM SEEMED bewildered by the turn of events. All except the other Asian, that is. His expression was set in place. I turned back to Johnny and stared at him. My mind was whirling, trying to digest what he had said. All that time we had been on his tail I thought he had been running for his life. In fact, he had been luring me here. But was he telling the truth now, or was this just an elaborate lie to throw me off balance? A ruse to avoid certain death?

He said, "I deliberately let the security camera see my face in the lab. I could have got in there without being detected; I'm familiar with the security system."

I snorted. "All to bring me here."

"Exactly."

"And what about the five men you sent to kill me?"

He raised a finger. "Not kill. Our first plan was to kidnap you. If that failed, I had to hope that Shanks would send you. That was a gamble that paid off."

I frowned. "And the *Fast Attack* that tried to sink us?"

"Not sink. Just damage you enough to board and bring you to me. That failed too. They're working with me; Sheng City doesn't know about them. They lost you and *Impaler* scared them away. This was my last resort."

Something about that just didn't make sense. I motioned to the French in the room. "And them?"

He shrugged. "A legitimate transaction. They don't know anything about you. They're here to purchase what I stole. It's the only way to stop Trieste from what they're attempting."

"Which is?" But I already knew what he was going to say.

"Independence, Mac. Trieste is going to declare independence, and it will trigger a world war. We have to stop that."

HE WAS WATCHING MY EXPRESSION INTENTLY, to see if I bought it. I realized there was a lot of truth to what he was saying, and Kat had basically said it already. Still, I hadn't known whether to believe her, as it seemed so farfetched. But now here was a foreign operative saying the same thing. Things were adding up, finally, but I wasn't sure what I could do about it just yet.

He continued, "You were never in favor of independence, even though your father died for it. You know what the problems are. If Trieste starts a war with the United States, other nations will try to help. In particular, China. They'd only be too happy to watch the great United States say goodbye to her only underwater colonies. They'd supply arms and troops, and the States would find out. Hell, the Chinese hate the fact that the movement in 2099 failed. The CIA action that killed your father took them completely by surprise. They've vowed to never let that happen again. If Trieste tries for independence, Sheng City and the other undersea colonies will throw their hats in the ring with you."

My jaw dropped. Johnny had hit me with two bombshells in only a minute. First, that he had engineered our meeting. Second, that the Chinese were banking on a Triestrian move for independence. And he was right—if they got involved, it would indeed start a war. And not just in the sea.

He could tell that he had hit a nerve. He sat back and watched the emotion cascade across my features.

"What proof do you have?" I finally managed.

"Intelligence reports."

"Do you have them with you?"

"No."

"And you expect me to just accept this and do . . . do what, exactly?"

"Go back to Shanks and stop it. Stop what they're trying. You're the only one I could think of to help."

I blinked. "But why do you want to stop it? I thought you hated Trieste."

"I hate Shanks, not Trieste. I love that city. I lived there for years."

I watched him closely. I could tell he was conflicted about his decision to defect, and that surprised me. He wasn't truly happy at Sheng, and he was trying to make amends with me in his own way. It wasn't exactly what I had wanted, but at least the realization that he was *trying* gave me a tiny bit of gratification. In some small way, I felt bad for him. "So you're trying to stop Shanks from declaring independence?" I fumbled, stalling. I wasn't sure what to think.

He nodded. "There would be too many dead. And Trieste would be gone."

I gestured to his companion. "And who is that?"

"A friend. Someone I work with at Sheng."

"And why would he help you? He should want war—it would give the Chinese a foothold in an American city."

"He has family there. I knew them. They could die if fighting broke out."

A piece of the puzzle clicked into place. That's why Johnny had defected to Sheng City; he hooked up with their people through a Chinese contact in Trieste—the family that had befriended him. He called them "cousins." And his dislike for Shanks and what Shanks had been doing to the Chinese prisoners had pushed him over the edge. It made sense now. At least, more than it had earlier.

"And what exactly has Katherine Wells invented that will allow Trieste to push for independence?"

He smiled. "She's brilliant, Mac. She did something that scientists have been trying for years. And Sheng City needs it. I have to take it back to them, regardless of what we decide right now."

I clenched my teeth. He hadn't answered my question. "I don't think you're going to get it to them."

"I think I am." His expression was calm again. Calculating. My friendship with Johnny had taught me a lot about him, and I could read his face.

He had a plan.

I said, "So you want me to go back and stop Shanks. And you want me to let you go and take this technology to the Chinese."

"That's right. After I share it with the French, of course, which are my orders."

Inside, my guts were churning. I had wanted to kill the man, and it would be easy enough to do so. But with this new information, I realized perhaps it would be better to question him more, to figure out what exactly was going on here.

I said, "You can't have both, Johnny. I need you *and* the stolen data."

"Do you know what's going on in the Storage Module at Trieste?"

The change of topic caught me off guard. I frowned. "What the hell could that—?"

"I think you should look into it." And with that his hand darted behind his back and he withdrew a gun. I could have fired, but he hadn't yet aimed at me.

Instead he held it in front of him, angled straight up.

"Don't point that at me or I'll shoot," I growled. "Put it down."

"Sorry, Mac. I think you should go back to Trieste now and check out what I've told you. I'm taking the technology to Sheng." He turned to one of the women of the French contingent. "I'm afraid we'll have to make the exchange later. This meeting is over."

And then he fired.

At the ceiling.

The skylight in the ceiling.

The shot reverberated through the room; we were all too stunned to react.

The acrylic cracked. Then it groaned. The weight of 1000 meters of water was pressing down on that window, and it was about to give way.

And then it did.

AT FIRST ONLY A STREAM OF water the width of the bullet hole shot downward. With the amount of pressure behind it, however, it thundered into the control room and punctured straight through the steel deck into the level below us. Sparks sprayed from the floor—the drilling water had sheared power cables—and the bridge lights flickered once and then went out. Emergency lights flashed on, turning the room a ghostly red, and a recorded voice pierced the station. It was in French, and was clearly a warning to vacate the facility at once.

The elderly Frenchman, unfortunately, had been too near the jet of water. His chair collapsed to the side and he fell toward it. He uttered one quick, incoherent yell, and his torso disappeared into the stream. Blood immediately sprayed out and his body jerked in sudden spasm. As he continued to move through the water, it sliced his body as easily as a saw. He hit the deck hard. Blood spurted from his massive wound—a slit from the center of his abdomen clear to the side of his body—and internal organs surged outward.

The remaining members of his group pushed themselves away and stared in horror at the scene. The sound of the water was deafening—it was a shriek not unlike a diamond-tipped drill boring into bedrock. Add to that the alarms, the continuing recorded warning, and the creak of a now-compromised hull, and the situation was beyond imagination.

The torrent of incoming water widened by another few centimeters. The water in the room was now knee deep, and I knew it was spilling down into level two as well.

We were in serious trouble.

Johnny had leaped to the side after he fired and was now sprinting to the hatchway at my back. I spun toward him and brought my gun to bear. I aimed low and fired at his legs. The spray kicked up from his long strides obscured them, however, and I missed. He could have fired back at me but didn't.

And then he hit me hard with a shoulder tackle and we careened out into the corridor.

The three French women ran past us and headed for the ladder down to the airlocks. Johnny put his shoulder to the hatch and forced it shut. I was now on my ass, hands behind me on the deck. I had lost the gun. The water there was also knee deep, and I struggled for a moment to get back to my feet.

Johnny had crouched before me, ready for a fight.

"Don't do this," he snarled. "We have to get out of here."

"I'm not going without you."

"This station could implode any second! You have to get back to Trieste and stop Shanks from starting a war!"

"I need the technology that you stole. You can't take it to Sheng."

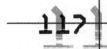

He shook his head. "You'd risk death over that? You'd obey Shanks when you know what kind of man he is?"

We had to yell over the sounds of the alarm and the flood of water into the facility.

"He may be an asshole," I said, "but he's a patriot. He wants to protect the city; that's the aim of TCI."

"We have to leave, *now*!" Johnny was growing frantic; the situation had cracked his stony resolve.

And with that he turned and ran for the ladder.

I dove for him and wrapped an arm around his neck. We went down, under the ice cold water.

I wasn't going to let him get away without a fight, even if it meant both of our lives.

HE TWISTED IN MY GRASP AND escaped within seconds. He was slippery and difficult to get a hold of. But as he pulled his head up to take a breath, I was waiting. I hit him with a hard right cross that sent him back under. He pushed himself up again and lashed out at me. I blocked three strikes and then his fourth finally landed; it hit my chin, and my vision went dark.

"There's no time for this!" he cried.

I shook my head to clear it. "Then we'll both die, and China doesn't get their hands on the technology. Sounds good enough for me."

"You're mad!"

"Just doing my job."

His face grew hard. "Damn you, Mac. I don't want to kill you."

There was a sudden *crack* and the hatch to the command module bent outward toward us. It was still on its hinges, but not for long. Water now spilled from its sides; the seal was no longer intact. The pressure from the flooded cabin was just too much.

I rose slowly to my feet. He remained on his knees, in the water. "You're going to have to, Johnny."

He watched me for a heartbeat. The groans of the dying station echoed loudly in the corridor. The water jet that he had unleashed from the skylight had punched down to level two, and it might have compromised the deck there as well. Water had probably now already reached the lowest level.

And the strain on the hatch beside us was increasing. It continued to bulge outward.

He got to his feet and we faced each other. My only hope was to knock him unconscious and drag him back to *SC-1*. However, the French were on their way down and we had connected our seacar to theirs. Kat would have to think fast and disconnect from their lock and reconnect to the station's umbilical.

I stepped in and feinted with a simple left hook. He attempted to block and I countered with a right. He anticipated, however, and dodged away. I began a barrage of elbows, which he narrowly managed to avoid or knock aside. At last I managed to land one: a crushing blow to his nose. There was an explosion of blood and his eyes lost focus for an instant. I saw white as they rolled up into his head. This could be it, I thought. I swung once more, hoping to put him out for at least a few minutes, but he managed to lurch to the side. It was a clear miss. I tried again, and this time connected, but it was only a glancing impact. He collapsed to one knee, dazed.

I realized suddenly that the cold had probably kept him from blacking out. I kicked at his head, but the water was now too high. The blade of my foot caught the surface, which slowed it down. He heard it coming and fell backward to avoid it. I stalked forward. He was lying face up in the water. I grabbed him around his shirt lapels and dragged him toward the ladder. Water was flowing down the ladderwell into level two, where it was halfway up the bulkheads.

Shit! Not much time left.

We slid down the steep ladder into level two and I stopped suddenly at the bottom. I was now swimming to stay afloat. The blows had disoriented Johnny, but he was managing to keep himself from sinking. I realized in shock that the breach had already flooded the lowest level of the base. The only thing we had going for us was that the pressure hadn't yet built to an unmanageable level. Once the station was completely full of water, however, that would quickly increase until it equaled the outside environment.

And if that happened, with such low air pressure in our lungs, the gigantic weight of a thousand meters of water would snap our ribs like kindling.

"There's still time to reach the seacars," Johnny gasped. "Take a deep breath—"

"You're coming with me."

He scowled and looked around him in desperation. Finally, he deflated. "Whatever we do, we have to do it *now*."

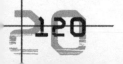

A tremendous shudder abruptly shook the station and the alarms increased in intensity. It was complete chaos. Only a foot of air remained in the corridor, blue pressure lights were flashing angrily, and the recorded warnings continued. We could barely hear them now; the shriek of stressed metal had become so loud that it was difficult to hear anything else.

"We go together," I yelled. "Side by side."

He nodded.

We began breathing deeply, oxygenating our blood as much as possible. Doing so gave us an extra thirty percent of swimming time; it was something we had learned during training, and it was a technique that I had used to evade security in foreign cities on the few occasions they had discovered me. Those had been scary moments, but it was a good feeling to dive into water and swim to freedom as those pursuing you had to pull up and watch you escape.

Together we took ten deep breaths. We felt lightheaded afterward, but it would pass quickly.

We plunged under and began to swim down to the first level.

THE EMERGENCY LIGHTS CAST A GORY glow over everything, and it was easy to find our way back to the locks. There were two, side by side. One umbilical led to Johnny's seacar, the other, hopefully, to *SC-1*. I pointed down the correct path and Johnny turned to me.

He shook his head in response.

I grabbed him around the throat and started to squeeze. My intention was clear: I would wait there and die with him, if need be, to protect Kat's secret.

And then a sudden pain lanced through my body.

My back arched uncontrollably and I released my grip. I clutched at the blade and wrenched it out. Blood swirled around me. The pain was excruciating. Dammit! Johnny's partner had known exactly where to hit me—at a point that was not fatal, but hurt like hell. He had been following us, and I had forgotten about him.

By the time I got my bearings, all I saw was the hatch to their seacar's airlock closing at the end of the umbilical.

Johnny had escaped.

I had only one chance now: get back to my own seacar and continue the chase.

Swimming with the injury was agonizing. Every movement with my left arm sent a shot of pain through my body. Kicking was okay, but in the end I could use only one arm.

My heart hammered in my chest.

My lungs burned.

My vision faded.

At last I entered the airlock, closed the hatch, and hurriedly rammed my fist on the CYCLE button. The water level began to lower almost immediately. I thrust my face up into the air space and took several huge breaths. Knowing that Kat would be listening over the comm, I screamed, "Disconnect from the station! Pursue Johnny, now!"

"Mac!" she replied. It was difficult to detect emotion through the tiny speaker, but I had the distinct impression she was scared. "The *Fast Attack*—it's here!"

Oh, shit.

I HAD ALMOST FORGOTTEN THAT THE Chinese *Jin* was still on our tail. It would probably try to damage us again to prevent us from capturing or killing Johnny.

The lock finished draining and I slammed the hatch aside. I sprinted up the passageway toward the control cabin—drenched, shivering from the cold, and bleeding profusely—and slid into the copilot's chair on the right. In the view before me, Johnny's seacar was accelerating away, and the French seacar with its delegation of government officials—minus one—was directly in our path.

I clenched my teeth. "Kat."

"Yes?"

"Fire a torpedo. Point blank detonation."

Her jaw dropped. "But that's not Johnny or the *Fast Attack*! That's *Patriote*, the French—"

"They're trying to prevent us from stopping him because they want your invention! Now fire!"

She paused for a moment; I could tell that she was struggling with the order. To fire meant killing people, and that was never easy. The mention of protecting her invention, however, must have convinced her. She opened a panel between us and pressed a button marked IMPACT DETONATION. Then she hit a green one labeled ARM. We had only one tube, on the blunt bow of the seacar; it slid open.

We were directly in line with the French vessel.

About twenty meters away.

The shock wave would hurt us too.

But we had no time to waste.

"Here we go," she muttered, and pressed the red button marked FIRE.

A surge of bubbles briefly obscured our view and a sharp whine reverberated through the ship. The torpedo was in the water, and it soared in front of us straight and true. It was two meters long and about thirty centimeters thick. It came to a point at its nose, at the trigger. The bubbles from the cavitating propellers showed its trail clearly; they rose to the surface behind the weapon and were out of sight within seconds.

Only a few meters to go.

The French vessel suddenly blew her ballast; vents on her hull had opened and bubbles frothed outward.

The ship started to rise.

But she wasn't fast enough, and we were way too close.

There was no hope for her.

The torpedo hit. There was a flash of white on the VID, and a shock wave emanated from the explosion, displayed as concussion lines on the projected image. Then everything seemed to crush in on itself, and the punishing water rushed in to fill the large volume that had vaporized to steam an instant earlier. The weight of a kilometer of water filled the void, and the hull of the ship, already weakened by the blast, gave way.

It collapsed like a tin can almost immediately.

Implosion.

Our own seacar trembled violently and I had to hold the yoke with both hands to steady us. A few lights on the main board blinked red, but they weren't critical systems.

The debris before us drifted to the plateau below. A single large bubble of air escaped from the hull that was now split in multiple places along the length of her axis, taking with it pieces of refuse and cushions and even what looked like a bed sheet.

There was a tinge of crimson in the waste rising to the surface, and I felt bile rise in my throat.

The force of shattered bulkheads and pounding water had crushed the bodies beyond recognition.

Kat had a look of horror on her face, but I knew that there had been no other choice. They wanted us stopped, and probably would have done the same to us. By firing we had ended the confrontation first, potentially saving our lives in the process.

No doubt Johnny had witnessed the entire incident on his sonar.

He knew I meant business.

The Chinese *Fast Attack* was somewhere nearby, and I slammed my hand on the ballast controls to make the ship positively buoyant. I slid the throttles to full on both thrusters.

"Prepare countermeasures," I barked.

The comm speaker crackled and a static-filled voice echoed through the cabin. "Let me go," Johnny said. "Head for Trieste. That warsub will leave you alone if you do."

I growled under my breath. "I'm coming after you. You're not getting away again, even if I have to use a second torpedo."

"You're going to find it difficult with that vessel on your tail."

"Then I'll take care of it first."

Kat had a perplexed expression on her face. "Is that the person who stole my invention?"

I nodded.

"You're a dead man!" she snapped at the speaker.

"Is that Doctor Wells?" Johnny asked. He paused for a moment, processing. "I'm sorry about what happened, but we have to do these things to preserve the balance of power, you know. That's how the intelligence business works."

"Unless I end this early," I said.

He sighed. "Try if you want, Mac, but that ship will destroy you if necessary. There wouldn't be any point to that." A pause, and then, "Oh, I forgot to tell you something. Remember I said that I set up that meeting? That I deliberately led you to it? Well, this seacar isn't quite as slow as I led you to believe either."

I shot a glance at the sonar. Sure enough, he was moving away at seventy-three kilometers per hour.

Faster than us.

Damn.

We'd never catch him.

"Fire a torpedo!" I cried. "We don't have much time!"

Kat's hands danced over the controls. I watched as she set the torpedo's mode to HOMING and quickly armed it. The automatic mechanism loaded the device into the tube, the hatch opened again, and she stabbed at the FIRE key.

Torpedo away.

"That was silly," Johnny said a moment later. But he sounded stressed. He knew he had to avoid a seeking torpedo that was seven kph faster than his seacar. He continued, "Now you're a dead man, Mac."

And my sonar blared. Another torpedo was in the water, headed straight for us.

It was a Chinese weapon, fired by the *Fast Attack*.

It was directly behind us, about a kilometer away.

I SNAPPED THE BALLAST TO NEGATIVE and pushed the yoke straight down. We would dive into the deep, into the canyon, and try to avoid the weapon near the bottom. If we couldn't, the pressure down there would at least minimize the explosion.

There were two torpedoes in the water now, both armed and homing on the sound of screws. Their traces were clearly visible in the VID; bubbles from each rose serenely to the surface. Strange that a grisly death marked the source of each of those trails.

I thought briefly of the French seacar.

I swallowed.

The same could happen to us within seconds.

The bow of *SC-1* was now at a ninety degree down-angle. Kat's hair hung toward the control console. Thrusters were on maximum. I had completely flooded our tanks. Our depth readout increased faster than I'd ever seen it. Soon we were at 2000 meters, but still the torpedo followed. Our speed was eighty kph—the same as the torpedo—and it was not closing.

But it was still behind.

The Charlie Gibbs Fracture was 4500 meters deep here. Just past our limit—even with the safety margin—but we had to do it. I looked behind me and tried to locate Johnny's seacar—difficult because it was straight *up* toward the shallows. It put tremendous strain on my neck. At last I saw his vessel on the display. He had deployed countermeasures—the devices were churning the water in an attempt to lure the weapon that we had fired in—and our torpedo soared by them without detonating.

I grinned.

He would be shitting his pants right about now.

The hull creaked around me; it sounded like a vicious snap followed by long, sustained thunder as the stresses built.

We can't keep doing this, I thought. *Eventually it'll give. It's inevitable.*

Then I checked our depth: 3800 meters.

"Countermeasures!" I bellowed.

I pulled up on the yoke with my right hand and blew ballast with my left. *SC-1*'s bow tilted upward, and at the bottommost limit of our dive, we hit a depth of 4410 meters.

We began to climb, still in the great canyon, but the floor quickly fell away behind us.

The Chinese torpedo followed, but the countermeasures were now in its path, calling its name.

Screaming its name.

I hoped.

Our up-angle was at almost seventy degrees now, and air filled the ballast tanks.

Thrusters were still at max.

We powered up like a rocket toward orbit.

Emergency ascent.

The torpedo detonated.

SC-1 vibrated angrily, but no new red lights appeared on the displays. I tested the ballast controls, changed our buoyancy to neutral.

They still worked. The detonation had not damaged the valves.

"You did it," Kat whispered. Her fingers were white on the safety straps that crossed her chest.

"They'll send another," I grunted. "We need to kill that ship if we're going to survive here. There's no other way now." We had six torpedoes remaining.

Kat began to prepare the next.

I searched the sonar for Johnny and easily found him. He was still running from our weapon. Three countermeasures were on the screen, and he was pulling around to take the homing torpedo through the first one that he had deployed.

Toward us.

He was bringing our own torpedo back at us!

"Smart guy," Kat muttered.

"That's the way TCI makes them."

Johnny and I were now heading directly toward each other. There was a torpedo on his tail. When our courses intersected, the weapon would lock onto us and detonate directly over our hull, crushing us in an instant. No matter what direction I turned now to avoid him, that torpedo would hit us.

There was only one thing I could do.

"Fire another one, Kat. Now."

She didn't hesitate. The torpedo had been ready in the tube, set again to HOMING mode. It lanced out of our bow and streaked toward Johnny's seacar.

There was a grim laugh from the comm. "Smart move, Mac," he said. "How many of those does that ship have?"

"Hopefully just enough to take you out."

He angled his seacar down to avoid the weapon, and I immediately took ours up. The whine of the thrusters filled the cockpit as I changed course; I hoped they could handle these kinds of stresses.

The missile surged toward his seacar, and, as he dove, the one that trailed him suddenly came into view. He launched more countermeasures, confusing the one behind him for a brief second. It didn't follow his plunge downward immediately, and instead powered toward the devices. The second torpedo, the one we had just fired, detected the high whine of the other, along with the countermeasures, and locked onto it.

The two torpedoes collided.

Johnny's seacar was below the explosion and screaming like hell down into the depths—the maneuver we had performed just a minute earlier. The concussion ripped out and pummeled the aft of his vessel. His thrusters stuttered for a moment, then began again, though weaker than before. He pulled level, on a course away from us, but his speed was slower now, only sixty-eight kph.

He had sustained some damage there.

Perhaps even some flooding.

Beside me, Kat swore.

"What's wrong?" I asked. "We hurt him."

"Not that," she said. "*That.*"

I glanced at the display, then jerked my head in the direction that it showed. Two kilometers away, on an intercept, was an attack warsub. It had been hiding somewhere nearby, silently waiting.

Not Chinese.

Not American.

This one was French.

And her crew had to know that we had just murdered French citizens.

"They're arming torpedoes," Kat said. She was watching the sonar readout that indicated what was happening with each contact on the screen. The computer listened to all vessels in the passive range and compared each noise to its extensive databank library of known sounds. "They've flooded four tubes and are ready to launch." She looked at me. "Mac, they mean to kill us."

CHAPTER FIFTEEN 十五

WE NOW HAD TWO ENEMIES TO evade: the Chinese *Fast Attack* and the French warsub. The French ship was a mid-sized attack vessel, *Requin*—or *Shark*—class. Top speed: seventy-two kilometers per hour. Two thrusters. Six tubes. Fifty meters long.

Deadly.

And her crew and captain would be out for blood.

"Jesus Christ," I muttered. This was not good.

On the sonar, Johnny's seacar was moving steadily away from us. He had blown his tanks and was rising above the lip of the canyon, headed north. Once he was over that ledge, his signal would disappear. He would be gone unless we could locate him while still in our active range.

But I knew we couldn't follow just yet. We had to deal with the French— and the Chinese—first.

I'd had a great deal of training in my twenties for my life in TCI, and had even been involved in a few small skirmishes like the one we'd just had with Johnny, but I'd never experienced anything like this. Once the French started firing, there'd be four torpedoes in the water at the same time, *at least*, and all headed for us.

Various strategies raced through my mind. There must be some way to level the playing field here, I thought. The French warsub was eight hundred meters away now. She could fire at any minute. In fact, she would probably fire before she was within three hundred—

Of course. That was it.

"Contact them," I said as I steered toward her. The VID now showed her directly in front of us, and I was closing the gap rapidly.

"Why?"

"To stall them. Do it, please. Put a filter on my voice." I gripped the yoke tightly. A second later they were on the line. I said, "To the French warsub in my path, may I ask your intentions?"

The response came within seconds. I assumed it was the French captain, a woman. "Our intentions are clear, as yours were only a few minutes ago when you destroyed a French seacar with government officials within." Her voice was icy cold.

"There must be some mistake." I glanced at the distance readout on the sonar. Six hundred meters. "Something destroyed her, yes, but it wasn't us."

Kat shot me a look.

Five hundred.

The captain continued, "We saw what happened. Our tracking computers have recorded it for posterity. Cut your thrusters and prepare for boarding."

"Say again?"

Four hundred.

"What are you doing?" Kat asked. She was staring at the large warsub before us; it now almost filled the entire forward segment of the canopy.

"Your transmission broke up a bit there," I said, ignoring her for the moment.

"Prepare for boarding. Cut engines."

Three fifty.

We were close now, but not close enough. We had left the seamount behind, and the ocean floor below was more than three kilometers down, four and a half in total. I was sure about this warsub's specifications: she could not reach a depth of more than 3200 meters. Once again, we could go deep, but their mines would eventually wound us.

And Johnny would get away.

Two hundred meters.

"We will fire if you don't surrender," the captain grated.

"Let me get this straight," I said, pausing between each word. "You think *we* destroyed that French seacar?"

"Yes! Now do as I've ordered!"

One hundred.

"But we didn't do that. Can't we talk about this?"

"Yes, *after* we board you."

Fifty.

Finally, we were close enough.

"Sorry," I said. "I don't think so."

"Then you risk certain death."

"We're too close now for you to fire; the missile will simply circle in the water and probably come back to kill you instead." I knew we could just piggyback on the big warsub and they would be powerless to stop us. I pulled up alongside her, banked hard, and matched her course and velocity. The disadvantages of such a large ship were numerous, but the most important was that she couldn't aim her torpedoes at our current location—she could only fire homers and hope that they would zero in on us.

But *we* were so small and maneuverable that we could fire into her hull at point blank range.

"*I order to you cease all activities!*" Her voice blared into our control cabin. She sounded mad and desperate at the same time; it was clear even through the thick French accent. She must have realized she should have fired when she had the opportunity. Her crew were probably furious with her.

I said, "I'm about to fire into your aft compartments. Please evacuate and seal those areas immediately."

Kat jerked her gaze to me and cut our transmission. "What are you thinking?" she snapped. She pointed out the canopy. "That's not just a seacar out there, that's the goddamned French *military*!"

"Kat," I said in a soft voice. "They're going to take us prisoner. Take us back to France. I doubt we'll see Trieste again for twenty years. We *have* to stop Johnny. There's no other option here."

"Are you going to sink her? Kill all those people?"

"No, just fill her aft section. She can try to pursue, or call for help, but they'll be too slow to keep up."

She looked away; the crease in her brow was obvious.

"We have to do it," I whispered.

The warsub suddenly shifted course twenty degrees to the south; the move was easy to match. Then she tried to dive. Then ascend. We stuck with her every step of the way. Her final move was to cut speed to only ten kph.

"Those big ships are powerful," I muttered, "but against us, like this, she doesn't have much of a defense." I keyed the comm. "What do you say? Are you through trying to lose us? I'm about to fire. Are your aft sections cleared of crew?"

"How dare you threaten such a thing!" the captain yelled back at me. "This is a vessel in the French Submarine Force! If you attack us, you risk war!"

"And who will you declare it on?"

Pause. "It won't be hard to figure out, I'm sure. You sound American."

"But I'm not working for the USSF, I assure you. I'm *independent*." I almost smirked at the irony of the word.

Movement suddenly caught my attention. Something off to port . . . outside the ship. . . .

I craned my neck to see better.

A fish? A shark? What could have made such a noticeable shadow?

I choked off a startled gasp. "Oh my God." There were people out on our port stabilizer.

Divers.

From the warsub.

They were trying to sabotage us.

"PREPARE TORPEDO!" I BARKED AS I hit the throttles to max. The divers must have exited the warsub from an airlock; they were attempting to access the mechanics of our thruster. That's why their ship had slowed so dramatically.

When *SC-1* had almost passed the giant sub's bow, I shifted to reverse but kept the power at one hundred percent. The seacar vibrated madly and Kat struggled to keep her eyes on the weapons panel. Bubbles streamed from the water around our screws as the pressure there dropped so low that gases boiled from it.

We reversed until we were just off the French vessel's stern. She stretched out before us, a clear target. I nudged the ballast to positive and we ascended fifteen meters. Usually when switching ballast, the computer kept the tank volumes equal to avoid affecting the pitch of the seacar. This time, however, I deliberately pointed the nose down by making it the heaviest part of the vessel.

I had angled our torpedo tube directly at the French *Shark*.

The divers were still on our port thruster. Holding on for dear life, probably, but they wouldn't stop trying to damage us.

"Fire," I hissed.

Kat winced as she pushed the button. She was clearly conflicted about the situation, but she understood our predicament.

With a high-pitched whine, the missile streaked straight for the warsub.

Three seconds later there was a thunderous explosion. A strong current rushed in to fill the void created by vaporized water, and the warsub's velocity slowed, wavered, then stopped altogether. Her hull had caved in at the detonation point; a large, jagged hole was now visible just forward of the aft stabilizer.

She was foundering.

Just don't sink, I screamed to myself. *The water is too deep here. No one will survive. Please let those watertight hatches in the sub hold.*

The divers on our hull watched their ship as she took on water. I could see their expressions through their facemasks; they were close enough so that the VID system didn't have to display them for me.

There were three of them there.

They turned their eyes to me.

One word could sum up their feelings at that moment: *rage.*

I gestured for them to leave our seacar and go back to their sub.

They ignored me.

I pointed down.

With buoyancy at negative now, we began to plunge into the depths. The divers could only last a few seconds of this before they had to start swimming back to their sub. Sure enough, they soon let go and kicked madly toward the stationary vessel now far above us.

"Are you going to make sure they get back?" Kat murmured.

"No."

Her eyes were narrow, angry. "And why not?"

"The *Fast Attack* is still here, Kat. And she's going to try to take us out." I gestured to the sonar. "Right now, in fact."

An alarm began to shrill.

Torpedo in the water.

THE CHINESE HAD WAITED UNTIL WE were away from the French warsub and the divers were off our hull. They, at least, did not want to start an incident between their two countries. I, on the other hand, was past the point of caring, especially as I watched Johnny's seacar reach the lip of the canyon and disappear over the edge. We still had time to find him, I knew, but we couldn't leave the *Fast Attack* to chase us too.

We had to deal with her, now.

And we only had four torpedoes remaining.

I hit the thrusters to max and steered for the guyot and the flooded base at its summit. The torpedo was headed toward us from the northeast at a

speed of eighty kph. It was nine hundred meters away. It would narrow that distance quickly, I knew, but we might just make it.

I watched our speed readout anxiously, begging for it to increase, but it held at seventy.

We were approaching the seamount.

"Dammit," I groaned. The tension was getting to be too much. My vision was growing dim, for some reason, and I wasn't sure why. Perhaps the sudden changes in g-forces were bothering me, but it had never happened before. I had trained for far worse. I hit the heater and desperately willed it to keep me warm enough to stop the shivering. I needed to get us through this. Only one ship left to get past. Johnny's seacar was slower than ours now . . . we should be able to get him, I thought.

My eyes closed abruptly and then snapped open an instant later. What the hell? *You have to focus*! I scolded myself.

Kat was watching, clearly worried. "What's wrong with you?"

"Nothing," I mumbled. My words were thick.

The torpedo was still coming. The alarm was shrieking now. I wished Kat would just turn it off, but I didn't have the energy to ask her.

She was still looking at me with that peculiar expression. "You don't look well. You're pale. Are you cold?"

"Damn right," I slurred.

"Is that all?" She leaned over to examine me. She grabbed my arm and looked under it, at my left side. She gasped. "Mac! You're bleeding!"

"Got stabbed."

"When?"

"On the station."

"You've lost a ton of blood! It's puddled on the deck—"

"No time," I mumbled. We were over the guyot now. I waited another twenty seconds until we were past it; the sides of the mountain descended steeply below us toward the ocean floor. I brought the thrusters to zero and made our buoyancy negative.

This time, however, I adjusted the ballast tanks and filled the aft ones only. I kept the bow ones clear. We began to tilt upwards.

Kat clutched at her safety straps. She was probably worried about me, thought I was losing my mind. I still had a few tricks up my sleeve, though. I had pitched *SC-1* at ninety degrees straight up, just below the guyot's summit.

Then I made our buoyancy neutral. It was tricky, keeping us on end like this, but I only had to do it for a minute. . . .

"Be silent now. . . ." I whispered. A burst of adrenaline had cleared my mind as I performed the maneuver, but I wasn't sure how long it would last. Hopefully just long enough. . . .

The torpedo sailed over the guyot and came into view. It crossed our bow ten meters above us, but we were completely silent. It had nothing to lock to. We watched it continue into the distance; it would eventually run out of battery power and sink to the bottom.

And there we held position, pressed back into our seats, beside the flat-topped seamount, the canyon floor far below.

"What are we waiting for?" Kat hissed.

And then it came into view.

The *Fast Attack*.

The bastards had tried to sink us more than once. She was directly before us now, her underbelly as clear as day in our VID system. She was making eighty kph and we didn't have much time.

"Kat," I whispered. "Torpedo."

She needed no urging. She quickly selected HOMING mode and fired.

It soared straight up, directly for the *Jin* class vessel. The ship tried to dodge and eject countermeasures, but they had been unprepared and were too late.

They hadn't expected us to be there.

The missile plunged into the ship, dead center, and a white flash illuminated the display. An instant later the hull fissured and its bow bulged enormously as water surged in. Debris and shattered steel sprayed out as it ruptured. The savage force of pummeling water crushed her crew to meat in an instant.

I had put a *third* vessel out of commission in only fifteen minutes, all to catch one man.

I BROUGHT THE SEACAR BACK TO level. Damn. I couldn't believe what we had just been through. The confrontation in the facility, the hand-to-hand fight with Johnny, the escape through flooding corridors, then the battle with multiple vessels. I felt dizzy with relief, and probably blood loss.

Only three torpedoes left now . . .

I leaned back and let out a long sigh. Doubt filled my mind. I was conflicted about everything Johnny had said. I wasn't sure if *anything* had been the truth. Some of it had corroborated Kat's claims, however, about Shanks and Flint, and I knew I needed time to decide for myself just what the hell was

going on. Was Johnny really trying to stop a war? Had he deliberately brought me to this place to ask for my help? Was he really doing it without his government's permission?

There was too much to think about just then, not the least of which was the death of at least five in the *Fast Attack*, three in the French seacar, and perhaps a few in the French warsub.

Was the technology that Johnny stole worth all of this?

Kat was watching me again with concern in her eyes.

"I'm okay," I grumbled. "Just need a bandage and some rest."

"It seems like a lot of blood."

"That guy deliberately hit me in a spot that wouldn't kill me. Just above the kidney. Hurts like hell, but I'll be okay. Feel weak, that's all." I gestured to the sonar. "Can you take over? Bring us back on Johnny's tail. He's heading north."

She nodded and took the yoke, then expertly applied thrust and adjusted our up-angle to hit the top of the canyon four kilometers away.

"If you can't see Johnny when we're up there," I said, "it means he's lying low. Use a pulse from the active sonar to try and find him."

"I'll be okay. Don't worry about me. Just get back there and put a dressing on that."

I dragged myself to my feet and stumbled to the back, trailing water and blood on the deck behind me. In the tiny washroom, I stripped off my shirt and studied the gash in my side. Blood still dribbled from it, but it had mostly coagulated and the arteries were undamaged. I pressed some gauze to it and found some white tape in the first aid kit. Gripping the end in my mouth, I tore off a long stretch and began to wrap it around my body as tightly as possible.

The pressure on the wound felt good, and I grabbed some dry clothes from my bunk. I removed the rest standing in the passageway, in plain sight of Kat, but I was so exhausted I just didn't care. I pulled on a pair of loose fitting pants, forgot about the shirt, and hauled myself into my bunk.

Sleep came before my head hit the pillow.

THIRTY MINUTES LATER, USS *IMPALER* ARRIVED at the guyot in the Charlie Gibbs Fracture Zone. Her four massive screws stopped turning as her crew took in the devastation and tried to make sense of what they had heard over the sonar. Something had damaged and flooded a domed facility. A

small seacar was in pieces on the plateau, a Chinese *Fast Attack* was lying at the bottom of the canyon, all hands dead, and a French warsub was limping away to the east. The Americans had heard multiple torpedo contacts and even a few garbled transmissions as they closed on the battle.

Her commander considered his options for mere seconds, then did the only thing possible at that moment in time: he followed the tiny seacar that his superiors in the USSF had ordered him to capture days earlier.

The *Reaper* class attack sub—fifty meters longer than a World War II battleship—sailed north, over the canyon wall, to continue the search for her prey.

CHAPTER SIXTEEN 十六

I DREAMED OF MY FATHER.

It was not a restful sleep.

I was fourteen years old again, and it was the year that the CIA assassinated him in the government's attempt to put down the independence movement once and for all. We were arguing. I, the surly teenager, sure of myself and confident that my beliefs were one hundred percent correct and anyone who disagreed with me was not only ignorant, they were *dumb*, and he, stubborn and irascible and confident that only he knew the correct path that the city should take.

We were probably more alike than I cared to admit.

He had just informed us, his family, of the city council's plans to stop exports topside and begin instead to ship our product to other nations in an attempt to control our own economy. He thought the US government would protest for a while, put on a show, then give in to our demands and grant us independence. I remember shaking my head at him; he was so sure that fair and equitable treatment by our colonizers was the only option open to them. He was working for the city council, together with people like George Shanks, who at the time was a young underling who rarely spoke and just watched and learned how things were done, perhaps in the hopes that one day he would take over that aspect of the city's operations.

Dad and I had argued late into the night. It grew to a screaming match at times, during which even Meagan got involved. She also disagreed with him.

We knew the dangers.

It was the last conversation we would ever have. The next day he was dead, and with him the city's dreams of independence.

Until now.

I woke up sweaty in the bed sheets aboard *SC-1*. I stared at the ceiling bare centimeters above my face, breathing hard, waiting for my heart to slow. I hadn't thought of that night in a long time. The people of Trieste actually still remember the day that the CIA killed him—February the twenty-third—and every year around that time I have to answer more questions from the curious and respond to more comments about the kind of man he had been. A legend had built up about him—about this fantastic freedom fighter who had given his life for his people, when in fact he was an irritable, stubborn, closed-minded obsessive who felt resentment toward the States because of the failure of the Second Korean War; a dreamer who desired to lead Trieste to the Promised Land. I couldn't convince people of the truth—that he had been deluded and destined to fail—and so instead just gritted my teeth and passed the days in February with great anxiety, just waiting for people to stop commenting about him and the events of 2099 until the same time the following year.

How silly he had been, I thought. He and the city council had built up a small security force that numbered only three thousand, equipped with only a few armed vessels, and they thought they could defend themselves against the most advanced military in history. Either he was indeed painfully ignorant of reality, or he was a total idealist.

Or both.

Minutes later, I stuck my head out of the curtain and peered up the passageway toward the control cabin. Kat was nowhere in sight. Then I heard her muted breaths, and realized that she was sleeping in the bunk just across from me. The vibration from the thrusters was smooth and steady; we were on autopilot, hopefully following Johnny and closing slowly but surely.

I pulled my legs out and hopped to the deck softly. In the control cabin, I slowly lowered myself into my chair—wincing at the pain in my side as I did so—and studied the controls. Sure enough, there was his seacar, twenty-five kilometers ahead of us, on a heading now slightly northwest toward the coast of Greenland. His velocity was seventy kilometers per hour, the

same as ours, and I stared at that for several minutes as the reality of the situation sunk in.

We could not catch him.

The distance between us would remain the same the entire journey back to Sheng City.

All would be lost.

Our only hope was that eventually whatever troubles he had experienced during our battle would grow worse as time wore on, and eventually his speed would drop.

The sonar displayed numerous other contacts, most of which were just seacars or surface vessels traveling between North America and Europe. Nothing of great interest, except, just at the limits of our passive sonar . . .

Oh my God.

USS *Impaler.*

On a course northward, she would be able to detect us any minute now, if she hadn't already.

I had to act fast.

I stabbed at the comm and signaled Johnny. "Listen to me," I hissed, hoping that he was there. "It's USS *Impaler.* She's right on our ass, and may or may not know that we're here. Respond."

Silence.

I repeated the message.

Finally, his voice came to me from the speaker, tired and weary. He was probably exhausted after repairs. "So what?"

"They're either after me, or they're after you. They've been on us since leaving Trieste." He didn't say anything, and I continued, "They must know something is going on. You don't want war, right? Well, we can't let them know a Chinese seacar is running with stolen US technology, can we? They'd hunt you down too!"

Pause. Nothing but static from the speaker. Then, "What are you suggesting?"

"She'll probably start using her active sonar soon to try and find us. We have to stop engines and settle to the bottom." I knew if I did and he didn't, he'd increase the gap between us. I couldn't let that happen. But he wouldn't stop and wait for *Impaler* to leave unless I did so too. "There's no choice, Johnny. We both stop and wait."

He hesitated, then, "You'll guarantee that you won't chase me until she's gone?"

"It's my only option, and yours too. You know we have to keep the USSF out of this. We can't let them know what's going on." They were probably

just suspicious, I thought, and were following to see exactly what we were up to. I had to get Johnny to agree to this, and *now*.

Finally, "All right. But if I hear you start your thrusters, I'm running. I don't care if *Impaler* hears; I'm farther from her than you are."

"Then shut down your engines, now."

"You first."

I sighed. "Fine." I pulled back on both throttles and drag with the water around the seacar quickly brought us to a stop. I then filled the ballast and we began to sink to the bottom, two and a half kilometers down.

Ten seconds later the sonar indicated that Johnny had followed suit. I lowered our landing skids, and a few minutes later finally hit bottom. We had to hope that the USSF warsub did not yet know our course or position, and that they were simply searching for nearby contacts to pursue in the hopes that it was us.

It was now a waiting game.

THE SHIP WAS SILENT EXCEPT FOR the sound of Kat breathing in the bunk behind me. The sonar kept a close watch on *Impaler*; they were still sailing northerly, and hadn't yet shifted to our northwesterly course.

They didn't know where we were.

In about twenty minutes they'd be off the screen, and Johnny and I could continue the chase.

I snorted. It seemed ridiculous for both parties to willingly set aside a dispute so they could continue the fighting later. It was Christmas on the Western Front, 1914, all over again. Only instead of German, British, and French troops, it was American and Chinese. Still, it was either this or the US warsub would be breathing down our necks the entire journey to the Pacific. They might even call in reinforcements, which would really add a wrinkle, for both of us.

The VID system was dark blue and there were no vessels currently within its five kilometer range. Then I noticed a shape appear, moving across our path two kilometers away.

Then another.

And another.

I began to sweat. What the hell were they? Seacars? Warsubs? The French maybe?

I shot a look to the sonar, and almost laughed in relief.

Whales. A pod of fifteen of them, swimming slowly westward toward the coast of Newfoundland, where the warm Gulf Stream and cold Labrador currents collided and produced the plankton-rich environment of the Grand Banks. Fish and mammals of all types often visited the area, looking for easy meals and shallow, sunny waters.

The whales were beautiful. The VID showed them clearly now, moving their tales and fins seemingly without effort, at one with the deep, perfectly adapted to the dangers of the intense cold and pressure thousands of meters down. Up there, on the surface, all that sailors ever really saw was a fin or a tail break the surface for a few moments before it disappeared. They never got to see the true beauty of life underwater. They simply traveled on the skin of a vast frontier. Only ocean dwellers ever experienced the true nature of the deep.

Independence.

The thought startled me. Funny, that it should suddenly pop into my head as I watched the graceful mammals swim away. Perhaps it was because I knew how precious and delicate life down here really was; our grasp on survival was tenuous at best. Independence was a dangerous thing to want.

Still, it would be nice not to worry about troops harassing our people and constantly watching us. To ship out fish and kelp and minerals and realize the benefits for ourselves. I understood what my father always wanted for the city; it was just the way he went about doing it that was so damn naive. I didn't want to end up like him. Not that I didn't believe in dying for something great—that's what this mission was all about, after all: to preserve Trieste's position in the oceans. Dying pointlessly, however, was entirely different.

Independence.

Could Trieste do it? Could Shanks and Flint pull it off? They'd need a large military force to fight off the USSF—which meant armed warsubs. Shanks had sent me on this mission supposedly to *stop* a war. Could it be that he actually *wanted* one? And what about the Chinese? Could they be working with Trieste? Had they been secretly negotiating with Flint and Shanks?

I snorted at the thought. No way. Otherwise Shanks wouldn't have sent me out after a Chinese thief to recapture stolen goods.

There was a sound behind me, and I turned to see Kat emerge from the bunk. Her hair was in her face, messy from sleep, and she brushed it to the side. She noticed the open curtain on my bunk, and then glanced into the control cabin. Our eyes met, and she flashed me a quick smile.

"You're finally up," she said.

"How long was I out?"

"Six hours or so, I guess. I went to sleep an hour after you, once I located Johnny and set course to follow." She squinted as she peered out the canopy. "We're deep. Why aren't we moving?"

I explained the situation, and she nodded. "Makes sense. Johnny for one shouldn't want the USSF anywhere near him. They'd skin him alive if they caught him." She peered at my bandaged side. "How are you?"

"Not bad. Stiff, sore, but I'll survive."

"You act like it was nothing."

"In the grand scheme, it really was."

She paused for a heartbeat. "I guess you've been through a lot worse." Then an odd expression crossed her face; it looked as though she wanted to ask something, but was afraid to.

I said, "Out with it. What do you want to know?"

She shrugged. "I guess . . . I guess I'm curious why you're doing this. Why put yourself through all of this? Going outside four kilometers down, trying to get Johnny from that French base, risking your life battling warsubs, dodging torpedoes. At the beginning I was skeptical about you, whether you really cared about recovering my work. After all, you quit TCI. I understand why now, after you told me the story. But I'm worried about you because you seem so driven. Is this really worth your life?"

I hesitated. She seemed like such a different person than she had that first day, when she had been so confrontational. I also understood her better now, though—and had even begun to like her. She was competent, intelligent, and not scared to take risks. I said, "Trieste is worth it. Shanks claims that if other nations get control of your invention, it could be the end of our place in the oceans. I'll do anything to stop that." *And to get Johnny*, I added to myself.

"Would you fight for independence?" She was watching me warily. As if she knew something that I didn't.

"No. That would only hurt the city. We've talked about it before."

"But what if Shanks tries for it? Would you fight then?"

Was she admitting it now? "I don't know."

"You wouldn't abandon Trieste, would you?"

"No. But I would resist, try to talk sense into people."

She shook her head. "It'll happen eventually, Mac. And when it does, you have to plan for it."

With a shudder, I realized it all came back to my father. To the legacy he had left for me. Live up to his legend? Step into his shoes? Or ignore it all and fight to stop dangerous people from ruining the city?

In the end, I didn't respond.

The reality of the situation was I had no idea what I would do if I found out Shanks was indeed pushing for independence from the United States. I knew what I *thought*, but if push came to shove, and it was out of my hands, what then?

Would I start a war myself?

No way.

But Kat made a valid point. If someone else started the fighting, would I die to protect my people? To save my city?

The answer to that was, of course, yes.

"The planet is replete with remarkable features. Most people don't realize the immensity of the ocean depths. To say we are like insects in that environment would be an understatement of the highest order. We could get squashed at any moment . . . and never see it coming."

—Richard Lancombe, Pioneer, Ocean Colonist, and Freedom Fighter

PART FOUR: THE ALEUTIAN TRENCH

seven

CHAPTER SEVENTEEN

IT TOOK US THIRTY-NINE HOURS TO reach the Davis Strait, the passage of water between Greenland and Canada. Time passed uneventfully; we spent the first few hours simply studying maps. Johnny was still traveling at seventy kph, and we remained twenty-five kilometers behind him. I was beginning to get frustrated. Unless something happened to his vessel and his speed slowed, there was no point to all of this. The journey through the Davis Strait would take us forty-three hours. Then the stretch across the Canadian archipelago, around the Alaskan coast, and south to the Bering Strait: forty-six hours. And then the long haul southwest to the continental shelf and Sheng City: eighty-nine hours. All told, the journey before us would be a *minimum* of 178 hours, or seven more days. *A lot can happen in a week*, I told myself. *Let's just hope we get a break here.* But I knew that once he made it through the Bering Strait, he would be far closer to Chinese territory. They might even have a welcoming committee there for him—and if they did, we were sunk. Literally.

It had been difficult to watch Johnny escape from me in that French base. I had been so close to him; I could have killed him right there. A big part of me still wanted to, but I was growing more conflicted, and it worried me. I needed to always be in control, and this whole situation was throwing me off balance. Johnny had had strong reasons for betraying Trieste seven years earlier, and he clearly felt he needed to lure me to the facility to ask for help.

He had a reason for everything he did, and in a perverse way I wanted to give him a chance. To prove he wasn't all that bad, that perhaps what he was doing could actually protect the citizens of Trieste. But until Kat told me everything she knew—about what Shanks was planning and what Johnny had stolen—I was in the dark.

But I had clues. I was perceptive. I kept my eyes open at all times and studied minor things, searching for anything that could be of help. Maybe that's why I had been such a good operative for TCI. I had worked for the agency from 2111 to 2122, and had been successful in the vast majority of my missions. And now, with this one, I had some theories, but it wasn't yet time to confront Kat. I would wait until the proper moment—until there was no other choice in the matter.

I decided to explore the seacar a bit more. The engine room was the only area I didn't know well, so I spent a few hours going through the equipment, the batteries, and the backup systems. It was in complete disarray following the events of the past few days, and I cleaned up the tools and got them back into their lockers. A few tanks of compressed gas were lying around, and I squared those away too. The batteries worried me; most ships could only go five days before needing a recharge at a station or a city, but when I checked the levels I was shocked at how much power was left. We had roughly ten days remaining.

There was also something else of note in there I hadn't seen earlier: a hatch set into the aft bulkhead with a digital keypad next to it. The seam of the hatch was flush with the bulkhead; there was no frame around the door. If it hadn't been for the keypad, I would never have noticed.

I decided to ask Kat about it later.

For the time being, I relaxed, unwound, and let my body heal. I also cooked a few nice meals for us. She looked surprised the first time I rummaged through the tiny kitchen, searching through the precooked packaged dinners and taking what I thought would make for a pleasant meal. Usually the food was so boring, but I used what we had, combined some other dishes, and created some things that were fairly unique and tasty. She was genuinely touched that first dinner. We spoke very little, but her little glances toward me said volumes, and I was feeling a definite attraction to her too. Her shapely body in that skin-tight suit was too much to look at sometimes, and sleeping in such close proximity to one another was often painfully difficult. We were in different cubicles, separated by the narrow hallway and our two curtains, but she was just an arm's length away, and at times I had the distinct feeling we were lying there awake at

the same time. I wondered what it would be like to forget all about this mad adventure, get into a bunk with her, strip off each other's clothing, and just enjoy this experience for a few hours.

Thoughts like that drove me crazy, and I found myself looking for things to do to keep my mind off of her. But it was difficult. She was no longer rude and abrasive; now she was kind and gentle and willing to speak about politics and ocean life and current events such as our country's difficulties with China. She had a sharp mind, and her observations often startled me. In particular was her theory that the current situation between the undersea cities—who were actively engaged in a cold war fought between intelligence services—could escalate to a war supplied with weapons from our colonizers; the similarities to the Spanish Civil War in the 1930s was what intrigued her. I agreed, but surprisingly, the potential of it actually happening didn't seem to bother her.

"But such a war could be disastrous for us, even if it doesn't spread to land," I said one evening during a dinner that I had prepared. "China and the US would test their weapons down here, just as Hitler was doing in Spain as his armies prepared for Blitzkrieg. The military would control our cities; we would lose what little freedom we have now."

"We could keep them away."

I blinked at that. "How? The US is the most advanced—"

"All we'd have to do is keep them from docking with the city, close the moonpools and airlocks."

I shook my head. "Kat, they could just set up shop outside and control things from there. Enter through a travel tube—cut a hole in. There's no way to keep them out." I snorted. "You sound like my father, you know."

"I've been reading about him. He was a great man."

"Not really, when you're familiar with the big picture. He was terribly naive. He didn't think they'd try to kill him, but of course that was the best—and easiest—move they could have made. He didn't even see it coming."

We were sitting at the small table in the living area; there was a large port overhead and the sigh of water across the hull combined with the drone of the thrusters made for a very comfortable—and romantic—setting. Kat had dug up some wine for that evening, and we were both on our second glass.

I sighed. "I hate to keep having this argument with you, but independence is a mistake, plain and simple. It will lead to war with the United States, *at the very least*. If other nations get involved, it could grow into something massive."

"You're referring to Johnny's claim that China intends to help Trieste fight the States?"

"Yes. He could be lying, he could be mistaken, or he could be stringing me along, to keep me from—" I stopped abruptly. "To keep me from taking him back to Trieste. But I can't for the life of me see why he would go to all this trouble to get me to that meeting."

She continued as if she hadn't noticed my stumble, "You believe him then?"

I shrugged. "Mostly. He could have escaped from us, you know. Before we damaged his seacar his speed was seventy-three kph. And yet he kept it at sixty the whole time and allowed us to find him in the Fracture Zone."

She pushed her plate away and leaned back in the chair. "We should tell Shanks. It might make a difference."

"You mean about China wanting to help? Fat chance. He *hates* China and her underwater cities. And I know the man. If he's planning on making a play for independence, he'll do it on his own."

We were silent for a long period. Our eyes met several times, and once she even smiled at me, as if to say, "I know what you're thinking; I'm thinking it too."

And yet we said nothing.

A FEW DAYS PASSED, AND FINALLY we approached the Alaskan coast. Decades ago the journey would have been almost completely under ice, except for short stretches through Arctic oases called polynyas. Now, due to the rapid warming the planet was experiencing, there was only open water overhead. It made surface shipping easier, but had taken a tragic toll on the wildlife of the region.

Johnny was ahead of us, still at the same velocity, and I was in the control cabin going over options for the millionth time. I couldn't fire a torpedo at him; he was just too far away and traveling too fast. The weapon would exhaust its batteries before it could reach him. I couldn't catch up to him. I couldn't get our seacar going any faster . . . Other than that, I had no ideas.

The comm buzzed and I stared at it in shock. It was from a local source, not from the global network. There were few seacars in this area of the world; despite being off the coast of one of the largest nations on Earth, there was a low population density at this latitude. All we detected were a few native settlements nearby on land, an abandoned oil derrick here and

there—supplies long since exhausted and the equipment left to rust—and the odd surface transport vessel.

There could only be one person on the other end of the transmission.

I accepted the call, but said nothing. The cabin was dark, Kat was sleeping in her bunk. It was an eerie sensation.

"Mac?" the voice said. "Are you there?" It was Johnny.

I hesitated before, "I'm here."

"We don't have to do this. You have no hope. As soon as I get to the Strait and through the Aleutians I'm essentially on home turf. You don't have backup. You don't want the USSF involved. Chinese forces are waiting for me."

Damn. Just as I'd feared. "Why are you telling me this?"

"I don't want you dead, Mac. I never did. I led you away from Trieste for a reason—to stop Shanks. To protect the city. Go back. Turn around now. I'm begging you."

"You're doing this out of the goodness of your heart, I assume."

"I know you don't believe me."

"After my four month stay in your city, I have my doubts."

A sigh. "I know it was tough. I hated every minute of that too. I wanted the prisoner exchange to happen sooner than later, but Shanks was stubborn. It took us a long time to convince him."

"So it's his fault."

"What do you think? He was holding and torturing Chinese prisoners."

I didn't respond; he was right. It's why I held such resentment for Shanks, why I had vowed to never work for him again. But then this had come along, and I had to accept the mission. Johnny was too important to pass up.

But why hadn't I killed him when I'd had the chance? I could have lied about how he died.

Because he could be telling the truth.

And I needed to know everything in order to complete the mission and protect the city.

I realized now, as I sat in that darkened cabin talking to my former friend, I had to keep him alive and get him back to Trieste to find out what exactly was going on. But once I did, Shanks would have him, and might even resort to torture once again. But shouldn't I want that? Didn't I want revenge? A part of me did—a *large* part—but strangely enough I also still cared about Johnny. I clenched my fists. The guy had betrayed me and imprisoned me and tortured me, and yet here I was thinking about the fact that I actually missed his friendship.

"Perhaps you're right," I said finally, "but you shouldn't have done it to me. We were friends."

"I know." His voice was soft, a whisper. "And I do regret it."

"Because you know I'm going to catch you?"

"No! Because I'm a human being, for Christ's sake! My superiors forced me—"

"I don't want to hear it, Johnny. I'm ending my transmission now."

"Wait! Don't!" He paused. "Did you think about what I told you?"

"Of course I have."

"And?"

"I have no way to confirm or deny it right now. When I've got you and we're back in Trieste, I'll look into it."

"Look, if you keep following me, I don't think you'll get back. You're in great danger. I'm trying to warn you."

"I'm not turning around."

There was a long break. "You always were stubborn as hell, Mac. But promise me this: if you do make it back, make sure you investigate that module."

I frowned. There he was again, mentioning the Storage Module "What is it?"

"They're not refitting it, or building new levels, or digging deeper. It's part of their plans."

"You mentioned that, but you didn't have proof."

"I *have* proof, just not with me."

"You thought I'd take your word for it, after all the good times we shared."

He was silent following the sarcastic bite. Then, "I guess so, yes. Goodbye, Mac. I hope you live through this."

"I hope so too."

We terminated the transmission.

THE NEXT MORNING, AFTER A FITFUL sleep, I sat with Kat for breakfast. I said nothing of my conversation with Johnny the night before. She was quiet, preoccupied with something, and kept shooting me looks I found hard to interpret. There was a definite sexual tension between us now, but I didn't think this had anything to do with it.

"What is it?" I finally asked.

She grinned at me, one of those warm, radiant smiles that showed her beautiful teeth and lit her entire face. In an instant, the sensation that she was worried was gone, replaced again by the feeling that she genuinely liked me now, and more than that, that she wanted to be with me. She put her

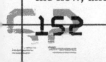

hand on my arm again, as she had been doing more often recently, and said, "Nothing really. Just hoping that we can get him soon, before we get too close to China."

"There's not much chance of that, Kat. We're almost at the Bering Strait now." I checked my watch. "A few more hours, then we're officially in the Pacific."

She sighed. "We have to get him . . . but I just don't know how we can do it." Then that look crossed her face again, just for an instant.

I said, "There's a space behind the engine room, isn't there?"

She looked startled. "Pardon?"

"The aft bulkhead of the engine room stops well before the hull does. There's a hatch in there with a coded access panel. What is it?"

She nodded. "Oh, that. It's watertight. Behind it is the access to the emergency ballast compartment. It's not important to get to. I'm not even sure why we have a hatch for it. We don't really have to get back there for anything."

Exactly, I thought. But I held my tongue.

THAT AFTERNOON, WE THREADED OUR WAY through the break between the landmasses of North America and Asia—a strait made far larger by the rising ocean levels—and forged south toward the Aleutian Islands that stretched from Alaska all the way to Russia. We had been in the shallow waters of the Alaskan continental shelf, but once through the islands and into the Pacific, the ocean floor dropped suddenly and dramatically into the Aleutian Trench. Here, where the Pacific Ocean floor collided violently with North America, driven by monumental tectonic forces, the oceanic crust subducted under the continental crust and the seafloor dipped downward to tremendous, crushing depths of up to seven kilometers. It meant that our seacar could not settle to the bottom if needed or if we experienced an emergency. It wasn't the deepest part of this ocean, but it was close.

And once over those great depths, we would finally get our chance to catch Johnny.

CHAPTER EIGHTEEN 十八

HE BEGAN TO EXPERIENCE ENGINE TROUBLE on his port side. At first the sonar detected merely a slight variation in sound output, and then his velocity began to decrease.

Sixty-eight kph.

Sixty-five.

Fifty-nine.

This was it. Finally.

Within minutes his speed registered zero. The ocean floor was 7000 meters below. Our sonar indicated all sounds from the vessel had ceased, except for one.

The airlock hatch opening.

He was outside the seacar.

The only thing we could surmise was that something had finally broken down on the vessel and he'd had to go outside for repairs. He was at a depth of fifty meters, and I noticed a few minutes later that the seacar was gradually descending.

He was sinking, slowly but surely.

We watched the DISTANCE TO TARGET readout change as we sped toward him. At our current velocity we would reach him in about twenty minutes. I could sense the anticipation radiating from Kat; I felt it too. Unless it was a trap, I reminded myself. He had sounded sure that if I continued to follow him I would never make it back to Trieste. This could be part of that plan. Whatever the case, I had to take advantage of the situation and hope for the best.

Kat stayed in the control cabin, watching his ship on the sonar, while I went aft and pulled on a wetsuit. I prepared the scuba tank for a depth of eighty meters; the mix was good for up to two hundred, just in case his ship continued to descend while I was trying to bring him in. I would have to depressurize in the airlock after the excursion, but not for too long. The needle gun that I had taken from one of my attackers at Trieste was in my bag, and I removed it gingerly and strapped it to my thigh.

It was time.

I STOOD IN THE NARROW AIRLOCK with the mask over my head as I waited for word from Kat. Within a few moments the sound of the engines changed; she was throttling down. I was so accustomed to the noise, after having listened to it for so long now, that the silence felt odd. Then the vibration in the deck tapered off to nothing.

"We're there," she said. "Put your mask on."

I pulled it off my head and sealed it around my face.

"I'm pumping the water in now. Get ready to equalize and begin breathing the pressurized gases from your tank."

I rolled my eyes at her comments. This was nothing new to me; after all, I was now the holder of the deepest scuba dive in the world. I could do this blindfolded.

The water thundered in and surged upward without any further warning from her. There was a sudden sensation of weight on my chest, and at that precise moment, I sucked in a breath from the tank. The tri-mix immediately filled my lungs and perfectly counteracted the pressure. The airlock was full of water within two seconds, and Kat's voice came to me now from the speaker in my ear. "Be ready for him; he must know we're here."

"Any movement from his seacar?"

"No. Thrusters are still down."

"What does the sonar say?"

"Nothing's happened since his airlock opened that one time. The hatch never closed."

Which probably meant that there was only one person outside. "Can you see him?"

There was a pause. Then, "No. He's not on this side of the vehicle."

"Can you take us around? Check for him?"

"Already did before I shut down. Either he's not out, or he purposefully stayed on the opposite side of his ship."

He was clever, all right. "Go ahead and open the hatch, Kat. Listen for me in case I need something."

She hesitated before, "Good luck, Mac. Go get him for me. I wouldn't want last night's dinner to be our final one together."

"Are you asking me on a date?" I almost smiled to myself, but the very real danger of what was about to happen had me on edge. Every muscle was tensed and ready, and the needle gun was tight in my hand.

"Sure."

"Then I accept."

She said nothing more, and the hatch swung out into the cold water of the north Pacific Ocean.

KAT HAD BROUGHT US IN PERFECTLY; his seacar was only ten meters away. It was similar in size to ours, but its hull was the shape of a cigar and the stabilizers were far stubbier. As a result, the two thrusters were closer to the ship than *SC-1*'s. I spent a few moments searching for him, but he was nowhere in sight. It was daytime topside and the sun was out, and a fair portion of light penetrated to this depth. The far side of his ship was in shadow, except for a sparkle of illumination from the aft section. The sun, perhaps, was glinting off something more reflective than the rest of the hull. Then again, I thought, the flashes were coming in spurts, which seemed odd.

I keyed my comm to Kat's frequency, and made sure that it wasn't a common one that Johnny could listen in on. "You're sure you didn't see anything on the far side?"

"Nothing."

"What about damage to the hull?"

"Hmm." She pondered that for a heartbeat. "I didn't actually look. I was searching for a figure."

"Tools or anything?"

"Didn't notice. Sorry, Mac."

The flashes of light were still there. I had an idea of what they were, and decided to check. I pushed out from the airlock and soared into open water. It was a daunting thing to do, knowing that the bottom of the trench was so far down. At the same time, the surface was so near, and a miserable death lay there as well—The Bends. Thankfully I was neutrally buoyant, due to the weights on my belt that counteracted my body's natural buoyancy; I stayed in place once outside the vehicle, neither rising nor falling.

"Kat, take *SC-1* around his vessel again. I'm going to watch from here." Hopefully if Johnny was indeed there, he would duck to my side to stay away from *SC-1*.

And I would have him.

The seacar's thrusters began to churn the water, but only at a fraction of max. She slowly circled Johnny's vehicle, and I remained there, still and silent. An instant later a figure in a dark wetsuit swam out from under the crippled seacar, hugging the hull and watching *SC-1*. He was using his own vessel to block Kat's view. But now that I had seen him, I knew what he was doing and how to get him.

"Stay there," I whispered.

"Roger," she responded. "I do see damage now. A charred mark on the hull at the aft compartment."

The flashes of light had been from a welding torch. He had probably suffered some minor leaking after the skirmish in the Fracture Zone, and had been pumping water out ever since. But the breach in his hull was in the engine room, and the water had most likely finally risen too high and damaged some electronics or shorted a bank of batteries. Johnny had to repair the hull before he could get underway again. It was a quick job to seal a small leak at this depth. He would just have to weld a hull plate over the crack and make sure the seal was watertight.

Luckily, we had caught him before he had finished.

I kicked out and my flippers snapped behind me. I closed the distance fast. The man was just a few meters away. He was peering out from under the hull at *SC-1*; he didn't even see me coming.

I wrapped an arm around his neck and tightened it with a savage jerk. Johnny went rigid, pulled his feet up and planted them against the hull of his ship, and pushed. It propelled us both away from the seacar. He began to turn his body, as he had before at the French dome, and once again I found it difficult to hold on to him. However, this time he wore a scuba tank, so I grabbed it with my free hand and held on. I clutched the needle gun in the other, and I brought it before his mask to show him.

It got his attention.

He stopped moving.

I relaxed my grip and allowed him to twist toward me. I kept the gun at gut level, prepared to fire in case he tried something dumb.

His face came into view.

It wasn't Johnny.

IT WAS HIS PARTNER. I SHOULD have known. Same build and hair, and I had just assumed.

I clenched my teeth and gestured with the gun.

Move back toward the ship.

He did so warily, watching me the whole way.

I pushed him until his back was against the hull. Then I keyed my comm to a standard frequency, so any divers nearby could hear my broadcast. "He's inside?" I said.

The other didn't respond, so I said it again, this time in Chinese. His face registered shock for a moment, then he finally nodded.

I wondered what I could do with him while I went inside to fish for Johnny. I couldn't leave him out here to do as he pleased. He might try to board *SC-1* and capture Kat. Then we'd really be in trouble. I had nothing to tie him up with, however, and nothing to secure him to his ship so that he couldn't move.

Then it came to me.

"Take a deep breath," I ordered.

His eyes grew wide. "No," he gasped. "I can't hold my breath for that long!"

"Then you better hope he'll come willingly." He understood what I was suggesting: leave him outside without a tank while I went in to get Johnny. And if Johnny put up a struggle, his partner would drown waiting. It would give Johnny incentive to move.

He looked away into the dark distance as he tried to think of another option. "I could call him out for you," he said finally.

That, of course, was what I had wanted all along. "How?"

"I'll tell him that I need help fighting you off. It'll even be true, in a way."

I snorted at that. "All right. But I'm watching your lips. If you warn him, I'll fire."

He nodded, then switched frequencies on his comm. A few seconds later he was back on my channel. "It's done; he's coming. He thinks I've almost got you beat, but just need a bit more help."

"Good." I glanced toward the airlock, just a few meters away. "Then when he comes out—"

I didn't finish the sentence. As soon as I looked away, he struck.

He knocked the weapon from my hand and I watched it sink into the blackness below. Then he lashed out at my mask and tore it from my face. Water flooded in, and the icy shock stunned me. I closed my eyes for a second, and when I opened them again, he had backed away with my face mask still in his hand. I reached for my secondary regulator; every tank had such a backup. But I was too slow—he had grabbed that too, and with a quick jerk ripped the mouthpiece from the tube. It disconnected with a *pop* and he looked at me with a hard expression on his face.

I was in serious trouble.

He held up both my mask and the backup regulator, and dropped them into the depths.

Shit! I nearly screamed. Air was streaming from my tank, and I had to reach back to yank the emergency valve shut.

It took only a second to decide what to do.

I kicked downward madly.

I COULD ONLY GO SO FAR. With each ten meters the ocean applied another kilogram of weight to every square centimeter of my body. My chest would begin to compress without an equal amount of pressure within, and once I was about thirteen meters down, the volume of air in my lungs would be insufficient to keep me from sinking.

The mask had already disappeared from sight, unfortunately. I needed it more than the backup regulator, but it was the heavier of the two. Now the regulator was my only hope.

I lunged after it with massive kicks and reached my hand out.

It was falling quickly, but I was moving fast and began to catch up.

I descended five meters within seconds.

My fingers stretched out, grasping for the precious device.

Seven meters.

Nine.

I touched the rubber, closed my hand, but it slipped out. *Damn! Come on, Mac! Get it!*

Eleven.

I tried again, reaching with everything I had.

My heart was pounding now, my lungs heaving. It felt like someone was sitting on my chest; the pain was increasing exponentially with each kick downward. I couldn't equalize, and a stabbing sensation had begun in my ears.

Thirteen.

Fourteen.

Got it! I pulled the regulator up and hurriedly began to connect it back to the hose. As I did so, I looked up at the seacars; they seemed so far above.

And still I was falling.

I was now negatively buoyant, and I began to kick frantically. I managed to maintain my position, but it was taking every bit of energy I had. The situation was pushing me to my limits—even more so than when I had been out on the bottom of the Atlantic abyssal plain. My vision began to cloud over.

The weights on my belt were there, I knew; I could simply release them and I'd soar upward. The problem with that, however, was that if I went too far up without decompressing slowly, I would die horribly. I would end up in the exact situation as now, only kicking frantically to keep myself from ascending.

The regulator finally connected to the tube and I greedily sucked it into my mouth.

Shit! No air—you turned it off, asshole! Quick, get it back on!

I reached behind me and turned the valve. A rush of compressed mix filled my lungs and my vision immediately cleared. I took breath after breath; my depth was now constant—my lungs were full of air once again at a pressure great enough to keep me neutrally buoyant.

Exhausted and with every muscle burning in agony, I kicked up toward Johnny's seacar.

And the man who had almost just killed me.

THE FLASHES OF LIGHT WERE THERE again; Johnny's partner was frantically trying to repair the hull so they could escape. No doubt Johnny was himself inside the engine room, trying to restart the thrusters.

The man stopped welding and glanced below him. Then he turned his welder toward me. I stopped advancing, faced him at a three meter distance, and gestured for him to release the torch.

He shook his head.

I no longer had a mask on, and it was difficult to see exactly what he was doing, but I could tell that his mouth was moving. He was talking to Johnny, inside the seacar. There was a sudden throbbing noise behind me, and I glanced at its source. Kat. She had brought *SC-1* to my back. Her bow was facing us.

The torpedo hatch was open.

There was a torpedo in the tube, ready to fire.

And she was in the control cabin, watching with a grim look on her face.

The man's jaw fell open, and he immediately stopped speaking. He put his hands in the air and released the welder. It dangled downward, but the tube and tank resting on the starboard stabilizer prevented it from falling toward the seafloor.

I couldn't help but admire Kat. She had seen everything transpire out there, and had probably thought I was already dead. She was ready to kill these two, not only to protect her secret, but to avenge me.

My respect and admiration for her climbed yet another notch.

I FIRST DECIDED TO SEND THE man into *SC-1*. He had to decompress in the airlock before he could enter the living area. Decompression would take an hour, and Kat made sure the inner lock was secured.

But the dilemma now became how to get Johnny out of his vessel. It was still sinking very slowly—we were now at a depth of 185 meters—but he didn't have to come out, and he didn't have to let me in.

The answer came to me quickly. To use an old expression, I would simply smoke him out.

I used the welder.

First I went to the spot on the hull where Johnny's partner had been trying to weld a patch over a small breach. I opened the torch to full, removed the patch, and began to lengthen the crack in the hull. When I felt it was large enough, I swam to the middle compartment. It was the living area of the seacar—I could see couches and a pair of small bunks through a porthole—and began to slice there too.

It took ten minutes, but soon water was spraying in at tremendous pressure.

Then I did the same to the control cabin.

The ship was sinking faster now; we were at two hundred meters, and I had a tight grip on a safety rung to keep me with the vessel. I would have to go back to *SC-1* soon—as my mix wasn't good for any deeper—but I also knew that Johnny's only hope was to come out.

Sure enough, within minutes, his airlock hatch opened. He stood in the small chamber, glaring at me. I pointed to *SC-1*, and he gave a single, angry nod.

I had him.

CHAPTER NINETEEN 十九

JOHNNY AND I HAD TO WAIT outside until his partner's decompression was complete. Then we had to stay in the airlock together for ninety minutes. According to the dive tables, my decompression was far longer than his, as I had been out longer, and he had to remain in the chamber's tight confines with me until I was done. It was awkward, to say the least. We had to stand and face one another. For the first few minutes he said nothing and simply fixed me with an icy glare. I didn't care. I was alive and had finally captured my elusive prey.

I just had to be careful now not to let the two of them overpower us and take control of the seacar.

He finally spoke. "My superiors are going to be very upset with me."

I snorted. "I hardly think that matters now. You're coming to Trieste."

He shook his head. "I can't do that."

"I thought you wanted me to go back there, to check out your story."

"Of course I do," he snapped, "but not with me. I have to—" He suddenly closed his mouth. I knew instantly what he had been about to say.

"You have to take the stolen information to your bosses." I crossed my arms. I assumed he still had it; he wouldn't have let it go to the bottom with the seacar. "I'm afraid that isn't going to happen now."

He brushed a hand through his wet hair. "Dammit, Mac. You can't do this. You're playing with my life here."

"At least you know where you stand. Seven years ago, you betrayed me. I've done nothing of the sort to you. You chose a side, and I've done my job."

"I've got a job to do too. My mission was to get that information. If I don't get it to them, they're going to come after it. And they're going to do everything in their power to get it."

"Are you saying they're on their way here?"

"Damn right! We're in tremendous danger right now."

I threw my head back and laughed. "Incredible. You'd better hope that we get to Trieste in one piece then. Unfortunately, when we do, Shanks will have his hands on you."

He reached out and clutched the front of my wetsuit. "I should kill you right now," he hissed.

"I beat you at the French base, it'll happen again."

"I wasn't trying to kill you then. Things will be different."

I sized him up for a moment. We had similar builds, though I was thicker through the arms, chest, and legs. He was more agile, however. It would be a close contest, but I knew he wouldn't try just yet. Kat would simply open the lock and flood the chamber if he did anything.

He seemed to realize that after a heartbeat; he glanced at the speaker in the ceiling, then released me. His face was a mask of anger and anxiety.

"Is that how your superiors treat you?" I asked. "Punish operatives for a failed mission?"

He seemed reluctant to answer at first. "It's different than at TCI. They are much more authoritarian. Operatives can't act as freely."

"Except you managed to convince the *Fast Attack*'s captain to kidnap me, without orders from China."

"True, but he is a friend." He pierced me with another look. "*Was* a friend, I should say."

"They tried to sink us."

"The first time they had instructions not to kill. They knew that I wanted to meet with you. Since they couldn't board your seacar and capture you, they left you alone and let you follow me to the meeting."

I had gone over his story multiple times, and yet something still didn't add up. "You're saying that they were working with you. That the five men who infiltrated Trieste were only trying to kidnap me. Then later the ship was just trying to damage us so they could board."

"That's right."

I shook my head. "You're wrong. They tried to kill me at Trieste, Johnny. And later, the *Fast Attack* tried to sink us. We were stranded on the abyssal plains at our maximum depth. They dropped four mines on our heads."

He frowned. "Are you sure?"

"No doubt about it. They were doing their damned best to take me out."

He looked away as he processed that. "That doesn't make sense. I specifically asked her captain *not* to hurt you. I just wanted to meet with you, to tell you about Trieste's plans."

I had a theory about all of this. It was the only thing that truly made sense. After Johnny had told me what was going on, I realized that the *Fast Attack's* actions did not fit the picture he was trying to paint. Either he was lying, or they had betrayed him. And for some odd reason, I had the sensation he was telling me the truth, that he would never lie to me again.

"Johnny," I said in a soft voice. "Is it possible that they're playing you?"

He blinked. "What do you mean?"

"That your superiors told the *Fast Attack's* crew to pretend to do as you asked, but instead kill me. Perhaps they were going to kill you too, after they got what you stole."

"That's insane." And yet he looked concerned; I had struck a nerve.

"Think about it. You defected to Sheng. But you aren't really Chinese. Sure, your parents were, but they were Chinese-Americans. Isn't it possible that your bosses don't trust you? That they never trusted you? After all, you betrayed us. Why not them too?"

His eyes flashed. "I've been a good operative for them!"

"When it suited their needs. But I'm telling you, that warsub was trying to kill us! There was no attempt to merely damage us so they could board. They were launching torpedoes and mines with the intent to kill. For Christ's sake, they chased us four and a half kilometers down, then kept at it! We could have imploded!"

He whispered, "Those were not their orders."

"No. And the men in Trieste killed Blake. Did you know that?"

His face went white. "Blake? Are you sure? You saw that?"

"He was right next to me. He took a dagger in the chest."

"You're sure he's dead?"

"Absolutely."

He swore. I watched him silently as thoughts churned through his head. To find out that his superiors had discovered his plans must have been

difficult. He had left one home for another, and now neither place was safe. True, he had made his own bed, but a part of me did feel sorry for him.

Eventually he said, "They'll be coming, Mac. They'll be trying to sink us soon. If what you're saying is true, they may not care that I'm on board. If they know that I deliberately tried to contact you, to *help* you, they'll want to kill me."

"You have the information though."

"They can retrieve it from a sunken vessel easily enough. They don't need me."

His eyes finally met mine, and in them I saw fear.

OUR DECOMPRESSION ENDED AND THE INNER hatch swung open. But not before Kat came on the speaker and warned Johnny not to give us any trouble. When we entered, she had a gun on his partner, who was on the couch in the living area. I hadn't known that she had one, but it made sense. Shanks probably made sure of it. She gestured to Johnny, and he went and sat next to the other.

She was fuming. She looked ready to shoot right then and there. I had to put my hand on her shoulder to keep her from doing anything brash.

"This is the asshole who started all of this," she snapped at me.

"Relax," I said. "He's got your data on him. It's okay now."

But she didn't respond; she was still glaring at him. "How dare you steal from me?" she grated. "That's *my* work, not yours!"

Johnny cocked his head to the side. "That's how things are in the underwater cities. Our intelligence services are always trying to one-up each other." He glanced at me. "Doesn't she realize that?"

"She was a topsider until a month ago."

"Really?" He looked shocked. "I didn't know that."

"Now give it to me!" Kat yelled.

"Easy, now." He was staring at the barrel of the deadly weapon. "It's right here." He withdrew a small plastic case from a zippered pocket on his thigh; it was a container with a chip inside for transporting digital information. He set it on the low table in front of him.

"I should kill you and dump you out the airlock!"

"Kat," I started, but she ignored me. That unpredictable and angry person was back, the one I hadn't seen in days.

She continued, "Shanks wants you at Trieste, but I say to hell with it! He'll just try again, Mac! I need to protect my work!"

Strangely enough, I was now trying to protect the man whom I had previously wanted to kill. I realized I could just let Kat do it, then destroy the information and save myself a huge headache. But I didn't.

"It's not worth it," I whispered. "You'll regret it later."

"To hell I—"

"*Kat.* I know about killing people. You never forget it. It's a part of an operative's life, but the killing never gets easier. Shanks will deal with Johnny. Don't worry."

He snorted. "By 'deal with,' you mean torture, right?"

I ignored him. "Please Kat. Let me have the gun. We're all in this together now. We have to get to Trieste safely."

"What are you talking about?"

"The Chinese know where we are. They'll be trying to sink us. It's in Johnny's best interests now to come back with us. The Chinese will kill him if they find him. His plan didn't work the way he had hoped, and they've shown their cards. They know." I turned to him. "Your only help is at Trieste."

"With Shanks." His tone dripped with sarcasm.

"Yes. And I'll look into your claims." I hesitated. "If you're right . . ."

"Then what?"

I chewed my lip. The fact was, I didn't yet know. I had thought a great deal about it, but I was conflicted about the whole situation. Kat's invention would enable Shanks to make a play for independence. If he tried that, however, it would start a war. I didn't want that, but my mission was to bring the chip back. A tough predicament, to say the least.

"Then I'll get you out," I heard myself say.

No one spoke. Johnny's face was blank. Kat was staring at me as if I were a madman.

"But why?" Johnny asked.

"Because I believe you. Because I think you were honestly trying to warn me about Shanks." I faced Kat. "You said that Shanks was planning a fight for independence. Are you ready to talk about it yet?"

She looked suddenly distraught. "I'm sorry, Mac. I can't say anything; I'm under orders."

I sighed. Until she did, I was still on my own.

And then something caught our attention.

Something that chilled us to the bone.

Ping.

The sudden high-pitched noise shot through the ship and echoed for ten seconds after it first arrived. We had all heard the sound before, but at that moment, it was the last thing we wanted.

"Holy shit," Johnny whispered. "They've found us."

A PULSE FROM ACTIVE SONAR HAD tagged us. Someone out there was searching, and they had just found their target. The burst of sound had reflected off our hull and returned to its point of origin, telling them our precise position and depth.

Ping.

Shit. Another pulse. Now they knew our course and speed.

I raced to the control cabin and threw myself into the chair. Kat slid into the other, and Johnny and his partner stood at our backs. I had the gun in my pocket now—I had taken it from Kat—and I glanced back at my former colleague. "Do we have to worry about you still? Should we tie you up?"

He shook his head. "No. You've convinced me. I'll go to Trieste."

"Good."

He looked at his partner. "I'm sorry, Lau. I have no choice anymore."

The man considered the situation for a brief moment. "If what he claims is true, then I'm also in danger. Our superiors know that I helped you." He spoke in Chinese.

"At least you have family in Trieste. Perhaps you can stay with them."

"Shanks will let you," I added. "After a lengthy debriefing, I'm sure." During which he'd have to tell Shanks everything he knew about Sheng City Intelligence, their operatives, procedures, and so on. Hopefully minus the torture.

Lines creased Lau's forehead. It was an enormous dilemma for him, but he had no other options. Even if he overpowered us and contacted the CSF, he was still a dead man. Finally, he nodded. "Then we go to Trieste."

"Good." I noticed that *SC-1* was already heading due south, toward the Panama pass-through. I scanned the sonar, searching for the source of the signal. It had come from the north.

From the Bering Strait.

It couldn't be the Chinese. Not from that direction.

"Switching to active mode," I muttered. I toggled it on, then sent my own pulse outward. With a range of a hundred kilometers, we should be able to see exactly who had tagged us.

Though I already had a suspicion.

An instant later we had our answer.

USS *Impaler*, on a direct course for us.

"DAMMIT," I SAID. "THEY JUST DON'T give up."

"They've been following you since you left," Johnny muttered. "I wonder why."

I frowned. "I thought they were just curious about us, but perhaps it's more than that. They must have seen the wreckage in the Fracture Zone. Either they're investigating that, or . . ." I trailed off.

"Or they know about the technology I stole. They could be after it too."

I checked *Impaler*'s speed—seventy kph. She couldn't catch up, but she was on our tail. If something happened, if we suffered some engine trouble as Johnny had, then they would have us, and the USSF would most likely get the technology and learn about TCI in the process.

I couldn't let that happen.

MINUTES LATER THE COMM BEEPED. THEY were calling. As a US seacar, we had to respond to a request from the USSF. We were also obligated to stop if they required it. It was law as a US citizen in the oceans; the USSF had total jurisdiction over us. It was one of the things Triestrians hated so much about them.

I glanced at the others, then pressed the ACCEPT TRANSMISSION button. I made sure our own signal was muted. A female voice filled the cabin. "Attention US seacar on a bearing one-eight-zero from this signal. This is USS *Impaler*. We demand you cease all thruster activity and wait for us to approach. We intend to board you. Do not continue on your current course."

Johnny swore. "You can't let them, Mac. They'll execute me and Lau."

"I know."

"And they'll steal my invention!" Kat snarled.

Clearly I couldn't stop. Despite the potential consequences, I had to ignore the order.

It repeated; this time, the woman on the other end sounded sterner than before. Then with the next message she added, "I have to stress this, unidentified seacar. We will not only board you—we will fire on you. We are a *Reaper* class US warsub. Respond."

We said nothing, and the comm went dead.

Ping.

We jumped in our seats. Damn. They would most likely continue that as we headed south. They might also call in reinforcements; USSF Command could dispatch other US warsubs based out of Anchorage or Seattle to intercept us.

Things could get very hairy, very soon.

And then I noticed Kat point at the sonar. "What is that?"

Our last active pulse had identified numerous contacts ninety kilometers to the south.

"Those," Johnny muttered, "are the forces sent for us."

Eight contacts, all Chinese, and we were sailing straight for them.

"ACCORDING TO THE SONAR THEY'RE *JIN* class warsubs," Kat reported, "with one *Han*."

Johnny shook his head. "Not *Jin*. They are the newer versions. *Mao* class."

I snorted. "Let me guess. More armor, just as fast, and they can go almost twice as deep."

"Yes. Same as the one that attacked you earlier. We still call them *Fast Attacks*. The CSF is phasing out the *Jins* and replacing them with *Maos*."

I blinked. "The CSF currently has sixty-one of them. You're replacing them *all*?"

"Over the next five years, yes."

I shuddered. They were far superior to their American *Hunter-Killer* counterparts. When the USSF found out, they were going to shit bricks.

The thought made me glance at *Impaler* on the screen.

They might just be finding out, very soon.

Our ETA to the Chinese vessels was thirty minutes, give or take. *Impaler* would arrive on the scene ninety minutes later.

Unless we could arrange for them to meet at the same time.

"Kat," I murmured. "Let's do what the US warsub wants. Bring us to a stop. Make our depth a thousand meters."

Her forehead crinkled. "But that would—" She let out a strangled gasp. "You don't mean to—"

I nodded. "We're going to need help to get by those Chinese. And *Impaler* is going to give it to us." Once we stopped, the Chinese force would hit us in seventy-five minutes. We would have to stay alive for just fifteen more until *Impaler* joined the battle. And the US warsub didn't yet know the Chinese were there; they were still out of her range. When they found out, however, they would want to defeat the Chinese to protect Kat's invention, then take it for themselves.

This could start a war, but it was our only hope.

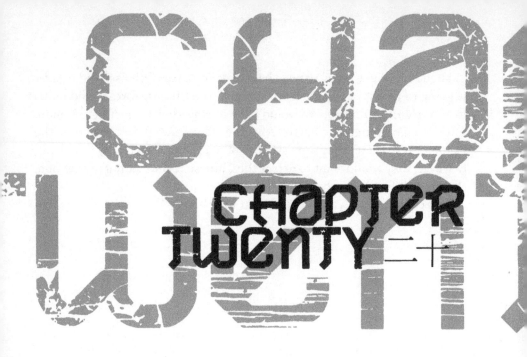

As soon as we cut thrusters and set the autopilot to keep the ship in place, Lau spoke up. He had a deep, resonating voice, and his English was perfect. Evidently Sheng City Intelligence had used him to infiltrate our cities, as he could have blended in perfectly as a Chinese-American. His accent wasn't Midwest, New England, or New Jersey. It was simply nondescript and did not stand out in any way. Based on his physical appearance, he was probably deadly in a physical confrontation. We had already had a few minor altercations—he had stabbed me, after all—but nothing like a knock-down, drag-out fight. I hoped we would never have one.

He said, "Will you trust me enough to give me access to your comm system?"

I frowned. "Why?"

"Chinese warsubs emit transmissions during battles or war games. The transmissions aren't strong and are hard to detect at a great distance, but they're crucial to strategy. They simply tell Chinese torpedoes and missiles not to detonate if they're approaching a 'friend,' so to speak."

I wanted to grin. *Perfect.* What he was describing was something our own military also used. Friendly fire was one of the biggest problems in battle, and it was even more problematic underwater where piloting and targeting was done largely by instrument. If a warsub launched a torpedo, any vessel without safeguards in the theater would be at risk. The system Lau had referred to cut that dilemma out of the equation. We could simply transmit a "Do Not Detonate" message and watch their torpedoes sail away into the distance.

"Do you know the codes?" I asked.

"A few. The captains will most likely realize the problem after their first volley, but it could give us the edge."

It might save our lives for the first fifteen minutes, which is all we needed. After that, the situation would be dramatically different.

The Chinese warsubs finally appeared on the projected VID; they had entered its five kilometer range. It had been a tense time waiting for them. As the warsubs approached, we received another transmission from USS *Impaler*. The Chinese force was now within their passive sonar range, and they had realized the enormity of the situation that they were sailing for.

"Unidentified seacar, we suggest that you engage thrusters and make your heading due north." The woman's voice now had a tinge of urgency to it. Perhaps trepidation as well. "You are in danger."

"Do you think they're actually concerned with our well-being?" Kat asked. "Or do they just want the stolen information?"

"We're Americans facing eight Chinese warsubs. Tensions between our countries are immense. They'll do their best to protect us, then take what they want."

But I wouldn't let it come to that.

The Chinese must have known *Impaler* was speeding toward us, but it made no difference. They pressed on, preparing to attack. They separated into four groups of two and placed themselves between 500 and 3000 meters. It would be hard for us to get through that net; if we tried, any torpedoes fired in the battle would be extremely close and difficult to avoid.

Thankfully, we had Lau.

He programmed the codes into the comm, and then we watched the warsubs on the VID, white shapes that grew larger by the minute.

Urgent warnings continued from *Impaler*, but we ignored them. When they arrived, all hell would break loose, and hopefully we could slip away undetected. The *Reaper* class US warsub contained smaller subs that could launch to join the fight. In that respect it was similar to an aircraft carrier. They dominated the seas, and most superpowers had such vessels. China had their version, as did France, England, Germany, India, Iran, and Japan. Numerous other countries had similar types under development.

"I'm taking us deep," I said at last. "Four kilometers." I hit the thrusters to max, pushed the yoke away from me, and switched ballast to negative. We dove quickly, and once more the creaks and groans of a stressed hull echoed through the ship. Johnny and Lau glanced around unconsciously, but they had been through it all before. In fact, according to Johnny, the voyage from the Fracture Zone had been a hellish exercise in keeping their engines going and their speed up against all the flooding they were experiencing. Our torpedo had hurt them more than we had thought.

Soon we were at 4000 meters, and the Chinese were overhead but still a kilometer away. They began to turn to match our course, and abruptly the sonar began to shrill.

Torpedoes, headed downward.

Four warsubs had fired two weapons each. They had angled their noses down, and the weapons raced toward us. The sonar displayed them as red streaks, and the VID system showed them as white cylinders with frothing trails of bubbles.

"Ignore them," Lau muttered.

A shock jolted my body. I realized dimly that this could have been a clever setup to a glorious suicide. If Lau and Johnny were willing to give their lives to prevent us from getting back to Trieste, then Lau could have fabricated the whole strategy of transmitting a code to nullify the torpedoes.

The thought chilled me to the bone.

I clutched the yoke and prepared to yank it to the side; I was an instant from ordering countermeasures—

When Johnny said in a soft voice, "It's okay, Mac. You can trust him. You convinced us both."

I stared into his eyes for a long moment. There was a great deal of history between us, and I wanted to see him begin to repair the damage he had inflicted on our friendship. But still, I had no idea what nation his allegiance was now to.

"I don't want to die, I promise you that," he continued.

I turned back to the VID. The missiles were so close now . . . barely 200 meters away. I loosened my grip on the yoke and leaned back in the chair. Kat stared at me, wide-eyed.

The whine of the electric-driven screws grew in intensity.

I watched the torpedoes, stony-faced.

If this was it, then he had betrayed me twice in my lifetime.

The missiles passed *SC-1* and continued into the depths. The sound of their engines diminished, and I breathed a sigh of relief.

The sonar emitted another warning. The deeper pair of subs had just released four mines in our path; they were falling before us and would intersect with our course in less than forty seconds. I could see them on

the VID; white stars trailing luminescent streaks. "Ignore these, too?" I muttered.

"They launched them too quickly to have changed the safeguards," Lau said. "We're fine."

I nodded. "Good. Then it's time to press our advantage." I pulled the yoke back and changed our ballast to positive. The two closest *Fast Attacks* were ahead and above, on the same course as us.

We closed the distance quickly.

"Prepare torpedo," I said. We only had three left; I had to hope that these would all hit their targets. Otherwise, there would be no choice but to go deep and try to avoid their weapons.

The mines passed before us silently; each failed to detonate. They disappeared into the darkness of deep waters, where they would eventually hit bottom, and sedimentation over the next few years would bury them.

The Chinese captains in the warsubs were probably screaming at their weapons officers, thinking they had screwed up. Logically there could only be one explanation for the failure of twelve weapons, but I knew from hard experience it was sometimes difficult to accept the truth.

"They'll be wondering what the hell just happened," Lau said. "They might now arm their weapons immediately before launching, and allow friendly fire."

Which meant every sub in the region would be at risk. Just as I wanted.

"Ready," Kat said. "A homer is in the tube."

"Fire," I said.

A *Fast Attack* was directly in our path, with another a few hundred meters to her port. If it missed the first, hopefully it would target the other.

There was a burst of bubbles across our canopy, and the deck shuddered slightly under us. It shot toward the warsub, and we held our breath as it churned through the water. The Chinese vessel began to blow ballast and her nose pitched up. It ejected countermeasures. . . .

And the torpedo went for them.

"Shit," I grumbled.

But it wasn't done yet. It passed through the cavitating devices and instantly locked onto another target: the nearby warsub whose captain had not thought to take evasive action. The missile closed on his screws, the distance decreased rapidly—

And then the captain finally acted. He angled his vessel away from the missile, increased speed to max, and blew his tanks. The ship started to climb at eighty kph, the speed of the weapon, and the distance stopped decreasing. The torpedo's computers instantly recognized it was at its closest possible point to target, and it detonated fifteen meters away.

The shock wave hurled the stern of the *Fast Attack* upward and the warsub's screws immediately seized, warped beyond the ability of their reactors to turn them. A surge of water crashed into the area vaporized by the explosion, and the concussion pounded the hull of the vessel.

It was hard to tell what had happened to her structural integrity, but she was dead in the water and out of the fight.

"Still seven more to go," I said. I checked the time. Only five minutes had passed since the encounter began; still ten until *Impaler* arrived.

The crippled warsub had begun a slow and lazy descent, and we watched it silently on the acrylic canopy before us. Bubbles were now streaming from her hull.

The comm abruptly crackled. "This is *Jia*, issuing a Mayday!" The voice was hurried and frantic. "Mayday, Mayday! We're taking on water and all systems are down! Approaching crush depth!"

There was no response from the others.

"Please! Captain Li, your vessel has grapples. There is still time to rescue us!"

The frenzied man was clearly appealing to the captain of the *Han* class vessel. I checked the sonar and saw the labeled specifications next to that target; the *Han* could only descend to a depth of 3150 meters. The sinking sub was already deeper than that.

There was no hope.

A part of me felt remorse for what I had just done—there was a crew of ten in that boat—but I knew that had I not, we would be the ones facing death. As it stood, there was a strong possibility we would not make it through this.

The warsub continued to sink, well past her listed crush depth, and still the radioman continued to plead, despite the fact that no one could help. Then there was the sound of wrenching metal, a burst of static, and the transmission ceased.

I glanced back at Johnny and Lau; their faces were somber. Lau had contributed to the death of the people aboard that warsub. However, they both knew the stakes.

They remained silent.

"Prepare another torpedo," I whispered.

Kat did so, and I searched the sonar for the other contacts. The *Fast Attack* that had run was coming around for another shot at us; the rest were still

at shallower depths, though they were now starting to drop mines. I had to assume they had removed the safeguards, and they would now damage a Chinese vessel as easily as *SC-1*.

I steered toward them.

Johnny said, "Uh, Mac, what are you doing?"

"Bringing that warsub toward those mines. They might damage him."

"And us too, you realize."

We didn't have many other options.

There were still seven minutes before *Impaler* arrived.

The mines were overhead now, and I reduced our speed. The Chinese vessel was on a course directly behind us, and clearly knew what I was attempting. They fired a torpedo and stayed well back.

I slammed power to full and blew all the tanks. We began to soar upward, and the VID's background color quickly began to lighten. "Countermeasures!" I snapped, and Kat stabbed at the panel. "Prepare torpedo!" I hoped I could catch the other captains off guard by firing while trying to escape. A warsub was in our path, at 2000 meters, and Kat pressed the FIRE button as we soared toward shallow water. The torpedo shot for the warsub, which immediately began ejecting countermeasures and taking evasive action.

Then I lost sight of her, and focused on what I was doing. I pushed on the yoke—there was a lot of resistance, and it followed my commands sluggishly—and switched back to negative buoyancy. We began to plunge into the depths.

"It's a hit!" Johnny cried. "You got him!"

I risked a glance at the sonar; sure enough, the warsub we had just fired at had turned gray on the screen, and a question mark had popped up in the box next to it. According to the readout, it was in pieces and now falling rapidly past 3000 meters.

Six warsubs left, and we only had one torpedo remaining.

And there was still one right on our tail.

I groaned.

THE WEAPON BEHIND US WAS SLOWLY catching up. Kat launched another set of countermeasures—I could tell from her expression we were low on them—and then I pulled back once more on the yoke.

The devices worked.

The explosion rocked the seacar, lights winked red on the panel, but we had survived.

By the skin of our teeth.

But I didn't get a chance to relax. The sonar called for attention once again; four more torpedoes were in the water, all coming for us.

Meanwhile, Johnny was looking over his shoulder, down the passageway toward the aft compartment. "Something's going on in the engine room. I'll check it out."

Lau went with him, and within seconds yelled back at us, "There's some flooding here! Not major, but it's building. Don't go deep."

The greater the pressure outside, the worse the flooding inside. One of the simpler rules of piloting a damaged seacar.

"Damn it!" Kat snapped. "The structural integrity of this vessel is crucial!" She thrust out her jaw and her eyes were daggers.

"Don't worry. If we make it through this we can weld some plates over the trouble spot." I didn't want to tell her the vertical stabilizer was worse than it had been just a minute earlier. The skirmish with the lone *Fast Attack* had first damaged it over a week ago, and now it barely responded to my commands.

I glanced at the time and let out a sigh of relief. Finally, USS *Impaler* was in range. I steered toward her, began to blow tanks, and brought *SC-1* to a shallower depth.

Trailing four torpedoes.

"She's taking evasive action!" Kat cried. "Launching multiple counter-measures!"

The comm blared. It was *Impaler*. "Do not bring those weapons toward us or we will be forced to fire on you!"

"Tough shit," I said.

I wasn't turning away.

The massive warsub did not exactly move on a dime, but she was able to flood her tanks and sink below us. Her four giant thrusters cut into the water viciously, and the wake tossed our little seacar about madly.

But her countermeasures had maintained depth, and I steered straight for them. *Impaler* had launched more than ten of them, and the disturbance they created was remarkable. The mass of bubbles completely obscured our canopy, and their powerful shriek echoed through every compartment in our vessel.

The four missiles on our tail entered the disturbance, and at least one of them detonated, setting off the others in the process.

The concussion shoved *SC-1* to the starboard, and the seacar almost completely rolled over. I compensated with the controls, but it was difficult with the damaged stabilizer.

Johnny and Lau were talking loudly in the engine room, and I risked a glance behind me. I could see a spray of water back there, and the sound was louder than it had been just before the massive detonation.

"Are the pumps on?" Johnny cried.

I glanced at the console; the light on the emergency flood-control system was red. "No, it's damaged."

He swore. "We have to get that working or we're going down!"

SC-1 was foundering, and the Chinese warsubs were closing.

KAT TORE OPEN THE PANEL UNDER the console and began poking around its innards. She was looking to see if the problem with the pump was a fault in the wiring. If not, something far more serious was likely. A few moments later, she had traced the circuit back to the main junction box, and turned to yell at Johnny and Lau in the aft compartment.

"It's not up here! The pump must have malfunctioned!"

I heard one of them swear, and then the sounds of a power tool dismantling part of the bulkhead reverberated up the passageway.

Meanwhile, I kept my eyes on the ships around us. USS *Impaler* had maneuvered between us and the six remaining Chinese warsubs. We had armed our last torpedo; it was currently ready and in the tube. The flooding in *SC-1* continued unabated. Hopefully the two back there could do something about that, and fast. I had already noticed I was having to flush more water from the ballast tanks to keep us neutrally buoyant; if we took on too much through flooding, it would eventually reach a point where even with the tanks empty, we would still be heavier than the water we displaced, and we would go down.

Into the trench.

I swallowed. This definitely wasn't the best place to engage in a battle like this. If we sank, we would implode. There were no nearby seamounts to land on this time.

The sonar made a noise I'd never heard before. *Impaler* was directly in front of us, and from the bottom of her hull multiple new contacts were appearing. They were her fighter submersibles: fast, maneuverable, and each armed with four torpedoes. They swarmed from the larger vessel and began powering toward the enemy. The Chinese now would have their hands full, I thought. They would have to forget about us for the time being. At least twenty of the fighters were in the water.

I left the controls in Kat's hands and sprinted to the engine room. The deck in the living area and central passageway was ankle deep with ice-cold water. In the engine room, it was spraying in from behind the recycling equipment and arcing across the compartment toward the banks of batteries. Johnny had pulled the waterproof tarp from the ceiling down across them, and the water was hitting that and flowing to the deck. It was under great pressure, and the noise was nearly deafening.

Lau was on his knees with a panel in the bulkhead open and a mechanical device dismantled and spread out over a crate next to him. It was the flood-control pump, and it was immediately obvious why it wasn't working: one of the concussions we had taken had burned out the motor. If he didn't get it running within minutes, the water would rise to the level of the batteries and begin to short out the system. I wondered if we should just accept the inevitable and close the watertight hatch. It would mean sacrificing engineering. If we did that, we would lose power for the living area and the environmental controls, including air circulation, carbon dioxide scrubbing, and heating.

I turned to Johnny. He was trying to locate the rupture in the bulkhead behind the recycling equipment; he had begun removing its ductwork to get back to the outside hull. His face was greasy and he was completely soaked. He was shivering.

Both men were working hard to save the seacar.

"We should go outside and try to weld a plate over the damage," I said. "Before it's too late."

Johnny stopped what he was doing and looked at Lau. "Any luck over there?"

"No," came the response. "The motor is dead. I'm trying to repair it, but I couldn't find a suitable part in the repair shelf."

"There isn't one," Kat called from the front. "Sorry. You'll have to make do with what you've got."

Johnny thought for a minute, then nodded to me. "You're right. We have to stop this flooding before it gets any worse. Let's go."

GEARING UP AND GOING OUT IN the middle of a battle was not exactly ideal, but we had no other choice. We were outside in minutes, at a depth of only fifty meters. Kat had set a southerly course, and I looked back at the fighting between the American and Chinese forces. Already another *Fast Attack* was crippled and out of the fight, and one was in the process of going down. Four of *Impaler's* fighters were gone as well, hit with torpedoes and blown to bits.

Johnny and I maneuvered a plate over the breach in the hull, which was a two centimeter tear in the engine room bulkhead. Not a huge hole, but enough to let in liters of water per second. The repair was simple enough—it was the same procedure Lau had been attempting before I interrupted him— but time was crucial. We had to get it done and be back inside in case an errant torpedo—or Chinese warsub intent on destroying us—came our way.

I held the plate in position as Johnny readied the welder. He had the flame going in a few seconds—white hot and vaporizing water as it melted the steel—and bubbles were streaming to the surface as he worked.

"Strange situation we're in," he muttered.

"You can say that again."

"Look, for what it's worth, I'm sorry that we're in this mess. I just wanted to warn you and send you back to Trieste to stop Shanks."

"Unfortunately, the material you stole is too important to let China have. Shanks was clear about that."

He grunted. "And what I did to you, seven years ago?"

I paused. I simply didn't know what to say. He had betrayed me and turned me over to Sheng City during a mission. He was a traitor to Trieste. Could I find forgiveness in me for what he had done? Could I welcome him back with open arms?

It wasn't that easy. The four months in that cell had been the worst of my life. The experience had changed me forever.

He had finished two sides and went to work on the third. Almost done.

"I'm not sure," I finally managed. "It's a tough thing to ask. Especially while we're in the middle of this." I gestured around us. The sound of overlapping explosions was like thunder. The ocean lit on occasion; some flashes distant and dim, some nearby and blinding.

"I'm actually happy I'm going to see Trieste again. It felt like home when I was there earlier. It was strange, actually. I hadn't expected to feel like that. But when I went into Doctor Wells's lab, it was all so familiar. The smells, the sounds . . ." He hesitated. "It really was a welcome sensation."

I realized perhaps his time in Sheng City hadn't been all that comfortable. He had alluded to the fact that his superiors weren't that forgiving, that their operatives did not work in the same way that TCI's did, but I still didn't know exactly what his life had been like. I would have to ask about it later.

He said nothing more and concentrated on his work. Within another minute he was done, and he extinguished the torch. There was a smile on his face.

Suddenly Kat's voice pierced out, "Torpedo dead astern!"

"We're coming in now," I said. I motioned to Johnny to follow me back.

"There's no time!" she continued. "Grab something!"

I shot a look over my shoulder. Sure enough, the distinctive trail of bubbles was only a hundred meters away, headed straight for us.

"Holy shit," I muttered. I grabbed a safety rung on the hull as Johnny did the same. "Hold on!" I barked.

With a lurch, the seacar tilted and the thrusters whined. I gritted my teeth against the pain in my hands; the acceleration threatened to throw us off the hull and leave us floating in open water. Then *SC-1* angled up, and Johnny and I swung downward as the g-forces worked to pull us in a different direction.

Johnny groaned against the stress.

"Sorry!" Kat exclaimed.

"Don't be sorry," he snapped. "Just get this thing off our ass!"

Behind us, the torpedo was noticeably closer; it had followed every move Kat had made.

"Countermeasures," I groaned.

"Only one set left!"

"Do it!"

There was a sharp *clunk* nearby, and a hatch on top of the hull opened and the devices shot upward. They immediately started releasing bubbles and turning in the water. I kept my eyes on them as they fell behind us.

The torpedo approached them.

Almost there.

Almost.

"Get ready," I said to Johnny. "When it goes, it's gonna—"

The explosion was massive. The amount of water vaporized was greater than any previous detonation we had seen. Either this one was an American torpedo, or the lower pressure at our current depth had resulted in a larger detonation. Whatever the case, the sphere of empty space created by the heat was so large that when the ocean crashed back in to fill the void, the concussion it created instantly hurled the stern of *SC-1* to the side. The pain in my hands was now excruciating. We slid back against the edge of the rung, and both of our legs now dangled upward, toward the surface.

The explosion had shoved *SC-1* down, into the depths.

Johnny cried out as he lost his grip. I let go with one hand, reached out to him, and grasped him around the wrist.

"Hang on!" I yelled. "Grab my arm!"

He did so, but he was struggling. My own grip on the rung was slipping. The seacar was still tumbling downward, and the stress of the plunge threatened to pull us both from the vessel.

The pressure began to mount. I could feel it in my ears. Equalizing was difficult under these conditions, and I could see my own pain mirrored in Johnny's features. "Hang tough, buddy," I whispered. "Don't let go." I had him by one arm, his body dangling behind. He clenched his teeth and locked his eyes to mine. His grip was tight, and within a few seconds the ship had stopped moving. Kat had cut the thrusters and was waiting for word that we were okay. I reeled him back to the hull. He was panting from exertion, too tired to speak, but he was unhurt. We had lost the welder, though—a small price to pay for survival.

"Say something!" Kat yelled. She had given up being patient, and sounded desperate to hear from me.

Somehow I managed to find the humor in the situation, and I grinned. "Say what?"

"You asshole! I thought you were gone!"

"You can't get rid of me, Kat. Haven't you figured that out yet?"

"Asshole," she muttered again, but I could tell that she was happy.

Johnny was staring at me, and I turned to him. "What's wrong?"

He shook his head. "Nothing," he whispered. But I could tell something deeply troubled him. The near-death had shaken him up, and no doubt emotions were roiling just beneath the surface. I said nothing, however, and merely grinned at his pale and shocked expression.

Together we moved toward the airlock, back into the safety of the seacar, and prepared ourselves for the short decompression.

LAU WAS STILL AT WORK ON the pump. He had locked himself in the engine room to work; the water was now over his waist—high enough to enter the control cabin at the bow of the ship. To keep it out of there, he had sealed the watertight hatch, placing himself in immense danger. We had repaired the breach and the water was no longer rising, but until he got the pump working, he was in there with the cold. He still had his wetsuit on, which gave him some protection, but I knew the working conditions were brutal. His hands were probably numb by now, his teeth chattering as he labored to finish.

Johnny and I sloshed our way through the living area—still ankle-deep—and found Kat in the control cabin, looking back at us with anxiety clear in her features.

"Sorry about that," she said. "Had no choice."

"Who fired it?" I asked.

"It was American, from one of those tiny fighters."

"Aimed at us? Or a stray?"

She shrugged. "Hard to tell."

I studied the sonar and watched the battle that still raged between the two forces. "Look at that, Johnny. China and America in open conflict. Lives are being lost."

"It's not the first time. It happens more often than you'd think."

"So I've heard." I recalled Blake saying the same thing minutes before he'd died at the hands of a Chinese assassin. Things were definitely getting out of hand. War now felt more likely than ever, especially as the rumble of distant concussions shook the ship.

Our speed was fifty kph, slightly slower due to our increased weight, but we were moving farther and farther from the battle.

We had escaped.

For now.

A different vibration suddenly started, and I glanced at Kat for confirmation. She peered at a control on the console, and a smile lit her face. "He did it. The pump is clearing the engine room."

It had been a close call—several of them, actually—but we were going to be okay. We had survived the battle. As the pump worked, our speed increased, and soon we were back at seventy.

And then Johnny spoiled the mood.

"It's not over," he whispered. "There are more forces on their way."

I paled. "How many?"

He turned to me. "*A lot.* Those eight ships were just the closest ones when I called for help. There's an entire fleet coming. They'll intercept us between here and Panama." He hesitated. "And when we meet, we won't have a hope in hell."

CHAPTER TWENTY-TWO

WE PUSHED SOUTH INTO WARMER WATERS. We left the Aleutian Trench behind and were soon over the Aleutian abyssal plain. Then over the Mendocino Fracture Zone, the Murray Seascarp, and, seventy-one hours after the battle, we were on approach to the Clarion Fracture Zone, 5000 kilometers from the Aleutians. The Hawaiian Ridge was to our west. We had all expected to immediately encounter a Chinese or American force, and yet the only traffic we passed were standard shipping vessels carrying cargoes of methane or hydrogen. It surprised us. We knew they would be coming, however, sooner or later, and every time I glanced at the sonar I expected it to be full of contacts identified with a CSF or USSF tag.

During that time, with the seacar seaworthy once again, we settled into something of a routine. The living arrangements were cramped. Johnny and Lau slept on the small couches in the lounge, while Kat and I continued to sleep in our respective bunks. The mood was sometimes tense, as Kat was still angry at the two men for stealing her material, and they did not pretend to be oblivious to it. They generally stayed out of her way and interacted only with each other or with me.

Days earlier I had been gunning for Johnny; I'd wanted nothing more than to catch and kill him. And then the meeting at the French base had changed everything. It was an odd feeling, to say the least. He had appealed to my love for Trieste as the reasoning behind his actions. Everything he had done, Johnny claimed, was the morally correct thing. And when I sat back and thought about it—*really* thought about it, objectively—I realized that he was absolutely correct. I could have done without the torture in Sheng City, but his explanation made sense. He had to prove to his new superiors he was obedient and willing to follow orders. Too bad for me, but for him it was either that or face death.

He had come to believe my assertion that Sheng City Intelligence was playing him, that they knew he had been trying to contact me to warn me about Shanks. But Chinese intelligence *wanted* us in a conflict with America so they could step in as our allies and pull us away from the States. Johnny was right—it would start a war, and at this point in our journey, I realized both sides seemed to want that pretty badly. It would be difficult to stop.

According to the news, things were not going well in The Iron Plains. NATO had backed the United States, while The East Asia Economic Block had backed China—two alliances squaring off against one another, as had happened prior to World War I. Tensions over the Plains were high. All it would take was one event to start another war. Back in 1914 it had been an assassination in Sarajevo. Now, with everything going on around us, the conflict we had just caused over the Aleutian Trench could very well be that trigger.

The first night following the battle, after Lau had repaired the pump and drained the water from the ship, I found Johnny sitting on the couch in the lounge. He looked downcast. I sat with him to talk; we kept our voices low to prevent the others from overhearing.

"What's on your mind?" I asked.

He glanced at me, pursed his lips, then looked away. "Why'd you save me?"

I shrugged. "To get you back to Trieste. Orders—"

"Don't give me that," he snapped. "You never obeyed orders you didn't believe in."

I paused. I knew I had to be honest with him. He could see right through me. "It's true that I never intended to bring you back."

"Then why do it now?"

"Because I realized that you deserve the chance to defend yourself. What you did back then, you did for a reason. It's taken me a long time to understand, but I guess I do now."

"You could have let me go out there. I would have been a goner. When the torpedo detonated . . . it would have incinerated me. It would have solved all your problems."

"That's not true. I still have to worry about Shanks. If he is planning war with the States, I have to stop it."

"Do you believe me now about that too?"

I paused. "Perhaps, though I need to see the evidence with my own eyes. But Kat said something earlier along those lines as well." I shot a look up the passageway toward the control cabin, where she sat silently with Lau. "She knows something she's not telling me. She's aware of Shanks's plans."

"Why won't she talk?"

"I think when he recruited her he told her everything. She's worked all her life for the colonies. She's dreamed of our independence since she was a kid. Shanks probably knew it and told her in confidence what he was planning. And now she feels obligated to keep the secret."

"Despite the fact that he's such an oily prick."

I snorted. "She doesn't know that yet. She doesn't have the same history with him that we do."

He looked at me. "Once again, thanks for saving my life back there."

"All in a day's work." Though taking him back to Trieste could be a death sentence. I knew it, and so did he. He was a traitor, after all.

He was still staring at me. He said, "Did you really mean that you would get me out if I was right about Shanks?"

I sighed. "Yes. But I'm not sure what I'm going to do about him. He'll have the support of a huge portion of the colony."

He thought about that for a beat. "Your dad was Frank McClusky. He's still adored by Triestrians. And you too, as a result. Surely you could capitalize on that."

I had already considered that and had come to the conclusion it would only help if I supported independence. If I didn't, they would most likely turn their backs on me. When I mentioned this to Johnny, however, he did not agree.

"They trust you," he said. "I don't think they would treat you lightly."

If it came down to a fight between me and Shanks, it would be tough for the city. Some people would side with him, and if some joined me, it could mean civil war, which might be far worse than the alternatives.

This was a tricky dilemma—something that, at that moment, I saw no way out of.

"I wouldn't want anything bad to happen to the city either," Johnny muttered. He knew exactly what I had been thinking; just like old times.

"Really?" I asked, with a touch of sarcasm to my tone. I immediately regretted it, but said nothing.

"Sure. I practically grew up there, like you. I worked for TCI for almost as long as you. We went on similar missions."

"But you just couldn't get past the fact that there were Chinese prisoners there."

His eyes grew hard. "No—it was the fact that he was torturing them. I couldn't get past that."

"Oh."

We sat in silence for a while, and eventually he started to talk about his life in Sheng. About how the authorities constantly watched him, despite the fact that he was one of their operatives. They watched everyone. Civilians especially. They were everywhere, just waiting for someone to say something derogatory about the life people were forced to lead. They took those caught away for re-education; those unfortunate souls later returned far different than the people they had once been.

The government there was very demanding. Citizens couldn't just pick an occupation; one was forced on them after a rigorous screening process that took education, training, and psychological testing into consideration. Press, religion, politics—it was all dictated. There were few freedoms and not many were happy with their lives. Johnny said it was the same in all their undersea cities.

I listened to all of this in dead silence. Part of me was incredulous at the fact he hadn't expected it. But then again, he had never thought the things we heard from our own media were one hundred percent accurate. He had thought it was all an exaggeration, that people would never treat others in that way. When he said that I almost jumped in shock; this coming from a man who had killed when necessary to avoid capture. Someone who had tortured his own friend!

His journey to Sheng City, needless to say, had been extremely difficult for him.

Despite his uncertain future, a big part of me felt Johnny was actually happy with our current situation. Happy that China had seen right through him, that he had been forced to turn his allegiance back to Trieste. And now here he was, on his way back, and for the first time in seven years, he actually felt normal again. Regardless of what might happen with Shanks, he was going home, and nothing Shanks could do could take that away from him. I shuddered at that, but said nothing and left him to his thoughts.

The following night we had our first dinner together. Kat was silent through much of it, and Johnny and Lau spoke only to each other. I asked them to use English for her benefit, and they accepted without complaint. They did not want to aggravate her further. I spoke with Lau for a bit about his family in Trieste, and he smiled as he remembered his visits to the city and the times he had spent with his cousins.

Later, when Johnny and Lau were asleep, I moved forward and found Kat in the control cabin. I slid in next to her and touched her arm. "Relax," I said. "It's going to be all right."

"Those two make me nervous," she hissed. "Shouldn't we tie them up or something?"

I glanced back toward the couches; the two were silent and motionless under their blankets. "I considered that. But I think I convinced them that the Chinese were onto them."

"Still, we can't be a hundred percent sure."

She was right about that. But I didn't want to travel the entire way to Trieste with the two of them tied up. "They worked hard to save the ship."

"To save *themselves*, more like it."

"True. But don't forget they helped us avoid the torpedoes and mines. We were able to sink two warsubs as a result. I don't think they would have let us do that if they meant to later kill us. They could have done it right there."

She was silent for a long moment as she stared out the canopy. Then, "I guess you're right. Still, I can't get over the fact that they were the ones who stole my material. I ought to hurt them for that."

"They're hurt, don't worry. They can't go home now, and all that waits for them at Trieste is a cold prison cell."

She had taken the theft of her work personally, and rightfully so. But Johnny had been correct in saying that it happened all the time. Our spies were constantly working to steal new technologies, to discredit others, to monitor military movements and elections in undersea cities around the world. French, British, Chinese—it was all the same. But at that moment, sitting with her in the control cabin, it would simply have been the wrong thing to say.

Instead I was silent, and I just sat and watched the ocean with her. For some reason, I suddenly found myself thinking about the United States and Israel, and how they had become independent nations. I couldn't shake the feeling it had something to do with all of this. Something about Kat and what she had meant when she first mentioned that . . .

"You think they'll be coming?" she said finally, interrupting my thoughts.

"Yes."

"Who? The Chinese, or the Americans?"

"Both, probably. But most likely the Chinese will get us first. They know what your secret is. We're still not sure if the USSF is aware, or if they're just curious about what the hell we're up to. The Chinese are more motivated." And Johnny seemed pretty sure of it, as well.

"How are we going to get away from them this time?" she asked. Her eyes held more than a hint of fear. And yet under it, I sensed something else. It was difficult to interpret.

I chewed my lip. "I'm not sure, to be honest." We had only one torpedo left, and no countermeasures. Our batteries were running low and would need charging in a few days. The damaged stabilizer was giving us more problems; it was growing harder and harder to steer because of it. It had been a grueling voyage, but I knew there were more obstacles before us.

It was night topside, and the moon could not penetrate to our current depth. Our running lamps and floodlights were off. The light from the control panels was the only illumination in the seacar. I noticed in the shadows that Kat's lips had parted slightly, and her eyes were focused tightly on mine.

"Thanks for all you've done," she said in the awkward silence.

"Just doing—"

"Please don't say 'your job.' It's more than that, I can tell. Your thirst for revenge drove you at the start, but now there's something else to it. I know you care about Trieste."

"Are you going to fill me in on what Shanks is planning?"

She shook her head. "Sorry, Mac. I can't. I'll leave that for him, when we return."

"He'll tell me then?"

She shrugged. "I'll force him to." She was still looking at me, and now it was her hand on my arm. She was caressing it lightly. And then she leaned in and kissed me. It was tentative at first, but quickly turned hard and passionate. Her tongue stroked my lips, and abruptly pushed deep into my mouth. I moved my arms around her and pulled her to me.

I'm not sure if it happened because there were real feelings between us, or if living together in the cramped confines had just developed into a physical attraction. The constant danger we'd been living under might have played a part as well, but I did have an emotional connection to her, there was no doubt about that. She was a caring, considerate, passionate, and deeply intelligent woman who had dedicated her life to underwater living. Sometimes she was rash, angry, and obstinate, but I understood her passion and her drive to see our underwater colonies succeed. I found it highly attractive.

We crept silently back to her bunk and the two of us squeezed inside. I closed the curtain and we hurriedly undressed one another. Her dark skin glinted in the dim light, and I eagerly pushed myself into her as she wrapped her thighs around me. She groaned slightly at first, then began to breathe harder as we made love.

SC-1 moved silently through the waters a kilometer down, cruising southward at maximum speed in the inky black, and within its cramped confines, two strangers thrown together on a deadly mission desperately made love as if it was the last night they would ever share.

THE NEXT MORNING WE ROSE BEFORE the others and slowly made breakfast. We exchanged fleeting glances, sharing a secret that neither Johnny nor Lau knew, smiling together at what had happened. Kat had been incredible in bed; I hadn't been with anyone for a long time, and in fact realized now I had been extremely lonely these past few years. Ever since 2122, the year of Johnny Chang's defection and my resignation from TCI.

We ate breakfast together, and finally Kat began to make small talk with Johnny and Lau. I noticed Johnny throw me a quizzical look—with eyebrows raised—and I merely shrugged and suppressed a grin. Then his expression turned to one of complete understanding, and I realized he really knew me better than anyone else.

Soon we had arrived at the Clarion Fracture Zone. It was a rift region, the separation point between tectonic plates, much like the Mid-Atlantic Ridge, but the undersea mountains here were far smaller. As a result, the waters below were deeper than they had been in the Atlantic, but the same intense geologic activity occurred there as in any rift zone. Geothermal vents, underwater volcanoes, earthquakes.

We were preparing to shift course southeast, toward Central America, when a shrill sound hit the ship and echoed through its interior.

"Oh, shit," Johnny muttered from my side. The two of us were in the control cabin, and both of us looked immediately to the sonar. Someone had pinged us from the southeast.

Someone who now knew our exact location.

Someone who was directly in our path.

I sent our own active pulse, and immediately the screen lit with multiple contacts.

Johnny swore. "Over fifty warsubs. All Chinese. Between us and the Americas."

And we had to go through them to get home.

"I reached the bottom in a state of transport . . . To halt and hang attached to nothing, no lines or air pipes to the surface, was a dream. At night I often had visions of flying by extending my arms as wings. Now I flew without wings."

—Captain Jacques-Yves Cousteau, Ocean Explorer, Inventor, and Innovator

PART FIVE: THE CLARION FRACTURE ZONE

Twenty

二十三 CHAPTER
TWENTY-THREE

THE FLEET WAS ONLY A HUNDRED kilometers away, driving for us at fifty kph. My eyes widened as I read the list of vessels in our path. They represented every attack class in the Chinese Submarine Fleet: twenty-nine *Jins*, three *Shangs*, seven *Yuans*, four *Hans*, a *Tong*, two *Kilos*, five *Soongs*, and two *Mings*. There were also a few SSBGN warsubs capable of carrying ballistic missiles such as the *Yans* and the *Xias*. Their presence was an implication of how far the Chinese were willing to take this; an indication they were escalating due to *Impaler*'s actions three days earlier. I had worried the battle over the Aleutian Trench could trigger a war, and it seemed as though my fears might come to pass. If those ships came into contact with a USSF force . . .

I swallowed.

"It's a goddamn barricade," Johnny muttered. "There's no way we can get through that."

I sat and stared at the sonar for long minutes. Then I got to my feet and walked to engineering. The others watched me, curious, but I ignored them.

All evidence of the flooding was gone; Lau had done a superb repair job, and Johnny had returned the recycling equipment to its previous state. I stood in front of the small, concealed, watertight hatch in the rear bulkhead and stared at the digital panel beside it. Kat had claimed it opened into the emergency ballast compartment. It was bullshit, of course, but I hadn't pushed her then.

It was time now.

I grabbed a tool from the rack and opened the panel quickly and efficiently. I located the proper wires, cross connected them, and within a minute it slid open at my command. It was a skill I had learned early in my career, and I was glad it was still useful.

There was a cabin within. It was part of engineering; the aft bulkhead simply separated the two chambers. Along the bulkheads on all sides were electronic gauges, readouts, and display screens that were currently dark. In the center of the enclosure was a freestanding control console of some sort. Piping snaked along the ceiling toward the rear of the room, where it entered a—

What the hell?

At first I had no idea what I was looking at. The pipes wound their way toward a metallic sphere. There were projections jutting from it at various angles, and wiring and tubing on its surface connected to sensors and equipment on the deck. On the far side of the . . . the *device* was a large cylindrical conduit—thick, reinforced steel—that extended a very short distance to the exterior bulkhead at the aft end of the ship.

I stared at the curious room and the bizarre contraption for what seemed an eternity. And then several things began to fall into place in my mind. Things that had happened over the last several days, things I had heard and seen.

And then it came to me.

I finally had an idea of what was going on.

THE OTHERS WERE IN THE LOUNGE. They had brought the seacar to a dead stop and were waiting for me to return to review our options. The Chinese fleet was steadily approaching; we didn't have much time.

But there was only one thing I wanted to discuss.

"Kat," I said slowly and deliberately. "It's time you told me about your invention."

She shook her head. "Sorry, Mac. I can't—"

"I said it's time," I ground out. She took a step back at my tone, shocked at the steel in my voice.

But she said nothing.

I grunted. "Then perhaps *I'll* tell you, shall I?" I gestured to a chair. "Sit down."

Stunned by the sudden change in my demeanor, she sank to the chair and waited.

I began to pace before the three of them, wondering how best to start my explanation. The only way to get Kat to talk was to prove I already knew the truth and there was no point holding anything back from me. There was a lot to discuss, and it took some time, but at last I had my thoughts organized. "I knew something was odd the night we first met, Kat. The first time I saw this seacar." Her eyes widened for just a moment, and in that brief instant, I knew I had her full and complete attention. "When I went to the Docking Module to see Shanks and Flint before we left, the shape of this vessel caught my eye. For one, the bow is unique. It's blunt, something that's not exactly frictionless in water. Furthermore, the thruster pods are located farther from the hull than is normal. I also noticed that the stabilizers are quite thick, which I had originally assumed was for ballast. I realize now I was dead wrong."

Complete silence met my comments. Johnny and Lau were staring at me, no doubt wondering exactly where I was going with this.

And I didn't disappoint. "And then *Impaler*'s First Officer entered the module. As he neared, Shanks gave you a very interesting order. Do you remember what it was?"

She nodded. "He asked me to descend a few meters."

"Which you did. You were trying to get the seacar out of his sight. What's more, when I mentioned the shape of the vessel, Mayor Flint immediately interrupted. She was quite rude about it. She was trying to distract me. Am I right?" She didn't respond, and I shrugged. "I guess it doesn't matter, because over the course of the next few days I noticed some truly bizarre things about *SC-1*. First, there's the obvious: it can dive deeper than any current military warsub and most civilian seacars. Second: it's *fast*, especially considering its shape. The only way it can get up to the speeds it's capable of is through its large arrays of batteries."

"That's true, but I already told you—"

I ignored her. "I noticed something else interesting that first day out of Trieste. When I commented on the poor engineering in the engine room—the proximity of ballast pipes to electronics—it set you off. At first I thought you were angry at our disagreement over the prospect of another fight for independence. But I was wrong. You've grown upset now several times, whenever I commented negatively about *SC-1*. At first I just figured that you weren't the most social person, but I know better now. My criticism of the seacar had *offended* you."

She clamped her jaw shut.

I pressed on. "You even claimed there was no problem having the pipes in the engine room. And this, from someone with a doctorate in aquanautic engineering, someone who knew the story of *Thresher*!" She still didn't respond, so I continued. "Furthermore, Kat, you even alluded to the fact that this seacar is experimental. When I asked about the VID system, which I had never seen before because of my long absence from the intelligence business, you said that 'not many private seacars have one.'"

"Well, that's true," she finally answered, "but we're on a mission for TCI now, aren't we?"

"But there's a reason we're using this seacar. Do you deny that?"

"I'm not saying anything about it."

"Then I'll keep going." I glared at her for a moment. She was still playing dumb, acting like I wasn't on the right track. "Then there's the large space behind the engine room. I had thought for a while it might be for emergency ballast, something you yourself claimed later. But why seal it with a digital keypad that needed a secret code? That makes no sense, if all that's back there are pellets of lead or osmium. So Kat, the question for you is: What exactly is in there?"

"I told you, it's just emergency—"

"Cut the bullshit. I've been there. I've seen it."

She bolted to her feet. "How dare you! You have no right to—"

"I have *every* right to!" I bellowed. "We're less than two hours from the Chinese fleet—and perhaps from *war*—and you need to fill me in on exactly what's going on!" I paused and took several breaths to calm myself. But I couldn't stop yet—there was so much more to say. "After the first battle with the *Fast Attack*, you were trying to repair the systems that shorted during a fire. There was damaged wiring in the main panel."

"That's right. I was replacing it."

"But when I looked closer, I saw you were repairing circuits that weren't even part of the main controls on the seacar! One was marked 'containment.'" As I said it I studied her reaction closely. "Containment for what, Kat?"

She looked flustered. "I don't know. I was just putting things back to the way they were."

I sighed. I was now growing exasperated by her act. "After being out at the bottom of the Atlantic, I decompressed and then passed out in my bunk. But you kept working on those circuits. You repaired them when I was unconscious. If they weren't important, why worry about them when there were more pressing matters?"

She stuttered as she said, "Just to get the ship back in working—"

"Bullshit. You're telling outright lies now. I think I deserve better."

She stopped suddenly at the jab and her eyes softened slightly. "Mac, I don't want to lie to you, really."

"Then why do it?"

She huffed and turned away. I glanced at Johnny and Lau. Both were watching the scene, intensely curious.

Back to Kat. "And during the battle with the *Fast Attack*, when it seemed as though we were about to sink, I saw you looking at the section of the console that's sealed with an unmarked panel. I noticed it my first night on *SC-1*. What's in there, exactly?"

"It's nothing; I was just concerned with the ship."

"Why?"

"Because we're in it, of course! If anything happened to it, we'd be dead!"

"Is that why you were so upset when the torpedo caused the breach in the engine room?"

She looked confused. "What? I was upset because our lives were at risk."

I shook my head. "Sorry. You said—and in anger, I might add—'*The structural integrity of this vessel is crucial.*' What did you mean?"

She snorted. "Just how it sounds. I didn't want to sink."

"No. There's more to it than that." I paused. "Like the thicker stabilizers and the thruster pods placed so far from the hull."

"I'd hardly call three meters far."

"Farther than most, then."

She shrugged. "Whatever. It doesn't mean anything."

"Maybe they're for increased support." I stared at her, waiting. Johnny and Lau were as still as death. They understood what I was doing, and had clearly decided to just sit back and let me do it.

"Why don't you finish this for me, Kat?" I said in a soft voice.

"How? Finish what?"

"Explain what field your education is in."

A frown. "I told you, my doctorate is in aquanautic engineering."

"Yes, but you never told me about the other one." She had mentioned to me on the first day that she had two doctorates, but had only told me about one. It had struck me as odd at the time, but not suspicious. Now, I needed to know.

Her mouth closed suddenly. She eyed Johnny and Lau, then turned back to me. "It's in theoretical aquanautic engineering."

Perfect, I thought. That made total sense. *Theoretical* engineering.

"And what were you studying after that?" There were still missing years in her story. She had been doing something for quite a while after her second doctorate, before Shanks had recruited her.

"Electrical generation," she whispered.

Ah. Another piece of the puzzle. "You also said you were in Florida, Kat, after agreeing to work for Shanks. Can you tell us what you were doing there?"

She was glaring at me now, and she snapped, "You're so brilliant, why don't *you* tell everyone what I was doing!"

I shrugged. "Easy. You were overseeing the construction of this seacar. The seacar that you designed."

HER NOSTRILS HAD FLARED AND SHE was breathing heavily. "How do you—"

"I put two and two together. You told me that a private firm in Clearwater had built *SC-1*. That's where you were when Shanks convinced you to come to Trieste. Am I right?"

She was silent for a long beat. She seemed to be hesitant because Johnny and Lau were there. However, she could tell I would not let up. Finally, she deflated, and said, barely loud enough to hear, "You're right, of course."

Something we had discussed earlier came back to me, and another piece of the puzzle fell into place. She felt a nation could not achieve independence without fighting for it. I said, "You designed and built this seacar, Kat, with one purpose in mind." I paused. The silence in the cabin seemed absolute. No one even breathed. "You built it to fight a war, didn't you? A war of independence against the United States."

She looked up at me, but not in anger. Her eyes were accepting now, as if she was ready to admit everything. She nodded. "Yes. I designed *SC-1* for war."

"And what is that in the compartment behind the engine room?"

"It's a device for energy generation."

Johnny stormed to his feet. "You mean that you've actually *built* it? That this seacar is *it*?"

I shot a look at him. "What are you talking about? Do you mean—" And then I stopped. A prickly sensation moved down my back. Of course. It all made sense now. The invention he had stolen, the one I was still in the dark about—it was in this very ship! Johnny knew what he had taken from her files, but hadn't actually realized there was a working prototype! No wonder he was so shocked.

"What is it exactly, Kat?" I asked. "What's so special about this seacar?"

She sighed. "I promised Shanks I wouldn't say anything. He threatened to kick me out of Trieste if anyone found out about it before he could set his plans in motion."

"For independence."

"Right."

"I don't think it matters now. We know all about it. I've *seen* it in the aft compartment." I gestured at Johnny. "He knows what it is too. If you don't tell me, he's going to." I grabbed her gently around the shoulders. "Please. Tell me now. What did you invent?"

She looked at each of us in turn. Then, "The thing you saw back there is a fusion reactor."

She said it in such a matter-of-fact tone that it caught me off guard. I almost didn't register the meaning for a few moments. "But the ones topside are massive. They're the size of buildings."

"Which is why this technology is so important for Trieste. And why China wants it."

I considered that. "But there's more, isn't there?"

"Yes. The fusion reactor isn't just used for power. It's a source of propulsion for *SC-1*."

I hesitated. "Fusion propulsion? Underwater?" I didn't understand.

She nodded. "It's actually a simple concept, Mac, something that scientists have been discussing for a while. The reactor produces enormous heat. The pipes you saw aren't for ballast—but they are for water."

It only took me an instant to figure out. I fell into a chair and gasped. "My God. They carry water to the reactor, which flash boils it to steam. The steam is forced from the aft end of the hull under enormous pressure. It creates thrust for the seacar. *Steam* thrust."

"Precisely." She extended a small smile. "Would you believe I've created a steam-powered seacar?"

I shook my head. "But that doesn't make sense. The maximum speed a sub can go is eighty kilometers per hour. We've already hit that. Friction and drag with water limit—"

"This seacar can go a lot faster."

I frowned. "But that's impossible."

"It's not Mac. It's very possible, and I did it. And *SC-1* has the technology." She reached out to give my hand a squeeze. Her expression said it all: she had been uncomfortable withholding this secret from me, but now that it was out, she was relieved. All the guilt and worry I had seen in her expressions over the past week or more had been because of this. Our relationship had

reached a level that dictated honesty. But now everything was all right, because I finally knew.

And she hadn't had to tell me—I had figured it out on my own.

Mostly.

Johnny now had a hint of a smile on his face. "I can't believe it. The Chinese government had no idea Kat had actually built the thing—and in a seacar this size! It's revolutionary!"

"I told you I would do anything for the undersea cities, Mac," she said. "And I did. I built this." She gestured around her.

"A seacar with a fusion reactor and an experimental propulsion system."

"That's right."

Several seconds passed as a thought slowly crystalized in my mind. After the fighting in the Fracture Zone around the French base, she could have activated the drive and easily caught Johnny, and yet she hadn't. I recalled seeing a look cross her face during the chase. She had been thinking then about using her invention, but knew if she did, I would learn the truth—and Shanks had ordered her not to let that happen.

And then something else occurred to me.

"Wait a minute!" I shouted. "You let me go outside four kilometers down to repair the thrusters! I didn't even have to!"

She lowered her gaze to the deck. "I'm sorry, Mac. But remember the fire had damaged the circuits to the fusion reactor. I still had to repair them."

"But we could have focused on that!"

"I couldn't activate it. I promised Shanks."

I ground my teeth. "I could have died, Kat." Going out had been immensely dangerous—a massive understatement!—but I had done so in order to catch Johnny and regain the stolen material. And it hadn't been necessary. I swore to myself. "Why risk my death?"

"I—I didn't want to. But there didn't seem to be any other option. You seemed so confident about it, and the drive was down. . . ."

I held my head in my hands and thought about it. She did have a point, but still, I had come close to death. Perhaps we should have just repaired the reactor and lied to Shanks about it. "Kat," I finally mumbled. "Just how fast will this thing get the seacar going?"

Her brow crinkled. "Oh, I'd say about 450 kilometers per hour."

OUR JAWS HIT THE DECK. EVERYTHING that we had previously learned told us that it simply wasn't possible.

"Four hundred and fifty kilometers per hour, *underwater*?" I muttered.

"Oh, drag with water is not an insurmountable problem," Kat replied. "Conventional propulsion has an upper limit, sure. But supercavitation is anything but conventional."

"Supercavitation?" I had heard of cavitation, of course—every conshelfer and submariner had—but had never heard the prefix *super* before it.

Cavitation was a relatively simple concept, but to fully understand it, one must first accept that the boiling point of water was not a constant. Under lower atmospheric pressures it will boil faster than at higher pressures, which is why it's quicker to make a cup of tea in Denver than in, say, New York. A similar process will occur underwater. Around a screw blade, pressures can reach a point low enough for water to boil at very cold temperatures. Poorly designed screws, or those that spin too quickly, generally caused it. In cavitation, when the bubbles emerge from the surrounding water into higher pressures, they will immediately implode and can damage the screw blades. This also creates unwanted noise.

"This seacar can use cavitation," she said, "but on a much greater scale."

Johnny's brow crinkled. "But what does a cavitating screw have to do with generating high speeds underwater? There's still the issue of drag to worry about. Water's a very dense medium."

"True, but as I said, there is a way around it. It was first achieved by the Soviets in the 1970s. They invented a torpedo called the *Shkval* that could travel at about 350 kilometers per hour. We can use the same process, but instead of a torpedo, we surround an entire seacar with something that is almost frictionless in water."

He frowned. "What do you mean, *surround*? With a coating of some kind? A layer of Teflon or—"

"No, you've got it all wrong. It's not something that's put *on* the vessel. But it is something that *envelops* it."

I thought about that for a moment, and began to put the pieces of information together. A cavitating screw created bubbles, which was why torpedoes and subs sometimes left trails in the water. Kat had said that something *surrounded* the seacar, something that could reduce a seacar's friction—

And then I realized what she meant—but it didn't seem possible.

She was watching me in silence. She could tell I had hit on something.

"Can surrounding *SC-1* in a *bubble* reduce drag?" I asked.

She grinned. "Exactly. That's what the Soviets did all those years ago. They created a torpedo that cut through the water in such a way that the water at the torpedo's nose reached extremely low pressures. A bubble formed—but not a series of small ones that shot to the surface. This was so large that it stretched back and encompassed the entire weapon! It then became almost exactly like a cruise missile or an air-to-air missile in the sky. It used a rocket engine for propulsion."

I swore. Avoiding a torpedo like that would be nearly impossible, especially in a seacar at such a relatively slow speed.

There were deep lines in Johnny's brow. "So the bubble encircles the entire projectile."

"Yes."

We digested that for a few moments. I said, "And *SC-1* is a supercavitating vehicle. You applied the concept to a far larger object—an entire seacar."

"Yes, but there have been others before me. One American back in the early twenty-first century reportedly created a submersible missile that traveled at over 5000 kph. Imagine such a velocity! It broke the speed of sound underwater—a remarkable feat."

I shook my head. The ramifications were enormous; the invention would change travel completely. It could also be as great an advancement in naval warfare as nations had ever experienced. It would, however, most likely be dangerous for animals. Speeds of that magnitude would create immense

noise—it was a rocket, after all—and the effects on marine life could be devastating. Many beached whales had shown signs of damage to the audio-sensory regions of their brains. Could supercavitation tests be to blame?

Johnny was now realizing the importance of the technology. "And the fusion reactor you invented for *SC-1* provides the thrust," he muttered. "The seawater is readily available . . . the process just turns it to steam."

"And the blunt nose creates the low pressure," I finished for him. "The bubble stretches back to surround the ship, and before you know it, you're flying underwater."

Kat smiled. "That's exactly it. It's not even that complicated a process. There was just one real obstacle to it. Well, two actually."

"Creating a reliable source of propulsion that didn't run out. And you've done it." Johnny exhaled forcefully. "It's fantastic, Doctor Wells. Really. The Chinese government had no idea. We just thought it was a new energy generator."

She snarled. "It's far more than that. And you took everything I had on it."

Her background now made complete sense. Her doctorates in aquanautic engineering, theoretical aquanautic engineering, and her studies in electrical generation contributed to *SC-1*'s design. The fusion reactor most likely provided electrical power for the ship at the same time as the thrust.

"What was the other obstacle?" I asked.

"How to pilot inside a bubble. With no surfaces interacting with water, steering became a major issue."

That's why the yoke looked more like it belonged on an airplane. I remembered thinking as much the first time I'd seen the control cabin. *SC-1* was literally a plane that doubled as a submarine. Or vice versa. It was difficult to decide exactly what it was, really. "The control surfaces on the horizontal stabilizers are similar to ailerons on an airplane. I even thought of them as such."

"Yes. They work in the same way."

Something else occurred to me. The name of the seacar, *SC-1*. I had thought that it simply meant *SeaCar-1*. It didn't at all. It stood for *SuperCavitating-1*. The secret had been right there all along.

It was a remarkable invention that would no doubt make a huge difference for Trieste in the political realities of ocean colonization. Shanks had said this, but I had thought it an exaggeration. But now I realized that *SC-1* and seacars—or warsubs—like her would tip the balance of power in our favor. No nation could stand up to a ship like it.

Not even the United States.

A jolt shot through me.

"Holy shit," I breathed. "Using this ship—and others like her, probably—Shanks will utterly destroy the USSF, and they won't even know what hit them."

Kat smiled. She didn't seem to object to the notion. "Most likely."

THAT WAS WHY SHE HAD SAID that her invention would help Trieste achieve independence. Shanks wanted the prototype back and the material out from Chinese hands. If they found out about *SC-1*—or *SCAV-1*—it would change everything.

I continued to think about that as we sat quietly in the lounge in the cramped living area. The Chinese fleet was approaching—their active sonar continued to ping us every few minutes—and yet what Kat had created had completely stunned us. Of course I assumed we could just use the drive to escape, but I realized if we did so, China would discover what we had.

An idea began to percolate in the recesses of my mind. Something that could get Trieste out of this situation. . . .

"How does the reactor work?" I muttered. "And the drive?"

"I'll show you," she said. "Come with me."

"THESE CONDUITS CONTAIN SEAWATER," SHE SAID, pointing at the pipes over our heads. We were in the secret engineering compartment, examining the reactor and drive. "It enters the seacar through the bow, right at the blunt nose. They carry it through the bulkheads, into this chamber."

I grunted. The pipes still carried water through areas they shouldn't, just like *Thresher*.

Kat noticed and blushed. "You were right to criticize it, you know. That's why I got so defensive. But the problem is there simply wasn't another place to put them. They *have* to come into this area, to bring water to the reactor. It's an unavoidable problem."

"Perhaps future models can improve on this one."

She frowned at that. "Maybe." Her tone was clipped.

"Is it just seawater that's boiled?" I continued.

"Yes, but some processing happens first. We need fuel for the reactor. Deuterium and tritium."

Both were types of hydrogen: H_2 and H_3 respectively. They were removed straight from the seawater.

"We do that here." She patted a device on the deck just before the reactor. "The oxygen created as a byproduct goes into the recycling system." She turned to the sphere. "This is the Vacuum Confinement Capsule, or the VCC. The projections you see here are injectors that introduce the fuel into the chamber. Our batteries heat it, and along with high frequency radio waves, the temperature increases rapidly to two hundred million degrees Celsius."

I gasped. I didn't understand much about fusion power, just that industrialized nations of the planet had made the switch in the 2060s. But the temperature created an obvious problem. "Why doesn't the capsule melt?"

"At that point the heat creates plasma, or a superhot gas. And because plasma consists of charged particles, we can manipulate them with magnetic fields. That's how we keep it away from the sides." She frowned. "It actually looks more like a donut inside. The magnetic field confines—or *contains*—the heated material."

Containment. That was the damaged circuit that had worried her following our battle with the *Fast Attack*. It was essential for the fusion process.

"Inside the capsule," she continued, "one deuterium and one tritium atom combine to form a single helium atom and a neutron. And of course a lot of energy. The neutron hits the inside of the sphere—which has a lithium coating—and produces more tritium for fuel." She shrugged. "A heat exchanger back there—" she pointed behind the capsule "—boils water to generate electricity to recharge the seacar's batteries. The exchanger then releases the steam through this conduit for propulsion. It keeps us going at a high velocity, and continues supercavitation. It's pretty simple, actually."

"Of course," I muttered. "Simple." I realized the reactor was the reason the vessel didn't carry enough emergency ballast—a fact that had shocked me earlier. It took up too much room.

"This is all just the basic fusion process, you know. I just refined it and made it smaller."

I couldn't help but marvel at her. She truly was brilliant. She deserved the Nobel Prize in engineering.

Another ping hit us and we all jumped. You'd think we'd be used to it by now. I checked my watch; the CSF warsubs would be on us in just over ten minutes. "Uh, Kat," I said. "How about we get this baby revved up and get the hell out of here."

Her smile faded. "I don't think we can. We might be stuck here with only our conventional drive."

HORRIFIED, I STARED AT HER FOR a heartbeat. "But why?" I finally managed.

She sighed. "Well, the big problem is the vertical stabilizer. The Chinese damaged it our second day out. It's been getting worse ever since. We need it to help control the vessel during supercavitation."

I swore. She was right. It had been problematic even at a speed of seventy kph, to say nothing of what it would be like at 450 kph.

Johnny said, "We have no choice. The fleet is almost on us. We have to at least get out of the area. Turn us around and activate the drive, even if just for a few minutes. Put some distance between us. Then we can figure out what to do."

His suggestion immediately gave me an idea. I knew someone who could help. "He's right," I said. "And we don't have much time to waste."

I SAT NEXT TO KAT IN the control cabin and watched as she removed a key from her pocket. It was small and thin, and slid easily into the slit just above the sealed panel on the console before us. Then she pressed her thumb to the scanner beside it. The section of console moved aside, revealing a set of gauges and controls that she had been right to hide from me. Labels such as THRUST, CONTAINMENT STATUS, WATER INTAKE, ELECTRICAL GENERATION, VELOCITY, and CAPSULE TEMPERATURE would have given *SCAV-1*'s secrets away, or at the very least, given me a direction in which to search. There were other buttons and readouts there as well, much of which I did not understand.

On the sonar, the CSF warsubs were closing. They were now well within passive range, but not quite close enough to show on the VID. *Impaler* was behind us as well, but only barely in range.

I pushed our thrusters to full and set our course: bearing 225 degrees.

"Australia?" Kat asked.

I grunted in reply. "What depth should I make?"

She shrugged. "Doesn't matter. Say five hundred meters." She reached down and activated a switch on the panel. I immediately felt the vibration of a hatch opening on the hull, and a display flashed yellow. It said: INTAKE

IN PROCESS. The water intake hatch was in the blunt bow of the ship. She pressed more buttons, studied some readouts, and remained still for several minutes.

I noticed that our speed had dropped to sixty. The increased drag with the open hatch was slowing us.

"What's happening?" I asked. I had images of the fleet closing and pulverizing us. The thought made me shudder.

"Takes time to heat the plasma," she mumbled. "Gotta get it up to two hundred for the SCAV drive, remember."

Two hundred million. Astounding.

At that point I realized that there was a deep throbbing hum from somewhere behind me.

Soon she said, "Opening stern thruster hatch. We're ejecting steam." Another vibration and our speed began to climb. "Uh, Mac, how are you at piloting a plane?"

"Never done it."

She glanced back at Johnny and Lau, who hovered at our backs. "You two better strap in. This could get rough."

OUR SPEED HIT EIGHTY AND REMAINED constant for a few minutes. I glanced at Kat, and she said, "Don't worry, the bubble has to form." She paused, and then, "I'm shifting ballast to negative; the heavier we are, the better."

Sure enough, gases were beginning to churn around the bow of *SCAV-1* and soar toward the surface. The filmy exterior of a large bubble had begun to stretch backward; it now almost reached the canopy.

Our speed began to increase.

I could hear Johnny and Lau behind us speaking heatedly; they seemed to be arguing about something, but I wasn't sure what.

"Ninety," she reported. "A hundred. Hundred-ten."

I gripped the yoke tightly, but my hands were slick with sweat. I wiped one on my pant leg, then the other.

Kat noticed, but didn't say anything.

The bubble continued to grow. It was now past the canopy; it seemed to be expanding by about a centimeter a second.

"The thrust is stable," she said.

The warsub captains out there would no doubt be listening to the drive over their sonars. In all likelihood they had never heard anything like it.

A high-pitched whistle now cut through *SCAV-1*, but the sound of the water slicing past the ship had decreased significantly. The hum at my back was intense and made my skin crawl.

"Thrust increasing," she continued. "Easy now. I'm about to shut down the screws." She had to do this, otherwise they would continue to turn but move only air, and likely overheat. I realized the pods were farther from the hull because of the SCAV drive. First, so the stabilizer acted more like a wing. Second, to keep the pods away from the steam exhaust. Kat said, "Mac, are you ready?"

Good question, I thought. *What will this feel like?* Air would completely surround us, so wouldn't we be permanently positively buoyant? Then I realized that was why she had flooded the tanks.

"Hundred-ninety," she continued. "Two hundred kph. Air now fully encircles *SCAV-1*. Two-ten."

A part of me wanted to push the drive even further, to see exactly what it could do. But I realized there was no need. We would be out of the fleet's grasp after only a few minutes of this. Also, with the damaged stabilizer, it would be stupid to stress the ship beyond its limits. I gestured to Kat to stop accelerating, and she powered back to an even 200 kph.

The controls felt light in my hands, as if the slightest move would start the ship spinning violently out of control, cartwheeling in the water and shredding her hull to pieces. It was a gut-wrenching feeling, and I almost told her to back off a bit more.

But I didn't.

Within fifteen minutes we were over fifty kilometers from the Chinese warsubs. I knew we needed more distance; we had to be out of their active sonar range so they didn't know where we were going. *Then again*, I thought, *anyone within fifty kilometers right now can probably hear us screaming through the water.* We were practically ringing an alarm bell begging people to look at us. It would be difficult to keep the SCAV drive a secret after this.

Soon we were more than a hundred kilometers from the fleet, and I asked Kat to cut the drive. She began the process—

And then all hell broke loose.

The yoke jumped slightly in my hands.

"Easy," she warned. "It's probably the stabilizer."

I hadn't changed course at all; just kept it straight and true. Still, the wobble had unnerved me. The bubble slowly receded from the ship, and suddenly I felt the stern yaw violently to port.

There was no way I could have kept her steady. At about 140 kph, we skidded to the side, the bubble collapsed around the seacar, and friction with the water hurled us forward against the straps. Kat swore loudly. "It's the stabilizer!" she screamed. "It buckled!"

I spun the yoke and tried to right our course, but the resistance was massive. The ship shuddered violently; it wrenched us to the side and only the straps held us in place. The impact no doubt had left severe bruises—but better bruises than fractures.

Finally *SCAV-1* was level and still, but it was more due to the lack of propulsion than from anything I had done.

I stared out of the canopy in horror; pieces of steel arced past my view as they fell into the deep. At the ship's aft, the stabilizer had bent at a twenty degree angle and the rudder was useless. It had folded completely and steel splinters projected from it. It looked almost like cracked balsa wood; the stresses on it had been incredible, and it had simply reached its maximum load capacity.

We could no longer steer the vessel.

And then the flood alarm went off.

CHAPTER TWENTY-FIVE

"It's the engine room again!" Kat shouted.

I spun to look, and sure enough a fountain of water was cascading from the bulkhead into the aft compartment. It was coming from the breach we had just repaired; the stress of the sudden stop had likely torn off the plate we had welded over the hull. Johnny and Lau quickly unstrapped, leaped to their feet, and sealed the engineering hatch. The water was rising just too damned fast. The pump was working hard, but couldn't keep up. It meant that the main batteries were now lost, as was life support. We would have to survive on what air was in the cabin or in the emergency tanks near the airlock. And due to our life in a saturation environment, we could not surface for air or rescue without first decompressing. We were trapped underwater.

I walked back and stared at the closed hatch for a while as I considered our options. The lights in the living compartment faded noticeably, and Kat grunted.

"We're now running on batteries from the two thruster pods only," she whispered. "We're not going to make a high top speed."

Which meant wherever we were going to go, we had to get moving, *now*.

I stalked to the control cabin and studied the console. Crucial systems were out and red warning labels had popped up on almost every display. The SCAV drive was also down. The fusion reactor had cut out during the flooding, and we had no idea what damage it had sustained.

But the larger problem now was the loss of the rudder. It would be difficult to steer without it, but it could be done. Passenger jets, for instance, had managed to navigate under similar circumstances by adjusting power to opposing engines—to steer right, increase thrust to the port engine, and vice versa. It would be hard, but it was our only choice.

I started the thrusters and the deck began to vibrate at my feet. It was hardly smooth, however; the seacar rattled as I applied acceleration and a distant screech replaced the cool *thrum* of power. I glanced at our speed and winced. Only forty-three kilometers per hour. We were simply carrying too much water weight, and battery power had diminished considerably. The blunt nose of the seacar was now clearly a detriment. I thought of mentioning that to Kat, but wisely reconsidered.

"Where are we going?" Johnny inquired as I adjusted the throttles to turn the ship.

I pointed at the navigation map on the screen at my side. "Australia."

He frowned. "Why? Are there Triestrian operatives there who can—"

"No, no. Not that. We need to repair *SC-1*. That Chinese fleet will be looking for us. We're out of their range now, but they'll be coming. They heard the drive and might suspect what it is. We need to get out of the area immediately."

"But why Australia?"

"I know someone there who can help with repairs." I swallowed as I thought about how to explain everything to Meagan—how I could convince her to help. She didn't want me involved in any sort of dangerous activity, especially after what had happened to our father. Her reaction to all of this wasn't something I could predict. "My sister lives in Blue Downs. She's a sub engineer, and a damn good one. I'm hoping she can fix the damage before the Chinese find us."

If she couldn't, the alternative was not something I wanted to consider just then.

BLUE DOWNS WAS AUSTRALIA'S ONLY UNDERSEA city. It was on the country's southern conshelf, just north of Tasmania. The country had established the city in the first years of undersea colonization, back in the 2070s, but it really hadn't grown at the rate other cities had. As a result, her people had a reputation of being more laid back and easy-going, but I knew that just wasn't true. The fact was the city had more potential for ocean floor mining than any other undersea city in the world; the entire southwest

Pacific was rich in manganese and iron nodules. The only obstacle to harvesting the rich deposits was the depth of the ocean itself. If the people of Blue Downs could overcome the pressures at six kilometers below, they would be at the forefront of ocean exploitation. Every inhabitant of the city knew it, and they all worked hard to realize the dream.

During the last few hours of the journey, *SC-1* limped toward Blue Downs at only twenty-seven kph. We could have declared an emergency and asked for help, but that would have set off alarms all over the region and announced *SC-1*'s arrival to the Chinese. So instead we focused on conserving our oxygen and trying to be inconspicuous. At the end we were all on bottled air; carbon dioxide levels in the seacar were poisonous, and we were relieved when we finally arrived.

The city looked very much like Trieste, only scaled down slightly. They only had three Living Modules to our six, though I understood they dug theirs deeper. The central module that contained the business, entertainment, and control offices was not quite as large, and their farms were also smaller. But all the differences ended there. It could have been our own city, and as we approached it at night, my heart thudded in my chest and I felt the ache of homesickness. It was going to be good to be back in a place where we could walk around in open space. It really felt like Trieste.

Especially once I saw Meg.

We crawled slowly into the Repair Module, blew our ballast, and surfaced in the very sector where she worked. There were other repair shops there, each with their own section of dock, but Meg's was the largest. I had called ahead, and there she was, waiting anxiously. The place was empty; at this time everyone was either asleep or enjoying the recreational areas of the city.

We shut down the thrusters that had been laboring so hard for so many hours, opened the hatch at the top of the hull, and climbed the ladder into fresh air. We threw our masks aside, stepped onto the dock, and an instant later she was in my arms.

"Tru!" she cried. "It's great to see you!"

It had been years since our last reunion, and I held her tight for a long minute. We had been a close family until Father's death, but once Meg left, things had fallen apart between us. There was a distance there now, and it wasn't just physical. Whenever we saw each other, however, the camaraderie, the sense of deep respect, and the caring all came back in a surge.

She was my twin, but we didn't really resemble each other. While I was thickly muscled with dark hair, she was slender and blond with freckles. There were wrinkles around her eyes from laughing, and I could tell immediately she was happy here. I had known that from her letters and messages, of course, but one look at her face and it was clearer than ever. To her, Blue Downs was home. That thought triggered an odd feeling within me—almost a sense of betrayal—but I fully understood her motivation for leaving when she had. Hell, the legacy Father had left behind still bothered me, even all these years later.

"You too," I finally managed. I pulled away and looked her over. "I've missed you."

She gave me another hug before stepping back. "This is really a big surprise. I thought you were taking your vacation around the US."

Her statement came across as innocent, but I recognized the tilt to her head that said so much. She was suspicious already. Her gaze darted to the seacar, and she frowned at the damaged vertical stabilizer. "Wow. What the hell did you do to—" She trailed off as she studied the vessel. In particular, the bow had caught her attention. "That's an interesting ship you've got there," she finally muttered.

"Doesn't belong to me." I gestured to Kat. "It's hers." I made introductions, and Meg immediately began to ask questions about *SC-1*. Kat seemed uncomfortable; she didn't know whether or not to openly discuss the seacar. Meg would have to know the truth, however, if she was going to fix the damage, and I would soon have to fill her in on everything.

And I wasn't looking forward to it.

"We need repairs, Meg, and we need them fast."

The request clearly intrigued her. "Is it okay to start in the morning, or is this the kind of problem that needs immediate help?"

I grimaced. "Immediate, unfortunately. Apart from that—" I pointed at the stabilizer "—there's also a hull breach, the engine compartment is full of water, and the batteries there are useless."

Kat stepped forward. "I'm going to have to oversee all work in the engine room."

Meg appeared startled, and she looked at Kat with a critical eye. "My workers are going to need access to every part of the ship in order to get her operational."

Kat glanced at me. "I don't think that's—"

I raised a hand. "We have to tell her. There's no way we can't."

"But Shanks ordered me—"

"*You* don't have to say a thing. *I*, on the other hand, am free to tell anyone I choose. And in order to do her job, Meg needs to know everything."

My sister watched the exchange intently. Then she turned to me. "Does this mean you're finally going to tell me exactly what you've been doing all these years since university?"

I sighed. "I don't think I have a choice anymore."

MEG GOT HER PEOPLE THERE FASTER than I could have thought possible. "We're used to important jobs coming in at weird times," she had muttered as she started the process of contacting them. "They know how vital our reputation is."

It made sense, so I remained quiet and sat with her in the small office on the docks as she got the repair effort in motion.

Two hours later she had a team of workers on the hull of *SC-1* removing the shattered frame of the old stabilizer and welding a new structure to the vessel. A crane overhead was lifting the damaged sections away; each revealed severe warping from the incredible forces the seacar had endured.

Finally, once the work was underway, she sat before me and locked her eyes to mine. A slight smile graced her features, and she said, "It's truth time, Truman."

I nodded. "I know. First let me say how grateful I am for your help."

"Anything for you. Your friend, on the other hand, needs a little lesson in manners."

I shrugged. "When you know the story behind that sub, her behavior will make sense. It took me a while to figure out too."

A period of silence fell over us, and she raised an eyebrow. "So?"

"I don't really know where to start. Shall I begin with the seacar?"

She looked out the window at where the work was being done. The office was situated in an elevated position over the docks so Meg could peer down at the ships as her people worked. Kat was clearly visible there, shouting and directing the workers, and many of their faces showed their increasing agitation. "Why don't you start with Dad's death?" Meg said in a soft voice.

That startled me. I had been prepared to tell her everything, but had hoped to slowly lead up to TCI and my involvement in the intelligence business.

"Are you part of the independence movement?" she continued.

Of course. That was what worried her most. "No. You know my feelings about that." But a part of me knew that the answer wasn't a hundred percent

truthful anymore. My mission involved the movement, just not in a way I supported.

"Then what have you been into?"

I exhaled. "I'm an operative for Trieste's intelligence agency. My job is to infiltrate other cities, keep an eye on their activities, and make sure that Trieste continues to prosper in the oceans."

She blinked. "I had no idea such a thing existed."

"Few do, but every city has one."

"Really?"

"It's a cold war, Meg, and believe it or not, I'm a part of it."

"But not the fight for independence," she pressed.

I chewed my lip. "I don't want anything to do with it. But this mission that I'm currently on . . . I've discovered things about TCI I'm not happy with. There is a movement, you're right about that, and I don't want to help, but . . ." I trailed off and didn't quite know what to say.

Her eyes flashed. "But you can't help yourself? Look what happened to Dad! Why put yourself in such a dangerous situation?"

I raised my hands in defense. "Whoa. Just wait a second. You don't understand. *I'm* not the one who wants independence. But her—" I glanced outside, at Kat "—she's part of it. My job is to get her back to Trieste, along with Johnny and Lau."

"And what happens then?"

"I don't know, to be honest. I have to find out exactly what's going on . . . and then I'll decide what to do."

"But Trieste won't fight the United States." Her eyes had narrowed and she was glaring at me.

"I don't want that, no. I just need to find out what's happening."

"So what the hell is that thing?" She gestured at *SC-1*.

She was my sister and deserved to know the truth. I had been so quiet about everything else for so long because of my allegiance to Trieste and the need to keep TCI a secret. However, she was helping repair the ship without even a mention of money. Other vessels were in the dock in varying states of repair, and they were now floating off to the side. For her, I was the priority.

I wondered how to explain. There was no other way than to just come out and say it. "Would you believe it's an experimental seacar that the Chinese— or *any* nation, for that matter—would kill to get their hands on?"

She stared at me in silence, then turned back to the vessel. "You're not joking, are you?"

"No."

"Tell me what's special about it. Why the odd bow?"

I told her everything. The fusion reactor—currently in the flooded aft compartment—and the supercavitating drive. Her eyes widened at that, and she whistled. "I've read a lot about it. The problem was always how to get a propulsion source that could last for longer than a few hours. Our subs need to stay underwater for months. There needs to be a lot of fuel, and we can't spare much extra space for bulky liquids." She paused. "But a fusion drive that vaporizes seawater—that's brilliant."

"That's Kat."

Meg frowned. "What's her full name?"

"Katherine Wells."

She nodded. "Ah. I've read some of her work. No wonder she's so protective of the ship."

Outside, on the hull of *SC-1*, Kat was yelling at a worker as he welded a strut for the new stabilizer into place. He did not look the least bit impressed, and he glanced at us as if to beg for Meg's intervention.

"How long do you think this will take?" I asked.

"Oh, the breach is easy. An hour to seal it, an hour to drain the compartment. You'll need new batteries, though, but we have those in stock. That's fairly simple stuff. Say three hours for that. The stabilizer will take the most time; we have to get it integrated to your control system." She screwed up her mouth as she thought about it. "Say four more hours there."

Nine in total. Not bad. I smiled. "Thanks, Meg. You've saved our lives."

"We still have to talk, you know. I need to know exactly what that thing is for." There was a look of intense displeasure on her face.

"I'm just trying to get those three people safely back to the city."

She was silent for a long while and I wondered what was going through her head. At last she turned to me; there was a look of pain in her eyes. "I'm scared of losing you, Tru."

"I've been in danger a thousand times since I joined TCI. You don't have to worry."

"But now, with this . . ." She glanced at *SC-1*. "Are people after you? How'd that damage happen?"

She was astute, that was for sure. "The Chinese are chasing us. We had to use the drive, and we had a small accident."

A shadow passed across her face. "Don't bullshit me. I know torpedo damage when I see it. A detonation and concussion wave did some of that."

I frowned. Damn. "We've survived a long trip now. We'll be fine."

"*Right.* They'll kill to get their hands on that drive. You said so yourself. You need help."

"Yeah, and I appreciate it. As soon as you're done, we'll leave."

"That's not what I mean. You need help to get the drive up and running, and someone to keep her seaworthy until you get back to Trieste."

I didn't fully understand what she was getting at. I must have looked confused.

She put her hands on her hips. "I'm coming with you, Tru."

I blinked. "What? No way, sis. That's too damn dangerous—"

She scowled. "You just said you'd be fine. And that means *I'll* be fine. Now shut up and just accept it. I'm coming with you. Besides, it'll be good to see Trieste again."

I stared at the determination in her features. In many ways she was just like me—stubborn and obstinate when it came to things that we had strong feelings about. A part of me was pleased she wanted to help get the seacar back to Trieste. But a larger part knew exactly why she wanted to come: she wanted to keep me out of trouble and away from Trieste's independence movement. She didn't believe me about not being involved. In the end, however, I realized there was little I could do but let her come.

I deflated. "Fine, but room will be tight with five of us on board."

Meg was looking out at the repair work again; there was a crease in her brow. "Four, you mean."

"Huh? No, there's five of us."

She gestured out the window. "That Lau guy left an hour ago. Didn't you notice?"

I bolted outside and found Johnny helping the efforts. He looked immediately guilty as I approached, and a surge of fear shot through me. Inside, I already knew what had happened.

Lau had taken off. He was going to warn the Chinese.

CHAPTER TWENTY-SIX

JOHNNY HAD BEEN WORKING HARD; HIS clothing was greasy and wet with perspiration. But when he saw me, he stopped what he was doing and stepped slowly down to the dock. His face was a mask of guilt and shame.

"I'm sorry, Mac," he said. "He's gone. I tried to stop him."

I wasn't sure what to say. I had trusted both of them, and now realized it had been foolish of me to do so. But here was Johnny, still with me. Immediately I knew that I had a decision to make.

He continued, "When he found out about the SCAV drive, he felt it was too important to keep from China. He intends to tell them about it. That's why I'm working so hard, so we can leave as soon as possible."

I recalled the intense discussion the two of them had had just before the stabilizer succumbed to the stress. The subsequent flooding and danger had taken my mind off of it, and I had forgotten to ask them what the disagreement had been about. Damn it! Stupid of me. Rookie mistake.

I snorted. "And you expect me to trust you now?"

"I know it doesn't look good. What Lau is doing surprised me too."

"They could kill him for helping us. We destroyed two Chinese warsubs with his help! *Twenty people.*"

"And he knew that. This information, however, could save his life. He'd been having second thoughts about going to Trieste."

"How long have you known?"

Johnny winced. "Since we came aboard."

I pondered that. "What's he planning, right now? What can he do?"

"We have operatives at Blue Downs, of course, but no one knows who or where they are except intelligence headquarters. His first step will be to contact HQ to figure out a way to get in touch with their people here."

"And when that happens?"

"He'll track them down, and probably try to stop us from leaving. They'll take *SC-1* and leave for Sheng City in it."

Which meant we would soon have a fight on our hands. I had previously wondered who would win in a physical contest between Lau and myself, and it seemed I might soon get an answer to the question.

I glanced at my watch. Still seven hours to go on the repairs. By then the morning shift would be arriving. Currently the docks were silent except for Meg's crew. If we could seal the module somehow, prevent anyone from entering . . .

Johnny was still a problem. I was unsure of what to do with him. I could leave him behind, but then Shanks would have my ass. I could bring him with us, but his loyalty was still a question mark.

Or I could just kill him and be done with it.

He was watching me with a frown on his face, almost as if he understood what was going through my head. He didn't seem nervous though. Perhaps he understood me better than I did and knew I could never kill him in cold blood. That, despite my previous intentions, I just didn't have it in me.

Finally I said, "We're going back to Trieste."

A glimmer of a smile graced his features. "You trust me?"

"I wouldn't go that far. I have to get you back, and I'm going to do that." I pointed at the repair efforts on the rear stabilizer. "Now get up there and get to work."

"Aye aye, sir."

Now he grinned, and I felt my stomach churn. I couldn't help but wonder: Was it because he had fooled me yet again?

I IMMEDIATELY TOLD MEAGAN OUR PROBLEM and she had the crew seal the travel tube hatch to the module. Two of her people engaged the lock code, then went back to work. The order clearly confused them, but they were professional enough not to ask.

There was only one way into the module now—through the large moonpool entrance that seacars used to enter the docks. Meg said that if we sealed

that, an indicator would alert the city controllers, and they would most likely send a security patrol to investigate. As it stood now, we had perhaps a few hours before Lau could organize a team of operatives to move on us. It was a tough decision, but I opted to leave the hatch open. I would stand watch with Kat's gun and shoot anyone who tried to swim in that way.

The stabilizer damage took the longest to repair. The crew had to completely strip it from the hull and weld a new one in its place, then install new hydraulics and link the control surfaces to the console in *SC-1*. I watched the crew work; they were highly efficient and knew exactly what to do. They'd probably done such jobs thousands of times in the past. In what seemed like no time at all teams had welded the new support structure into place and repaired the breach in the hull. They too worked quickly; it was done in less than forty-five minutes.

Pumps were working to clear the engine room at the same time, and I could hear Kat yelling from within the aft compartment. She had no doubt kept the repair team out of there, but was probably having difficulty keeping an eye on all of them at the same time. Meagan soon went into the vessel to mollify her, and the yelling dropped a few decibels.

Hours passed and the stabilizer began to take shape. The crew welded plates over it. They attached the control surface and tested it using the pedals in the seacar's control cabin. Kat emerged from inside and watched with a drawn and angry look on her face. All of this had been stressful for her, but I had to admit, Meg's team had done remarkably well in such a short amount of time. The new structure was a dull gray that didn't exactly match the rest of the vessel, but the workers designed it to be the same configuration as the previous one. Finally they were clearing their tools from *SC-1*, looking tired, exhausted, and angry at having had to endure Kat's screaming.

And then a low rumble reverberated through the module.

Meagan, who had been at my side telling me the specifications of the new stabilizer, abruptly closed her mouth and cocked her head at the sound. "That's the moonpool hatch, underwater."

A shock coursed through me. "Closing?"

"Yes. They're trying to keep us in here."

Lau. He had either convinced his government to go to the city officials, or he had done it directly. Smart move. They had trapped us now, and he had all the time in the world to wait for his own people to arrive.

Unless we forced the issue.

A voice came over the module's public address system. The ceiling was high over our heads—about fifteen meters—and the sound echoed in the

large chamber. "Attention work crews in the Repair Module. Unlock the travel tube hatch immediately. Failure to do so will result in arrest and imprisonment."

Meg's workers stopped what they were doing and stared at the speaker on the bulkhead.

Then they turned to her.

"This is my responsibility," she said in a loud, commanding voice. "You're on my payroll, and you've only done as I asked. None of you are in any trouble."

The one closest to her said, "Should we do what they want?"

She glanced at me. "No. Please go and sit on the dock by the office. This will be over soon."

I started at that. We could only be so lucky.

THEY REPEATED THE MESSAGE SEVERAL TIMES. Johnny, Kat, Meg and I feverishly worked to replace the ruined batteries in the engine room, but I knew the city officials would soon act. They would come in to get us, and before that happened, the ship had to be ready.

We heard a cry from outside, and I rushed up the ladder to see what had happened. One of the repair crew—a woman sitting on the dock as Meg had asked—was pointing at the hatch into the module. Her face was white.

A fountain of sparks was arcing into the chamber. They shot across the docks and showered into water where they sizzled and smoked.

Someone was cutting their way in.

I shouted into the ship, "Get the thrusters up and running! Prepare to dive!"

"Dive?" came the bewildered response. It was Kat. "To where?"

But I didn't respond. I simply leaped to the dock and sprinted to the hatch. I had to shield my eyes as I approached to prevent a burn. I studied the progress that they had made. The hatch was solid steel. No windows; its purpose was to hold back water in case the module flooded.

They were nearly through.

I heard footsteps, and turned to see Johnny at my side.

"What are you doing?" I asked.

"Here to help." He shrugged. "You have doubts about my motives, Mac, and with good reason. I haven't been a good friend. But I'm committed to going back to Trieste. And so here I am."

I hesitated for a heartbeat. "There could be a dozen people on the other side of that hatch, and we have no way to get the ship out into open water."

A smile. "I'm sure you'll come up with something."

"That's a lot of pressure, you know." I stared at the spray of sparks and considered our options. "How much time until the seacar is ready?"

"Ten minutes, maybe. They're wiring the last batteries now."

"I don't think we have that long." The torch was cutting the locking mechanism from the bottom of the steel hatch. The top one was already gone. "Five, perhaps, at most." I thought some more and then gestured for one of Meg's workers to come over. He jumped to his feet and ran toward us. I pointed to the panel beside the frame. "Can you unlock this hatch for me?"

He blinked. "Uh, sure. It's fairly simple. I used a code when I sealed it. I just have to reenter—"

"Do it."

"But they'll be in here in a—"

"That's fine." I knew what would happen. The hatch would slide open before the people on the other side were ready. It would surprise them.

Then I could go to work.

Johnny looked at me and nodded. "I'm ready."

We stood side by side in front of the hatch as Meg's crewman moved to the panel. "Are you sure about this?"

"Just do it, then get back to the dock as quickly as possible."

He swallowed, then very calmly and deliberately keyed in the code.

He turned and bolted back to the others.

The hatch rumbled aside.

IT CAUGHT THE PERSON WORKING THE torch completely off guard. The visor over his face obscured his features, and he barely had time to look at me before I kicked him in the head. He slammed into the bulkhead and slumped to the deck.

In the corridor behind were three Chinese and two city security men. And Lau.

They all had weapons.

They took an involuntary step back as the hatch ground open, but Lau reacted first. He raised his gun, but I already had mine aimed and ready.

"Stop what you're doing," he said in an even voice. "You're under arrest."

"Why is a Chinese operative giving orders in Blue Downs?" I said.

One of the city security detachment said to me, "He's right, sir. Stop work on that vessel immediately. We're impounding it."

"Because Chinese officials asked?"

The other frowned. "The mayor ordered us, sir. I'm not sure about Chinese involvement in this matter. I'm just doing what my superiors tell me."

I grimaced. "Then I'm sorry for what I'm about to do." At my feet, the welder operator was unmoving and unconscious. The torch was still lit, however, and the two large tanks containing its fuel were behind him on a steel dolly. One was red, the other yellow. I lowered my gun and aimed at the red tank.

I fired.

An instant later an explosion filled the corridor. Lau and the other operatives all shielded their faces as they spun away. The two city security men who had been closest to the tanks ended up meters from where they had stood a second earlier. Both hit the deck heavily. I had to put an arm over my own eyes for protection, and as soon as the flames dissipated, I lunged at Lau.

He was blinking from the explosion and I caught him with three quick strikes to the face. He finally got his arms up to block my blows, and I countered with a sudden kick to his midsection. He stumbled back, attempting in vain to raise his gun. I spun savagely and hit his wrist with the blade of my foot, and the gun clattered away to the deck.

An elbow abruptly caught me in the temple, and my vision darkened. I barely managed to see another approaching, and I ducked under it. I shook my head to clear it just in time to see a foot inches from my face. I avoided it, stepped in toward him, and lashed out with an uppercut to the chin. He looked stunned for a moment, but managed to reach out and wrap his long, muscular arms around me. I had gotten too close to the large man. I brought a knee into his gut, but it barely hurt him. He squeezed and I felt the breath forced from my lungs.

Shit—he was going to squeeze me to death.

I still had the gun in my hand, but didn't especially want to use it in a foreign city. It could cause a huge political problem for Trieste—and for Meg. I had to avoid murder.

I stomped on his shin at a sharp angle and he cried out in agony. His grip loosened, and I smashed my palm into his neck. He made a strangled noise and fell to his knees.

I raised the weapon again. "Now stop what you're doing," I rasped.

Johnny had already incapacitated one of the Chinese operatives; the other two had backed off and were watching the melee.

"We can't let you go to Trieste," Lau gasped as he clutched his neck.

"We're leaving."

His eyes were steel. "How? They've closed the moonpool hatch. Chinese forces are on their way. The city government has agreed to hold you until they can resolve the matter." He sneered. "Face it, you're stuck."

I cocked the pistol and moved it toward his face. "I say we're not." He didn't respond, but some of his confidence drained away. "You don't think they're going to welcome you back with open arms, do you, Lau?"

"I belong at Sheng. I'm at outsider at Trieste."

"But after helping Johnny warn me, you're going to be on the outs with your superiors. Damaged goods. Untrustworthy."

He gritted his teeth. "I guess we'll see."

Johnny's anger was clear in his face. "You have family in Trieste. You realized how important it was to stop Shanks. They could die during a war. Why back out now?"

Lau's voice was hard. "China needs the SCAV drive. Otherwise America will be the dominant nation in the oceans. We'll lose the Plains. We'll lose everything."

For what it was worth, I understood his position. He was right to want to keep the drive from America. Tensions between the two governments were just too damn high already, and knowledge of Kat's invention could increase hostilities even more. I said, "I promise you I'll try my best to stop Shanks and his plans. For now, however, you have to leave." I tightened my grip on the gun. "Or I'll shoot."

He knotted his fists. "This isn't over, McClusky."

"We're even. You stabbed me. You tried to kill me over the trench. And now I'll let the Chinese take you to their finest prison cell." He scowled but said no more. I could tell it had hurt. "Now get the fuck out of here," I growled.

The operatives turned, and with a last glare at Johnny, marched down the corridor and away from the Repair Module. There were still three people lying on the deck; all were unconscious, but they would survive.

"Let's leave while we can," I muttered.

WE BOARDED *SC-1* AND SEALED THE hatch. In the control cabin, I lowered myself into the chair next to Kat. Behind me, Johnny and Meagan watched

anxiously. I brought the ballast to negative and the seacar disappeared under the surface. With the thrusters on reverse—their vibration was once again smooth and steady—I brought us to the main moonpool hatch that led outside. It was ten meters across and six high; the largest hatches in undersea cities were those designed for seacars to pass through. I maneuvered to face it directly.

"Kat," I said. "Prepare our last torpedo."

The others' jaws hit the deck. My intention was clear: the torpedo would blow the hatch to bits and we would leave through the hole. Since the moonpool was normally open to the outside anyway, there was no danger to the city or the module. Still, Kat was aghast.

"Are you *serious*?" she hissed. "We just repaired the seacar! The concussion could kill us!"

"We have no choice. It's either take the chance or wait for Australian forces to arrest us. Then your invention would be lost. Are you prepared to lose *SC-1*?"

She stared at me, wide-eyed and angry. Then she said in a quiet, more controlled voice, "There's no other option?"

Meg said, "City Control operates that hatch. We can open and close it from here, but they can override at any time." Her voice was calm and clear, but I could tell she was nervous about firing a torpedo in her own city.

Kat considered that for several heartbeats, and Johnny said, "They're probably preparing their warships now, Doctor Wells, to come and get us. We have to do this."

Finally, she sighed. "Very well. We'll use the torpedo."

She reached to the panel with trembling fingers and prepared the last weapon. She set its function to IMPACT DETONATION.

She took a deep breath, and pressed the button.

The torpedo shot from the bow of the seacar.

THE LARGE HATCH BLEW TO BITS before our eyes. First the white eruption of water and steam churning violently, then the collapse of the void, and finally the disintegration of the steel structure. I had been holding my breath, and released it only once the ship had stopped rocking to and fro in the maelstrom. No damage. We had survived.

With *SC-1*'s thrusters on max, we powered through the jagged hole and into open ocean. The sonar immediately detected two vessels on approach—city security. They would be fast and most likely armed. We had no countermeasures or torpedoes remaining. I swore. Out of the frying pan . . .

I heeled the seacar to port and the two vehicles fell in behind us. They were a hundred meters behind, but were easily keeping up.

Then they started to overtake us.

The comm crackled. "Attention unidentified seacar. Halt immediately. We are preparing to fire on you. This is your only warning."

The woman who had spoken sounded angry. We had fired on her city. To her we were no better than terrorists. Perhaps someone could criticize me for what I had done, but in my mind there had been no other choice. I needed to get Johnny and Kat back to Trieste as soon as possible. We had to get out before the Chinese captured us or got their hands on the seacar.

"Prepare the drive, Kat," I muttered as I took *SC-1* low to the seafloor and moved eastward toward the continental slope.

She shot me a horrified look. "It's not online! What are you thinking? The reactor has been underwater for hours!"

My mouth hung open and my heart hammered in my chest. "Are you serious? You can't start it?"

"No way. We spent all that time on the—"

"How long until it'll be ready?"

She frowned. "I have to run it through its pretest, check the fuel, make sure the connections are—"

"Dammit—get on it then!" I regretted being short with her, but the situation was tense. I had a tight grip on the yoke, and was now entering a narrow undersea valley. Strong currents flowed through it—runoff from the continent—and they were beginning to toss the seacar like a toy.

She growled, unstrapped her belt, and stormed back to the engine room. I glanced at Meg; she was already headed there as well. No doubt she would be a great help.

Johnny climbed into the chair beside me. "What are you planning?"

"I really have no idea. I guess just stay out of their way until the drive is functioning. Then we bolt. But until then . . ."

"Avoiding torpedoes is going to be difficult without countermeasures."

I watched the two vessels' profiles on the sonar; they were cutting the distance between us rapidly. Damn. The only thing that would save us now was stealth and piloting.

The gully twisted southeast toward deeper waters. The currents here were generally fast and turbulent, and the trench meandered with some very tight turns. This would be interesting.

The seacar jerked upwards and I pushed on the yoke to compensate. *SC-1* sank quicker than it should have, and I had to wrench it up suddenly. "Easy, there!" Kat yelled from the aft compartment. "We're working!"

"I'm trying to keep us alive!"

Johnny suddenly bit out, "They're opening their tubes!" He was watching the sonar as I piloted. "Torpedo in the water!"

"Shit!" I banked the ship with a quick turn of the yoke, pressed on the pedals, and the vessel moved quickly and smoothly. We darted to the side as the torpedo zoomed by, just past our underbelly. The high-pitched distinctive whine was far louder than our own screws.

I clenched my teeth and waited for the explosion.

It never came.

"They must have triggered it for impact," Johnny muttered.

He was right. Normally a torpedo was a homer. However, the ships following us were so close—to us and each other—that they were obviously

worried about friendly fire. Instead they aimed and hoped to actually connect with the weapon. Had it been a homer, it would have come right in on our screws, and just as ours had destroyed the Chinese warsubs over the Aleutian Trench, it would have detonated at close range even had we started to extend the distance between us and the weapon.

But it didn't do that.

It simply churned away and disappeared into the turbid waters before us.

"That was damn lucky," Johnny said.

"They'll probably back off a bit and try a homer next."

Sure enough, as I said it, the sonar indicated a drop in their speed. They were getting ready to launch again.

"They're really pissed about what we did to their access hatch."

"Can you blame them?" I mumbled as I concentrated on piloting. The controls really felt great now. I wasn't sure if it was because of the repair job, or if I was just getting better at it, but I was beginning to feel more confident with every second that passed.

In fact, I suddenly had an idea.

I pushed the ship lower to the seafloor—so low, in fact, that Johnny seized the arms of his chair—and watched with satisfaction as the screws disturbed the loose sediment in the gully. Behind us the already murky water began to grow more laden with sediment. It was no doubt getting difficult for our pursuers to maintain visual contact with us. They would soon be forced to use instruments only—which were not especially good for close distances. For instance, if I changed my depth, a two-dimensional readout had to show that in some way. The standard ones did so with markers next to the symbols. As a result, those pilots would have to keep their eyes glued to the sonar, which was hard in a place such as this, with the sides only meters from the boat.

And so, as it grew more difficult to see, I abruptly yanked the yoke back and clutched it close to my torso. Then I blew ballast. We began to rise rapidly. But instead of angling straight up and shooting to shallower depths, I held the yoke back. Thinking of *SC-1* as more of an airplane had given me the idea. Ever since we'd learned about the SCAV drive, I had thought a great deal about how to control her. It had a larger number of control surfaces than a standard seacar; most only had bow planes, but we had stern ones as well. And so, like an airplane, I decided to do a loop.

Underwater.

And come up behind the security seacars.

"Hold on back there!" I bellowed.

We climbed to ninety degrees, and then passed it. I heard someone yell from the engine room, but wasn't sure if it had been Kat or Meagan. Then we hit a hundred . . . a hundred-thirty . . .

And kept right on going.

The straps held us in place, but we were soon hanging completely upside down. Our rear ends were a few centimeters from the seat cushions and our hair hung toward the ceiling.

And still I held the yoke back.

I slammed a hand on the ballast controls and switched to negative. Our tanks flooded, and we quickly became heavier.

There was a now a constant scream from behind me. I thought at first it was the engines, then I realized it was Kat. They would be on the ceiling back there, and I hoped that no equipment or tools would hurt them.

We almost hit the surface of the water—we were still quite shallow here—then continued to arc back until we were angled straight down. We disappeared back into the gully, and I kept my wet grip tight on the yoke. Finally we started to draw close to level again—

And the two ships were directly before us.

Too bad we couldn't fire a torpedo. Not that I would have, anyway. These people were innocent. I was just trying to buy us time until we could activate the SCAV drive. I had only given us about ten minutes, however. Still not enough.

And then the two ships separated.

"Oh, shit," I murmured.

ONE WENT UP AND LEFT, THE other up and right. Their plan was obvious—each would circle around and close behind me again. If I followed one, the other would have me. If I stayed on course, both would have me. I wondered for a moment what to do. *SC-1* was more maneuverable, but their seacars were faster—and armed. We could most likely go deeper than them, but we were on the conshelf and the precipice and abyss were still a few hundred kilometers to the east.

I decided to get a progress report on the drive. "Kat!" I yelled. "Give me a time to shoot for here!"

Her voice came back to me, "It'll take hours to do everything properly, to make sure there won't be a malfunction during the start up."

I shuddered at that. "What if we started it without worrying about that?"

Pause. "Forty minutes maybe."

That was better, but still too long. We would be dead or captured by then. But even if we survived for that length of time, there were no guarantees that the containment capsule would even work.

The sonar indicated the directions in which the two seacars had gone, and I decided to simply stay on course in the gully. We were hugging the bottom—about three meters from it—and on a slight downward angle. Our depth was only fifty-three meters. I kept the ballast tanks flooded to give us more weight, and used the vessel's control surfaces to keep us from hitting the floor. That, along with the current, gave us a little more speed—seventy-two kph now—but the fast little security vessels still outclassed us.

"Come on," I muttered as I watched the sonar. "Stay off our tail."

"They might just give up after a while," Johnny said.

"Not likely. We fired a torpedo inside the city. They want our skins." Thankfully, the Australians wouldn't know what city we had come from. If we could hide from them in some way, however . . . find a ledge or an overhang to stop under, we might be able to avoid them for a bit. On the projected VID, the gully's steep sides were clearly visible. However, there were no places to conceal ourselves. The swift flow of water ensured steady erosion that kept the valley smooth; undersea landslides probably occurred frequently here.

The two seacars had regrouped and were back on our tail. They were closing the distance, and knew exactly where—

The sonar shrieked abruptly. I shot a glance at it; each vessel had fired simultaneously.

"Hang on!" I yelled as I pulled the seacar up. It was slow with the tanks flooded, and I hit the ballast controls and started to clear them of water. We began to rise more quickly, and I watched as we approached the top of the gully. The slopes were only a few meters on either side of our thruster pods—

And then an idea suddenly hit me.

Of course.

We were in what was essentially a narrow trench on a slight downward angle. The material on the bottom was loose, unconsolidated sand and debris from the continent. Our thrusters could churn it into the water easily enough, and I realized a torpedo detonation could easily collapse one of the walls.

And so I crested the gully but maintained our course, paralleling the trench but just over the ridge. The two torpedoes were approaching, still in the canyon, and when they were only ten meters behind us—the sonar was screaming now—I yanked the ship to the starboard, over the flat bottom

of the Australian conshelf. The torpedoes were homers, as I had expected, and they tried to follow. They were too close to the side of the trench, however, and one or both actually collided with the wall. The explosion lit the entire area, and the gully collapsed. Tonnes of sand and gravel and boulders cascaded down—

Onto the pursuing vehicles.

I held my breath as I watched the sonar. A cloud had obscured the area in the valley where we had just been; debris and aftershocks from the detonations reverberated the entire region and material continued to rain down on the two seacars. Their thrusters had stopped, and they quickly settled to the bottom beneath the cloud. I hoped we hadn't injured anyone— that the falling rocks hadn't breached their hulls and that they weren't flooding—but if they were, I knew with a heavy heart there wasn't anything we could do for them.

I held my course to the east, and kept to the bottom as we moved into the deeper waters of the Pacific.

SOON KAT WAS ABLE TO RESTART the SCAV drive and our speed shot to 200 kph. Meg's eyes widened at the velocity—she had never expected to see such a speed underwater in her lifetime—and within moments they were talking a mile a minute about the reactor and the drive and how everything worked. Meg's respect for Kat increased almost as fast as our speed had, and Kat seemed enormously proud of her invention. I could tell that she was pleased with the attention.

"Why only two hundred?" Kat asked me a while later.

I was piloting the seacar, and the controls felt far more stable than they had during our earlier attempt at this velocity. I wondered what it would be like to perform the same maneuvers we had just completed at such a speed—a loop, for instance—but decided to just fly straight and true. "When we pass the Chinese force, I don't want them to know our true capabilities. They'll hear us and suspect what we've got, of course, but there's no need to show them everything."

I'll save that for later, I thought.

WE THREADED THROUGH THE FIJI ISLANDS, over the Tonga Trench—nearly the deepest place on the planet, with a depth of 10,822 meters—over the

Austral Seamount Chain, through Polynesia and the Tuamotu Ridge, and back toward the Clarion Fracture Zone. It was clear sailing; only 6000 kilometers until we reached Panama, which meant only thirty hours at our current speed. And if we pushed it to maximum, we would be there in only thirteen. It was incredible. I shook my head at the thought.

The Chinese fleet was out there, somewhere. They knew Panama was our destination, and would no doubt try to barricade us again.

The ocean floor in the region was remarkable. Below us, geothermal vents towered upward and released large plumes of black mineral-choked dust. The heat of the asthenosphere penetrated the thin ocean crust easily at diverging tectonic plates, and the vents were everywhere on the seafloor. Dark clouds filled the water, sometimes right to the surface, and currents pushed the material along in their unending cycle through the world's ocean basins. The dust would eventually settle to the bottom where it would grow as nodules—gravel-sized balls of minerals miners could simply scoop up and take directly to processing facilities. The Iron Plains was only one such region among countless others.

I had often wondered what the colonies would be like, what they could achieve, if the troubles between land nations could be eliminated from the equation. If there was no cold war. If we could live peacefully and see each other as friends rather than enemies. Work together to harvest ocean resources. People often talked about such a nation of undersea dwellers. They called it *Oceania*.

I wanted Trieste to continue to grow, but still, I was becoming more and more sure that I wanted *all* the cities to flourish, not just my own. At one time in the past, when I had been working for TCI before Sheng City captured me, I had wanted Trieste to be better than the others. Now, I realized that the oceans were too dangerous without anyone else. We needed to continue the colonization of the deep to keep the human race alive. Sure, one day space would be a realistic place in which to expand, and attempts were well underway, but for now, we needed the oceans.

I sighed. It was a pipe dream, I knew. But worth thinking about.

KAT AND I SPENT LESS TIME with one another now, but I could tell from the look in her eyes she was still interested in me. Despite the differences of opinion regarding Shanks and his plans, despite her temperamental nature, I still found her nearly irresistible. Our lovemaking had been intense and

had calmed my nerves somewhat—this mission was one of the toughest I had ever had—and I found myself missing it immensely. But Meg was on the ship now, and for some reason I felt I should stay away from Kat for a little while. I sometimes sensed that she resented this, but I tried my best to ignore it and focus on other things. But still she shot me those looks on the odd occasion—the ones that made me long for another night together.

Kat and Meg were developing a strong relationship. Their common interests had helped them bond. While Kat's knowledge was extensive and highly theoretical, Meg's was practical and developed from experience. The two made a good pair, actually. Together they might even create seacars more remarkable than *SC-1*. Already they were discussing a variation—one with a more powerful reactor and multiple steam outlets that might reach higher velocities.

It was all very interesting, except, of course, when I realized what Shanks would use it for. If he got his way, the SCAV drive would be the cornerstone of his bid for independence.

Sometime later, I discovered with a flash of anger that Lau had taken my Personal Communication Device with him. The PCD had belonged to Blake; it had all of his contacts in its memory, and would be a valuable prize for Sheng City. Perhaps Lau could even trade it for his life. I wasn't looking forward to telling Shanks about it.

MEG AND I WERE IN THE living area, having a bite to eat. The other two were piloting the vessel; both Kat and Johnny were taking turns, and getting quite good at it. There hadn't been any major issues—just a bit of turbulence as we soared over some intense geologic activity. The seacar seemed to glide through it easily now, with barely a shudder as we passed massive undersea eruptions kilometers below.

Meg said, "You and Kat have been on this seacar together for a while now."

I couldn't help but laugh. She always got right to the point, and she was quite perceptive. "We're closer now than we were at the beginning, that's for sure. But still, there are issues between us."

"She has a strong and domineering personality."

"Sometimes. Mostly when it comes to this ship."

Meg nodded. "Otherwise she's pleasant and charming."

I recalled the times when Kat had snapped at me for criticizing *SCAV-1*. Or when she had yelled at Meg's work crew.

"Why is she like that sometimes?" Meg asked.

I told her the story about Kat's dad, about how his illness had prevented her from achieving her dream until now. "As a result," I said in a quiet voice to keep the others from overhearing, "I think anything that threatens her work or what she's doing can set her off."

"What is she planning?" Meg's eyes narrowed. Perceptive indeed.

"She and Shanks have something cooked up. I have to figure out what it is once we hit Trieste."

"What if you find out it'll cause trouble?"

I hesitated before, "Then I'll have to stop it."

She tilted her head. "And your relationship?"

The truth was there really wasn't one. We had a physical connection and a common interest in the oceans, but her desire to fight for independence would always keep us apart. I didn't know what to say, so I didn't answer.

"Well, whatever happens, Tru, she is definitely a genius." She exhaled. "This vessel is marvelous. And I can't believe that we're only going at less than half of our top speed!"

I frowned. "She had mentioned to me earlier that the Soviets first invented supercavitation back in the 1970s."

"That's true."

"But why isn't the technology used? Why aren't all torpedoes like it?"

"Ah. Do you remember an incident over a century ago involving the Russian sub *Kursk*?"

I did indeed. It had happened in the year 2000. An explosion in her forward compartments had vaporized the bow section and all the crew in that area. She sank in over a hundred meters of water, and because of the secrecy of the Russian government—echoes of the Soviet era—the country took days to request help. By then it was too late. Over a hundred crew were lost, and the country's president had taken a beating in the press.

I gasped when I realized what she was implying. "You think it was a supercavitating torpedo?"

"Those are the rumors. The Russian report on the incident cited that a torpedo caused the initial explosion, and several subsequent ones also occurred. From other torpedoes, they said. Anyway, since then, nations have stayed away from those sorts of weapons. Having large warheads is dangerous enough. But add in volatile rocket fuel, and it makes for a dangerous combination."

"So they just don't exist now?"

She raised a finger. "I didn't say that, Tru. It's possible some vessels have them. Just not all of them."

JOHNNY SOON CALLED US TO THE control cabin, where I noticed a swarm of contacts on the sonar. My visions of clear sailing until Panama disappeared almost immediately.

My stomach dropped.

The Chinese Fleet.

Directly before us.

"Well, we expected it, didn't we?" I mumbled. Still, a part of me had been hoping . . .

"We should be able to shoot straight past them, shouldn't we?" Meg asked.

I didn't respond. They could hit us with a lucky shot or drop a perfectly placed mine. The slightest impact could damage the SCAV drive.

"Send out an active pulse," I ordered. Johnny did so and the screen lit with contacts. There were three times the number that had tried to intercept us before, just waiting for a chance to capture or destroy us. Either they had realized that we were using a SCAV drive—we emitted enough noise now for them to figure it out—or Lau had contacted his people in time.

Damn.

And then I noticed something on the other side of the fleet. It was a US contact, a USSF warsub.

The same one that had been chasing us since we'd left port.

USS *Impaler*.

"How the hell do they know where we are all the time?" Johnny whispered.

I had a theory about that, but this was no time to check it.

"Prepare to engage that fleet," I said. "We have to get through them to get back to Trieste."

If we didn't, the politics of the undersea colonies would be far different than they were today. China would emerge on top, and would probably win the cold war.

And the rights to The Iron Plains.

And all the resources in the ocean depths.

And domination over every other undersea colony.

CHAPTER 二十八 TWENTY-EIGHT

THE CHINESE WARSUBS—OVER ONE HUNDRED AND fifty of them—had spread themselves out over an immense area. Each was at a different depth in an attempt to cover as much ocean as possible. They were doing the only thing possible to stop us. I knew what was coming.

I also knew how to get through their net.

I hoped.

As we closed to within ten kilometers, the mines started dropping. They had timed it perfectly. As we passed under their ships, the devices would detonate whenever one got within range. The explosions might damage us enough to disrupt the SCAV drive, then it would be conventional thrusters only, and it would be over for us.

We watched in silence as the white stars slowly descended. It didn't matter what depth we made; multiple ships in our path had dropped the mines, and even if we descended to four kilometers, they would still be in our way. There was only one solution.

I increased speed.

Kat had switched the thruster controls on my left from conventional to supercavitating, and I pushed them forward slowly. The vibration of the venting steam grew to a dull roar. I watched the speed increase as I held the yoke steady.

Two-twenty.

Two-forty.

Two-seventy.

Three hundred.

I let it continue for another fifty before I stopped. The controls were stable in my hands; the yoke hardly bounced at all. We weren't even at maximum, but we would shoot right under their vessels and mines before any of them were close enough to detonate.

And hopefully travel straight to Panama, unmolested.

And then the alarms began to sound.

Johnny barked, "Torpedoes! Multiple sources! I count—" His voice cut off in a startled gasp. He turned to me. *"One hundred.* Headed straight for us."

We were going so fast that we would collide with them at any second. I had to immediately veer to starboard. The CSF warsubs occupied over four hundred square kilometers of ocean, and since so many had fired, their chances of connecting were very good. Even at our present speed it would take five minutes to clear the field of weapons. And with a hundred of them in the area . . . it would be tricky.

I gingerly turned the yoke and pulled it toward me. We banked smoothly and shifted to a more southerly route. The g-forces pushed us into our seats. The torpedoes closer to us began to detonate as we pulled away, and the concussions rattled the seacar.

"Come on, baby, hold together," I muttered. The sonar showed us moving south now, with the fleet to our port. They were continuing to fire, but the weapons were falling behind. Whenever one blossomed into steam it took the nearby ones with it; there were now puffs of white all over the screen. The warsubs were maneuvering toward us, but they were just too slow and cumbersome. Nothing could keep up with us. It felt great to pilot *SCAV-1.* I imagined us as a fighter jet arrowing through the sky. Both types of craft flew in air, after all. The only difference was the air around us was merely a single bubble that stretched back from the low pressure zone at the bow.

Some of the ships to the south had set a course due west rather than head for us. It had been a smart move. We were now heading right for three warsubs, and I couldn't turn east to avoid them. The warsubs' depths were between 1000 and 3000 meters, however, so I pushed on the yoke. We rocketed down faster than we ever had before, and the hull groaned ominously. Even though a bubble surrounded us, it was still under pressure. It was dangerous, but the hull held. It was truly a remarkable vessel.

All three of the warsubs fired torpedoes simultaneously as they dropped mines. The mines wouldn't fall fast enough, but it had been a shrewd tactic.

It cut off the shallower waters as an option for me. The torpedoes were diving toward us at nearly a sixty degree down-angle. I peered at them on the VID for a brief moment and my heart suddenly strobed in my chest.

They were going to intersect with our course.

Damn.

I hit the rudder to steer farther to starboard—now on a southwesterly course, *away* from the Americas—and attempted to put some distance between us and the weapons. They were a hundred meters behind, and the distance closed a bit before my course correction.

Then they detonated.

All three at the same time.

The explosion was gargantuan.

I wondered briefly if they had planned the simultaneous detonations, or if one had gone and just taken the other two with it. But it didn't matter now. The concussion crushed into *SC-1* and the yoke jumped in my hands. I yelled in surprise as I tried to control the seacar, but the turbulence was just too much.

Next to me Kat said, "The bubble is collapsing! Hold on!"

The shock waves had collided with the air around us; it was enough to destabilize the void. And once they compromised its integrity, the entire thing imploded around us with a tremendous shudder. We immediately slowed under the increased drag, and I watched the approaching vessels in horror.

We were sitting ducks.

"Is the drive down?" I asked.

Kat was studying the readout with a tight expression. "No. The reactor is still working. The bubble just needs to reform. Push the throttle—"

She didn't have to finish the sentence. I rammed it forward and watched as the turbulence at the bow of the seacar began to boil into air that stretched backward rather than rise to the surface.

The three ships fired again. Their missiles were right on our ass. I sensed they would explode together again, and interfere with the supercavitation process.

"Come on," I hissed. "Form, dammit." The bubble was over the canopy now, and still moving—

The torpedoes detonated.

The pressure wave hurled the aft end of the seacar upward and I suddenly found us on a thirty degree down-angle. I pulled up desperately—we were already near our maximum depth—and in those few seconds we plummeted

over two hundred meters. The hull creaked again—a sharp *snap* echoed through the ship—but we soon began to rise. The bubble paused for a moment under the relentless shock of water that churned toward us, then it began to grow once more.

I sighed.

It had held. The explosions hadn't been close enough.

Still, it had been scary. The Chinese had come up with a method to destabilize the drive, and it had almost worked.

We changed course due east, and bypassed the massive fleet.

And moved closer to USS *Impaler*.

"TOO DAMN CLOSE FOR MY LIKING," Johnny muttered from my side. Kat was back in the engine room with Meg, checking over the containment capsule.

"Tell me about it," I answered as I watched the sonar. I wanted to give *Impaler* a wide berth. She had known precisely where to position herself in our path.

The comm beeped. It was the USSF warsub. I shrugged inwardly. There was no point answering. We would pass the enormous vessel in minutes. Her four thrusters were incredibly powerful, but her size limited her speed to seventy. She just couldn't keep up, and I had nothing to say to her captain.

And then he came on the line.

"Attention *SC-1*," the captain said in a deep, gravelly voice. It was one honed from years of giving orders and demanding nothing but perfection. I knew that type well, after all my time spent training and working for TCI. It couldn't be faked. He continued, "If you stay on your current course and velocity we will have to destroy you."

I snorted. *Good luck*, I thought. There was no—

But his next sentence turned my blood to ice.

"We have supercavitating torpedoes in our arsenal. I'll fire within twenty seconds if you don't respond."

Our velocity was still 350 kph. There was a possibility that he was bluffing. . . .

"The top speed of our torpedoes is over 1000 kilometers per hour," he said. "Continue at your own peril."

The seriousness to his tone was unmistakable.

"Bullshit," Johnny muttered. "He's just trying to get us to stop. I've never heard of an American ship with that technology."

I tended to agree, but still, Meg had mentioned the possibility earlier. It was conceivable that he was indeed telling the truth.

I keyed the comm. "Prove it first. Then we stop to talk."

There was a long pause. Then, "Very well. Firing now."

The sonar alarm abruptly shrilled and a streak of red screamed from the contact at our port. They did not aim it at us, but it was across our path.

And it was moving damned fast.

The label on the display indicated its velocity at 1050 kph.

"Holy Christ," Johnny whispered. His mouth hung open.

"Stop your drive immediately," the captain repeated, "or the next one will follow your wake and you'll be nothing but a cloud of sinking scrap."

RELUCTANTLY, I DID AS HE ASKED. We were ten kilometers from him; the Chinese were over a hundred farther on his other side. I knew that eventually I would have to push the drive to max and try to outrun the supercavitating torpedoes, but for now, I wanted to see what exactly this man wanted.

"If you come closer we'll run," I said.

"And we'll fire, and you'll die."

"I'd rather scuttle the ship than see you with the technology."

He laughed, but it sounded more like a bark. "We already have the technology."

"Not for seacars. That's substantially more difficult." The fusion reactor was what provided our unlimited propulsion. That's what they needed to make it practical for manned vehicles.

"So we're at an impasse," he finally growled. "But I have a suggestion."

"Go ahead."

"Stay where you are. My executive officer and I will come out to you."

I frowned. "Why?"

"To talk. Face to face."

I considered that. "And *Impaler*?"

"She'll stay right here. Schrader and I will take a fighter over to you. We'll dock, and simply chat. Then we'll leave. I promise you'll be interested in what we have to say."

I had to admit, I was intensely curious about them. Their motives, their reason for being there. Why they had followed us from Trieste. Answers would be nice for a change, I thought. "Very well," I heard myself say. "We'll set our controls to station-keeping. Follow a straight line toward us. Don't

make any sudden deviations or we'll destroy you." I chewed my lip. We didn't have any more weapons, but he didn't need to know that.

"If we were planning to trick you, we'd have killed you by now. I promise."

I clenched a fist. "We'll be waiting," I finally managed. I slammed my palm on the button to terminate our transmission.

"Very odd," Johnny breathed. "I wonder what the hell they want."

To negotiate our surrender, probably. They wanted *SC-1*. I couldn't give it to them.

I'd kill us all first.

THIRTY MINUTES LATER THE SMALL VESSEL approached *SC-1* and docked neatly with our airlock. I had brought the ship to a depth of five hundred meters, and all four of us had been absolutely silent during the wait. During that time, a great many things had crossed my mind. I had been wondering about something for a while now, and it seemed as though I was about to finally discover the truth.

Eventually the two men stood in the living area of our cramped seacar. I had the gun in my holster—plainly visible—and I saw the captain's eyes dart to it.

They, on the other hand, seemed to be unarmed.

I gestured to the couch, and they slowly lowered themselves to it.

The captain was an older man, balding with a fringe of hair around his head. He wore round glasses with steel frames. He was thin, but sinewy muscles beneath the blue USSF uniform were clear. He carried himself with great confidence; a silent aura of power radiated from him. He was unquestionably a leader—even had he worn civilian clothes, it still would have been obvious. His name was Heller.

His first officer was Commander Schrader. I had already met him. On the night that I had first boarded *SC-1* at the start of the mission, he had come to the Docking Module at Trieste to ask about the fight that had occurred outside the city. That night Mayor Flint's attitude had rubbed him the wrong way; he did not have a good poker face, for his ire had been quite visible. He was large with broad shoulders—probably 200 pounds, all muscle. He was glaring at me now, most likely angry at the chase I had led them on. Or perhaps at the way I had set them up to take the Chinese warsubs out for us over the Aleutian Trench.

"What do you want?" I asked without preliminaries.

"We don't have much time," the captain said. "The Chinese are approaching. They know we destroyed their ships earlier. They'll most likely engage us, and try to capture you."

"They've been trying for days now, without much success."

He shrugged. "They might still succeed. I can't allow that to happen. My intention is to take you and your ship with us back to the States."

That startled me. "And what makes you think we'll agree to that?"

"Simple. We'll kill you."

Schrader had a smug look on his face, as if we didn't have a hope in hell. My hand was drifting to my gun, and he eyed it. His expression grew dark. "Don't even think about it."

"You come onto our ship and order us to surrender? Give me a break."

"Then how's this for incentive," Captain Heller said. He shot a glance at Johnny. "I know about Trieste City Intelligence. I know about George Shanks. And I know what he's planning."

THE WORDS HIT LIKE THUNDER. IT was everyone's worst fear in the intelligence business at Trieste: TCI was no longer a secret organization.

The American military *knew*.

Shit. This was a disaster. And now they knew that Trieste had a supercavitating drive.

And, to make matters worse, they knew that Shanks was planning to fight for independence.

It meant the end of the city.

I was speechless. The blood had drained from my face.

"We've known for a decade now," he continued. "We're aware of your operatives and your missions. We routinely monitor you."

"What about Shanks?" Johnny asked. His expression was like ice, and I could tell from his stance that he wanted nothing more than to crush these two with his bare hands.

Heller scowled. "He's planning a war. A stupid idea. We'll destroy Trieste before that happens. In fact . . ." He paused for a moment as he eyed me. "Our job is to stop it. When we return, we intend to. A fleet of USSF warsubs is moving toward the city now."

I felt like he'd punched me in the gut. My dreams for the city were gone. That idiot Shanks, along with Mayor Flint, had led us all to certain destruction. And there was little I could do about it.

The fucking US military knew about TCI.

I said, "You put a tracking device on this seacar, didn't you?"

Kat shot me a look. *"What!?"*

With difficulty, I thrust my anger aside. "They've been behind us every step of the way. Even when we were out of active range. They knew where to wait for us while we were at Blue Downs." In fact, the idea had come to me as I had guarded the moonpool in the Australian city. It had reminded me of my last night in Trieste, when I had first seen *SC-1*. I had noticed a shape under the seacar then, and had assumed that it was a shark or a dolphin.

In fact, it had been a man.

Planting a tracking device.

I glared at Schrader. "You were there to distract us. Not talk about what happened."

He offered an oily grin. "Of course we knew what had happened. You fought with two Sheng City operatives outside Trieste and killed them both. You fought with others inside as well." He motioned to Kat. "We had suspected there was something odd about this seacar. Doctor Wells spent a lot of time supervising construction in Clearwater." He laughed at the looks on our faces. "Yes, we know everything. We've followed you this entire time. Even after you destroyed the *Fast Attack* in the Charlie Gibbs Fracture Zone we knew where you were, but we let you continue so we could see what you were up to." And then he rose to his feet and stepped toward me. "And now it's time for you to surrender."

"Never," I said between clenched teeth.

"Then you'll die."

"So be it."

Heller also stood. "That would be a stupid move, McClusky."

"Get the fuck out." I didn't know what else to say. My hand was on the gun.

The two USSF officers stared at me for a long minute. Then, without another word, they turned and marched through the airlock into their own vehicle. Schrader shot me a last glance, and in his eyes there was something other than anger. It seemed to be almost . . . understanding. Compassion, perhaps.

I slammed my fist on the CLOSE button, and their vessel detached from ours.

Meg swore. "That asshole Shanks. His maniacal dreams of independence are going to kill thousands!"

I had to try and stop it. I knew it, deep inside. There was nothing else for me but Trieste. And if Heller destroyed it . . .

I couldn't bring myself to even think about it.

"We have to beat that force to Trieste," I growled. "We need to start the SCAV drive and get there, *now*."

Kat's eyes were wide. "But *Impaler* will sink us. We can't outrun those torpedoes."

"We have to. We have no other choice." I turned to Johnny. "Let's start the drive and get moving. Maximum speed. This is going to be rough."

WE BARELY GOT BACK INTO SCAV drive before *Impaler* fired a missile. It was on an intercept, and I realized with a pit of hot fear in my gut that this could be it. It was shooting toward us at over 1000 kph.

No one spoke. Our eyes were on the sonar.

The range closed rapidly.

Our speed was 450 kph; for the first time, I was piloting at max velocity. My hands trembled on the yoke. There wasn't much I could do except attempt to evade it. We were more maneuverable than it; at that missile's speed, it would not be able to turn on a dime. We might just be able to circle and make radical course changes until it ran out of fuel.

The problem was *Impaler* most likely had a large arsenal.

I considered ramming the tiny fighter that had carried the captain and his exec over, but the moral side of my character prevented it. It was that same side that had spared Johnny's life earlier. Besides, I knew that another officer on board the warsub would just take over, and would be more determined than ever to destroy Trieste for what we had done.

To evade the missile, I needed room to maneuver. Great depth was the best place for that, and I rapidly brought us down to 3000 meters. The torpedo was only a kilometer away now, and coming on fast. I watched the sonar carefully . . . waiting for the best time.

"Mac . . ." Meagan muttered.

"Don't worry," I whispered. "Strap in back there. You've got ten seconds."

They scrambled back to the living area and I heard safety straps quickly ripped into place.

"Here we go," I said. I pulled back on the yoke and we ascended remarkably fast. We were at a forty-five degree up-angle, and still the torpedo followed.

Only fifty meters away now.

I kept the yoke back. We were almost straight up, shooting for the surface.

And then I wrenched it toward me and we arced backward at 380 kph. My vision dimmed as the blood rushed from my head. I moaned through grinding teeth as we performed the loop. Johnny also groaned; his fingers were white on the arms of the chair.

And then we were all the way around. I leveled us off and continued east. The missile was still on the sonar, but now a kilometer above us. It hadn't been able to turn as rapidly as we had, and now it was trying to reacquire. It made a wide circle toward us, and the nose dipped down.

It had us again.

I swore. The thing would just keep coming until we were dead. Or *Impaler* would just fire two at the same time. That would be impossible to survive.

Impaler. An idea had suddenly come to me. What if I could destroy her with her own missile? I wrestled with the notion for only a brief moment. I hadn't wanted to kill the two officers; they had come to speak to us under a truce. However, *Impaler* was fair game. In fact, if we *didn't* kill her, we might never make it back to Trieste.

The USSF would know what we had done, but they already knew everything anyway.

We had no choice now.

I heeled the seacar over until the warsub was dead center on the VID. Its image grew rapidly.

The comm came to life. "*SC-1*, turn away immediately! Do not come any closer!"

"Do you think we're going to listen to you after you tried to kill us?" I snarled. I kept her directly before us. The missile was at our back, and closing.

Impaler was diving now, trying to get away. At the last second, I yanked the yoke up and we shot over her hull. She rocked back and forth in our violent wake; the move had most likely tossed her crew about like rag dolls.

And then the missile approached. It closed on *Impaler* . . .

And darted right over her.

It had *known* not to hit her. It had a friendly fire avoidance program, of course.

Shit.

Behind us, it quickly closed the gap. I had to get deep again in order to evade . . .

Or did I? Why go down? Why not try up?

It was worth a shot.

I brought us to the surface; in seconds we were only twenty meters below the water line. The missile was the same distance behind us. Our speed was back up to 450 kph. I pulled back a fraction more on the yoke—

And we broke the surface.

We rocketed out into open air.

"WHAT THE HELL ARE YOU DOING!?" Kat screamed, but I didn't care. It was our only option left.

Bright light immediately filled the seacar; the blue sky and noon sun were simply dazzling, especially after living meters underwater for so long. In fact, I hadn't seen the sun like that in over ten years. It was magnificent. We were in the middle of the South Pacific, the water flat around us to the horizon in all directions. The fierce glare sparkled off the surface.

Our speed fell rapidly; with no water to suck into the engine room, there could be no steam propulsion. We simply hopped into the air, and within seconds had hit the zenith of the arc.

We started back downward; we were only about five meters above water.

But it was enough.

The missile had followed us and also soared into the sky.

We hit the surface with tremendous force and water surged back into our fusion intake system. It vaporized under the high temperature and the steam exhaust began nearly instantly. We plunged down, and I watched the sonar intently. No contact yet, but it would be coming. "Everyone hang on!" I bellowed.

The missile completed its arc—a much larger one than ours—and hit the surface of the water well in front of us. The impact was hard, and the computer—thinking it had hit the hull of a ship—did the only thing it knew how to.

It detonated.

The blast shoved us violently to the side, but no red lights appeared on the console. I quickly regained control of SC-1, and sent us hurtling to the east once more.

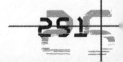

And away from *Impaler*.

They fired twice more, but with each one, I performed the same maneuver. Kat had stopped protesting, but the massive concussions when we hit the surface were hard to ignore. She was gritting her teeth at the potential damage we were taking, but I saw no signs of any on the control consoles. In fact, within fifteen minutes, we were safe.

We had escaped.

WE BREATHED A SIGH OF RELIEF when *Impaler* disappeared at last from our sonar display. Johnny had a huge grin on his face, and even Kat seemed impressed at what I had done.

"How did you think of it?" she asked. The two women had unstrapped and were behind me, just over my shoulder.

I shrugged. "There was nothing left to try."

She shook her head. "You astound me, Mac."

"Me too," Meg added.

I remained silent for a while and simply piloted the vessel as I considered what had happened. Heller knew everything. He had a tracker on us. He knew we were going to Trieste. When *Impaler* arrived, the USSF would come down hard on Shanks and Flint and most likely take Trieste under their complete control. The Chinese were on their way as well. And according to Johnny, they *wanted* us to fight, so they could back us and pull the city away from the States. It would destabilize the entire situation, and perhaps even give them more of an opportunity to take over The Iron Plains. The US might just let China do what they wanted in the Pacific while they were busy with us.

Then again, once China got into it, there was no telling what would happen.

Meg said, "Shanks is going to bring the city down with him."

"His plans are big," Kat muttered. "As soon as he sees a fleet closing on him, he'll start early."

And that would be the trigger.

The problem was, I had no idea what to do.

We surged through the ocean, toward the Panama pass-through.

Toward home.

Toward the final confrontation.

"The dream will continue long after I'm dead."

—Frank McClusky, Citizen of Trieste, Mayor, and
Freedom Fighter

PART SIX: THE GULF OF MEXICO

THE PASS-THROUGH WAS A TUNNEL THAT paralleled the Panama Canal; it pierced the isthmus of the continent from the Pacific to the Gulf. It was for submersible traffic only, and as we approached it we shut down the SCAV drive and reactivated the screws. As soon as we were in the Gulf, we brought the fusion reactor back online and pushed the ship to maximum speed. No doubt every listening device in the area and every seacar and warsub heard us and realized what we had, but we were past the point of caring. We had to get back to the city.

On the way, I pulled Johnny aside to talk with him. We sat in the lounge, and I said, "Are you willing to come with me?"

His face registered shock. "What do you mean? We're going to see Shanks, aren't we?"

"Not yet. I have to see the Storage Module first." It was what he had warned me about, days earlier at the French base. He thought something odd was going on there, something that had to do with the bid for independence.

"You still don't know?"

"No."

"Kat won't tell you?"

"She doesn't want to get sent back topside for betraying Shanks."

He winced at my choice of words. "About all of this, Mac, I'm truly sorry."

"You've already explained yourself. I told you it made sense."

"But still, what you went through . . ."

I sighed. Shanks had mistreated prisoners in our city too. "What I need to know is: Can I trust you completely?"

"After what Lau did, I wouldn't blame you if you didn't. But you have my word. I'll do whatever you want."

What I wanted now might mean his death. Would he agree to that?

"Tell me what's in the Storage Module," I said.

He laid it all out, along with how they had gotten the information in the first place. He didn't have evidence with him—it was all back in Sheng—but he seemed to have minute details about what Shanks was doing and how exactly he and Flint had pulled it off.

After he finished, I left him sitting on the couch and pulled myself into my bunk to think about our predicament. I felt massively conflicted about things, more so than ever in the past. I knew independence would destroy Trieste. Meg knew it too. Hell, our father was proof of what could happen to someone who defied authority. He had been so completely ignorant about the whole situation. I had promised myself that I wouldn't be, but events had pulled me to a place I didn't want to be in. There was really no solution to this mess. Even if I managed to somehow stop Shanks and Flint, the USSF was still going to crush the independence movement, once and for all, and then they would be in our city—more of them than ever—and likely controlling our municipal government. Say goodbye to all of our hard-earned industry. To what little income we generated for the city. After the takeover, it would *all* go to the federal government.

Eventually I pulled myself from the dark confines of the bunk and found Meg in the engine room. She had left the control cabin and was now going over the fusion reactor. She could study the equipment for years, I knew, and never grow bored. She loved technology that allowed us to live underwater, and here was the biggest leap forward since Cousteau had invented the aqualung. She was checking over the device after its long period of operation at maximum output. All signs were that it was perfect.

"Meg," I said as I entered the chamber. I closed the hatch behind me.

She lifted her head and stared at me from her crouch beside the containment capsule. "Feeling better?"

"Worse, actually. I'm not sure what to do. How to get us out of this."

She appeared confused. "We have to stop Shanks, of course, then appeal to the US government."

I sighed. "They won't listen. You know that. They've been watching us since 2099. This is just a repeat of that. They won't make the same mistake twice."

She frowned. "Then what do we do? Just walk away and watch the city die?"

"Dammit, that's my problem! I can't do that. But I don't think stopping Shanks will help either. We're in a real fix here. There doesn't seem to be a way to save the city."

She rose to her feet and put her hands on my shoulders. "I have faith in you. You've astonished me in these past few days. You'll figure something out."

My jaw dropped. "You think there's an easy solution?"

A shrug. "I'm not sure. But if there is one, you'll find it."

I wasn't sure about that. I did have a glimmer of a plan, but didn't think she'd agree. And my sister's approval was damn important. When I presented the idea to her, I thought she might just want to kill me.

If I wasn't dead already.

WHEN WE WERE LESS THAN FIFTY kilometers from Trieste, we shut down the SCAV drive and our speed dropped to seventy. It was daytime, and the sun penetrated right to the floor of the continental shelf south of the United States. As we approached, the waters grew more and more shallow. Trieste was thirty meters down, clearly visible, and a feeling of intense worry welled up within me as it came into view. The familiar modules and travel tubes were all there, and I thought again of how I would do anything for her citizens. But this dilemma would change the city forever. The decisions I made in the next few hours would have massive repercussions.

But before I could confront Shanks and decide what path to take, I needed to see the Storage Module.

"What do you think is in there?" Meg asked as I brought the seacar toward Trieste. We were closing on it from the southwest, and the module was now only fifty meters ahead. We had identified ourselves to the city controllers—they had us on sonar and were requesting our ID—and they were no doubt notifying Shanks and Flint at that precise moment.

We had maybe an hour, at most, before security came out to get us.

"I have a suspicion," I finally answered, "but I need to see it with my own eyes." I knew what Johnny had said, but there was still a chance his information had been false. Perhaps even propaganda from his superiors. The module seemed so small it was doubtful anything odd was happening there. Still, that might be why Shanks had chosen to use it—to avoid USSF suspicion.

The thought made me realize that there was a fleet bearing down on us; it could arrive within hours. We needed to move.

Johnny and I went through a very familiar procedure: we prepared to infiltrate a city. As we pulled on our wetsuits and attached daggers to our thighs—I had lost the needle gun during my fight with Lau—I noticed him glancing at me with a smile on his face. Like him, I couldn't help but feel the thrill of adventure once again; despite our troubled past, he had once been a great friend and we had done this many times before on missions to other undersea cities around the world.

In the central passageway, just under the ladder that led to the hatch on the top of the hull, was the seacar's moonpool. Because the pressure inside the vehicle was equal to the outside, water didn't rush into the car, and the air didn't go out. The two balanced perfectly at this depth, and it was far more convenient than the airlock.

We sat on the edge of the pool and dangled our feet in the water. Our tanks were strapped to our backs, and our facemasks were on.

We were ready.

"No comm chatter," I reminded him. "Hand signals only."

"Roger."

I glanced at Meg and Kat; they stood next to us as we prepared to exit. They were going to set the seacar on the bottom and wait for us to return. Kat had a look on her face that was hard to interpret at first, but I eventually recognized it as trepidation. She knew what was there, of course, what I was finally about to see. Her refusal to speak still annoyed me, but I respected her decision. At the very least, it made me realize if I ever needed her confidence or help for anything, she would be there. She was loyal.

She nodded to me, her lips tight. Meg winked at us, and we slipped quietly under the surface.

Once again I was back in the water outside my home. The last time I had been here, I had killed two Chinese operatives as they'd attempted to escape. It had been night then. Now, as we began to swim toward the module, the sun was at its zenith and the waters around me were fully lit. At this depth it was still fairly cool, but the wetsuits protected us. Soon our muscles were pumping as we kicked ourselves forward, and I felt absolutely comfortable.

I eyed Johnny as we moved toward the module's moonpool. In a way I felt bad for him, for he was a lost soul. His actions seven years earlier had led him in a direction I sensed he now regretted. Forgiveness for what he had done was difficult; I wondered if I could trust him as I'd used to, before he betrayed me.

I would have to watch him carefully here.

Soon the moonpool was in sight. It was in the lowest level of the module, but raised slightly over the seafloor. We simply had to move under the lip and swim upward. We would break the surface and officially be in Trieste once again.

The module had been off limits for over two years. The official explanation was that it was undergoing refitting. People were beginning to grow curious about what exactly was happening, however, because what refit for storage could possibly take so long? The team of construction workers had been isolated in a separate temporary habitat. Funny that I had never wondered why, although now it seemed obvious: Shanks was worried that if they interacted with Triestrians, someone might accidentally spill the beans.

The workers came and went every single day. I had hoped that we could just do exactly as they did—enter at the moonpool—and have a look around.

But I hadn't counted on a guard.

He was in the water below the pool, wearing scuba gear. He saw us swimming toward him and immediately turned to us. "Halt. This area is for workers only."

Johnny's reply was immediate. "The foreman asked us to come."

There was a slight hesitation. "Where's your access card?"

That startled me. No request for ID—but one for some sort of computer chip that could open hatches.

"He's going to meet us just inside," Johnny replied. "He's got them for us there."

We were now directly in front of the man. He was big. He was holding a needle gun, and he touched the side of his mask with the other hand. "I'm going to confirm first. You two, don't move."

We floated there before him, pretending to wait, but I knew from past instances like this exactly what was about to happen.

We couldn't let him make that call.

With a flick of my flippers, I began to drift to his right. Johnny did the same, but to the guard's left.

He noticed, and his face grew hard. "I said stay where you are."

"Sorry," I said. "The currents."

He frowned at my explanation, but before he could say more, Johnny was at the man's side. This was no professional, that much was certain. He should have fired as soon as we'd disobeyed his order.

In a flash, one of Johnny's arms was around his neck and his other hand grabbed the needle gun.

"Hey!" the guard cried. He wrenched his arm down to aim at me, but Johnny's grip was strong. I heard a strangled gasp from the man.

"Don't hurt him," I muttered. He was innocent. And a Triestrian. I disarmed him and pushed the weapon into his back. "We're going into the module. You're going to show us around. Then we'll leave. If you give us trouble, I'll be forced to kill you. I don't want to, but I will if I have to. There's too much at stake here to let you give us away. Do you understand?"

His eyes were like daggers, but after a moment he nodded. He didn't think it was worth it.

"I'm a Triestrian," I said. "You know me."

"Bullshit."

"I'm McClusky."

His eyes widened behind his mask. "But why the hell would you do this?"

"I'm trying to save the city."

He said no more. Together we swam to the ladder. Johnny went up first, the guard next, and I brought up the rear.

We entered the Storage Module.

THE ENCLOSURE IMMEDIATELY INSIDE WAS THE moonpool room, with lockers for scuba gear and wetsuits. Here workers would change to either go farther into the module or back outside. On the only hatch in the room was an electronic keypad with a slot for an access card. I turned to the guard and held out my hand. In my other was the needle gun. When the hatch was open, we stepped forward into the single chamber. It was at least five levels deep. Catwalks ringed each level; the center of each deck was open to the ones above and below. Along the exterior bulkheads on each were cranes and conveyers that held machinery for the manufacture of—

Of what?

I squinted as I tried to peer closer. What exactly was Shanks building here? What were they—

"Holy shit," I said. I turned to Johnny.

"Now do you believe me?" he asked.

MINUTES LATER HE AND I WERE outside and swimming furiously for *SC-1*. We had simply left the guard in the module, bewildered at our sudden

departure. My breath was coming fast and my face was flushed. I was filled with rage and wanted nothing more than to get to City Control to confront Shanks. How dare he do this? How dare he bring Trieste to this point? The looming confrontation was his fault, and moreover, it would further exacerbate the situation in the Pacific. He was playing with people's lives—and with the fates of nations.

Inside the seacar I kept silent as I ramped up the thrusters and powered us toward the Docking Module. The landing lights stretched out before us, and I coordinated our entry with the city controllers in a tight, clipped tone. Meg and Kat watched me warily; neither had asked what I had seen.

Once we were safely in our berth and had shut down the ship, I rose to my feet shakily and clenched my fists. "Johnny and I are going to City Control now. Are you coming?"

Kat nodded. Meg looked first to her, then at me. "Yes."

I led the way from the ship and we stepped onto the docks outside. The trip through the travel tube to the Commerce Module was quiet. The others could sense the anger radiating from me. My heart was thudding; I felt like it might soon explode. Within minutes we were standing inside the offices of the administration, traffic control, and maintenance departments. There were various displays and schematics of the city around the room. Some showed the atmospheric composition of each module, others minor variations in pressure. Computers and personnel monitored everything, just as in a space colony. A large map on the far wall showed the Gulf and Caribbean; there were symbols and lights located all over it. In the corner, standing before some screens and control boards, was Shanks. His broad figure and salt-and-pepper hair were easy to identify. His posture and jerky movements betrayed his tension; he was wound as tight as a spring.

I stalked toward him with the others at my side. As I grew closer, I could hear him barking questions.

"Well, where are they then?" he was saying. "They arrived forty-five minutes ago, but they didn't dock until now. What were they doing?" A short pause; I couldn't hear the response. He continued, "I ordered you to watch them for me!" He swore and slammed his fist on the comm to terminate the exchange.

And then he turned and noticed me.

And Kat. And Meg.

And Johnny.

His mouth twisted when he saw the Chinese agent. "There you are, you son of a bitch! I've got you now, and you'll never see Sheng City again!"

"Not so fast," I ground out. I raised the guard's needle gun and aimed it directly at the director's face. "We have to debrief first, don't we?"

THERE WERE ABOUT TWENTY OTHER PEOPLE in the room, sitting at their desks and control stations, and they turned at my voice. Their jaws dropped when they saw the gun.

Shanks's face was red. "What are you talking about, McClusky? I ordered you to get Johnny back here, and you've done that. Dismissed."

I raised my voice and spoke to the room. "You people know who I am. I would never do anything to hurt the city, or anyone who lives here. You're in no danger." And then to Shanks, "Except maybe you."

"What are you talking about?" His eyes flicked to the hatch; there was something there. The guard we had left behind in the Storage Module must have finally alerted someone.

"Johnny," I muttered. "Check the entry."

He glanced behind us. "Uh huh. Security. Four."

"Keep an eye on them."

"Got ya."

Shanks snarled, "You'll do no such thing! You're a traitor and a Sheng City agent!"

"Shut up!" I snapped. "He's more a patriot than you'll ever be!"

Shanks's eyes narrowed. "I worked with your father, McClusky. He would never have put up with this sort of insolence from a supposed operative."

"Cut the shit, Shanks. Enough talk about my father. He was an idiot. He was stupid enough to think that the US wouldn't act on his threats. Well, they did, and now he's dead. And because of the crap you've pulled, they're on their way right now. They mean to stop you before you can act."

His mouth clamped shut for a heartbeat. Then, "What are you talking about?"

"I spoke with *Impaler*'s captain. The USSF knows about TCI. They know about your plans, and have all along."

He frowned. "That—that can't be." His voice had grown quiet.

"The Chinese are also on their way. They mean to join the fight on our side. It means war, Shanks—and one that will spill over onto land. And it's all your fault." A long silence stretched out between us. He turned from me and stared at a closed circuit monitor of the ocean outside the city. When next he spoke, his tone was normal, controlled.

"So be it. We'll have to act sooner than later, but there will be no difference. The war against the States will begin in hours instead of weeks. And when it's over, we'll be free. Trieste City will be an independent nation."

It seemed odd to finally hear him admitting this. After all, when he had originally sent me out on the mission, his stated motivation had been that Kat's stolen invention could start a war. As it turned out, that was exactly what he had wanted all along.

Meg had watched the whole exchange quietly, but now she just couldn't contain herself. "What are you talking about?" she said. "They'll crush us! They're going to destroy the city!" She turned to me and grabbed my arm. "What the hell did you see in the Storage Module? What's he doing over there?"

Shanks said, "You were in the module? How did you—"

"Johnny warned me about what you were doing. I was skeptical, but even Captain Heller told me you were planning something. And once I saw it, I knew they were telling the truth."

"Truman," Meg grated. *"What is in the module?"*

I glared at Shanks. "Tell her, Director."

He remained silent and simply stared at me.

I sighed. "Fine. I will." I turned to her. "Ships under construction. Lots of them. I counted forty."

"Ships?" she asked, slightly mystified. "Seacars, you mean?"

"Yes, but ones for battle. Militarized."

She knotted her fists. "He means to fight with them."

"That's how he thinks he can win."

She snorted. "Fat chance. Forty ships against the entire USSF. A single *Reaper* could probably take them—"

"There's more, Meg. They aren't ordinary seacars. They're supercavitating vessels, like *SC-1*. They all have fusion reactors—Kat's design." That was why Kat's invention was so important to him. If the Chinese or Americans got their hands on the technology, they would all have their own vessels equipped with SCAV drives. It would be another stalemate. But with Trieste as the only holder of the technology, she could dictate what would happen in the future exploitation of the oceans. And with a fleet of forty seacars like *SC-1*, Shanks could destroy any nation that opposed him underwater. I said to him, "Johnny told me you've been dealing more produce than normal to some nations in exchange for building material. You've also been buying torpedoes in large quantities. How long have you been doing it?"

He sneered. "Years. But we've only recently started installing the reactors. We're almost done now."

Something I had heard long before suddenly came to me. I snapped my fingers. "That's why the large imports of lithium! You needed it for the lining on the containment capsules!"

He seemed proud of himself. "Very good, McClusky. But those ships in that module are superior in every way to any other warsub out there. They're even better than *SC-1*. They're equipped with SCAV torpedoes too! No one can compete with our forces."

Meg's eyes were like lasers. "What gives you the right to do this to the people of Trieste?"

"Do what?" he barked. "I'm giving them their freedom! I've been working on these plans since your father died. I'm doing it for the city, don't you see that?"

"This city will be dust in a few hours! Don't *you* see that?"

He shook his head. "You're naive. The Americans can't stand up to—"

"You fucking asshole!" she yelled. "You have no right!"

"I have every right! I'm working with Mayor Flint! She is fully behind this, which means the people of the city are!"

Meg was angry as hell and having a hard time controlling herself. I put my hand on her shoulder to help calm her. I said, "If they knew you two were bringing them to the brink of war, surely they would object, Shanks."

"It's too late now, McClusky. If what you say is true, that the Americans and Chinese are on their way, then we have to prepare."

The room was deathly silent. Everyone in there had heard the exchange, including the controllers and the security Johnny was holding back with his gun. And they were not happy; I could see it in their faces. I pointed at one of them, a woman at Sea Traffic Control. "You. Do you want independence so bad that you're willing to go to war for it?"

She shook her head. "No way. We're too vulnerable here. One missile from topside could finish it all in an instant."

I turned back to him. He was speechless for a moment, completely flustered by anger. Then he said to me, "I sent you to get a traitor back, and instead you've come back one yourself!"

"I've always resisted independence because of the dangers that it brings. For one, the US would crush us. For another, we're simply not ready for it. Not without good government, anyway, and simply put, you ain't it."

He stepped toward me and bared his teeth. "We'll see then, won't we?"

I paused for a long moment. "I guess we will." I pointed at the map of the Gulf and Caribbean high on the bulkhead next to us. It had on it every seacar, vessel, and warsub detected in the area by a vast network of listening devices. It compiled its results together and displayed them with different symbols. "Look—do you see the dangers now?"

Massive clusters of lights had appeared at the edges of the map. From the west—the Panama pass-through—the large force of Chinese warsubs was en route. And from the east, the USSF fleet.

"Here comes your war, Shanks. I hope to hell that you're ready for it."

Meg turned to me. "What are you talking about? We have to stop this, right now!"

"I'm sorry, Meg, but there's no way. We have to fight for independence now. There's no going back. Those forces are coming, and we need to be ready." I paused to steel myself, and then, "I can't believe I'm saying this, but we have to join Shanks."

CHAPTER THIRTY-ONE

DEAD SILENCE. MY SUGGESTION HAD SHOCKED them. Only Shanks was pleased; he had a tight grin on his face as he watched the others.

"How can you say such a thing?" Meg hissed. "You're sentencing the people here to death!"

Kat stepped in. "He's doing the only logical thing possible. The Federal government has persecuted the people here for too long. It's time someone did something about it, and Mac knows that this is the right decision."

I watched her with a sinking feeling in my gut. The truth was that I didn't think it was time to make our move at all. In fact, it was a colossal mistake. We could never beat the United States, SCAV technology or not. It didn't matter how many *SC-1*'s Shanks had. We were easy prey.

We might all be dead in just a few short hours.

And the world would be at war.

"No," I finally whispered. "That's not true, Kat. This is wrong."

"Then why help Shanks?" Meg injected, clearly confused.

I sighed. "The fact of the matter is that they're coming, regardless. They know we have SCAV technology now. They'll come here and take over, and most likely arrest Shanks and Flint."

Shanks chortled in derision. "I doubt they'll make it in."

A surge of disbelief passed through me. "That's inevitable, Shanks. They'll penetrate your defenses easily. You see, their ships may not have the SCAV drive, but they do have SCAV torpedoes. Your warsubs will last longer than a conventional fleet, but in the end it won't make a difference."

His tone grew sharp. "I say that it will. And we're going to find out."

"Yes, we will," I said, resigned. "Listen, the US is going to win here. But I see a chance to lay the groundwork for independence for some time in the future. I can't sit back and wait for them to just obliterate our dreams. I have to help." I turned to Meg. "Don't you see, sis? Whether I sit back and do nothing, or fight and die, the end result is going to be the same. But if I fight, there is a great opportunity here."

"For what?"

I hesitated and glanced at Shanks. I didn't want to come out and say it yet in front of him until there was no turning back. And by then he'd be gone—taken by US troops most likely—and once that happened I could begin a logical and more realistic drive for independence. And so I settled on, "I can't say just yet. But trust me on this—it's the *right* thing to do." She still seemed shaken by my decision—almost *hurt* by it, in fact. I added, "You said you had faith in me, Meg. Trust me in this."

Her jaw clamped shut and she glared at me. Then, "You're only going to exacerbate the problems! You're going to bring the city down with you!" She pointed to a nearby comm console. "Call the USSF now and declare our surrender before the fighting begins."

"Dammit, I can't do that!" I snapped. "Don't you understand that they *know* about TCI? I have to *prevent* the damage from being too excessive!"

But she was breathing hard and refused to back down. The others were staring at us now—at brother and sister engaged in a childish shouting match. She had clenched her fists at her sides. "I guess you're going to do what you want, but I can't support you in it."

You'll see, I wanted to say. Instead I kept my mouth shut against what I so desperately wanted to tell her. A hard moment of silence later, she spun on her heel and stormed out. I watched her go, feeling as if someone close to me had just died.

Shanks faced me in the stunned silence. "What are you talking about? You're going to fight for us, aren't you?"

He knew the effect that my presence would have on the battle. The Triestrians who piloted and crewed the new warsubs would most likely rally around me. They would see my actions as an attempt to achieve what my father had been unable to do.

I said, "I'll pilot *SC-1*. Have it fully armed with torpedoes and countermeasures. Johnny will be my copilot."

The director's face grew red again. "He's a spy! A traitor!"

"He's coming with me, or I won't help, Shanks. We'll deal with his actions after the battle." I shrugged. "Hell, maybe he and I will both die out there. That would solve your problems, wouldn't it?"

He was glaring at Johnny. "Fine, but afterward report immediately back to me."

"Agreed." I looked at Kat. "It seems you were right all along about independence." I paused. "And now I have to fight for it."

A smile split her face and she put her hands around my neck. Her dark eyes locked to mine. We hadn't been physical or had much of an intimate relationship since Meagan had come on board *SC-1*. The escape from the Chinese, as well as *Impaler*, had distracted us, as had the upcoming confrontation. Nevertheless, I did have a desire to see her happy, and I hoped that what I was going to do would please her.

But I knew deep inside that there was a chance she could hate me forever—perhaps even enough to kill me.

AFTER THE CONFRONTATION WITH MEG, I stalked toward my cubicle in Living Module B. She had left City Control in a huff; I wasn't sure where she had gone. I was angry at her reaction, but understood why she had responded in such a way. I just prayed she would agree with me when this was all over. I hoped I would see her before I had to leave.

Shanks had already left to organize the efforts to launch his fleet of supercavitating seacars, and I found myself without a whole lot to do until we could leave. The CSF and USSF vessels were on an intercept course in the Gulf, and until they met, I had some time.

I soon found myself standing in the corridor where some two weeks earlier Chinese operatives had attacked and killed Blake. All evidence of the fight was of course gone, but still, he had been a friend, and although I hadn't seen or talked with him in years, the loss had been difficult to stomach.

Inside the cubicle, I sat before my computer and switched on the global news. From the looks of it, there was continuous coverage of the converging fleets. A male voice was narrating over stock footage of warsubs firing torpedoes.

" . . . the two fleets will meet within hours now, and tensions are high." A scene of Chinese politicians at the United Nations in an angry confrontation with the American delegation appeared. "Troubles in the Pacific Ocean have led to this, although it's unsure why it has escalated so rapidly. But sources within the Chinese government are claiming the loss of at least eight vessels at the hands of a single USSF ship, the *Reaper* class warsub *Impaler*. The US government has remained silent about the accusation. Speculation is rampant that there was indeed an incident over the Aleutian Trench days ago, and that the increasing tensions are a result of that confrontation. No doubt the dispute over mining rights to The Iron Plains has played a large role as well." An image of Trieste City suddenly appeared, looking peaceful and serene in the bright waters of the continental shelf. "The conflict also seems to involve the US undersea colony of Trieste, although few officials are speaking about it. The two forces are due to meet near the city within twenty hours, and calls to Trieste's mayor and city councillors have gone unanswered." The image shifted to a serious-looking news anchor who sat in front of a large display of a CSF warsub in the process of simultaneously launching six torpedoes. "One can only hope cooler heads will prevail, but with both China and the States having now severed diplomatic ties over the incident, things are not looking good."

I snorted and cut the feed. *Cooler heads.* Such a thing didn't seem to exist in government anymore.

A knock at the partition startled me, and I opened it to see Kat standing just outside.

"Busy?" she asked.

"Just watching the news."

"It's insane, isn't it?"

I frowned. "This is what you wanted, Kat. A fight for independence."

"I didn't want China involved. It's snowballing because of my invention." She stepped inside and sat on my bunk. "This isn't exactly what I thought would happen."

I studied her for a moment; her face showed her emotions clearly. She was nervous and scared about what was coming. "But how did you think it would go? A quick decisive battle between just a few ships?"

"Perhaps."

That's what my father had thought too. "Kat, this is going to be *massive.* Thousands of people are going to die, and that might just be the start."

"I know," she whispered. "Because of me."

I sighed. "You created something incredible. I wouldn't want that invention to go unrealized. But it's not your fault that China is pressing."

"But I am responsible for giving it to Shanks."

I shrugged. "True. But if you hadn't, we wouldn't have the SCAV drive,

would we? We disagreed about independence, but you haven't caused this."

She considered that for a moment. "How is this going to end, Mac? If you don't think the city will be free after this, why get involved?"

I started at that. "I've been involved since Johnny stole your material. I have to see this through to the end now. And I have an idea. . . . I think I can start us on a path to independence . . . but it's going to take some time. It won't happen overnight."

She looked up at me. Her dark eyes were sad. "I don't want to lose you. I know I'm temperamental sometimes, but only when it comes to my work. I've really enjoyed being together these past weeks. And the night that we spent together . . ." She trailed off but kept her eyes locked to mine.

I sat beside her. "I feel it too," I said. "Despite the fact that you're so hardheaded, I had a real attraction to you almost immediately." I hesitated. "In fact, I think we're very similar. I have strong beliefs too—I just don't blow up when I'm challenged."

She smiled. "That's probably because of your training. It helps you suppress your emotions, right? To be a better operative. Colder."

I mulled that over. "I guess. It helped when the Chinese captured me, that's for sure."

"And what about Johnny? Do you still blame him?"

"Yes. But I've forgiven him. I understand him better now."

"Will you keep him safe from Shanks?"

"I'll try my best."

She fell silent for long minutes as we sat there. She had looked away again, but eventually tilted her face to mine. She whispered, "You truly amazed me while we were chasing Johnny and trying to get back home. During the last few days, I was upset that Meg was there. She took your attention away from me. It was childish, I know, but it's how I felt." She paused. "I want to make love again, Mac, for as long as possible before you leave, if you're still interested."

At that moment, there wasn't anything that I wanted more.

I took her in my arms.

HOURS LATER, AFTER KAT HAD LEFT for City Control to monitor the battle, I met with Johnny and we headed for the Docking Module. As we walked back to *SC-1* to confirm the loading of the new weaponry, he said, "You really think we don't have a chance?"

"We can't beat the States, Johnny. Not like this."

"Then why do it?"

I glanced at him and pondered the question for a few heartbeats. Around us in the travel tube Triestrians were on their way to work despite the looming danger. Nothing could stop them from fulfilling their responsibilities. I could be sacrificing their lives for my plans, but in the end I felt that it was the right thing to do.

In fact, it would shock them.

If only I could come out and tell them about it.

But not yet. I couldn't risk someone overhearing and informing Shanks or the mayor.

"Because we have no choice," I replied in barely a whisper. "Meg's idea has merit, but it's the wrong thing to do." I grabbed his shoulder. "You'll see, Johnny. In a few hours, it will all make sense to you."

I looked around the docks before we boarded the seacar. Still no sign of her.

"Don't worry," he said. "She'll forgive you."

I grunted. "I hope so." We descended the ladder into the ship and sealed the hatch above us.

WITHIN HOURS THE TWO FLEETS HAD assembled just south of Trieste over the shallow continental shelf. The water was clear and bright, and almost four hundred ships faced off across the immense battlefield. The line of vessels was nearly ten kilometers long. Warsubs from the smallest American *Hunter-Killers* and Chinese *Fast Attacks* to the largest *Reapers* and their counterpart *Mings* were there. Each side had placed their ships at varying depths—some at only a few meters, and some very close to the bottom at 150 meters. One kilometer separated the two forces. The sea was alive with the sounds of ships' thrusters as they maintained their positions in the line.

There was not a single living creature within range of the fleets. The Chinese and the Americans faced each other as two armies would have in the middle ages. And when the torpedoes and countermeasures started launching, it would be a chaotic scene, full of destruction and death.

Marine creatures knew better than to stick around.

Johnny and I were in *SC-1*, leading the pack of forty SCAV warsubs that Shanks had built. They were slightly larger than our own seacar and were the same design, but these were grayish-blue and difficult to identify visually.

Even at close range in the middle of the afternoon it was hard to spot one. The noise from the SCAV drive would give them away, of course, but in a pinch they could settle to the bottom and hide quite effectively. Shanks called them *Stingrays*. It was a fitting name for the deadly little ships.

Beside me, Johnny gasped at the scene. Neither of us had ever seen anything like it. The VID projected it all before us; the line of opposing ships passed even beyond the system's five kilometer range.

"I hope you know what you're doing," he muttered.

"Me too." I turned to him. "Are you sure you can find Lau in there?"

"I think so."

Lau was the lynchpin to my plan. The last time I had seen him had been at Blue Downs, after our quick and violent confrontation. As he left he had said that things weren't over between us, and he had been right. But he had no idea how different our next interaction really would be.

According to Johnny, there would actually be two groupings of warsubs in the Chinese Submarine Fleet. The first would be those associated with mainland China—the official navy operating under the government, the CSF. The other would be those subs that represented the six Chinese undersea cities. Lau would most likely be among that group—in particular, the Sheng City warsubs.

"How can you find his vessel?" I asked as I positioned *SC-1*. We were at the northernmost end of the theater of battle, with both fleets before us stretching away into the distance. It implied very clearly that we had not taken a side. Our force of forty subs was substantial, I knew, despite our size, and both the USSF and the CSF would be quick to realize it.

"Each sub transmits a signal, just as with Triestrian seacars. The transponder identifies the warsub and its port of call."

"Let me guess—you know the codes."

He grinned. "I can find the Sheng City warsubs for you. But to find the precise one that Lau is in—*if* he's there—I just can't do."

"We'll contact them randomly then. You do that while I try to keep us alive." For my plan to work, there was something that I needed. "I want our forces to target mainland Chinese and US warsubs only. Can you send a message to the *Stingrays* to tell them?"

He nodded. "I'll have those warsubs show as red on their sonars."

"Do it."

"But will they listen to you?" He was looking at me, then a flash of embarrassment crossed his features. "Right—you're a McClusky, after all. They'll listen."

"Let's hope so."

I stared at the huge numbers of warsubs before me. Each side had close to two hundred vessels present. There had never been a battle of this magnitude in the history of submarine naval warfare. One had expected such a conflict to break out near The Iron Plains in the Pacific, but not here, so near to the tiny city of Trieste. Our SCAV drive was clearly so important to the future of nations that they were willing to kill—and *die*—for it.

China had sent a signal and openly invited us to join their fleet—as Johnny had indicated earlier—but I had refused. We would target Americans and Chinese alike, but avoid the ships of the Chinese undersea colonies.

Until I could contact Lau.

If he was there.

A DEEP AND RESONATING VOICE ABRUPTLY came over the comm. I groaned. It was the Commanding Officer of the USSF in the Gulf region, Admiral Taurus T. Benning. His presence indicated the USSF's position in no uncertain terms: they were going to attempt to annihilate the CSF from these waters. There would be no negotiating.

Sure enough, all he gave was one quick warning. "Attention CSF warsubs and those of Trieste." I jumped at that, for he had clearly noticed us. "Leave immediately. Trieste forces, return to your port of call and wait for USSF warsubs to impound your vessels. This is your only notice. If you don't depart within one minute, we will interpret that as an act of hostility and engage."

I snorted. He had geared his message in every way to inflame the situation.

Then the response from the CSF. It was a woman. "This is Admiral Yan of the Chinese Submarine Fleet. We require the return of our kidnapped citizen and also the surrender of the seacar *SC-1*, along with her pilot and crew. We will interpret a failure to do so as an act of war."

There was no way either side would accept the demands of the other. These two fleets were about to start shooting. Tensions over The Iron Plains had finally grown too great, and *SC-1* and her unique drive had pushed the two sides over the brink.

"Any luck?" I muttered to Johnny. He was attempting to locate Lau in the Sheng City warsubs.

"Not yet. I'm still trying."

I frowned as I studied the waters before me. I wondered who was going to act first—

And then it happened. An American vessel fired a torpedo. An instant later, other American warsubs fired. All at once there were fifty torpedoes in the water, churning across the kilometer-wide battlefield toward the CSF.

"Holy shit," I muttered.

ALMOST IMMEDIATELY TWENTY CHINESE WARSUBS LAUNCHED a series of small torpedoes. They arced quickly out between the two forces and detonated midway between them. In each torpedo's place a series of frothing bubbles and devices that emulated the sounds of spinning propellers had appeared.

Countermeasures, placed in the middle of the battlefield.

Brilliant.

The US torpedoes angled toward the devices and one by one began to detonate. Light strobed into the control cabin of *SC-1*, and I dimmed the VID system slightly in order to see what was happening.

The explosions were simply gargantuan. The sea around them flash boiled and water crushed into the large cavities that formed. At the surface, massive fountains shot fifty meters into the air all along the ten kilometer line of ships.

It was astonishing.

A few of the USSF weapons made it through, however, and the CSF warsubs took evasive maneuvers and ejected more countermeasures.

Then they returned fire.

Their weapons lanced through the churning maelstrom straight for the USSF ships. Torpedoes began to detonate on the hulls of vessels, and within seconds warsubs of each fleet had merged to fight battles in groups of four or five. It was hard to keep track of what was happening. To the port, about a kilometer away, a USSF warsub disintegrated instantly when a massive detonation pulverized her entire aft section. And to starboard, two Chinese warsubs hit bottom after blasts cracked their hulls in multiple locations.

The commander of Shanks's fleet gave an order to the *Stingrays*, and our ships powered into the battle. At the stern of each, a surge of bubbles had begun; the wakes stretched twenty meters behind each vessel.

Their SCAV drives were on.

That was really going to get some attention out there, I thought.

THE *STINGRAYS* QUICKLY ACCELERATED TO OVER 200 kph and rocketed through the debris-laden turbulent waters of the battle. Explosions continued to flare around them and errant torpedoes circled masses of ships, but for a moment I had the distinct impression that warsubs on both sides of the fight halted momentarily as the small vessels tore through their lines. No doubt the Chinese and American commanders had never seen a manned contact move so quickly underwater.

And then our sonar screamed.

"Torpedo!" Johnny yelled. "Coming up fast on our stern!"

I hit the ballast control and *SC-1* plummeted to the bottom. Once there, I skimmed the sandy floor and ordered our own SCAV drive initiated. Johnny's fingers darted over the controls as Kat had shown him, and within a minute a jet of steam erupted from the seacar. Our velocity increased rapidly, and I watched as we pulled away from the torpedo.

Then I halted our acceleration.

The torpedo stayed on our tail, and I brought our speed back down to eighty.

I banked hard to starboard and moved toward an American warsub, a *Typhoon* class vessel. She was thirty meters long with a crew of seventeen. I didn't want to destroy her, rather just put her out of commission for the battle. I cut right across her stern. She was blowing ballast as I approached— her sonar operators probably recognized what I was doing—and trailed the torpedo straight to her screws. As I passed I cut hard to port and disappeared behind the hull of the vessel. Then Johnny ejected countermeasures. The torpedo followed and—

Detonated on the screws of the *Typhoon*.

The twisted steel of the propellers would never push water again. Her aft hull split from the shock wave instantly and her engine room began to flood.

Bubbles streamed to the surface as the warsub's rear compartments tilted toward the bottom.

She was out of the fight.

Meanwhile, torpedoes were *everywhere*. There were too many countermeasures in the water to count; so many, in fact, that some torpedoes didn't quite know what to do. They would lock onto one set, then turn away as another caught their attention. Explosions were flashing through the water like lightning, and here and there warsubs fell silent, victims to the concussions.

I shook my head. I was participating once again in open combat between the world's two greatest superpowers. I hoped it would remain confined to the sea—perhaps to this particular battle—but with tensions as high as they were, it would be remarkable if it did.

I also prayed that no one was stupid enough to use a nuclear weapon.

"Did you find Lau yet?" I asked.

"Still searching." Johnny had been calling Chinese warsubs—using his own codes to bypass security—but hadn't yet located the operative. There was a chance that Lau was on one of the destroyed subs, and if so, my plan would fail before I ever got a chance to put it into action.

As we darted over a battle being fought between three CSF and two USSF warsubs, my breath caught in my throat.

Directly before us was USS *Impaler*.

And her supercavitating torpedoes.

WE WERE ENGAGED IN THE MOST deadly underwater naval battle in history, and yet all I could think of was the *Reaper* before us. Her 250 meter hull dwarfed the other warsubs around her. She was a dominating ship in this battle. Captain Heller had told us that he intended to take Trieste down because of Shanks, and now I had the opportunity to eliminate him from the equation.

And yet I couldn't do it.

There were 400 crew on that ship, and they were innocent in this. Destroying a vessel in order to save yourself was one thing, but needlessly killing that many because of a personal vendetta was something else entirely.

I decided to leave her alone and continue to avoid trouble while Johnny searched for Lau.

And then two missiles shot from *Impaler*.

They were SCAV torpedoes; they quickly accelerated to 1000 kph.

The sonar alarm blared.

They were headed directly for us.

"Hold on!" I blurted as I heeled the ship to port. I then shifted to starboard, blew the ballast, and shot for the surface at max speed. We were at 450 kph within seconds, rocketing past other CSF and USSF warsubs as the torpedoes steadily closed.

It was difficult to pilot at such a velocity with so many ships in the water. Avoiding them—and other torpedoes—was difficult, but somehow I managed.

The comm sounded and a voice echoed in the cabin. "Hello again, McClusky." It was Heller, and I swore at his miserable sense of drama. "You escaped earlier, but I told you I'd be coming."

I clenched my teeth as I neared the surface. I checked the sonar; the missiles were nearly close enough now so that I could try the same maneuver as before.

Two hundred meters.

One-fifty.

"I wonder if you can evade *both* of our torpedoes this time," he said in a smug tone.

"I'm gonna try," I grunted.

One hundred.

Fifty.

Thirty.

"Now!" Johnny yelled.

I pulled back on the yoke, and we broke the surface and soared into the brilliant afternoon sky. We arced up into the air and quickly descended back to the water. We plunged downward heavily—slamming against our straps in the process—and I pushed the yoke away and willed the explosion to occur well behind.

It never did.

"They didn't follow," Johnny said in horror. He had watched the sonar the whole time. "They stayed below the surface!"

Heller: "We reprogrammed our supercavitating torpedoes, McClusky. Can you avoid them now?"

"COUNTERMEASURES!" I BARKED. AN INSTANT LATER they were in the water, churning violently in our wake. The devices fooled one missile, which detonated almost the same instant Johnny launched them. *SCAV-1* shuddered from the blast, but the bubble around us remained intact.

"There's one," Heller said. "Still one more though."

"Shut up!" I roared. Sweat was dripping from my forehead. My arms were aching from the strain of holding the yoke and maneuvering the seacar at this velocity. Still, I realized this might be the perfect time to do what I had intended. . . .

"How far away is Trieste?" I asked.

"Three klicks."

I turned the seacar and stared at the torpedo contact on the sonar. Large parts of the display were simply white blotches from all the underwater detonations, but right behind was the unmistakable red line that represented the dangerous threat. I banked *SC-1* from port to starboard and back again to force it to keep adjusting its course; it slowed substantially, but still managed to close the distance.

Trieste was clear in the VID; her modules and travel tubes before us seemed like an image that belonged on a postcard.

And I was going to ruin it.

Deliberately.

I tilted our bow down and fixed my sights on the Storage Module.

The one where Shanks had built the *Stingrays*.

"What are you doing?" Johnny gasped.

The missile was only thirty meters behind us now. "Countermeasures ready!" I snapped. He nodded. I paused another fraction of a second, and then— *"NOW!"*

He stabbed at the button and two of the devices launched from *SC-1*. I had skimmed the module just as I ordered the release, and they hovered directly over the structure, luring the last missile in.

It exploded.

On top of the module.

The roof of the manufacturing facility collapsed instantly. A massive bubble burst upward from it and a rush of water surged down into the open cavern. Inside the five story module, I knew alarms would sound only a millisecond before the crushing water pulverized the equipment. Watertight hatches would seal immediately and protect the rest of the city, but for a moment I wondered how I would live with myself if they failed. I would be responsible for the destruction of a large part of Trieste and the death of thousands of people.

I held my breath as I watched the image on the canopy. It took a few seconds for the bubbles to finish venting and the water around it to calm enough to make out details, but when I could finally see again, my jaw

dropped at the sight. The sides of the module were splayed outward, cracked in multiple places vertically, almost as if a giant had sat on the structure and shattered it under its enormous weight.

Johnny was staring at me. "Is this part of your plan?"

I nodded. "It is."

"Huh." He thought about that for a few seconds, then shrugged. "I guess you'll fill me in later. I'll continue trying to get Lau. Keep us away from *Impaler*, if possible."

"Don't worry. I will."

I knew that Shanks would be wondering what the hell had just happened. It would only take him a few moments to review the records and see I had deliberately used the countermeasures to destroy his facility. When next I saw him, he might just try to kill me himself.

TEN MINUTES LATER JOHNNY HAD TRIED without luck to contact every Chinese warsub that belonged to an undersea city. He said, "Most comm technicians won't even tell me if he's on board." He grunted. "It makes sense though, you know. They *are* in the middle of a battle."

He was right. I didn't know why I had thought we could contact him. Hell, he might not even be here. I had figured he would be, at least until his superiors had a chance to debrief him. I thought there was a good chance that he would have joined one of these crews in an attempt to prove his loyalty. But for my plan to succeed, his presence was crucial. Maybe there was another way to contact him . . . if we had a more direct method of—

I swore. We did have a direct way of getting him.

The Personal Communication Device that he had stolen from me.

Blake's PCD.

Johnny thought of it at the same instant. "It just might work," he muttered. "He might still have it on him."

I gave Johnny the code, and he fed it into the comm. A minute passed, with no response. Then another. I was about to give up, when finally, he answered.

At last.

"What the hell do you want?" Lau hissed at Johnny. His surprise evaporated rapidly; within a few seconds he was clearly angry. He spoke quickly and barely let Johnny get a word in. "You made your decision when you chose to stay with McClusky. Why bother me now? Are you trying to change your mind—"

"It's me, Lau," I said in a calm voice. I had to fight to keep it so; we weren't exactly on the friendliest of terms.

He stopped for a long moment. Then, "Are you trying to get me in trouble with my superiors? We're a little busy—"

"I know what's going on—we're in the battle too. But I needed to talk with you."

Pause. "Why?"

I wondered exactly how to come out with it. I had been thinking about it since we had escaped from Blue Downs. Now here was my opportunity, and I didn't quite know what to say.

I noticed Johnny watching me again, this time with a worried expression on his face.

"Lau," I finally managed. "I have a proposition for you."

"We have nothing to discuss." In the background I could hear shouting voices; he was close to the bridge, if not on it.

"I think we do. Have you noticed that none of the Triestrian warsubs have targeted a vessel belonging to a Chinese undersea city?"

"Actually, no."

"Check if you want, but it's true." Earlier I had asked Johnny to send the request to our subs; I had no doubt that their captains had complied. Although I didn't command them, I figured that my clout would be enough to influence their strategy. Besides, there were plenty of targets out there for them to fire at.

"What if it is?" He sounded suspicious.

"There's something I want you to ask your superiors."

"About?" He was curious now, and I knew I had him.

"Simple. I want them to leave, along with every other vessel that belongs to the underwater cities."

"Are you mad?"

I smiled to myself. "No. But I have some compelling incentives."

CHAPTER THIRTY-THREE

THE BATTLE WORE ON. WARSUBS OF every class were involved, *Impaler* had launched her tiny fighters, and the Chinese equivalent—a *Ming* class—had done so as well. Small *Hunter-Killers* and *Fast Attacks* swarmed the larger ships and pummeled them with multiple torpedo strikes. The ocean was alive with movement as vessels evaded weapons, dropped mines, and launched torpedoes. The sonar indicated the noise of several small screws near the seafloor. I peered closer, and—

I gasped. There were twenty figures near the bottom on tiny self-propelled sleds! Portable scooters. They moved under a Chinese *Tong* class warsub that was hovering near the bottom. They stopped beneath her, detached from their vehicles, and began to swim in groups of two. Each pair had something slung between them; they were struggling to drag the objects upward.

They were mines.

The swimmers were lifting the explosives to the underbelly of the warsub!

I watched as they attached several to safety rungs on the hull of the ship. Then the divers began to swim back to the seafloor and their waiting scooters. A moment passed, and then—

The mines detonated and instantly crushed the vessel's hull plating. The ocean flooded into the large warsub, and within moments it began to sink to the bottom.

I swore. Infantry, under water. I recalled that the French had tried to do the same thing to *SC-1* just before we fired on her in the Charlie Gibbs Fracture Zone. Perhaps submarines everywhere now had detachments of special forces troops who were prepared to go out and conduct such activities.

As I thought about that, a small hatch slid open on the stricken warsub's hull. It was an airlock.

There were divers within.

They spilled out and immediately moved toward the American troops. The two groups merged violently, and a deadly hand-to-hand battle began underneath the sinking sub. Some divers reached to their thighs to remove daggers and I saw the flash of blades. Others held needle guns. The recoil as they fired was unmistakable. Within seconds blood clouded the water around the skirmish. Other divers met and began to grapple with one another. They tore off masks, sliced regulator tubes, and bubbles began to stream toward the surface.

My guts churned. It was grotesque.

We were moving slowly now through the battle as history unfolded before us, watching the fleets of warsubs firing at one another and other subs sinking. Then a sonar warning pierced the control cabin.

"Three torpedoes on an intercept!" Johnny barked.

I slammed the throttle to full and glanced at the screen, expecting to see the torpedoes disappearing quickly behind as we accelerated away.

They didn't.

They were SCAV torpedoes.

Damn.

"What warsub just fired those?" I roared as I began a desperate run to evade them.

"A *Soong* class at two-hundred-thirty-seven degrees, six-hundred-ten meters! Torpedoes are at nine-hundred-fifty kph and still accelerating!"

"*Chinese?*" I said, alarmed. Holy shit, the Chinese had SCAV torpedoes too!

I banked hard and the g-forces pushed us into our chairs. The alarm was still blaring, and Johnny pushed the INTERRUPT button to silence it.

The warsub appeared before us. It was 143 meters long and had a crew of over eighty. I swallowed when I saw her; it was simply massive, and for a moment I found it difficult to launch our own weapons and potentially kill so many people.

But I didn't have much choice.

The torpedoes were right on our tail and coming on strong.

"Twelve hundred kph now!" Johnny screamed. "Incredible!"

Damn, they were better than the American ones.

"Is that a Chinese naval sub, or does it belong to the undersea cities?"

He checked the label next to the contact on the sonar. "Mainland China. Her listed port of call is Lushun."

So be it. I would have to take her out of the battle. "Prepare a torpedo, Johnny," I muttered. We only had SCAVs now; that was what Trieste City forces were using.

"Ready," he whispered. I shot him a quick look, and wondered for an instant if I could trust him to do this. He noticed, and said, "Don't worry, Mac. I fight for Trieste now."

I nodded. "Then fire."

He stabbed the button and the torpedo rocketed from our tube. A bubble formed around it almost immediately, and flames and smoke seared from the rear nozzle.

It lanced out toward the warsub.

"And another," I said. "Fire."

Johnny had set the first to HOMING. This one he set to IMPACT DETONATION and selected the ship's bow as the target. The homer would hit the screws and flood the rear compartments. The other would flood the forward compartments. Ships of that size were difficult to sink, however, due to their ability to seal large compartments.

She was trying to evade now, and within seconds countermeasures dropped from her hull. But our torpedoes were too quick, the ship too close, and her crew had been unable to react fast enough. Our first weapon blazed straight for the screws and the explosion rocked the ocean around us. The seacar rattled violently, and a few lights blinked red on the console.

Then the second torpedo hit.

I closed my eyes momentarily during the tremendous eruption. When I opened them again, I watched as the sea closed into the void. The bow seemed to wrinkle under the pressure. Then a fracture opened—just a small one—but it was enough. The hull suddenly swelled outward as the collapsing water pried it open. The power of the sea is merciless, even at this shallow depth, and the explosion had allowed it to worm its way into the vessel.

The warsub—which had been attempting to power away—stopped suddenly as debris and bubbles surged from the two large gashes in her hull. Her engines ground to a halt. She was out of commission, but still not damaged beyond repair. But that was good enough. As long as she couldn't destroy any Triestrian forces, I was satisfied.

And then we shot over her, trailing the three Chinese SCAVs, and I frantically pulled back on the yoke to take us to the surface. We reached it in only seconds. The torpedoes were closing fast, and as it looked like they were just about to hit, I brought us out of the water and into the air.

They followed.

They crashed onto the water's surface and detonated; the explosion was gigantic. The bubble around us collapsed instantly, and we slammed to a near stop. It shoved Johnny and I forward, and the impact of already-bruised shoulders against safety straps was agonizing.

It took a moment to focus through the haze of pain. When I finally stopped gasping, I studied the sonar. The strategy had worked, but just as with *Impaler*, I was sure that the Chinese would quickly adjust their missile programs to forbid them to leave the water.

More red lights had appeared on the control console as *SC-1* rocked back and forth in the mighty turbulence. I scanned them quickly and my heart thudded in my chest.

The containment capsule had suffered a power loss and was no longer operational.

The SCAV drive was out.

Damn.

I started the conventional thrusters and spun the ship to face the continuing battle. There were still over 250 vessels involved, and explosions flashed sporadically throughout the lines of fighting ships.

The comm beeped, and a voice filled the control cabin. It was Shanks.

"McClusky!" he barked. "What the hell are you doing? You destroyed the Storage Module!"

He had finally reviewed the tapes.

"We were avoiding a SCAV missile," I replied. "Sorry about that." I paused, and then, "But we just took out a *Soong* class warsub." I hoped that would distract him from what we had done earlier. It did not.

"But it was deliberate! Why?"

I pursed my lips. I had to put him off somehow. "We were running from that torpedo and launched countermeasures too late. We had a small malfunction on board. Sorry."

"That facility took us years to get up and running!"

I glanced at Johnny; he seemed to be enjoying Shanks's fury. I asked the director, "How is everything in the city? Any casualties?"

"The watertight hatches closed immediately. They held. No other damage." In the background I could hear someone yelling. There was a long break,

and when he came back on he sounded calmer, but somewhat confused. "A large number of Chinese warsubs seem to be moving away."

I shot a look at the sonar; he was right. About fifty vessels had shifted course and were powering to the southwest, toward the Panama pass-through.

"They're retreating!" he screamed, suddenly excited as he realized what was happening.

Easy now, I thought. It was just the forces that were affiliated with the six undersea cities. It wasn't the whole fleet.

But Lau had done it.

He had listened to me, and my argument had convinced his people.

Damn, it had worked.

THIRTY MINUTES LATER THE REST OF the Chinese forces withdrew. No doubt they were furious at the departure of Lau's group; the much larger American fleet had begun to batter them. Six more *Kilo* classes were almost immediately sunk, ten *Fast Attacks* disintegrated in torpedo explosions, and three *Hans* joined the others already resting on the bottom.

The battle had also left multiple American vessels damaged beyond repair. Many lifeless and shattered hulls now lay on the ocean floor. Others were limping away toward repair docks, heavy and sluggish due to flooded compartments. But there were over a hundred USSF warsubs remaining, of all classes, and they now turned their sights on Trieste.

They would arrive within minutes.

WITH THE CHINESE NOW OUT OF the picture, the *Stingrays* focused their attention on the USSF. The fast ships were zooming around the fleet, and conventional torpedoes just couldn't catch them. *Impaler* fired one SCAV missile after another, and they were having a dramatic effect. They had destroyed at least twenty of the tiny warsubs, and still more continued to fall silent under the *Reaper's* onslaught. There was no doubt that Shanks's fleet had been powerful, but they couldn't evade those torpedoes effectively. It didn't take a military mastermind to see what the end result of this would be. The Triestrian forces would inflict great damage, but in the end the Americans would be the victors.

I had to stop the carnage before it was too late.

I called City Control and within moments Shanks was on the line. "You have to signal your surrender," I said. "We don't have a chance here."

The suggestion offended him. "We fight to the end! Now get back to it and leave me alone!"

"But we can't win. *Impaler*'s torpedoes are just too fast. And—" I peered at the VID and watched a second USSF warsub launching the same weapons. "There's a *Matrix* out here that also has them."

"Then focus your attacks on those two subs!"

"The more damage we inflict—the more sailors we kill—the harder they'll come down on us. We have to stop the bleeding now. We'll deal with the aftermath, Shanks, and work to achieve independence another day. You weren't ready for it this time."

"We beat the Chinese! What are you talking about?"

"They left because of me."

"What?" he asked, bewildered. "Explain."

"I will, but not until this is over."

There was a long pause, and when he finally spoke, his voice was an angry rasp. "When this is over, I want you and that traitor back here to face discipline. Now finish this battle!" The transmission cut abruptly.

I sighed. I would have to do it on my own.

"There's a conventional torpedo headed for Trieste," Johnny said. He had just noticed it on the sonar. "It came from *Devastator*."

That was the Admiral's flagship. He was commanding their forces from that vessel, a missile boat. I snapped my gaze to the screen, then located the weapon on the canopy's projection. Sure enough, there it was, its trail of bubbles clear. It was on a northeasterly course, its nose on a slight down-angle. It would hit within seconds. It looked like it was headed for the Commerce Module—the largest in the city, and the location of City Control.

We were the only ship close enough to stop it. I turned the yoke and pushed the throttle to full.

Then a jolt shot through my body.

Our SCAV drive was down. The fastest we could go was seventy.

That torpedo was going to hit.

Had Shanks been smarter, he would have designed some anti-torpedo defenses to protect against just such an occurrence. But he had placed all of his efforts into the *Stingrays*, and as a result, Trieste was now a doomed city.

I watched the weapon in horror.

It continued to descend.

And then it detonated.

IT HIT THE NUCLEAR POWER PLANT. There was a massive flare of white in the VID, and the module collapsed under the shock wave. In an instant the concussion twisted and warped the metal bulkheads into shapeless scrap, and water pounded into the facility killing everyone within in an instant. The plant shut down immediately, and the bright lights in the city's windows winked out.

It was a deliberate strike against Trieste's power source. I breathed a sigh of relief. It had appeared as though the weapon had been headed for the Commerce Module, but Benning had actually aimed at the power plant. Clever, indeed.

Their next move was to invade.

Had I been in charge, I would have moved the plant, I thought. I would probably have buried it to keep it protected from such an attack.

But Shanks clearly hadn't thought this thing through.

The same mistake my father had made.

A voice came over the comm. It was Admiral Benning. "Attention people of Trieste. Your attempt at independence has failed. The Chinese have retreated. We're decimating your warsubs. Your power is out. We'll aim our next torpedoes at your government, economic, and control modules. You have one minute to comply."

I didn't waste any time. "This is Truman McClusky of Trieste. We surrender. Cease all hostilities."

Shanks came back online in an instant. "Belay that! That man does not speak for the people of this city! Continue the battle!"

"It's over, Shanks," I said in a calm voice. "We have to save the city."

"We'll save the city once we destroy those ships!"

"That's not going to happen. This is only a portion of the American fleet. More will come. Besides, our *Stingrays* will be gone soon. We have to surrender."

There was a tortured stretch of silence before Benning responded. "There seems to be some confusion regarding my order. All hostilities have to cease immediately or we fire on the city again."

I switched the comm frequency to address only Triestrian vessels. "Listen," I said. "This is McClusky. You all know me. We have to back down now so we can live to fight another day, which we'll do, I promise. But for now, if we don't stop, Benning will level every module we've got. There won't be anything left to fight for! Ignore Shanks and return to the Docking Module immediately."

I held my breath as I watched the sonar display. At first none of the ships shifted course, and my stomach dropped. They weren't going to listen to me, after all. They were going to—

"There's one!" Johnny cried. "It's headed for home!"

Then another turned. And another.

I had been holding my breath, and I finally released it. Within thirty seconds, the *Stingrays* had all shifted course back to Trieste.

Shanks was furious. He sent out several more signals, all of which we ignored. Then Mayor Flint tried, but still no one listened.

It was over.

The Second Battle of Trieste was over.

And we had lost.

Sort of.

As we pulled into the Docking Module, passing the corpses of Triestrians floating in the bloody waters around the city, and we'd finally shut down the thrusters, Johnny said, "Well Mac, you stopped the war, but what have we really accomplished today?"

I slumped back in my seat, completely exhausted. "We saved the city."

"True. But you realize that the USSF is going to flood Trieste with troops now." He glanced at his watch. "There are going to be a few thousand of them in here, probably within the hour."

"Which is why we have to work fast." I slapped his shoulder. "Come up top with me. I have something for you."

Together we climbed the ladder, cracked the hatch, and stepped out of *SC-1*. As we stood on the docks, I looked back at the little seacar that had been my home for over two weeks. We had almost died in her on multiple occasions, but the vehicle had pulled us through every time. Kat had done an incredible job designing her. No doubt the Americans would be more than happy to have the ship—with the SCAV engine and the micro-fusion reactor technology—in their hands.

Around us *Stingrays* were surfacing and shutting down their drives. There were only about ten left, which meant we had lost thirty. It would take a long time to rebuild that force, if at all possible.

I turned to Johnny. "When I started this journey I wanted to kill you. But instead I've realized that I've missed you since you left."

His eyes lowered. "Since I betrayed you, you mean."

"Perhaps. But you've made up for that. You came back to Trieste to face Shanks, to atone for what you did. It's been an adventure, but it's not over yet."

He frowned. "What do you mean? The war's done."

"When the USSF troops get here, Johnny, they'll most likely arrest you as a spy and an enemy combatant. You can't stay here."

He looked away and nodded after a moment. "I think you're right. I could try to hide, but they'd probably find me."

"I have a better idea." I pointed to a nearby *Stingray*; her crew had already left the module.

He looked perplexed. "You want me to take her?"

"Yes. I have something I'd like you to do for me."

The lines in his brow deepened as he processed that. "I won't be seeing you for a while, will I?" He seemed sad as he stared at me. Images of our friendship—both good and bad—flashed through my head. All the missions we'd been on, the happy times in Trieste, the fight in the French base, the repair on the hull of *SC-1* while a warsub tried to sink us, the fight today against the USSF. We'd been through a lot together, but despite our troubled past, I knew I was going to miss him. He had made up for his actions, but to be at peace myself, I too needed to move on.

Then I told him what I wanted him to do, and his face reflected the shock that he surely felt. Eventually, however, he nodded. "It's the right decision. I'll leave immediately."

"Good luck," I whispered. "I hope to see you soon."

We embraced as we said our goodbyes, then he stalked away from me and climbed onto the hull of the militarized seacar. He turned, gave me a quick wave, then disappeared into the sub. A few minutes later it submerged and its SCAV drive propelled it from the module and away from Trieste.

I WALKED TO CITY CONTROL. THE lights were off in the city—replaced by a dull red emergency glow—but in Control all seemed normal. The displays and maps along the bulkheads were still lit. A low hum reverberated through the chamber—a generator, located somewhere nearby.

As I entered, Shanks stalked over to me immediately. Kat, Meg, and Mayor Flint were at his side. He clenched his fists. "How dare you declare our surrender! I should have you locked up for what you did!"

Meg said, "We were losing the battle, Shanks. Did you want to fight until every last ship was gone? At least now we have a chance at rebuilding."

He snarled. "If the USSF lets us, and I doubt they will. They just broadcast a message about offloading troops!"

I shrugged. "We had no choice. You'll see that soon. I saved a lot of lives by surrendering. I also built the foundation for independence in the future. *Real* independence this time, not the phony and poorly thought-out kind that you aimed for."

Mayor Flint glared at me. "What are you talking about? We had forty ships in this. Each was superior in every way to a USSF warsub!"

"Our ships were close to being completely defeated. They were good, but the SCAV torpedoes hurt us."

Shanks ignored me and simply pressed his attack. "And where the hell is Johnny? He's going to prison now that he's back."

"I let him go."

The words dropped like thunder. Their mouths hung open.

Only Shanks could utter a sound, but even that took a long time. "What are you talking about? You spent two weeks getting him back here! Now you've just let him go?"

"Yes."

He and Flint both looked as though they wanted to kill me. They might even try, I thought suddenly. I had walked into the lion's den here, and I still wasn't even done telling them the news.

"But why?"

"I figure he has a debt to repay the city," I said, "and he won't be very productive sitting in a prison cell. So I've found a better way."

Flint growled, "What gives you the right to decide policy, McClusky? Living off your father's name will only take you so far!"

"If I have to use my name to make some changes around here, then so be it. You two have squandered our chances at achieving independence. Now it'll take years longer."

Meg's eyes were piercing. She was still quite angry with me. "Why are you suddenly fighting for independence? You swore to me that you weren't a part of that movement."

I faced her. "And at the time it was true. But when I found out that the USSF knew about TCI and the director's plans, I realized that it was too late to stay on the fence. I had to take a side."

"You picked the wrong one." Her tone was hard.

I grabbed her hands. "No, I didn't. And you'll pick this one too, Meg, when you hear my proposition."

Kat stepped forward. "You said that you'd 'built the foundation.' You mentioned that before the battle too. What do you mean?"

I studied her. Despite the stress of the battle, she looked radiant. I'd never seen her so beautiful. I said, "What Shanks was trying is never going to work. We simply can't fight the United States. Not as a single city." I examined each of them in turn. "But what about all of the cities, working together?"

Silence. And then, "You mean the three US colonies?" Kat asked.

"No. *All the cities*. All over the world. Every undersea city."

No one spoke. They glanced at each other, clearly perplexed. Finally she said, "It sounds wonderful, actually. But there's no way we'll be able to do that. Not with the USSF taking over."

"Actually," I said, "I've already started the process. Or, to be more precise, *Johnny* has. I sent him out as our envoy. Our Ambassador, if you will, to the other cities. He'll start with Sheng, try to convince them to turn against China."

Meg suddenly gasped. "That's why our *Stingrays* only targeted the mainland's navy, and not the colonies' forces!"

I smiled. "Exactly. I didn't want to give them more reason to hate us."

Shanks snorted. "Fat lot of good that'll do. Sheng City Intelligence will kill him as a traitor when he gets there!"

In many ways Johnny was an outsider in both Sheng and Trieste, and that's why it was the perfect job for him. He didn't feel one hundred percent comfortable here, and he didn't feel it there either. So perhaps working for *both* of us would ease his mind, give him some inner peace for a change. He would be representing us first, and if Sheng agreed, he would then travel to another city to represent both of us. He would convince them to join our alliance and rise against our mother nations to finally achieve independence. It would take time, but if it worked, it would mean a far different life for every undersea dweller on the planet.

"Actually," I said in a measured tone, "I'm confident that Johnny will be able to convince Sheng. You see, I've already told them what we have to offer."

Meg said, "That's why their ships left, isn't it?" Her expression softened somewhat as she realized what I had done.

"Exactly. They were chasing us the whole time to get their hands on the information that Johnny stole from Kat. Then, when they found out what *SC-1* really was, they knew they needed the ship too." I steeled myself. "And now Johnny's going to give them what they want."

Shanks's face was blank for an instant, then his eyes went wide. "You mean the SCAV drive? The fusion reactor?"

I nodded. "Johnny is taking the material that he stole from Kat to them. I've also given him a *Stingray*. If they join us, they can create a whole fleet of them—just as you tried to do, Shanks."

They didn't know what to say. At first Kat seemed angry. I had wondered earlier how she would take it. Then a bemused look crossed her face. "You're using my technology to get the cities to band together."

I nodded. "Imagine all the undersea cities acting as one. We can exploit the oceans together without worrying about the nations topside! Without sending them vast supplies of resources while our own people suffer. We'll *sell* them our products, and we'll continue to colonize the ocean floor."

Meg shook her head. "My God, Mac. It's brilliant."

I exhaled. "It's the only solution I could come up with. When both China and the States got involved in this, I realized it was the only way to stop the fighting and ensure independence for us at some point in the future. The undersea cities will create a new nation together—*Oceania*—and settle the seafloors peacefully. And *we'll* control the oceans, not China, and not the States. *We'll* mine areas like The Iron Plains, not them."

Shanks was now looking away, thinking furiously. He didn't seem that mad anymore. Flint too was deep in thought. I shrugged inwardly, for it didn't matter what either of them thought anyway. I would work my hardest to become the new leader of Trieste. I might not have much power for the first few months, as the USSF would be in charge, but eventually I would. And when Johnny returned with the results of his efforts, we would begin the fight again.

Only this time we would do it properly.

MY FATHER HAD WANTED THIS FOR us. I had thought earlier that he would have disagreed with my decision to leave TCI seven years ago. However, it had led me to this place, and I knew that he would be proud of me. I would fix his mistakes, and I would bring freedom to the people of Trieste. And in a hundred years, when historians wrote books about this day, instead of describing our defeat at the hands of the USSF, they would write about the mission I had sent a former traitor on. An outcast. A man who had betrayed *both* of his cities, only to realize that he could do something better with his life and change the course of history for not only those two colonies, but also for the ten million people who lived in the oceans.

Shanks and Flint left City Control soon after. Neither spoke to me. Somehow, I knew I would never see either again.

I moved to a large viewport and looked out at the ocean. Nearby, USSF warsubs were pulling into position as they prepared to offload troops to enter the city and take over. It was a scary sight, but it was necessary in order to save Trieste.

I had no regrets.

Kat and Meg approached to stand by my side. I turned to them.

Meg said, "I think you did the right thing, Tru."

I smiled at her. "I was hoping you'd say that. I was worried earlier. Had I died in the battle, you would never have known what I was planning. You'd have thought that I had turned into Father."

She shrugged. "I guess you know what you're doing after all." She paused, and then, "What will happen to TCI?"

I sighed. "I'll have to tell the USSF everything. But I'll keep our intelligence agency going, quietly. I'll rebuild. And when the other cities are ready, we'll make our move." I glanced at Kat. "Are you okay with what I've done? I gave your invention away, after all."

A frown. "You know, at first I was mad, but now I realize independence for *all* the people in the oceans is what I truly want. That would be incredible." She chuckled. "*Oceania*. I've dreamed of it all my life. And now I can play a part in it."

"A big part. Your invention will give us the edge over the topsiders. For a while, at least."

Meg gasped again. "That's why you deliberately destroyed the Storage Module! To prevent the manufacturing facility from falling into USSF hands!"

I nodded. "The US can still reverse engineer one of the *Stingrays*, but it will take time. By then some of the other cities will have the technology." Especially with the memory chip that Johnny had taken with him.

I pondered the events of the past weeks. During the first days of our mission, an updated version of the *Fast Attack* had tried to destroy us. I realized later there was only one reason for China to have built that ship: war. But *SCAV-1* had been built for the same purpose. It was dangerous having so many enemies. By giving away the technology, I was preserving the balance of power and making friends in the process. Tensions between the US and China had almost led to full scale war today. The Second Cold War had gotten out of hand, and I wanted out of it. Let the nations topside fight it out. The people in the oceans would band together, peacefully.

And if we had to fight, it would be side by side, as brothers.

Kat said, "Mac, why didn't you kill Johnny when you had the chance?"

That took me aback. I had never told her that I had been planning to kill him.

"You almost let it slip once," she continued. "I noticed, but didn't say anything."

Suddenly, I remembered. After the meeting at the French base, I nearly said what I wanted to do. "I guess I understood his motivations, even though I got caught in the middle. Shanks was the one I should have blamed."

A long silence descended over us as the events of the day slipped slowly into the past. Trieste would be a far different city tomorrow, and we would have to endure an occupation, but one day it would be better. Of that I was sure.

"Meg," I said finally. "What are you going to do? Are you going back to Blue Downs?"

My sister pursed her lips. "I was happy there, you know. I had a purpose. But I think I have a purpose here as well." She turned her eyes to mine. "It seems only fitting, our family name and all."

I blinked. "You want to help?"

She grinned. "You couldn't chase me away. Besides, I have to keep you from getting into trouble."

Kat said to me, "I guess you're not going back to your job on the farms."

I grunted at her joke. There was much to do now that I had taken a side and made a decision about my future. I would learn from our past mistakes. And we would plan and prepare.

"Independence is inevitable," I muttered. "History shows that. But the trick is *how* it's accomplished. We're going to have to go about doing it in a way that will result in a properly structured nation with good government for her citizens and a strong economy to lean on in the tough times. We can't just attack and win without fully preparing our social structure as well as the military one. What Shanks was trying—what my father tried back in 2099—had been to use brute force. That won't work." I would continue on the path that had killed my father—the path I had once abhorred—and finish what he had started all those years ago. But I would think it through far more carefully.

"We'll be part of Oceania one day," I continued. "Just not today."

And with that I walked out of City Control to meet the occupying forces, with Kat and Meg at my side, to begin the long and difficult process.

a noTe To THe
ReaDeR

Thanks to my agent Carolyn Forde of Westwood Creative Artists, and also to Sandra Kasturi and Brett Savory of ChiZine Publications for publishing this underwater thriller series. A special thanks to Leigh Teetzel, my editor on this book, Erik Mohr of Made By Emblem for the cover art, and Jared Shapiro for the brilliant interior design.

Any errors in regards to marine biology, the physics of cavitation and supercavitation, the effects of water pressure, sonar systems and SCUBA diving are mine alone.

The JFK quote is from his message to congress on 1 August 1963.

The Cousteau quote is from Page 6 of:

Cousteau, Jacques-Yves and Dumas, Frederic. (1953). *The Silent World*. New York, NY: HarperCollins.

The information about USS *Thresher* is from:

Thresher Down. (1987, February). *Mechanical Engineering Magazine*. Retrieved April 24, 2007 on the World Wide Web: http://www.subsim.com/ssr/thresher.html

Supercavitating technology does indeed exist, though not for a submarine, as far as I know.

There are some physical laws that are important in the realm of diving which I thought I'd include for those interested:

HENRY'S LAW: As pressure in the outside environment increases, the gases absorbed by human tissues also increases. As a diver moves back to the surface, this gas has to leave the body (naturally, through the lungs) to avoid decompression sickness, or "The Bends." This law also explains oxygen toxicity and nitrogen narcosis, meaning that under great pressure more oxygen enters our blood stream, which is toxic. Also, under great pressure more nitrogen enters our bodies, which is a narcotic.

BOYLE'S LAW: As pressure in the outside environment increases, the volume of gases in any spaces in the diver's body (lungs, sinus cavities, ear canals) decreases. Therefore, in order to breathe from a scuba tank underwater, the gasses within need to be at a similar pressure as the outside environment. Otherwise a diver's lungs would collapse and he/she would be unable to breathe.

DALTON'S LAW: The total pressure exerted by a mixture of gases is the sum of the partial pressures exerted by each gas alone.

In many ways water pressure and its effects on people and the gases they breathe is far more dangerous than the hazards in outer space. I have tried to be accurate with the science behind deep diving and submarine technology, but for fiction's sake, it was necessary to sometimes distort the reality of living and working underwater. The sequence in the novel where Mac ventures outside over four kilometers down, for instance, is a serious stretch of the imagination even for me. However, I found it to be an intense scene, very fun to write, and quite compelling to read. There are, however, experimental systems to achieve great depths, such as liquid-breathing apparatuses, that are far more realistic. Water is difficult to compress, you see, and filling one's lungs with an oxygenated fluid makes more sense than pressurizing with an exotic gas. However, the dilemma of creating a gas from very little material was a problem that I wanted to tackle. My apologies to those die-hard experts who sneer at such a scene, and I ask for your understanding for this work of fiction.

People generally refer to the region that includes Australia, New Zealand, and the surrounding islands as Oceania. When I came up with

AFTERWORD

the story and setting for this novel, however, I realized that there could only be one name for the future nation of people who live in the conshelf cities, and it too was Oceania. My apologies for any confusion between the two.

The details regarding fusion power are based on research and currently operating fusion reactors. The process of creating energy in this way is very real; the only limitation at present is that the amount of energy required for operation is greater than the output. Scientists predict that in only a few decades, however, the first fusion reactors will be online to generate electricity for public use.

I decided to combine the idea of a fusion steam-producing furnace with supercavitation for submarine propulsion. I believe the idea is valid; however, such a system would be far too loud for vessels that are primarily designed for silent running. Nevertheless, it's possible that such a thing might exist at some point in the future, and we might one day see crewed vehicles achieve incredible speeds underwater.

I have always had a fascination with the ocean; I'm not sure why. I am not a sailor. I prefer to swim in freshwater. I've only been on boats a few times in my life. And yet I find the lure of a life on water—or under it—extremely compelling. Stories about survival at sea are among my favorites to read. The oceans are relatively unexplored; in fact, scientists believe we have only discovered about five percent of the species that live there. The pressures at great depths make most areas of the seafloor unattainable to us. The continental shelves of the world, however, are well within our grasp. The total area of these regions is greater than the landmass of Russia and Canada combined! There are massive amounts of resources there that we might harvest—and one day, exploding populations and global warming may very well force us to reach to the oceans for our survival. That was the driving force behind this novel.

Deciding to do a story set underwater was easy for me, however, there were clearly many obstacles. I knew I had to create a level of technology that could overcome these problems. For instance, the military vessels in *The War Beneath* can descend to far greater depths than those that currently exist. I also wanted to increase their speeds to make the battles faster, and supercavitation was a good way to do that. I also wanted the combat to be easy to describe, and therefore created the VID system for *SC-1* so it was more of a fighter jet than a submarine. This way Mac could see what was happening at great distances around him. I also standardized the air pressure in all vehicles and outposts to better facilitate travel through the

AFTERWORD

oceans. I love thrillers that are set on land, in the air, or in space; I wanted to tackle the challenge of doing one under the oceans. I think I succeeded.

At its core this book is exactly what I enjoy reading: it's a grand adventure, a thriller with a technological component in an interesting and seldom-used setting, with a conflicted character on an emotional journey. Mac is a changed man by the end of *The War Beneath*, and he will return in *The Savage Deeps* and *Fatal Depth*.

Check out my futuristic murder mysteries *The Furnace* (2013), *The Freezer* (2014), and *The Void* (2015) published by Carina Press.

Visit me on Facebook @TSJAuthor, Twitter @TSJ_Author and my website *www.timothysjohnston.com* to learn about my thrillers and upcoming projects, and also to register for news alerts.

Thanks for investing your time in this novel. Do let me know what you think of my thrillers.

Timothy S. Johnston
tsj@timothysjohnston.com
31 December, 2016

AFTERWORD

ABOUT THE
AUTHOR

Timothy S. Johnston is a lifelong fan of thrillers and science fiction thrillers in both print and film. His greatest desire is to contribute to the genre which has given him so much over the past four decades. He wishes he could personally thank every novelist, screenwriter, filmmaker, director and actor who has ever inspired him to tell great stories. He has been an educator for twenty years and a writer for thirty. He lives on planet Earth, but he dreams of the stars. Visit *www.timothysjohnston.com* to register for news alerts, read his blog and reviews, and learn more about his current and upcoming thrillers. Timothy is also the author of futuristic murder mystery/thrillers *The Furnace, The Freezer,* and *The Void.*